D0049226

Divine Secrets of the

YA-YA SISTERHOOD

Also by Rebecca Wells:

Little Altars Everywhere

Divine Secrets of the
YA-YA SISTERHOOD

A NOVEL

REBECCA WELLS

HarperCollins*Publishers*

Deep Purple, music by Peter DeRose, lyrics by Mitchell Parish. Copyright © 1934, 1939 (renewed 1962, 1967) EMI Robbins Catalog Inc. All rights reserved. Used by permission of Warner Bros. Publications U.S. Inc.

My Buddy, by Gus Kahn and Walter Donaldson. Copyright © 1922 Warner Bros. Inc. (renewed). Rights for extended renewal term in U.S. controlled by Gilbert Keyes Music and Donaldson Publishing Co. All rights for the rest of the world controlled by Warner Bros. Inc. All rights reserved. Used by permission of Warner Bros. Publications U.S. Inc.

ISBN 0–06–017328–9

Designed by Nancy Singer

This book is dedicated to

TOM SCHWORER, my husband, helpmate, and best friend

MARY HELEN CLARKE, midwife of this book and steadfast buddy

JONATHAN DOLGER, my agent, who keeps the faith.

And to the Ya-Ya Sisterhood, in all its incarnations.

We are not born all at once, but by bits. The body first, and the spirit later. . . . Our mothers are racked with the pains of our physical birth; we ourselves suffer the longer pains of our spiritual growth.

—MARY ANTIN

Forgiveness is the name of love practiced among people who love poorly. The hard truth is that all of us love poorly. We need to forgive and be forgiven every day, every hour—unceasingly. That is the great work of love among the fellowship of the weak that is human family.

—HENRI NOUWEN

Penetrating so many secrets, we cease to believe in the unknowable. But there it sits, nevertheless, calmly licking its chops.

—H. L. MENCKEN

Prologue

$\mathscr{S}$idda is a girl again in the hot heart of Louisiana, the bayou world of Catholic saints and voodoo queens. It is Labor Day, 1959, at Pecan Grove Plantation, on the day of her daddy's annual dove hunt. While the men sweat and shoot, Sidda's gorgeous mother, Vivi, and her gang of girlfriends, the Ya-Yas, play *bourreé,* a cut-throat Louisiana poker, inside the air-conditioned house. On the kitchen blackboard is scrawled: SMOKE, DRINK, NEVER THINK—borrowed from Billie Holiday. When the ladies take a break, they feed the Petites Ya-Yas (as Ya-Ya offspring are called) sickly sweet maraschino cherries from the fridge in the wet bar.

That night, after dove gumbo (tiny bird bones floating in Haviland china bowls), Sidda goes to bed. Hours later, she wakes with a gasp from a mean dream. She tip-toes to the side of her mother's bed, but she cannot awaken Vivi from her bourbon-soaked sleep.

She walks barefoot into the humid night, moonlight on her freck-led shoulders. Near a huge, live oak tree on the edge of her father's cotton fields, Sidda looks up into the sky. In the crook of the crescent moon sits the Holy Lady, with strong muscles and a merciful heart.

She kicks her splendid legs like the moon is her swing and the sky, her front porch. She waves down at Sidda like she has just spotted an old buddy.

Sidda stands in the moonlight and lets the Blessed Mother love every hair on her six-year-old head. Tenderness flows down from the moon and up from the earth. For one fleeting, luminous moment, Sidda Walker knows there has never been a time when she has not been loved.

1

Tap-dancing child abuser. That's what *The Sunday New York Times* from March 8, 1993, had called Vivi. The pages of the week-old Leisure Arts section lay scattered on the floor next to Sidda as she curled up in the bed, covers pulled tightly around her, portable phone on the pillow next to her head.

There had been no sign the theater critic would go for blood. Roberta Lydell had been so chummy, so sisterly-seeming during the interview that Sidda had felt she'd made a new girlfriend. After all, in her earlier review, Roberta had already proclaimed the production of *Women on the Cusp*, which Sidda had directed at Lincoln Center, to be "a miraculous event in American theater." With subtle finesse, the journalist had lulled Sidda into a cozy false sense of intimacy as she pumped her for personal information.

As Sidda lay in the bed, her cocker spaniel, Hueylene, crawled into the crook formed by her knees. For the past week, the cocker had been the only company Sidda had wanted. Not Connor McGill, her fiancé. Not friends, not colleagues. Just the dog she'd named in honor of Huey Long.

She stared at the phone. Her relationship with her mother had never been smooth, but this latest episode was disastrous. For the umpteenth time that week, Sidda punched in the number of her parents' home at Pecan Grove. For the first time, she actually let it ring through.

At the sound of Vivi's hello, Sidda's stomach began to cramp.

"Mama? It's me."

Without hesitation, Vivi hung up.

Sidda punched automatic redial. Vivi picked up again, but did not speak.

"Mama, I know you're there. Please don't hang up. I'm so sorry this all happened. I'm really really sorry. I—"

"There is nothing you can say or do to make me forgive you," Vivi said. "You are dead to me. You have killed me. Now I am killing you."

Sidda sat up in bed and tried to catch her breath.

"Mother, I did not mean for any of this to take place. The woman who interviewed me—"

"I have cut you out of my will. Do not be surprised if I sue you for libel. There are no photographs left of you on any of my walls. Do not—"

Sidda could see her mother's face, red with anger. She could see how her veins showed lavender underneath her light skin.

"Mama, please. I cannot control *The New York Times*. Did you read the whole thing? I said, 'My mother, Vivi Abbott Walker, is one of the most charming people in the world.'"

"'Charming *wounded*.' You said: 'My mother is one of the most charming *wounded* people in the world. And she is also the most dangerous.' I have it here in black-and-white, Siddalee."

"Did you read the part where I *credited* you for my creativity? Where I said, 'My creativity comes in a direct flow from my mother, like the Tabasco she used to spice up our baby bottles.' Mama, they ate it up when I talked about how you'd put on your tap shoes and dance for us while you fed us in our high chairs. They loved it."

"You lying little bitch. They *loved* it when you said: 'My mother comes from the old Southern school of child rearing where a belt across a child's bare skin was how you got your point across.'"

Sidda sucked in her breath.

"They *loved it*," Vivi continued, "when they read: 'Siddalee Walker, articulate, brilliant director of the hit show *Women on the*

Cusp, is no stranger to family cruelty. As the battered child of a tap-dancing child abuser of a mother, she brings to her directing the rare and touching equipoise between personal involvement and professional detachment that is the mark of theatrical genius.'

"'Battered child!' *This is shit! This is pure character-defaming shit from the most hideous child imaginable!*"

Sidda could not breathe. She raised her thumb to her mouth and bit the skin around the nail, something she had not done since she was ten years old. She wondered where she'd put the Xanax.

"Mama, I never meant to hurt you. Many of those words I never even uttered to that damn journalist. I swear, I—"

"You Goddamn self-centered liar! It's no Goddamn *wonder* every relationship you have falls apart. You know *nothing* about love. You have a cruel soul. God help Connor McGill. He would have to be a fool to marry you."

Sidda got out of bed, her whole body shaking. She walked to the window of her twenty-second-floor apartment in Manhattan Plaza. From where she stood, she could see the Hudson River. It made her think of the Garnet River in Central Louisiana, and how red its water flowed.

Mama, you bitch, she thought. You devouring, melodramatic bitch. When she spoke, her voice was steely, controlled.

"What I said was not exactly a lie, Mother. Or have you forgotten the feel of the belt in your hand?"

Sidda could hear Vivi's sharp intake of breath. When Vivi spoke, her voice had dropped into a lower register.

"My love was a privilege that you abused. I have withdrawn that privilege. You are out of my heart. You are banished to the outer reaches. I wish you nothing but unending guilt."

Sidda heard the dial tone. She knew her mother had broken the connection. But she could not lower the phone from her ear. She stood frozen in place, the sounds of midtown Manhattan down below, the cold March light of the city fading around her.

After years of directing plays in regional theaters from Alaska to Florida, after numerous Off-Off-Broadway productions, Sidda had been ready for the success of *Women on the Cusp*. When the play finally opened at Lincoln Center that February, it was to unanimous golden reviews. At the age of forty, Sidda was eager to bask in the light of recognition. She had worked on the play with the playwright,

May Sorenson, since the play's first reading at the Seattle Rep, May's home turf. She'd directed not only the Seattle premiere, but productions in San Francisco and Washington, D.C. Connor had designed the sets, and one of her best buddies, Wade Coenen, had done the costumes. The four of them had been a team for years, and Sidda had been thrilled to sit back with her pals and soak up some glory.

Roberta Lydell's initial review of the play had fawned over Sidda's work:

> Siddalee Walker has directed May Sorenson's *tour de force* about mothers and daughters with gutsiness and compassion. In Walker's hands, what could have turned maudlin and overly comic is instead stunning, heart-breaking, and deeply funny. Walker has heard the purest tones of Sorenson's rollicking, complex, sad, witty play, and has shaped these tones into a production that is more a force of nature than a stage production. The family—its secrets, its murders, and its miraculous buoyancy—is alive and well at Lincoln Center. The American theater has both May Sorenson and Siddalee Walker to thank for it.

How could Sidda have known, a month later, that Roberta Lydell would snake her way into her psyche, extracting information that Sidda normally shared with only her therapist and best friends?

After the offending profile, Vivi and Shep, Sidda's father, and the rest of her family canceled their block of tickets to the play. Sidda set aside the elaborate plans she'd made for their visit. She often dreamed of Vivi crying. Dreams from which she, herself, woke crying. Sidda did not hear from her brother Little Shep, or her sister, Lulu. She heard nothing from her father.

The only relative she heard from was her baby brother, Baylor. He said, "It's nuclear, Sidd-o. Vivi Dahlin always wanted to be in *The New York Times*, but this ain't what she had in mind. You could give her your blood and she wouldn't forgive you. Besides, you're the one who's the star, not her. And it's killing her."

"And Daddy?" Sidda had asked. "Why hasn't he called?"

"Are you kidding?" Baylor said. "Mama's got him under her thumb.

I asked him why he didn't at least drop you a note. You know what he said? He said: 'I'm the one who has to live with Vivi Walker.'"

Sidda did not want to hang up the phone after her baby brother said this. She wanted someone to shake her out of this feeling of being orphaned. She wrote Vivi:

April 18, 1993

Dear Mama,

Please forgive me. I never meant to cause you pain. But it's my life, Mama. I need to be able to talk about it.

I miss you. I miss your voice, your crazy sense of humor. I miss your love. It breaks my heart to know that you have divorced me. Please try to understand that I cannot control what other people write. Please know that I love you. I'm not asking you to stop being angry. I'm just asking you not to cut me out of your heart.

Sidda.

The personal publicity from the profile on Sidda boosted ticket sales. *Women on the Cusp* became an even bigger hit. Sidda was featured in *Time* magazine in a piece on women in theater. She was hired by American Playhouse to direct the television adaptation, and CBS was on the phone to her agent about series work. Theaters across the country who'd turned her down for years were now begging her to direct shows for them.

In the midst of all this, May had acquired the theatrical rights to Clare Boothe Luce's *The Women* and was adapting it into a musical. The Seattle Rep had been awarded a sizable grant to hire May, Sidda, Connor, and Wade to do a workshop production.

As the date for their temporary move to Seattle approached, Sidda's neck was in constant spasm. She felt like a walking nerve end. She did not know which hurt worse: the spasms in her neck or the sadness that was released when Connor massaged her. Sidda had the life she'd always dreamed of: she was a hot director, engaged to marry a man she adored. But all she wanted to do was lie in bed, eat Kraft Macaroni and Cheese, and hide from the alligators.

Just before leaving for Seattle, she tried a different approach with Vivi. She wrote:

June 30, 1993

Dear Mama,

I know you're still furious with me. But I need your help. I will be directing a musical version of Clare Boothe Luce's *The Women* in Seattle and I have no idea where to begin. You know *everything* about female friendship. You've been bosom buddies with Caro, Necie, and Teensy for over fifty years. You are the *expert*. And your innate sense of drama is unimpeachable. It would be enormously helpful if you could send me ideas, memories—anything about your life with the Ya-Yas. If you don't want to do it for me, do it for the American theater. Please.

Love,
Sidda

Sidda and Connor left for Seattle in mid-July. As she stepped onto the plane, Sidda told herself: I have a great life. I'm marrying the man I love on December 18. My career is taking off. I am successful. I have friends who celebrate my success. Everything is fine, really it is.

❧

In the middle of the night of August 8, 1993, while the moon outside her window shone down onto the glassy surface of Lake Washington, Siddalee Walker gasped and woke in a sweat. Eyes wet, mouth dry as sand, skin itching, she knew for certain that her Connor, her beloved, had died in his sleep as he lay in the bed beside her.

I *know* it, she thought. He has left me. He is gone. Forever.

Every atom of Sidda's rigid body strained to discern if Connor was still breathing. Her tears came in hot, silent stabs, and the crazy drumming of her own heart drowned out all other sounds.

She pressed her face against her lover's. When the tears from Sidda's eyes dropped onto Connor's chin, he woke up. The first thing he did was kiss her.

"Love you, Sidd-o," he murmured, still half-asleep. "Love you, Sweet Pea."

Such a sudden sign of life startled her, and Sidda jumped.

"Sidd-o," Connor whispered, "what's wrong?"

He sat up, pulled her toward his chest, and wrapped his arms around her.

"It's all right, Sidda. Everything's fine."

She let him hold her, but she did not believe that everything was fine. After a while, she lay back down beside him and pretended to sleep. She lay that way for three hours, praying. Holy Mary, she whispered silently, Soother of Troubled Hearts, pray for me. Help me.

When the sun rose over the Cascade Mountains and angry crows noisily fought in the Douglas firs, Sidda stepped out onto the deck with Hueylene. It was a cold gray August morning in Seattle.

When she and the cocker stepped back inside, Sidda knelt down and rubbed the dog on her belly. Maybe, she thought, I'm a woman destined to love only dogs.

She walked into the bedroom and kissed Connor on the forehead.

He smiled when he opened his eyes. She looked at his blue eyes, and thought how they were always darker when he first woke up.

"I have to postpone the wedding, Connor."

"Connor. Just listen to me, please," she said, sick at the expression on his face. "I don't know if I can bear it."

"Bear what?"

"The fact that you're going to die and leave me alone."

"I am?" he asked.

"Yes, you are. Eventually. I don't know when and I don't know how. But it's going to happen. And I don't know if I can bear it. Last night you stopped breathing. Or at least I thought you did."

Connor stared at her. Sidda Walker was finely wired. He knew this. He loved this.

"My God, Sidda. I'm in perfect health. I didn't stop breathing last night, I was sleeping. You know what a deep sleeper I am."

Sidda turned to look at him.

"I woke up last night and I was convinced you had died."

He lifted his hand to her cheek. She turned away, and kept her eyes focused on her hands, which sat clenched in her lap.

"I cannot bear to feel the way I felt last night ever again. I do not want to be left."

"What is this all about, Sidda?"

Connor pulled back the covers and got out of bed. His tall, lanky body had the wrinkles of sleep, and he smelled like cotton and dreams. He was forty-five years old, fit, agile, light on his feet.

Hueylene thumped her tail against the wood floor. Connor reached down and stroked her. Then he knelt down on the floor in front of Sidda and took her hands in his.

"Sidda, it's not news that I'm going to die one of these days. You are too. This is not news, Sweet Pea."

Sidda tried to take a deep breath. "It's news to me," she said.

"You're spooked, aren't you?"

Sidda nodded.

"Is it the thing with your mother?"

"No," she said. "This has nothing whatever to do with my mother."

"You know," he said, "I have to deal with the fact that you're going to kick the bucket one of these days too, Sidda. I mean, you could die before I do. I could be the one who is left."

"No, that's not how it will happen."

Connor stood up. He took a green flannel bathrobe off the rocker and wrapped it around his body. Sidda followed Connor's every move with her eyes.

"You want to call the whole thing off?" he asked, softly. "Is this some polite Louisiana way of telling me it's over?"

She got up from the bed and went to him, wrapping her arms around his waist, leaning her head into his chest. The top of her head fit neatly under his chin.

"No," she whispered, "I don't want us to be over, Connor. I love you. I will always love you. I'm sorry for this."

Connor lowered his head next to hers. Sidda could feel his heart beating.

"How long we talking here, Sid?"

"I don't know. Not long. I don't know."

He broke away and walked to the window.

Sidda waited, terrified she might have pushed too far.

"I'm not interested in hanging out in limbo forever," he said, staring out at the Cascade Mountains. "Don't mess with me, Sidda. I'm not a masochist."

Please God, she prayed, *don't let me lose Connor.*

"All right," he said, finally turning back to her. "Okay. I'm not happy about it. But all right."

They crawled back into bed, and Sidda curled against Connor. They lay that way for a long time, without speaking. It had taken four years of friendship, four years of working together in the theater, before she would admit she had loved him from the first day they met. She'd been directing a production at the Goodman Theater in Chicago, and Connor had been the scenic designer. She'd wanted to kiss him the first time she saw him. Something about his slow smile, the shape of his jaw, that long, lean body, that imagination. Something athletic and relaxed about the way he moved, something unhurried about his whole attitude.

Now, cuddled against each other, Hueylene's adoring face propped on the edge of the bed staring up at them, Sidda sighed.

"I thought I might go away for a little while. When we arrived in Seattle, May offered me her family's cabin at Lake Quinault, on the Olympic Peninsula."

"How far is that from Seattle?"

"About three hours, I think."

Connor studied her face.

"Okay," he said. Reaching over to rub Hueylene's ears, he said, "Are you taking the governor with you or can she stay with me?"

"I'd like to take her along," Sidda said.

Connor brought his lips to Sidda's, and kissed her long and slow. She felt herself being pulled into a warm, fluid place. Sex heals, she told herself, anxiety kills. It was a struggle for her to surrender to such pleasure, such comfort.

Four months before she was to have married Connor, Sidda felt a heavy black stone inside her chest blocking the radiance. Her limbs felt tense, as though she were keeping vigil. As though she were locked in an endless Lenten season, waiting for the boulder to be rolled back from the opening of the cave.

2

*V*ivi Walker walked down the tree-lined drive at Pecan Grove to get the mail. She had been lying on the window seat in the den, reading a novel and listening to Barbra Streisand when she heard the mail truck turn around. At sixty-seven, she was still fit from playing tennis twice a week. She'd put on five pounds since she'd tried to quit smoking, but she still could have passed for a much younger woman. Her legs, though not tan, were muscular and strong. Her subtly colored ash-blonde hair was cut in a French bob, and over it she wore an expensive black straw hat of the best weave, which she had bought thirty-five years ago. She wore linen shorts, a crisp white blouse, and tennis shoes. Her jewelry consisted of a single twenty-four-karat-gold bracelet, her wedding ring, and a pair of tiny diamond earrings. This was her summer uniform, and had been since anybody in Cenla could remember.

Catalogs from every outdoor outfitter in the country filled the mailbox. Shep Walker, her husband, would never get over the country-boy thrill of mail order. There was a bill from Whalen's of Thornton, where Vivi had just charged a gorgeous new white silk pantsuit.

And there was a gray envelope, nice paper, postmarked Seattle. When she saw her oldest daughter's handwriting, her stomach tightened. If Sidda was asking for Ya-Ya-rabilia again, the answer was no. She wasn't giving that child anything, not after the way she'd been hurt. Standing in the driveway, Vivi slit open the envelope with her thumbnail, took a deep breath, and began to read.

The letter read:

August 10, 1993

Dear Mama and Daddy,

I have decided to postpone my wedding to Connor. I wanted to tell you before you hear it from someone else. I know how word spreads in Thornton.

My problem is, I just don't know what I'm doing. I don't know how to love.

Anyway, that's the news.

Love,
Sidda

Shit, Vivi thought. Shit, shit, shit.

Back inside her kitchen, Vivi pulled a stool and climbed up to reach the out-of-the-way cabinet where she'd hidden a pack of cigarettes. Stopping herself, she carefully climbed down. Reaching up to her cookbook shelf, she pulled out her roux-splattered copy of *River Roads Recipes* and opened it to page 103. There, next to Mrs. Hansen Scobee's recipe for crawfish *étouffée*, was the photograph of Sidda and Connor that Sidda had sent when she announced her engagement. It was the only photo Vivi hadn't destroyed. She studied the photo for a moment, put a piece of Nicorette gum in her mouth, and reached for the phone.

A half hour later, she popped the Barbra Streisand CD out of the player, snatched up her purse, climbed into her navy-blue Jeep Cherokee, and sped off down the long drive that led from Pecan Grove to the wider world.

Necie and Caro had already arrived at Teensy's house when Vivi pulled up. Teensy's maid, Shirley, had pulled together some sandwiches and two thermoses of Bloody Marys. Climbing into Teensy's red convertible Saab, they took the same positions they had been taking in Teensy's convertibles since 1941: Teensy behind the wheel; Vivi, shotgun; Necie just behind the driver; and Caro in the backseat behind Vivi. Unlike in the old days, Caro did not kick her feet up on the seat back in front of her. Not because she was worried about propriety, but because she was traveling these days with a portable oxygen tank. She didn't need to use it all the time, but it had to be near, just in case.

Teensy turned the air conditioner to high, and the Ya-Yas took turns reading Sidda's letter. When they had all finished, Teensy put down the top and Vivi slipped the Barbra Streisand CD into the CD player. Each of the women put on a hat, scarf, and sunglasses. Then they blasted off in the direction of Spring Creek.

"All right," Vivi said. "I stood there at the mailbox and began composing a prayer—an 'ultra-tomato,' as Sidda used to call ultimatums. I said, 'Listen, Ole Padnah.' Not *'Please* listen.' Just *'Listen.'*"

"I thought you only prayed to Mother Most Merciful, *cher,*" Teensy said. "Didn't you eighty-six the Old Fart?"

"Please, Teensy," Necie said, "stop it. You do that just to shock me."

"Well, that's true," Vivi explained. "I did give up on God the Father—the Ole Padnah—as Shep calls Him. But I just thought in this case I better cover all my bases."

"Always a good idea," Caro said.

"It can never hurt to keep praying to them all is what I say," said Necie, the only one who still thought the Pope wasn't senile. "Since the Holy Trinity *does* still exist, even though yall have reinvented the Catholic religion to suit yourselves."

"Come on, Necie," Teensy said. "Don't get preachy. You know we're all still Catholic girls *au coeur.*"

"I just think it's a little *gauche* to refer to God Almighty as the 'Old Fart,' that's all," Necie said.

"Bien, bien," Teensy said. "Don't get carried away, Saint Denise."

Vivi unscrewed a thermos and poured the Bloody Mary mixture into a plastic go-cup. "Caro Dahlin," Vivi said, reaching back over the seat to hand the cup to Caro.

"Teensy," Vivi said, "let's take the old road instead of the interstate, what you say?"

"Sure, *Bébé,*" Teensy said.

The old road was a single-lane state road that cut through farming country, and wound around part of Bayou Ovelier. It was quieter than the interstate, and cooler, too, with trees on either side.

"I figure God owes me extra favors with Sidda, since He took her twin," Vivi said. "I mean, don't I qualify for a discount?"

"Yes, you do," Necie said. "Sidda gets to have all the favors God would have granted the twin if he had lived."

"So there," Caro said. "Sister Mary Necie Explains It All For You."

"Teensy," Vivi said, "are you The Designated?"

"Hell, no," Teensy said.

"They could check us into The Betty for this," Vivi said as she poured Teensy a drink and carefully handed it to her.

"They could check us into The Betty for a lot of things," Teensy said, steadying the wheel. Teensy had christened The Betty Ford Center "The Betty" years ago, and now it was part of the Ya-Ya lexicon.

"Necie?" Vivi asked, raising her go-cup. "Sippie-poo?"

"Just a drop."

"Tell Babs to pipe down, will you?" Caro said. "I can't hear what yall are saying with her carrying on like that."

Teensy adjusted the volume on the CD player, and caught Caro's eye in the rearview mirror.

"They make them so they don't even show, you know, Caro."

"For the umpteenth time, Teensy, I do not need a hearing aid."

Vivi turned her head to face Caro and began mouthing words with no sounds. Necie immediately and silently joined in.

"Crazy fools!" Caro laughed. "Yall cut that out!"

"I am still mad as hell at Siddalee Walker." Vivi took a long sip of her Bloody Mary. "*Slaughtering* my reputation in the largest newspaper in the country. Who wouldn't be livid? But I am picking up beeps on my Mama-radar."

"I say *always* listen to your beeps," Necie said.

"It was that photograph," Vivi said. "This engagement-announcement picture," she added, slipping the photograph out of her purse. She handed it over the back of the seat.

"She looked so stunning in that shot," Necie said, "even if it was rather casual for an engagement announcement."

"No, *look* at that picture," Vivi said to her friends.

Caro and Necie both studied the photograph, then handed it to Teensy, who was snapping her fingers in a command to have the image passed to her.

Caro was whistling Bach's Brandenburg No. 6. Suddenly, in the middle of a measure, she said, "It's the smile."

"*Exactement!*" Vivi said, turning around in her seat. "Siddalee Walker has not smiled like that in a photograph since she was ten years old."

Teensy signaled and slowed down as they approached an old grocery store, its front gallery caving in on itself. The building had been taken over with kudzu, and vines grew out of the rusted Esso pumps like strange Medusa hair.

Then Teensy turned left onto a smaller road, where the canopy of the live oaks on either side met in the middle at many spots, so that the four women felt they were entering a magic tunnel. These trees were old sixty years ago, when the women were children. They grew silent and let the old trees wrap around them.

Not one of them could have said how many trips they had made under these trees on the way to Spring Creek. First as little girls with their parents, then with dates and each other, stealing gas-ration stamps to reach the sacred creek waters. Then all the summers when the kids were growing up, when they'd stay a full two or three months, putting on makeup only when their husbands came out on weekends.

"She's smiling that smile they smile before they grow bosoms," Teensy said.

"The kind you smile for yourself, not the guy with the Goddamn camera," Caro said.

"I had that smile too," Vivi said. "I know I did. Before I worried about my freckles and holding in my stomach."

"The Goddamn sonavabitch point is that Sidda isn't *posing*, for God's sake," Caro said. "She's not *impersonating* a woman who's getting engaged."

"Caro," Necie said, "you sound so—so—*strident.*"

Caro reached her hand over to Necie's and squeezed it gently.

"Necie, Pal, I'm sixty-seven years old. I can be strident if I fucking feel like it."

"Malissa says her therapist says I am afraid of stridency. She says I am addicted to sweetness. I do not understand why it is an *addiction* simply because I do my best to think pretty pink and blue thoughts," Necie said.

Caro lifted Necie's hand and gave it a quick kiss before pulling back into herself.

"Never listen to your child's therapist," Caro said.

"Wait until *their* kids' therapists start weighing in," Vivi said. "Oh, revenge will be sweet."

Necie was smiling and looking at Caro, who now sat with her eyes closed.

Vivi was wondering if her own mother, Buggy, ever smiled like that. She remembered a picture she'd found with Buggy's things after she'd died. An old picture from around 1916. Her mother had this huge bow in her hair and was staring soberly into the camera. On the back she had written her name. Not "Buggy" or "Mrs. Taylor C. Abbott," the only two things Vivi ever heard her called. But "Mary Katherine Bowman," her real name.

"*Maman* used to smile like Sidda's smiling there," Teensy said, gesturing to the photograph, which now lay on Vivi's lap.

What does my smile look like now? Vivi wondered. Can you reclaim that free-girl smile, or is it like virginity—once you lose it, that's it?

At the creek, the women got out of the car. Necie carried the basket of food, and Teensy pulled a fresh thermos of Bloody Marys from the trunk. Without offering, Vivi helped Caro with her oxygen tank, and without acknowledgment Caro accepted her help. The four Ya-Yas walked down a short path, then slowly, carefully scrambled down to the creekbank, where Vivi spread out an old pink-checked blanket. They lowered themselves into sitting positions on the blanket, and listened for a moment to the insects.

"Thank God for this cool spell," Caro said. "Otherwise, we would be *barbecued*."

Willow trees and cottonwoods leaned out over the creek, and behind those trees were loblolly pines. The sun was long past its prime, but still it was hot.

Necie handed out Shirley's oyster muffalettos on fresh French bread. Teensy poured each of them a refill on drinks.

"What should we do with Sidda's request for us to help her with the Clare Boothe Luce play?" Vivi asked. "The nerve of that little bitch asking for our *Ya-Ya-rabilia*. She *must* be kidding. After what she's done to me, I wouldn't send her a g.d. recipe for tuna-noodle casserole."

"Well, *I'd* be really flattered!" Necie said. "But that's just my opinion. My daughters only ask for municipal bonds."

"We *would* be helping the cause of legitimate theater," Teensy said.

"The kid knows prime source material when she sees it," Caro said.

"We are *nothing* like those cats in *The Women*," Vivi said. "They hated each other. *And* we were only *children* when that movie came out."

"Mere *bébés*," Teensy said.

"But we do have a sense of history," Necie said. "Wasn't Norma Shearer wonderful in that movie? They don't make actresses like her anymore."

"To Ya-Ya-rabilia," Caro said, raising her cup in a toast.

"What?" Vivi asked.

"Life is short, Pal," Caro said. "Send the scrapbook."

"It is not my fault if she's chickening out of her wedding," Vivi said. "I am *not* sending her my scrapbook."

"I'm the godmother," Caro said. "Send the 'Divine Secrets.'"

"It *would* be the well-mannered thing to do," Necie said.

"Send the 'Divine Secrets,' *cher*," Teensy said. "Send it *tout de suite*."

Vivi looked at each of her friends. Finally, she raised her glass.

"To Ya-Ya-rabilia," Vivi said, and raised her glass.

Then, each of them in turn met each others' eyes as they clinked glasses. This is a cardinal Ya-Ya rule: you *must* meet each person's eyes while clinking glasses in a toast. Otherwise, the ritual has no meaning, it's just *pure show*. And that is something the Ya-Yas are not.

3

*B*ack at Pecan Grove that night, Vivi sat in her bedroom. The air conditioner was on, the ceiling fan was whirring, and the windows were thrown wide open to the night sounds of the bayou. She turned off the bedside lamp and lit a candle in front of her Mary statue.

Mother, Most merciful, she prayed, hear me in my prayer. You are the Queen of the Moon and the Stars. I don't know what I'm the queen of anymore.

There is no excuse for that period in my life. These days, if you start to drop your basket, somebody sees it coming. And you fly off to someplace sweet like The Betty before things get too bad. Those days, well, those days I took the Goddamn Dexamyl, and confessed to the priest three times a week. Those days there was no Oprah.

That Sunday afternoon I had my husband's belt, the one with SHEP tooled in leather, the ruby set in the sterling-silver buckle, a sterling-silver tip on the other end. When I beat my children, the worst marks would have come from where that silver tip landed.

I can see their beautiful bodies as they were that day. I have been told what I did. Their baby bodies were such naked, easy targets.

Can you see the scar on Sidda's body now? Does Connor McGill see it when he loves her? If I could pass my hand over my daughter's back, over that entire Lent, over entire seasons of her childhood, I would erase it all. But I cannot do the godlike things I wish I could. This may be the only thing in my life I have learned.

Sidda should have stopped me. But she stood there and took it. Like I did, as a girl, with Father.

Does she dream of the leather against her thigh, against that spot on her shoulder?

And then I left. When I came back from the hospital that nobody called a hospital, we said I had been tired, that I had needed to rest. No explanation, ever. It was never discussed.

It was not the only time I hit them. But it is the only time I hit so hard they bled. It is the only time that Sidda lost control of her bladder.

I made Caro tell me this. I made my best friend tell me what I did.

Does she still sleep with all the covers pulled tight under her chin, a second pillow clenched in one arm, her other arm flung over her head? Does she wake with her old nightmares, gasping for air? Have I done this to her? Will I never be absolved? When she was little, I told her that her twin brother who died was her special guardian angel. Does she still believe that?

Is it my punishment now to watch my oldest one turn away from love? Holy Mary, you are a Mother, Lady of the Fields and Prairies. Give me some kind of sign, will you? Some kind of comfort. *Indemnify* me, too, while you're at it, will you? Must I carry my daughter inside me all my life? Must I be responsible for her till the day I die? I do not want this guilt, I do not want this weight.

Mary, Mother of the Motherless, intercede on my behalf. Make God listen like only you can. Take this message to your Son:

Jesus Christ, Our Savior and Lord, bend your ear to Our Holy Mother as she beseeches you on my behalf. I'm still mad as hell at my loudmouth daughter, but I'm willing to bargain. Here are my terms: You stop Sidda from chicken-

*ing out of love, and I'll quit drinking. Till the day she and
Connor say "I do." And I'll throw in the Ya-Ya-rabilia too.
I hear you laughing. Knock it off. This time I'm serious.*

*Make Siddalee turn around and walk through the fire. If
she starts that "I-don't-know-how-to-love" crap, don't fall
for it.*

*One caveat: they have to get married before October 31,
got it? No abstinence guarantees past Halloween. It's
August now. You have plenty of time.*

Let my oldest smile that real smile.

*Through the intercession of Our Lady of Shooting Stars, I
pray. Amen.*

After she made the Sign of the Cross, Vivi lit a cigarette. She
wasn't supposed to smoke inside the house, she wasn't supposed to
smoke at all, but hell, Shep wasn't home. She thought better with that
red tip glowing in the dark. Her bedroom was dark. She made the
Sign of the Cross again, this time with her cigarette, and when she
did, it gave her an idea.

She walked down the hall to the kitchen, and opened her firecracker drawer, the one where she stashed firecrackers from New
Year's and Fourth of July. She kept a supply around for special, unoffi-
cial celebrations. Vivi pulled out two sparklers and carried them outside with her.

No one else was home at Pecan Grove. Vivi walked down to the
edge of the bayou and lit her sparklers. She watched the little slivers
of light as they shot out into the night sky.

Then she began to wave them around in the air, and, without
questioning why, she began to run up and down the bayou, holding
the sparklers up above her head.

*If anyone sees me, they'll say, Well, it's finally happening. Vivi
Abbott Walker has gone over the edge. What they don't know is that
I went over the edge years ago, and lived to tell the tale. Although not
to many.*

Vivi ran until she was almost breathless, then she stopped and
held the two sparklers out in front of her. Staring at them, she
thought: *These are all I have. I do not have the wide, bright beacon of
some solid old lighthouse, guiding ships safely home, past the jagged*

rocks. I only have these little glimmers that flicker and then go out. Let me see my daughter like my mother could never see me. Let her see me, too.

Back in her room, she lit another candle and set it with the sparkler stubs in front of her statue of the Virgin Mary. Then she wiped off her feet and climbed into bed.

I'll burn the candle for my daughter all night while I sleep, she thought. I don't care what the fire department says about fire hazards. I have lived through fire before.

4

*S*idda stood on the upper deck of the Bainbridge Island ferry and watched as the Seattle skyline receded. The snow-tipped Cascade Mountains rose to the east. To the south, Mount Rainier watched over the city like a giant guiding god. When Sidda turned to face west, she could see the jagged peaks and shining glaciers of the Olympic Mountains, which shot up to the heavens from the Olympic Peninsula.

Sidda was only vaguely aware of the smiling tourists who ambled by her as she stood on the deck peering out across the water. She was remembering a day the previous February when the view in front of her had been quite different.

It had been a cold sunny day, midweek. The glowing major reviews for *Women on the Cusp* had just come out, and the disastrous personal profile was yet to come. Sidda and Connor had played hooky to celebrate their success, taking Hueylene for a long walk in Central Park, then returned to Sidda's apartment and opened a bottle of champagne in the middle of the afternoon.

As the sun dropped in the sky and evening's chill set in that February afternoon, they made love. She leaned down and smelled the skin at Connor's shoulders right at the spots where, as Martha Graham might have said, his own wings might have been attached. She crawled higher on Connor to smell his hair. Thick black hair, with gray hairs around the temples, soft, as though washed in rainwater the way her grandmother Buggy used to wash her hair. His lean muscled body was sexier than any twenty-year-old's could have ever been.

She'd had more lovers than she cared to count, years of couplings that had left her feeling raw, slightly lost, and emptied of sweetness when she woke up. She'd had two long-term relationships, but it was not until Connor that she felt fully met and deliciously cherished.

After they made love that day, they lay naked next to each other, their skin warm and flushed. Sidda sank down into the wide flannel embrace of their bodies, and she rested. For a moment she died a good little death, they died it together. And then her eyes began to fill with tears. She cried. At the beauty of what she had stumbled onto, at the fear that something terrible would happen because she was not vigilant enough. She cried at the fear of something so good that she would not be brave enough to bear it.

When she stopped crying, he kissed her eyelids. Then he asked her to marry him.

She said yes.

She had decided years ago never to marry. Anyone. Ever. She had sworn she would never sign on for what she had witnessed in her parents' marriage.

But she said yes to Connor.

He lowered his hand to her belly, laying it on the small rounded place, so that when she inhaled, her belly pushed up against his palm. Her instinct was to suck in her stomach so it would seem flatter, but she didn't have the energy. Love had worn her out.

Later, they had pulled on sweaters and heavy socks, and stepped out onto the small balcony of her twenty-second-floor apartment, with Sidda's old Rolleicord camera in hand.

They set the camera on the tripod and let the automatic timer capture their image. Smiling. Wind blowing their hair. Not leaning on each other, heading to trouble, but standing side by side, holding hands like in an old-time photograph.

Sidda drove off the ferry and headed west toward the Olympic Peninsula. An hour or so into the drive, she began passing vast corporate "managed forests," where the land had been logged, burned, then replanted. Through small towns with sad-looking houses with Day-Glo orange signs in windows which read, THIS FAMILY SUPPORTED BY TIMBER DOLLARS. She drove past wide, angry swaths of clear-cuts where bleached-looking tree stumps and gnarled branches looked like human bones. She passed a poster in a gas-station window that showed three generations of robust loggers. The caption read ENDANGERED SPECIES/SUPPORT THEM. At one point, Sidda almost drove off the road at the sight of a logging truck, stacked high with old trees, rolling past her. On the front of the truck a tattered spotted owl hung in effigy from the grille.

Late that afternoon, Sidda turned onto the dirt road that led to May's cabin. It was an old white clapboard from the thirties set up off Lake Quinault, on the edge of the rain forest. From its deck, Sidda could see almost the entire lake. To her right she could see the lush growth of the Quinault River's floodplain as it disappeared into rugged, snow-laced Olympic peaks. The sky was gray, and it was so quiet she could hear a loon as it surfaced on the flat water.

Inside, the cabin was dark and cozy, with old knotty pine paneling that gave off a golden glow even on the darkest Northwest days. A kitchen, one sizable bedroom, and one great room lined in windows and glass doors that opened out onto a deck comprised the building. Along one wall in the great room were photos of May Sorenson and her family. Sidda felt welcomed by the sight of books and overstuffed chairs, and the jigsaw puzzle of Venice that was still set up on a small table in the corner.

After she had hauled her bags in from the car, Sidda made a cup of tea and immediately began to regret her decision to get away. She itched to call her agent and check in. She kicked herself for not having brought along a cellular phone. She was too used to being plugged in.

Once she'd forced herself not to run out in search of a telephone, she decided to go out to the car and bring in an unfamiliar box that Connor had put in at the last minute. She set the box in the middle of the big room of the cabin, on an old pink-and-faded-green hooked rug, in front of the sliding glass doors that led onto the deck overlooking the lake. The doors leading to the deck were open, and a light breeze blew in off the lake.

Hueylene was circling the box, sniffing with curiosity. It bore Vivi's handwriting and Pecan Grove as a return address. Following Hueylene's example, Sidda too began to circle the box. She thought about bending down and sniffing it, along with her dog, but stopped herself. That thing is emitting Mama-rays, she thought. It had FedEx stickers plastered on it, and the word "Fragile" written large in Vivi's hand.

Sidda leaned down and picked up the box. She leaned her ear to it. Not ticking at least. It weighed perhaps twenty pounds, and didn't have any odor. She placed it on the table and walked into the kitchen, where she slowly drank a glass of water. Then she walked back into the big room and stared at the box again.

Hueylene went to the door and stood with her ears pricked up and tail wagging, waiting to go outside.

Sidda changed into her swimsuit and led Hueylene down a set of rough steps until she reached the dock that jutted out into the lake. She stuck her foot into the water and immediately pulled it back out. She was not about to dive into such cold water. It invited a heart attack for any Southerner. So she sat on the dock and watched her dog run, delighted, up and down the dock, until the cocker came to rest at a spot beside her.

Back inside the cabin, Sidda unpacked the books she'd brought— from Chekhov to Cirlot's *Dictionary of Symbols* to a biography of Clare Boothe Luce to a book called *On the Way to the Wedding: Transforming the Love Relationship*. She unpacked her clothes: khaki pants, shorts, some linen shirts, a pair of sweatpants, and one voluminous soft white cotton nightgown. She unpacked the talismans she always traveled with: the feather pillow she'd had since infancy and could not part with; the framed engagement photo of her and Connor; a frayed stuffed bear that May Sorenson had given her at the first staged reading of *Women on the Cusp*; a Ziploc bag with two cotton bolls grown on Pecan Grove Plantation; and a tiny antique vial found in a shop in London.

Sidda arranged her talismans on the mantel above the fireplace, along with a sanctuary candle with a picture of Saint Jude, and one with a picture of our Lady of Guadalupe surrounded by roses.

She put away fresh pasta, apples, cantaloupes, and Gouda cheese; she refrigerated the bottles of champagne; and she laid out Hueylene's travel bed.

But she did not touch her mother's box. Not yet.

It was not until she woke up in the middle of the night and could not fall back asleep that Sidda gave up trying to resist Vivi's box. She pulled on her robe, a poodle-and-rose-patterned creation that Wade Coenen had whipped up from a 1950s chenille bedspread, which made her feel a little like Lucille Ball on acid. It had begun to rain, and the air was chilly. August in the Northwest was like November in Louisiana.

Hueylene followed her from the bedroom into the great room. Sidda stood frozen for a moment. Then she pulled the lamp that hung over the table closer to the tabletop, sat down, and opened her mother's box.

What she found inside was a large, heavy-duty plastic garbage bag sealed carefully with strapping tape. Taped to the bag was an envelope with Sidda's name written on it.

Inside the envelope was a letter, written not on Vivi's monogrammed stationery, but on Garnet Bank and Trust Company notepaper, which always sat next to the phone in Vivi's kitchen. The note looked like it had been dashed off quickly, then ripped from the pad before Vivi could change her mind.

Pecan Grove Plantation
Thornton, Louisiana
August 15, 1993
5:30 A.M.

Siddalee—

Good God, child! What do you mean, you "don't know how to love"? Do you think *any* of us know how to love?! Do you think anybody would ever do *anything* if they waited until they knew how to love?! Do you think that babies would ever get made or meals cooked or crops planted or books written or what goddamn-have-you? Do you think people would *even get out of the bed* in the morning if they waited until they knew how to love?

You have had too much therapy. Or not enough. *God* knows how to love, Kiddo. The rest of us are only good *actors*.

Forget love. Try good manners.
—Vivi Abbott Walker

P.S. Have decided to send along some Ya-Ya memories. You lose this album or give it to *The New York
Times* and I'll put a contract out on you. I want it
returned to me safely and in impeccable condition.

P.P.S. Don't think this means I'm giving you all my
secrets. There is more to me than you will ever know.

Sidda put the letter back inside its envelope, as though to restrain
all her mother's question marks, exclamations, and italics. She turned
instead to the plastic garbage bag.

From the bag she pulled a large brown leather scrapbook, stuffed
fat with papers and various little items falling out. Its spine was
cracked, and the leather was scratched and scarred. It appeared that
the album had been taken apart and rebound after more pages had
been added, and that those extra pages could barely be contained
within the binding. The cover of the book was edged in gold, and in
the lower right-hand corner, embossed in gold, was the name Vivi
Walker.

The first thing Sidda did was to smell the leather. Then she held
the album to her chest and hugged it. She wasn't sure exactly why, but
it occurred to her that what she wanted to do, what she *needed* to do,
was light a candle.

Bringing the sanctuary candles to the table, she lit them and set
them on either side of the scrapbook. She stared at the tiny flames for
a moment, then she opened the album. On the first page of brownish
tan construction paper, written large in a youthful hand, was the title:
"Divine Secrets of the Ya-Ya Sisterhood."

Sidda smiled at the grandness of the scrapbook's title. How *Ya-Ya.*
Running her hands across the cracking leather, she vaguely remembered seeing the album as a girl, but being forbidden to touch it. Yes,
she recalled, Mama kept it stored on the top shelf of one of her closets, next to her winter hats.

Gently, not wanting to tear the old paper, she opened to a page at
random. The first thing she saw was a photo of her mother with the
Ya-Yas and two teenage boys on a beach. Her mother sat on the
shoulders of a dark-haired boy, whose face was radiant with laughter.
The smile on her mother's face was one of sheer delight.

She looked at her mother's face. How old was she in the photo?
Fifteen? Sixteen? The cheekbones were higher than Sidda recalled

them, the skin unwrinkled, the blonde hair curly, the eyes unmistakable with their sassy glint. She found herself smiling automatically at the sight of her mother's smile.

She wanted to devour the album, to crawl into it like a hungry child and take everything she needed. This raw desire made her feel dizzy. It mixed with the excitement of the voyeur and the curiosity of a dramatist. Her hands all but shook at the sight of the cornucopia that lay before her: clues to her mother's life, evidence of her mother's life before children.

This is ridiculous, Sidda thought. Calm down. Act like an archeologist sifting for clues among the artifacts. And remember to breathe.

She carried the album to a large overstuffed chintz-covered reading chair, the kind with arms wide enough so she could sit with her legs slung over the side.

She sat down, and Hueylene came to lie at her feet, sighing with the delicious effort of her dogly job. Sidda pulled an afghan over her legs, and began in earnest to look at the album. She allowed herself to simply turn pages for a while. No order, no plan—something that did not come naturally to her.

While Vivi had started the book chronologically, she had apparently begun to stick things in at random when she ran out of room. So there was a photograph of Vivi and the Ya-Yas, out-to-*here* pregnant, striking cheesecake poses on the creekbank, next to a newspaper clipping that read, "Miss Vivi Abbott, daughter of Mr. and Mrs. Taylor C. Abbott, of Thornton, is at home for a visit from Ole Miss. Miss Abbott was recently elected most popular girl on campus. She will be home for a week before returning to Oxford, Mississippi."

Sidda took a moment to contemplate Vivi, Caro, Teensy, and Necie as they stood in their swimsuits with their swollen bellies.

These were the faces Sidda scanned for clues to the world from the moment she could see. She learned what clothes, movies, hairstyles, restaurants, and people were "Ya-Ya" (read: *charming*) and which were "Ya-Ya-No" (read: *pathetic*). She had heard this so many times that she actually began to assess things to see whether they were "Ya-Ya" or "Ya-Ya-No."

In fact, there were times when these words just flew out of Sidda's mouth. She recalled a night when she and Connor were at a painfully self-conscious evening of performance art, during which they were forced to watch twenty-seven televisions at once and endure sugar cubes being set on fire and thrown on piles of Barbie dolls. Without thinking, Sidda had whispered to Connor, "*Très* Ya-Ya-No!" It was as though the Ya-Yas occasionally channeled themselves through her in spite of all the barriers she'd tried to place between their coven and herself.

She held the scrapbook in her lap. Why do I dwell on my mother and the Ya-Yas?

Because I miss them. Because I need them. Because I love them.

Sidda came upon crushed corsages, faded and powdery. Next to one was written "Cotillion w/ Jack. Wore yellow gown." Stuffed in the crack of the same page was a faded handwritten receipt from some place called The Lucky Pawn. Sidda wondered what it could have been for. She had a hard time imagining her mother at a pawn shop.

She found tickets to movies that cost only fifteen cents to get into. She found Coke bottle tops; she found an old IOU that read: "IOU 3 back rubs," but no clue whose back was on the receiving end. One page opened naturally to three blue-and-white raised school letters for cheerleading and tennis from Thornton High School for the years 1941, 1943, and 1944. For some reason, the 1942 was missing. Sidda wondered about that year—what had happened?

There were countless snapshots from the '30s, '40s, '50s, and '60s, many of them fading with time. It took Sidda a few moments before she realized she had yet to come across one picture of her father. But she was surprised and pleased when she stumbled across a little poem she'd written as a girl. It was folded into an envelope that read TO THE YA-YAS FROM A BOHEMIAN GIRL.

Then there was a cardboard foldout frame from The Court of Two Sisters in New Orleans, which contained a photo of Vivi, Teensy, and Genevieve, Teensy's mother. Genevieve was gorgeous in a young Jennifer Jones sort of way.

There were printed and engraved invitations to dances and luncheons and balls and afternoon teas.

She particularly liked the "At Homes," like the one that read simply:

Mr. and Mrs. Newton Whitman
At Home
Tuesday, the twenty-ninth of June, nineteen hundred and forty-three
from eight until eleven o'clock.

On that invitation Vivi had scrawled "Wore the apricot tulle."

There was a photograph of an achingly handsome young man in a World War II Army Air Corps uniform. There were many photos of men in uniform, of course, but this one caught Sidda's eye and forced her to linger. She wondered if it was Teensy's brother.

There were dance cards filled with gentlemen's names. Sidda had heard of many of them and had known some of them when she was growing up in Thornton. There were a few fading mimeograph sheets from a class called "How to Be Smart and Charming." There were holy cards, a red veteran's poppy, and a clipping from the classified section of *The Thornton Monitor*, thanking Saint Jude "For Favors Granted."

As Sidda looked at these various objects, her imagination kicked into full gear, and she could feel the *life* that her mother's keepsakes held. For a moment, she felt overwhelmed with gratitude toward Vivi for sending the scrapbook. She felt almost ashamed at being presented with such an embarrassment of riches. Sidda wanted to cry because she could not bear the thought of how *vulnerable* the scrapbook had been as it voyaged across the country in planes and trucks.

Mama parted with these Divine Secrets because *I asked her to,* Sidda thought. The reason I feel like crying, Sidda realized, is not just because this scrapbook is vulnerable, but because Mama, whether she knows it or not, has made herself so vulnerable to me.

Sidda returned to the snapshot of the Ya-Yas pregnant and posing creek side. She scrutinized the image. Each one of the women was laughing, and the longer Sidda stared at the photo, the closer she came to hearing their four distinctly different laughs. She studied each woman's pose, her swimsuit, her hands, her hair, her hat. She closed her eyes. If God hides in details, Sidda thought, then maybe so do we. She took a deep breath in through her nose, held it for a moment, then let it out very slowly through her mouth. Her eyes remained closed, but Sidda was far from being asleep.

5

*T*aking out the journal she'd packed, and intending to make some preproduction notes on *The Women*, Sidda began to write instead about the Ya-Yas. Her hand moved across the page swiftly. Sidda did not stop to correct herself, or to analyze why she was doing this. She simply glanced at the creekbank photo, sat at the cabin's table, and wrote from the heart.

Oh, how Mama and the Ya-Yas laughed! I could hear them from the water where I played with my brothers and my sister, Lulu, and the other Petites Ya-Yas. We'd plunge into the creek, then burst back up and hear their laughter. Caro's chortle sounded like a grin doing a polka. Teensy's giggle had a bayou flavor, as if somebody sprinkled Tabasco on it. Necie's hee-hee-hee sounded exactly like that. And Mama's head-thrown-back, open-back, open-throated roar always made people turn around and look at her when she laughed in public.

The Ya-Yas laughed a lot when they were around each other. They'd get going and not be able to stop. They'd laugh till big, fat tears rolled down their cheeks. They'd laugh until one would accuse the others of making her tee-tee in her pants. I don't know what they laughed about. I only know that their laughter was beautiful to hear and see, and that it is something I wish I had more of in my life right now. I like to pride myself on doing many things better than my mother, but she was always better at giggling with her girl-friends.

This is how the Ya-Yas used to be on the creekbank in the summers of my childhood. They'd coat their bodies with a baby-oil-and-iodine mixture, which they shook up in a big Johnson's Baby Oil bottle. The mixture was heavy, reddish-brown, an almost bloodlike tint. They'd coat their faces, arms, and legs, then take turns rubbing the solution on each other's backs.

When my mother lay down, her hands went under her chin, her head rolled to one side, her eyes closed, and she'd let out a long sigh that said how much she loved it all. I loved seeing my mother so relaxed.

This was in the days before anybody worried about skin cancer, long before the rays of the sun were thought to be anything but healthy. Before we killed the ozone that stood sentry between our flesh and the sun.

Mama and Caro usually wore striped tank suits, replicas of ones they used to wear when they were lifeguards at Camp Minnie Maddern for Southern Girls, before they married and had babies.

My mother was a beautiful swimmer. Her stroke was the Australian crawl. Watching Mama swim was like watching a woman who knew how to waltz perfectly, only her partner was not a man, but creek water. Her kick was strong, her stroke fluid, and when she rolled her head from side to side to breathe, you could barely see her mouth open. "There is no excuse for a messy swimmer, any more than there is for a messy eater," she told us. My mother judged people by how well they swam and whether they made her laugh or not.

Spring Creek was not wide like the Garnet River or huge like the Gulf of Mexico or long like some lakes. It was just a small brown body of water, well suited to mothers and children. While the creek was perfectly safe, we were warned about the areas out of sight. Out where the creek curved, where it was too deep. Past where old logs divided the swimming area from a darker, deeper one. Alligators that could eat a kid whole lived out there. They waited for bad little chil-dren who disobeyed their mothers. They crawled into your dreams at night. They could eat you, they could eat your mother, they could pull the rug out from under you when you least expected it, and then gobble you whole before you knew it.

"Even *I* can't save yall from the alligators," Mama used to say. "So don't push your luck."

When Mama swam her laps—ten times around the circumference of the swimming hole—she made the creek seem larger than it was. I marveled at her solitude as she swam those laps. She called it her "swim around the world," and I couldn't wait until my own stroke was strong enough for me to follow in her wake. Mama would conclude her swim by coming back to the shallow end, where the sandbar beach was. She'd emerge from the water, shake her head, and jump on one foot to shake the water out of her ear. Then she'd do the same on the other side. I marveled at her beauty, all wet and cool, her hair slicked back, her eyes shining, proud of her strength.

Mama and the Ya-Yas carried a big red ice chest down to the creek with them every day. The old tin kind with a lid that snapped off. Inside were chunks of ice chipped off large blocks of ice that we'd buy at the Spring Creek Shop and Skate, the local grocery and roller rink across the road from the creek.

That ice kept their beer and our Cokes cold. On top of the beer and Cokes were our ham and cheese sandwiches wrapped in wax paper. The crusts were cut off the sandwiches for the four of us, who wouldn't touch bread if the crust was left on. Paper napkins sat on top of the sandwiches, and when we opened the chest and lifted them out, they had a papery, powdery coolness that disappeared instantly, so we would quickly raise them to our cheeks as soon as we could in order to savor the chilly darkness of the ice chest.

Mama still drank beer when we were little. It was not until I was a teenager that she gave up beer altogether because it was too fattening. But even back then, when we were little, Mama would often forgo a beer in favor of a vodka and grapefruit juice, which she kept in a squat aqua-and-white thermos. Across the front of the little thermos she had written with a freezer pen: RE-VIVI-FICATION TONIC. She described the concoction as "a cocktail and diet aid rolled into one."

Mama and the Ya-Yas were always using different plays on my mother's name. If Teensy walked into a party that lacked pizzazz, she might announce, "This party needs to be *Vivi-fied*." Sometimes they declared things to be "Re-Vivi-fication projects," like the time Mama and Necie redesigned the uniforms of my Girl Scout troop.

When I was young, I thought my mother was so internationally well known that the English language had invented words just for her. As a child, I would turn to the skinny "V" section of Webster's and study the many words that referred to Mama. There was "vivid," which meant "full of life; bright; intense." And "vivify," which meant "to give life or to make more lively." There were "vivace," "viva," "vivacious," "vivacity," "vivarium," and "viva voce." Mama was the source of all these words. She was also the reason for the phrase *"Vive le roi"* (which she told us meant "Long live Vivi the Queen!"). All these definitions had to do with life, like Mama herself.

It was the word "vivisection" that baffled me: "A surgical operation performed on a living animal to study the structure and function of living organs and parts." It seemed to come out of left field. Its very sound gave me chills. I constantly asked Mama to explain it, but I was never satisfied.

Ever on the lookout for any words that might refer to me, I would paw through any dictionary I could get my hands on. There had to be at least one word that concerned *me*. At least a "Siddafy," like "Vivify." But the closest I could find was "sissified."

It was not until I was in second or third grade that my friend M'lain Chauvin told me that Mama had nothing to do with those words in the dictionary. We got into a fight about it and Sister Henry Ruth intervened. When the nun confirmed M'lain's claim, I was heartbroken at first. It changed my whole perception of reality. It began the unraveling of unquestioned belief that the world revolved around Mama. But along with my disappointment came a profound relief, although I could not admit it at the time.

I thought my mother was a star for so many years that when I found out she wasn't, I was stupefied. Had she once been a star and her bright burning had dimmed? Maybe because she had us? Or had Mama never been a star to begin with? Somewhere guilt developed whenever I seemed to eclipse Mama in any little way. Even winning a spelling bee made me worry, because I never trusted that I could shine without obliterating her.

I did not understand then that my mother lived in a world that could not or would not acknowledge her radiance, her *pull* on the earth—at least not as much as she needed. So she made up her own solar system with the other Ya-Yas and lived in its orbit as fully as she could.

My father was not included in this orbit, not really. All the Ya-Ya husbands existed in a separate universe from the Ya-Yas and us kids.

In our summer world at Spring Creek, we plotted against the men, made fun of them, listened to our mothers as they did imitations of our fathers around the campfire. We watched them treat our fathers like bosses or fools or sometimes sweethearts. But we did not watch the Ya-Yas treat their men like they were friends.

Perhaps Mama, more than Necie, Caro, or Teensy, depended on her girlfriends to give her what her marriage did not or could not. I do not doubt, for all their problems, that my mother loved my father, in her way; and that father, in his way, loved her. It's just that the ways I saw them loving each other left me terrified.

Much of the Ya-Yas' time on the creekbank was spent chatting, dozing, reapplying their sun-grabbing tincture, and keeping an eye on us. They took turns being responsible for watching us as we splashed, dove, cannonballed, jackknifed, dunked, kicked, floated, and fought in the creek water. The Ya-Ya who was on watch could only keep one foot in the conversation because she had to concentrate on how many heads were visible in the creek. Altogether, there were sixteen of us Petites Ya-Yas. Necie had seven kids; Caro had three—all boys. Teensy had a boy and girl. And then there were the four of us. Every half hour, the Ya-Ya in charge would stand up, look out at the water, and blow a whistle hanging from an old costume jewelry necklace. At the sound of the whistle, we immediately had to stop whatever we were doing and count off.

Each of the Petites Ya-Yas had an assigned number, and the Ya-Ya on watch would listen for our voices as we called them out. Once we were all accounted for, we could resume our playing, and that Ya-Ya, her half-hourly job done, could settle down on the blanket. Although the ladies did not stop drinking while they were on lookout, it must be said that not one of us Petites Ya-Yas drowned during all those endless summer days spent on the creek.

At least twice a summer, Mama would make one of us pretend to be drowning in Spring Creek so she could practice her rescue technique. Mama learned how to rescue drowning people long before we were born. She got recertified by the Red Cross every three years, but proclaimed it her responsibility to test herself every single summer. We begged and screamed and fought to be the drowning victim. We loved the special attention.

Basically, what you had to do was swim to the deep end and bob up and down in a panic, flailing your arms and screaming like you were about to take your last breath before sinking.

Mama would be up on the creekbank as planned. She'd be wearing her shorts and camp blouse over her swimsuit, and as soon as she heard your screams, she'd raise her hands to her eyes to block the glare. Then she'd scan the horizon like an Indian princess, and spot you. Even as she was searching, she'd start ripping off her blouse and shorts, and kicking off her tennis shoes. Then she'd run to the edge of the creekbank and plunge into the water, employing one of her famous shallow lifeguard dives. At the sight of Mama's leap, you would quiet down a little and watch her swim, fast and sure, to the spot where you were drowning.

When she'd reach you, she'd shout, "Flail more! Dahlin! Flail more!" And you'd flap your arms harder and kick and scream with increased vigor. Then, with great assurance, Mama would hook her hand under your chin, lean your head back against her chest, and begin the rescue, using her mighty inverted scissors kick to propel the two of you through the water in short little bursts.

Once back on the sandbar, Mama would lean over you with her ear to your chest. Then she'd feel around in your mouth with her fingers to make sure there was nothing blocking your throat. After that began the most dramatic component of the rescue: mouth-to-mouth resuscitation. The Kiss of Life. Or as we called it, "mouth-to-mouth re-Vivification." This was the crucial part of the rescue attempt, which could mean the difference between life and death. She'd clamp your nostrils together, put one hand on your chest, and begin to breathe into you. She'd breathe, then pump your chest with her palm, then breathe again. Then, when she was satisfied, Mama would stand up, her hands on her hips, her hair slicked back like a mermaid-lifeguard, and announce with a proud smile, "You were almost a goner, Dahlin, but now I think you'll make it!"

Occasionally the staged rescue would scare one of the little kids, who did not understand that it was pretend. So Mama had gotten in the habit of inviting each Petite Ya-Ya to lean over you, the rescued one, to feel the breath coming out of your nostrils. After the last kid had been reassured, everyone would start clapping. Then Mama would jump on one foot, shake the water out of her ears, and say, "Knew I hadn't lost my touch."

For days after Mama saved you from a watery death, you would recall over and over again the thrill of such a close call. You would remember how confidently she pulled you through the water, and you would recollect the taste of her mouth and the smell of her breath. For days you felt unsafe venturing near the deep end, because the "near-drowning" was so vivid. *So Vivi vivid.* You would begin to fear the alligators even when you were in the safe areas. You would wonder, What would happen if you were drowning and Mama wasn't around to dive in and save you? Say she *simply went away.* Like the time when you were little, getting over bronchitis, and it wouldn't stop raining. That time you went to the window again and again and she was not there. You were bad and she hit you, then just went away.

Mama wasn't the only strong swimmer. Caro had been a lifeguard too, and had even more stamina when it came to certain strokes. With her smart red-highlighted brown page boy and her olive skin, Caro grew up swimming in the Gulf, and she could swim for hours. Her dips in the creek were minuscule adventures compared to her ocean swims. Mama always said, "Caro is indisputably the strongest lady endurance swimmer I have ever known or ever *will* know."

Caro brought out Mama's intrepidness. She was close to five feet nine, which was terribly tall for a woman in an era that worshipped petiteness. She had long legs and her body was perfectly built for Hattie Carnegie suits, which she still wore in my childhood, even though she'd bought them years before.

With her flat chest and square shoulders, she looked terrific in clothes, although of all the Ya-Yas she cared the least for them. She had one black strapless evening gown with a slit up the back, which showed her calves when she danced. She wore that dress to every Ya-Ya party I remember from my childhood. She wore the gown with a feather boa, which my sister, Lulu, and I followed around like it was alive. For Mama's birthday one year, Caro teamed a pair of cowboy boots and a cowboy hat with the gown, looking like a cross between Marlene Dietrich and Annie Oakley.

Caro is my godmother, and I have always been told the story of how, at the end of my Baptism, Caro, out of the blue, whistled "When You Wish Upon a Star." She called everyone "Pal." "Hey, Pal," she'd say. "What's cookin?" Some people might think of New York City taxi drivers calling folks "Pal" or maybe gangsters from the thirties, but when Caro called you "Pal," she was including you in her own special Bohemianism.

She was the reason I became a Bohemian at the age of eight. Refusing to wear anything except my black dance leotard and tights, and a pair of dark sunglasses left behind after one of Mama and

Daddy's cocktail parties, I changed my name to Madame Voilanska. When people called me Sidda, I refused to answer. When the nuns called Mama to complain, she told them if I said my name was Madame Voilanska, then that's what they better call me. The minute I got home from school, I changed into my all-black ensemble, and added a cigarette to my overall look. I put my hair up in a ponytail, and sat for hours on a stool in front of the sliding glass doors that led onto the enclosed patio of our house, studying my reflection. I did not pretend to smoke the cigarette. (That was the kind of thing that Lulu would do.) Instead, I employed it as a prop with which to gesture. I held the cigarette between my thumb and index finger and used it to stab the air as though I were making some important, unassailable point. These points were expressed in my original poetry.

My mother has included one of these poems in the scrapbook. It is written in my young Palmer Method longhand, and it's dated 1961, which meant I was eight years old. I was shocked and touched to see it. My mother is nothing if not a surprise.

Freedom
by Madame Voilanska

26 times I have walked around the house!
I clapped my hands and sang!
Then my hair stood up!
And I did not go back in!

I had loved "bats and balls" ever since the nuns introduced them to us. I could not for the life of me understand why I couldn't use exclamation points to end every other sentence I composed. Sister Rodney Marie would circle them with mean red marks and write, "Use period, not exclamation point." At school I finally made myself cut down to using only one exclamation point per paragraph. But in my own private poetry, I used them all over the place. Later, in high school, I discovered that the magnificent Walt Whitman loved exclamation points as much as I did. That, along with his wondering and exaltation, and tender nursing of dying soldiers, made him one of my heroes.

I knew that to be a true Bohemian you had to wear sunglasses. This was the most obvious thing that had established Caro as the leading (and only) Bohemian of Thornton. Back then Caro had to wear sunglasses everywhere. Granted, when they had hangovers, all four of the Ya-Yas wore sunglasses, even at Sunday-morning Mass. Caro, however, developed a temporary condition in which even the least bit of direct sunlight in her eyes could make her sick. For a while she had to wear sunglasses all the time, even at night. She would do her errands, even on the cloudiest wet day, wearing her shades. Thorntonites began to get the idea that Caro was weird in an out-of-town kind of way. Many people did not know that she had a medical problem, they just thought she was being a snob, trying to act like a movie star. "Who does she think she *is*?" they'd say. Some of the more obnoxious people—"grown men," according to Caro—would actually walk up to her and say things like "Take those sunglasses off right now and let people see your eyes." Like Caro was breaking some kind of eyeglass law.

But to me Caro's sunglasses were simply the cat's pajamas. I would try to copy her and wear my sunglasses at night at Pecan Grove, even though it meant I bumped into furniture.

Teensy had jet-black hair and eyes that were almost as dark. Barely five feet tall, she had an olive complexion and tiny feet, almost like a child's. She and Mama first met at the age of four in the doctor's office. The story has become legend in Thornton because it involved a large pecan that Teensy had stuck in her nose "to see if it would fit." It did fit, and it took Dr. Mott's delicate skill to remove it. That pecan is mounted behind glass in a display case in Dr. Mott's office entitled "Foreign Objects Removed from Children's Bodies." Under the pecan it reads, "Nut from Teensy Whitman's left nostril. June 18, 1930." When we were growing up, this gave Teensy a sort of fame among school kids.

Teensy had a perfect body, and we all knew exactly what it looked like. One of her eccentricities (when the gang really got going, when the bourbon was flowing, when the time seemed right, when she received the call) was to stage an elaborately drawn-out, sexy, and very funny striptease. We had seen her do it at numerous Ya-Ya parties, and had heard talk about the time she did it at the Theodore Hotel during Caro and Blaine's fifth-anniversary bash. We Petites Ya-Yas were taught to simply refer to it as Teensy's *deshabillage*.

Teensy always wore the skimpiest swimsuits. The Ya-Yas called her the Bikini Queenie and she was the talk of Garnet parish with her risqué little numbers. I always imagined that she received those bikinis in the mail straight from Paris.

She swam only on her back. On her back in her un-Catholic bikini. Every once in a while she would give a furious flutter kick and white water would rise in a fume from her precious tiny toes. She'd cruise with this momentum for a while until she came to a standstill. Then, extending her arms wide in the water, she would gracefully move them as though she were conducting the legato movement of a water symphony. When she grew tired of that, she'd flip over and dive neatly into the water, her toes pointing up like arrows to the sky. Then she'd swim under water for what seemed like days, and we'd all place bets on where she'd surface. When her pretty black head popped up like a seal, we'd all say: "Where *does* Teensy *put* all that air?!"

Teensy always had money, and she gave it away to any of us who needed it. When her father died, he left her a fat bundle of Coca-Cola shares. Her husband, Chick, had inherited money as well, so much that the only reason he went downtown to his office was so he could drink coffee with the other men at the River Street Café. It was Teensy who staked Lulu when she started her own interior-design business. And it was Teensy who—no questions asked—wired me $10,000 when I called her at the end of my first year in New York, broke and scared, with not a job in sight. Teensy is also the one who offered—she was fairly tipsy at the time—to pay for each and every Petite Ya-Ya to go into therapy. She made this offer at my high school graduation party, which was held to jointly honor Teensy's son, Jacques, Caro's son Turner, and me.

Not one of us took her up on the offer at the time, a fact I've often regretted, since it could have saved me enough money to buy a small country somewhere. Teensy's only daughter, my childhood friend Genny, had by that time already undergone more therapy (both inpatient and out) than the rest of us could imagine. In fact, at the time we were graduating from high school, she was already in a private mental hospital for the second time. But that is another story. Her fine, fragile craziness that bordered on visionary reminded me of stories I'd heard about Genevieve, Teensy's mother. That family had its share of sadness.

All of us, so interwoven, so braided, growing up Ya-Ya in that backwater, third-tier state, where our families were the *haut monde*, their sins charming and mostly unnamed. So many stories in the Ya-Ya clan.

When the Petites Ya-Yas—minus the Walker kids—showed up *en masse* at performance of *Women on the Cusp*, I felt like I'd been granted a partial reprieve from my status of orphan. Even though Mama's anger prevented the Ya-Yas themselves from seeing the play, the Petites Ya-Yas came. Somehow they even managed to check Genny out of McClean in Boston long enough to come.

Mama's scrapbook is filled not only with her life and the lives of the Ya-Yas, but inevitably overflows into the next generation. We were a communal tribe, a little primitive matriarchal village. Especially during those summer days at Spring Creek, when the men stayed in town and worked all week, coming out only to visit on the weekends.

Necie was the Ya-Ya who looked most like a mom. But she, too, had her peculiarities. For one thing, she was the only mother from my childhood who had long hair. Her hair was the principal thing about Necie's looks that let you know she was a Ya-Ya. Wives and mothers in the fifties and early sixties just did not have long beautiful hair like that. Not in Thornton.

Necie's hair was thick and brown and luxurious, and when she let it down, it was her crowning glory. On summer mornings at Spring Creek, when she had just awakened, Necie's hair tumbled down onto her shoulders and caught the early sun as she sat on the porch and drank coffee with the others. She would let me play with her hair for hours, taking no notice at all. I would sit, with the sound of the ladies' voices rolling over me, and simply play with Necie's hair, heavy and clean and smelling of Breck. I loved lifting her hair and burying my nose in it, just to smell it. I took a soft pleasure from this simple, innocent, sensual act with a woman. Pleasure I wish had not passed out of my life as I grew older.

I loved seeing the Ya-Yas when they climbed out of the creek, with their hair all wet. They looked sleek and elegant and beautiful, like some kind of exotic water animals, some wild water women with secret lives somewhere at the bottom of a lagoon.

In those creek days, Mama never worried about her hair. It was cut very short in a "pixie," which she called her "Four-Kid Coif." Her hair was naturally blonde, and without makeup her eyebrows and eyelashes were the same shade. Years later, when Mia Farrow cut all her hair off, the Ya-Yas claimed she was imitating my mother.

Mama's eyes were a dark reddish brown, and they gave her face a power, a counterbalance it would not have otherwise had. Her fair skin and hair made people at first think she was fragile. Her eyes told them she meant business.

When Mama stepped out of the creek water, she would towel dry her hair for a moment, put on fresh lipstick, and reach for her large white sun hat, because—as Mama instructed us—true blonds can lie in the sun but only with a *very* wide brim. My mother loved very wide brims.

In those days I knew Mama's body down to the shape of her toes, her toenails covered in her trademark "Rich Girl Red" polish. Her blonde complexion with tiny cinnamon freckles on her upper arms, on her cheeks. A kind of milky whiteness lay underneath the freckles like a layer of thin cream. Sometimes, in certain light, you could see *through* my mother's skin to the lavender and blue veins underneath. When I saw this, it terrified me.

Mama's legs moved like the tennis player she was. They looked fine in shorts, which she wore places that most ladies wouldn't dare. She wore shorts, a camp shirt of crisp cotton or old linen, tucked neatly in, white crew socks, and white round-toed Keds. She called it her summer uniform. All white, like a tennis player.

My mother was a big woman in a little woman's body. She stood about five feet four inches tall in her bare feet and never weighed more than 115 pounds—except when she was pregnant. She prided herself on her weight, and took great pains to maintain it. She had the limbs of a taller person. Not that they were actually too long for her body, but they seemed to have a willowiness about them—a willowiness that encased a tightness. It seemed like the life inside my mother's body was too hot and fierce for her fair skin. "I am going to jump out of my skin," she always used to say. And as a girl, I feared she would.

She was not like the kind of mother I saw in books and movies. Except for her breasts, which were surprisingly full for her frame, she was not plump or round in any way. She was muscular and somewhat wiry. Any roundness that tried to sneak its way onto her as she began to age was promptly exercised or starved off. Once Necie turned to Mama and asked mildly, "Vivi, why do you insist on staying so thin? We're not *eighteen* anymore." My mother responded, as though it made perfect sense, "I want light baggage when I decide to blow this joint."

When I close my eyes, I can see my mother's body in front of me exactly as it looked in my childhood. I can hear her part-Scarlett, part-Katharine Hepburn, part-Tallulah voice, in all its rich, smoky nuance.

I know nothing of her naked body as it is now. I have heard rumors that she finally "filled out a little," but I have no proof. I have not seen her body without clothes in over twenty years. I do not know if I would recognize her body if her face and voice were hidden from me, and this makes me sad.

When I think now of the Vivi of my girlhood, I am overwhelmed. She gave birth to four children—five if you count my twin who died—in three years and nine months. That means from the time she married, her body never had a chance to settle down from the wild hormonal tangos of pregnancy. It means that she was sleep-deprived for five or six straight years. And Lord knows Mama is a woman who loved her sleep (as I do mine). She used to say she could *taste* sleep and that it was as delicious as a BLT on fresh French bread.

Even as a child you knew that she was not the kind of woman meant to have four stair-step kids. You would stand next to her and know you were asking too much even as you tugged and begged and insisted, "Look at me, Mama! Watch me do *this*, Mama. Now watch me do *this*."

But during those summers, my mother was a goddess of the creekbank with her girlfriends. Some days I worshipped at her feet. Some days I would have split her wide open just to get the attention she gave the Ya-Yas. Some days I was so jealous I wished Caro, Teensy, and Necie dead. Other days, from their spots on the picnic blankets, Mama and her buddies were the pillars that held up the heavens.

Here in this cabin, twenty-five hundred miles from Louisiana, and many years from my girlhood, if I close my eyes and concentrate, I can smell my mother and the Ya-Yas. It is as though my own body keeps the scents of the Ya-Yas simmering on some back burner, and at the most unexpected moments, the aroma rises up and joins with the fragrance of my current life to make a new-old perfume. The soft aroma of old worn cotton from a linen chest; the lingering smell of tobacco on an angora sweater; Jergen's hand lotion; sautéed green peppers and onions; the sweet, nutty smell of peanut butter and bananas; the oaken smell of good bourbon; a combination of lily of the valley, cedar, vanilla, and somewhere, the lingering of old rose. These smells are older than any thought. Mama, Teensy, Necie, and Caro, each one of them had an individual scent, to be sure. But this is the gumbo of their scents. This is the Gumbo Ya-Ya. This is the internal vial of perfume I carry with me everywhere I go.

The four of their scents were *in key*. Their very bodies harmonized together.

Surely this made it easier for them to forget things and forgive each other, not to have to constantly "work" on things, the way we do now. This has never happened for me with a group of women. It is hard for me to even imagine. Yet I have seen it. I have smelled it.

Mama's perfume is a scent that was created for her by Claude Hovet, the *parfumier* in the French Quarter, when she was sixteen. A gift from Genevieve Whitman, it is a scent that is softly shocking and deeply moving. A scent that disturbs me and delights me. It smells like ripe pears, vetiver, a bit of violet, and something else—something spicy, almost biting and exotic.

Once the scent caught me on the street in Greenwich Village. I stopped in my tracks and looked around. Where was it coming from? A shop? The trees? A passerby? I could not tell. I only know the smell made me cry. I stood on the sidewalk in Greenwich Village as people brushed by, and felt suddenly young and terribly open, as if I were waiting for something. I live in an ocean of smell, and the ocean is my mother.

6

*A*fter writing in her journal, Sidda felt sleepy. She let her head drop down over the table and dozed off. Vivi's scrapbook slid from her lap, and a small key slipped from between the folds of the old pages, and fell on the floor next to her foot.

When Sidda woke, the first thing she saw was the key. It was a small, tarnished thing, dangling from a chain, about the size of a pecan. What could it unlock? A jewelry box? A small suitcase? A diary? She padded to the sliding glass door and let Hueylene out. It was dawn, but the lake was shrouded in fog so thick that Sidda could not see the opposite shore.

The key lay in her palm as she stood on the deck looking out into the fog. A few tiny letters appeared to have once been printed on it, but Sidda couldn't make them out. Stepping back out on the deck to call Hueylene, she pressed the key between her palms and blew into her hands. Then she did a strange, childlike thing: she smelled the key, and licked it. It had a metallic taste that made her shiver slightly, made her feel a surge of Nancy Drew–like excitement.

She spent the rest of the day walking, eating, and napping. She had no idea she was so tired. Finally, around four, she walked down to the Quinault Mercantile, the small general store that served the area, to use the pay phone.

She made a little Sign of the Cross, then she dialed her parents' phone number.

It was midway into cocktail hour in the state of Louisiana when the portable phone rang at Pecan Grove. Vivi Walker was sitting at the edge of Shep's vegetable garden in an Adirondack chair, watching her husband pick vegetables for supper.

"Hello," Vivi said.

"Mama, it's Sidda."

Vivi took a sip of her bourbon and branch water. She immediately felt a stab of guilt at having broken her vow of abstinence so soon. She drew a deep breath, and said, "Siddalee Walker? *The New York Times* oft-quoted Siddalee Walker?"

Sidda swallowed. "Yes, ma'am, that one. I called to thank you, Mother."

"Since when do you call me Mother?" Vivi asked.

Shep looked over from a row of green peppers. When Vivi mouthed the word "Sidda," he moved over to the bean poles, farther away from his wife. He'd been the one who had to live with Vivi's reaction to the *Times* piece. Vivi had scared him so bad he'd taken her off for a trip to Hilton Head. Shep figured it was better than a doctor-ordered trip, which was what Vivi had seemed headed for.

Shep Walker didn't understand his wife, never had. To him, she was another country that he needed a passport to visit. He had given up on ever knowing what made her tick. She was harder to live with than a cotton crop, and Lord knows, cotton needed tending. But she could still surprise him, after forty-two years, and she knew how to make him laugh, something not many people did. When she rode in the back fields with him, sitting shotgun in his pickup, she still really *listened* when he rambled on about his rice or cotton or crayfish or soybeans. And once in a while, when she turned to him the way she did, tilting her head to ask a question, Shep felt like a young man again. There had been a mighty sexual attraction between them when they were young. An attraction that had waned—not so much with years, but from the exhaustion of trying to survive each other.

"I never trusted women who called their mamas Mother," Vivi said into the phone.

"Sorry. I called to tell you that I'm—well, Mama, I'm over-whelmed by your sending me the scrapbook. It's incredibly generous."

"It's the least I could do for the legitimate theater," Vivi said. "But remember that Clare Boothe Luce was much, *much* older than the Ya-Yas. And the Ya-Yas *love* each other, unlike those she-cats Luce wrote about."

"I'm really touched that you would part with 'Divine Secrets,' Mama."

"After the way you butchered my reputation throughout the United States of America, I do think it was rather *big* of me."

"Not simply big, Mama. *Grand*."

There was a short silence in which Vivi waited for an apology.

"I'm sorry about it all, Mama. I didn't mean to hurt you."

"I do not want to discuss it," Vivi said. "Now, what about the wedding?"

"I do not want to discuss it," Sidda said.

"Everybody's driving me crazy asking me questions," Vivi said. "I mean, I *have* given countless wedding gifts for the past twenty-some-odd years to every girl in your class, some of them for three different marriages. People want to know where to send the gifts."

"Your scrapbook is the gift I need right now, Mama."

"I always thought I'd use that thing to write my memoirs," Vivi said. "But who has time to write memoirs? I'm still *living* my memoirs."

"It would be wonderful if you'd write about all those memories, Mama. I have so many questions. I mean, the things in the scrapbook are wonderful, but there is so much I don't know. So many stories. I found this key, for instance. It just fell right out of the book, and I'm dying to know what it's to. Has a little chain attached to it."

"Oh, really?" Vivi said.

"Do you have any idea what it's to?"

"Could be to anything."

"Mother, it would be so helpful to me if you would just sit down and *write* about your life for me. What formed you, what went into creating the lifelong friendship you share with Caro and Teensy and Necie. What you felt, what your secrets were, what were your dreams? The stories underneath all this Ya-Ya-rabilia."

"I *asked* you not to call me Mother. It sounds so Northern. In fact, I believe I asked you not to call me, period. I am under no obligation to write an essay about my life for you. Especially since you seem to feel it *your* obligation to broadcast lies about me to the free world."

"God, Mama. I could not control that. Let's not fight, please."

Vivi took a sip of her drink.

Two thousand miles apart, Sidda could hear the ice cubes clinking against Vivi's glass. If anyone ever made a movie about her childhood, that would be the soundtrack. She glanced at her watch. How could she have forgotten that it was cocktail time in Louisiana?

"Forget it, Mother."

"No," Vivi said. "*You* forget it. You want to pick *yourself* apart, go right ahead. But you're not going to pick me to pieces. I sent you my Ya-Ya 'Divine Secrets,' for God's sake, what else do you want— blood?!"

"I'm sorry, Mama, I didn't mean to sound like I'm not grateful, but—"

"Do you remember how horrified you were as a little girl when you found the word 'vivisection' in the dictionary? Came running to me in tears, remember? Well, I'm not a Goddamn frog, Sidda. You can't figure me out. *I* can't figure me out. It's *life*, Sidda. You don't fig- ure it out. You just climb up on the beast and *ride*."

"I'll take good care of the album," Sidda said, "and get it back to you like you asked."

"I want it back before my birthday, you hear me?" Vivi said.

"Yes ma'am."

"And do me a favor, will you?" Vivi said. "Don't call me again act- ing like a researcher for *This Is Your Life*. I don't need the kind of pub- licity you come up with."

Late that night, after Sidda had race-walked for five miles down a long, flat road that led into the Quinault Valley, she sat out on the deck and stared up into the sky. The whole day had been overcast, and no stars were to be seen. She sipped a mimosa and nibbled on some cheese and bread, wondering what Connor was doing at that moment. Her body missed his. She thought of the time in his small office at the Seattle Opera when he'd reached down into the waist of her slacks while she stood at his drafting table, looking over drawings. How he stroked her and how he smiled and how she groaned, Oh, these drawings are so lovely. She missed him, she wanted him. She resented the fact that each time she thought of him she grew simulta- neously moist in her groin and tight in her chest.

She turned to look inside the cabin. Vivi's album sat on the table.

She took a step closer and leaned her face against the screen of the door, like a child might do. She raised her glass to the scrapbook in a private little toast. The album drew her back inside.

Leaning over the scrapbook, she opened to a page near the front. What she found was a cardboard placard with the number 39 written on it. Next to it was a piece of paper on which a childish hand had written the following, so that it looked like the beginning of a newspaper article:

VIVI'S VERY IMPORTANT NEWS

ISSUE NO. 1

SATURDAY, DECEMBER 8, 1934

GIRLS POOT AND GET DISQUALIFIED

BY VIVIANE ABBOTT. AGE 8

Sidda smiled and turned the paper over, but it was blank. No story followed, there was only that heading. She scoured the nearby pages for more, but she could find no further information from "Vivi's Very Important News." She knew exactly who those girls were. 1934. The depths of the Great Depression. Huey Long was Governor of Louisiana—or dictator, depending on your viewpoint and your parish. She knew that Eugene O'Neill's play *Days Without End* had premiered that year, and that Pirandello received the Nobel Prize for Literature. But she did not have the faintest idea what her mother had been disqualified from, or who had done the disqualifying.

Shaking her head, she absentmindedly reached down to stroke Hueylene. If only that scrapbook could talk, she thought. Our Lady of Cherubim Chit-Chat, if only that scrapbook could talk.

7

$\mathcal{V}$ivi Abbott Walker knew she wasn't supposed to be drinking, and she knew she wasn't supposed to be smoking. That is why, after she'd cleared the dinner things and said good night to Shep, she felt a little thrill as she stepped out on the back patio with a snifter of Courvoisier and a cigarette. She sat down at the wrought-iron patio table where she'd set up the Ouija board. She lit candles on the silver candelabra, which had been one of the many wedding gifts from Teensy's mother, Genevieve. Then she went into a little trance.

She didn't pose any questions. She just sat there with the candle-light and the Ouija board and the sounds of the cicadas and the appealing idea that she was some kind of medium.

One hand rested lightly on the pointer, and Vivi smiled as it slid across the board and spelled out the numbers "1," "9," "3," and "4."

Ah yes, Vivi thought, my first encounter with Hollywood.

Vivi, 1934

You have got to have *exactly* fifty-six curls if you want a chance to win the Shirley Temple Look-Alike Contest. Me and my best buddies Caro and Teensy and Necie spent all morning at the beauty parlor getting our hair *just perfect*.

Miss Beverly's Beauty Parlor was so busy you would have thought it was New York City. Teensy's mama, Genevieve, took us there to have our hair changed from rags to curls. Genevieve is the one who helped us all get our hair and costumes ready for the Shirley Temple Look-Alike Contest. Yesterday morning she rolled our hair in rags and we were supposed to keep them in all day and all night.

But Caro ripped her rags out in her sleep. When we got to the beauty parlor, her hair was lying there straight as little boards. She said, "Those rags made my scalp itch and they pulled my eyes back like a Chinaman's, so I ripped them out and threw them in the garbage."

I know what she means. I've still got twitches around my temples that I sure hope go away before I grow up.

"I'm gonna wear Lowell's aviator cap," Caro said, and she whipped out her brother's cap, plopped it on her head, and tucked her hair underneath.

"What a splendid idea," Genevieve said. *"Très originale!"* Genevieve always says things like this because she grew up on the bayou, near Marksville. She makes everyone call her by her first name, even kids. Whenever all us girls are together, she says, "Gumbo Ya-Ya!" This means "everybody talking at the same time," which is what we sure do.

Genevieve wouldn't even be here if she hadn't married Mr. Whitman, who owns the Garnet Savings and Loan. She met him in New Orleans, where a rich friend of her father sent her to the Ursuline nuns to learn to be a lady. Oh, but thank the Lord she came to Thornton! We adore her. She has jet-black hair and eyes just as dark, and her skin is smooth and she can dance any dance in the world. Besides the Cajun two-step, she has taught us all the jitterbug, Praise Allah, and Kickin' the Mule. Genevieve is the most fun of any grown-up I know—except when she gets her *attaque de nerfs* and has to stay in bed with the shades drawn. I want to be just like Genevieve when I grow up.

I made sure to count each curl when Miss Beverly took the rags off my hair and spun out curls with her fingers. I didn't want her to mess up and give me thirty-eight curls instead of fifty-six.

Then, in walked Jack, Teensy's brother. He came right into the beauty parlor, where boys never come.

"Hey!" he said. "Brought yall some donuts. Just out of the oven at Mr. Campo's Bakery. Vivi, I got you a chocolate, like you like."

That Jack is so sweet. Not sissy-sweet. Just sweet. He is the best baseball pitcher in town. And the way he hits, people call him T-Babe, short for Little Babe because he can slug like Babe Ruth. Jack also plays the Cajun fiddle, but his daddy won't let him play at home. Mr. Whitman won't even let Jack be called by his real name, Jacques. Mr. Whitman forbids Genevieve to speak Acadian French around him. He says, "Speak English, Genevieve! For God's sake, speak the King's English!"

"Yall are a whole lot prettier than Shirley Temple," Jack said. "She looks like a little skunk compared to yall. *Mais oui*, yall are gonna bump old Shirley's name right off the marquee."

Caro was the first to hear about the Shirley Temple Look-Alike Contest, because her father owns The Bob—one of the two movie theaters in Thornton. Mr. Bob also owns The Bob in Royalton and The Bob in Rayville, both down the road. His biggest movie theater is in New Orleans: The Robert. It's the fanciest of all The Bob Theaters in the world.

A month ago it was formally announced that The Bob would sponsor the contest, with a Shirley Temple man coming all the way from Hollywood. The girl that wins the contest gets to go down to New Orleans on the train and represent our town in the statewide Shirley Temple Look-Alike Contest. And that girl also gets to stay at the Pontchartrain Hotel and be treated like a princess the whole entire time.

Girls just came out of the woodwork. Even some little colored girls tried to sign up, but the contest rules say only white girls could apply. It costs a dime to sign up, but Mr. Bob let some girls sign up without paying. Some people who came to The Bob today paid him with eggs or potatoes. All those eight Nugent kids get to come to the Betty Boop Club Saturday matinee by paying with one bushel of collard greens.

Genevieve had her dressmaker, Cecile, do up all our costumes. I have the darlingest little blue-and-white-plaid dress with a little red tie that fits me to a tee. Over it, I'm wearing a matching little blue coat and a black cap, all just like the outfit Shirley wore when she sang "Good Ship Lollipop." I modeled it for Father last night, and when he saw me, he said, "Come on over here and give your father a hug." He doesn't usually like to be hugged when he gets home, so I was surprised. I went and wrapped my arms around him, and then he gave me a two-dollar bill.

Caro's outfit is so spiffy! She has a little brown leather jacket that she borrowed from her brother, and she's wearing it over a pair of baggy dungarees, with an aviator cap on her head. Just like Shirley wore when she met Loop's plane in *Bright Eyes*. Oh, Caro is so beautiful. All my friends are beautiful.

Necie has a bright yellow coat and a white tam over her curls. And that Teensy, she has a pink ballet tutu, like Shirley got for her birthday in that movie.

I secretly think that I look the most like Shirley Temple. After all, I am the one with the blonde hair. But I wouldn't dare tell anybody this.

When Genevieve brought us to the theater this afternoon, they made us check in at the door, where a lady gave each one of us a piece of cardboard to hang around our necks on a string. The cardboard has our official contest numbers written on them. Mine is 39, Caro's is 40, Teensy's is 41, and somehow things got mixed up because Necie is number 61. I hate this cardboard hanging around my neck. It covers up the buttons on my little blue coat.

The Shirley Temple Look-Alike judge spends his whole life riding trains all over the country judging who looks like Shirley Temple and who doesn't. His name is Mr. Lance Lacey, but Caro just calls him Mr. Hollywood. He arrived yesterday, and Caro and her mother and father went to meet him at the train station. They took him back to Caro's house, and he changed out of his suit into a powder-blue shirt and loose, baggy pants that Caro said looked like pajamas. During supper, he received three long-distance calls. We don't get three long-distance calls in a month at our house! They all sat there, Caro and her parents and Lowell and Bobby, her brothers, just waiting for Mr. Hollywood to get off the phone so they could finish eating. Then this morning he got another long-distance call before breakfast!

I have always always wanted to be up on the stage of The Bob, and now here I am! Oh, I was meant to be a star! Standing up in front of the footlights, high above the audience. Lights, lights, lights! It's better than Christmas. It's hard to see out into the audience, but I can tell exactly where my brother Pete is sitting because he yelled out, "Hey, Stinky!"

I want to step out in front of all these other little ringlet-headed girls and break into a dance. Make everyone look at me, only me! But you have to stand in line. All we're supposed to do is stand up here and try to look like Shirley Temple. I hate it when I have so many other talents! I can sing, dance, spell "prestidigitation," recite "The Ancient Mariner," whistle, and act out stories I made up myself. These folks don't know what they are missing.

Mr. Hollywood's voice flows out all velvet from the microphone. "Shirley Temple represents what is best about America," he says. "Her innocence and smile are a ray of sunshine that beams across these forty-eight states. And when times look down and regular Joes have trouble buying a cup of coffee, Shirley's dimples can cheer up even the saddest Depression hobo. 'Little Miss Sunshine' has danced her way into the hearts of millions, lifting up our land with her unique brand of sweetness."

He glances back at us girls for a second, and then gestures our way. "Now it is my pleasure to be in your fine town and look over your crop of little girls. It's my job to judge which one of these young ladies comes closest to Shirley Temple's wholesome charm and innocence. Which one of them is adorable enough to cheer up this great nation of ours like America's Sweetheart?"

Oh, if only they would let me show my real talent, I could cheer up this nation! I would tell my story about Alligator Girl with the head and shoulders of a girl, and the rest of her body pure alligator. Kind of like a mermaid, but mean. Oh! I am the world's best scary-story teller!

If I could only strut my stuff, I would not only win this contest, but I'd win the one in New Orleans too. I would get my own private rail car with my own bathtub in it and velvet curtains, and then I'd invite Caro and Teensy and Necie to come with me on my trip around America. We'd go to Washington, D.C., where the President and Mrs. Roosevelt would be waiting, begging me to come have tomato sandwiches with the crust cut off. I'd tell them this Great Depression has gone on too long and I'll give them my ideas on how to help the poor folks at Ollie Trott's Trailer

Paradise who lost their real homes. Oh, I'll wave to everybody and they will forget Shirley Temple ever existed!

Mr. Hollywood turns to us, with his hands up to his mouth, stretching out his lips. Has he hurt his lips? No, he is trying to make us smile wider. He gives a signal to the piano player, who starts playing "On the Good Ship Lollipop." Then he circles around us and stops at one girl who's wearing a fuzzy white fur coat. He makes her turn in a circle, then he writes something down on his clipboard. He doesn't say a word, just sort of examines her like you do a horse.

"My mouth is starting to hurt from all this smiling," I whisper to Teensy. Then, I don't have the slightest idea in the world what gets into her, but she hauls off and steps on my toe. So I step right back on her toe and grind down a little.

"Ouch!" Teensy hollers. She loves stuff like this. It's what keeps her going. She turns around at one of the other little girls and sticks her tongue out. Well, that makes that little sissy start crying.

"Titty-baby! Little sissy titty-baby!" Teensy whispers. Then out of nowhere, nowhere at all, Teensy *poots!* One of the biggest poots you have ever heard! You would not think that a poot that big could come out of a girl that small. The look on her face is shocked. She looks behind her like she can't believe she did it. Like when our dog poots and it scares him.

All the other girls heard it, though, and they back away from us. Like Teensy's poot is alive and might knock them down and crawl all over them. Teensy and I start laughing and we cannot stop. If you know of something funnier than pooting, then I wish you'd tell me about it.

Mr. Hollywood himself must not have heard the actual poot. He's still on the other side of the stage, still examining girls. But when he hears us laughing, he looks over our way, and I can see his lips moving, mouthing the words, "Be quiet."

Well, that makes us laugh even harder, and Caro and Necie start cracking up too.

"Shhh!" Mr. Hollywood signals, his Shhh! finger in front of his mouth. Then he takes that same finger and uses it at the corner of his lips to make a big smile, trying to make us do the same thing. The sight of Mr. Hollywood smiling like that just pushes us over the edge and we start howling, the kind of laughing that makes our mothers send us outdoors.

Then, all of a sudden, Mr. Hollywood turns on his fancy heels and heads our way. By this point, there is no stopping us. We couldn't stop laughing even if we wanted to.

Mr. Hollywood stops right in front of us. "Pipe down this very instant!" he says.

His eyes are popping out and his mouth is wide open, and we can see that he has not one, not two, but *three rotten brown teeth!* The front ones are shiny white, but those back ones are rotted! This just makes us scream with laughter. When we don't quiet down, he throws his clipboard slam-bam right on the stage floor, and takes a step toward us, and for a second I think he's going to hit us. But then he changes his mind.

He signals to the piano player to play a little softer. Then Old Rotted Teeth steps up to the microphone and says, "Some of our would-be Shirleys seem to think something is very funny. Numbers 39, 40, 41, and 61, would you please step over here to the microphone?"

When we get over to the microphone stand, Pete yells out, "It's Stinky!" I throw a kiss out to the audience.

Mr. Hollywood Rot-Tooth looks at us and smiles this big old fake grin. "Girls, since you know something so funny, I want you to tell it to the rest of us."

The four of us look at each other. Then Caro steps closer to the microphone. She reaches up and takes her aviator cap off and holds it down at her side. Her hair is flat as a rug. "Do you really want to know what is so funny?" she says into the microphone.

Mr. Hollywood leans into the microphone and says, "Yes, Number 40, we do."

"Well, okay," Caro says, and looks straight out into the audience. She opens her mouth and says loud and clear: *"Teensy farted."*

Well, the whole theater just busts its seams! They start laughing and hooting, and a whole gang of them up front—led by my brother, I bet—starts making poot noises with their hands. And pretty soon other sections of the theater join in making the same noise until it sounds like we're in one giant theater full of pooters! The few that aren't making poot sounds are screaming out things like "Yay! Teensy!"

All the other contestants have clumped together at the back of the stage. I am laughing so hard I can hardly breathe.

Mr. Hollywood shakes his clipboard in Caro's face and booms

into the microphone. "What are your names, little girls? Girls Number 39, 40, 41, 61, give me your names immediately!"

We just stare back at him. It is so much fun to see a grown-up get this mad.

"I said: Tell me your Christian names!"

I am still dying to talk into the microphone all by myself, so I take a step forward. I take a deep breath and give a big smile to the audience. "My name," I announce, "is Pooty Pootwell."

The whole audience breaks into applause! For me. Waves of applause just wash up on the stage and crash against my new shoes. I knew they would love me if I had half a chance!

Old Mr. Hollyrot pushes me away and leans into the microphone. "All four of you are disqualified! Do you hear me? Disqualified!"

His hands are shaking so hard he can hardly hold his clipboard. His mouth is all pinched together, and the veins in his face are about to pop! All because of me!

The place is going completely wild. Popcorn flying all over the place, JuJuBes landing on the stage, and a group of boys standing up yelling, "Go Pooty!" Ushers are running up and down the aisles trying to make kids stop throwing their Coca-Cola cups in the air. They're yelling, "We want Pooty! We want Pooty!" and climbing over seats and stomping on the floor! It's wonderful!

The other little girls are crying and calling for their mothers. Some of the mothers rush up to the stage. You can hear them saying to us, "You should be ashamed of yourselves!"

But I am not ashamed at all. The whole theater is going mad and *it's all because of me.*

"Bring down the curtains!" Mr. Hollyrot says into the microphone.

And then Mr. Bob is at the microphone saying, "All right now, boys and girls, pipe down. I know you're a little stirred up, but I've got a special treat for you. Listen up now. Who wants to see an extra installment of *Flash Gordon*? If you all will settle back down, I'll show a special, unplanned screening of next week's installment, *Flash Gordon and the Planet of Mongo.*" He signals to the piano player, who starts playing something soothing. The popcorn stops flying and kids start back to their seats. When you mention *Planet Mongo* around here, people shut up and listen.

Then Mrs. Bob steps up to the microphone and says, "Mothers, would you please come out and get your daughters? And those of you girls whose mothers aren't here, please come on back to the dressing room with me. Everything is just fine."

Teensy and Caro and Necie and I start to walk off the stage, but Teensy cannot stand it. She runs back to the center of the stage, turns and sticks her little booty out at the audience, and wiggles it for all she's worth.

Well, Mr. Lance Toothrot Lacey storms over to Teensy and yanks her arm so hard he just about pulls it off. And there he is, leaning Teensy over his knee with his hand in the air, about to give her a spanking right on her tiny little behind!

But Mr. Bob stops him. "Son, I think you better watch your manners. This child doesn't belong to you."

"I don't care who the hell she belongs to," Mr. Rottenteeth says. "She has ruined the official Shirley Temple Look-Alike Contest! This has never happened to me before!"

Old Hollywood's voice has changed. He doesn't sound like a movie star with a velvet-curtain voice anymore, but like one of those fellows who come to town with the circus and spit out of the sides of their mouth.

"Well, that might be true, son," Mr. Bob says, "but you still don't take a hand to one of our daughters. Her own father can spank her if he sees fit."

Mr. Hollywood straightens his ascot and pulls down the cuffs of his sleeves. "Well, I'm glad *you're* the one who runs a hick movie house in this hick town with that bunch of under-age hick vixens. I'm on the next train out of here."

And then he turns to leave, but not before Mr. Bob says, "I'll be sure and call your Twentieth Century Fox pals and let them know you're on your way. When they ask me who won the contest, I'll just tell 'em our gals were too pretty to pick just one."

Genevieve is standing backstage, holding our coats, and oh, she looks mad! "*Que méchante*, Teensy!" she says. "You went too far with that last little butt shake! *Que faiseur d'embarras!*"

Genevieve pushes open the stage door and we step outside into the cold fresh air. Jack is there to meet us, blowing on his fingers, stomping his feet, and laughing.

"Go, Pooties," he says, "Garnet Parish Pooties are the best!"

"We are Temples of the Holy Spirit," I say. And we all crack up again.

"That is enough," Genevieve says. "I am taking you girls home. Jack, please go find Mr. Bob and Mrs. Bob and let them know that we'll be over at their house later."

"Yes, ma'am," Jack says, and turns to go. But not before he gives me a wink and hands me a box of JuJuBes. Oh, I like that Jack.

Our curls are gone.

All 168 of them.

Genevieve brushed them out. Hard.

At Caro's house, the four of us are standing in the living room. Mr. Bob is in his easy chair, Mrs. Bob is sitting in her rocker.

"Bob," Genevieve says, "I want you to give these girls their punishment."

For the first time I get scared.

"Girls," Mr. Bob says, "I have thought about this long and hard. The four of you—well, the four of you behaved simply terribly in my public theater. You ruined the day for a lot of little girls, and their mothers too. I am not going to hear the end of it. They've already been ringing my phone off the hook."

Genevieve says, "Think of *les petites pauvres*. Yall ruined it for the poor children. Nothing to eat but onions and turnips in months, *non*? Some of them, *pères* haven't had a job in two, three years. Sharecropper *enfants* coming to town once a week for to see *Flash Gordon*. They don't want to see your *derrière*, *filles*. *Comprendez-vous?* You show those poor little girls the respect."

I look at Genevieve because she always makes me think things I want to forget about.

"Genevieve is right," Mr. Bob says. "There is a depression going on in this country, even if you four princesses don't see it."

"One of these days you girls have got to start behaving like ladies," Mrs. Bob says. "You're not babies anymore. You are young ladies. And there is a right way and a wrong way to act. What you did today was definitely wrong. You don't want to get reputations for being bad girls, do you?"

"But, Mrs. Bob," I say, before I can stop myself, "it's so much *fun* being a bad girl."

"Vivi," she says, "do you want me to call your mother and father and have them talk to you instead of me?"

No, I don't want her to call my mother, and definitely not my father, because he doesn't *talk*. He just takes off his belt and lets it do his talking for him.

"No, ma'am," I say.

"You all have got to start acting like ladies if you expect to get along in this town," Mrs. Bob says. "How can I get that through your head, Caro?"

"But, Mama," Caro says, "we can't *help* it if Teensy pooted."

"I know, I know," Mrs. Bob says, "you can't fight Mother Nature. But the four of you couldn't just leave it at that."

I drop my head, but I am secretly thinking about how very *original* the name Pooty Pootwell is.

"Thought I was going to have to call out for help," Mr. Bob says. "Never in my life have I had that much trouble trying to calm a theater down. Yall are not going to get away with this scot-free. For the next month—that is four straight Saturdays—you bad little girls are going to clean up The Bob after the Saturday matinee. Yall are going to sweep up every single piece of popcorn and pick up every candy wrapper that's left on the floor. Furthermore, you will not be allowed into The Bob except to clean. No movies during the whole time of your punishment. And I'm going to talk to Mr. Hyde over at the Paramount too, ask him to give his ticket people and his ushers strict instructions not to let the four of you into his theater either. Not until the month is up."

Back home in my bedroom, I sit down and think about what all has happened. And the more I think about it, the madder I get. It is all so unfair! I get so mad that my brain squeezes together and pushes out the most brilliant idea of my life to date! I will start my very own newspaper where I can print NOTHING BUT THE TRUTH! The name of my newspaper comes to me in a flash! It will be called *"Vivi's Very Important News!"* V.V.I.N. for short. Pronounced "Va-Vinn." I sharpen a pencil, get out my Big Chief tablet, and just start writing. I must reveal the news of this terrible injustice.

8

*I*n spite of the light drizzle that evening, Sidda was possessed with the idea of building a fire at the edge of the lake. She hadn't built an outdoor fire since she was a nine-year-old Girl Scout—the year Vivi and Necie had led Troop 55 and backed into the flagpole with Necie's County Squire station wagon.

She toyed with the twigs and newspapers, used up eight kitchen matches, and blew until she was hyperventilating. Then she gave up, sat back on her feet, and felt foolish. She only required a small fire. She wasn't cold, it's not that she needed heat. She had no plans to cook anything over the flames. She simply wanted to build a little fire outdoors and watch it burn. Her incompetence made her feel out of place in the great Northwest. She missed the screeching urban comfort of Manhattan.

If her *mother* were here, she'd have built a fabulous fire. Mama *or* Caro. Nights at Spring Creek, they'd build fires for hot dogs, s'mores, maybe toss in a firecracker or two. They'd sing, tell ghost stories, host talent shows, and compete in limbo contests, that broom lowering till it all but touched the pine needles. Later, their skin coated with 6–12, the kids would lean back against their mothers' bodies and watch the flames of the fire and the citronella candles burning, and the smoke curling up from the mosquito coils.

"Piney pitch is the secret to starting a fire," Vivi used to say. "Unless you have kerosene, of course."

Sidda hadn't thought she even remembered that instruction.

"Get hard pitchwood from the center of a loblolly pine stump if you can find it, Sidda, and you can't go wrong."

Well, Mama, there aren't any loblolly pines around this place.

She stood up and looked around her. All around her were Sitka spruce, Western red cedar, and hemlock, but she didn't know which was which. She'd never thought much about trees before. Except for the old live oak tree at Pecan Grove, with its hundred-and-twenty-foot-branch spread. That tree could make any member of her family weep when they talked about it. When Sidda was a girl, she believed if she ever got married it would be under that tree.

Pitch, Sidda thought. I'm looking for pitch. Perfect pitch.

There was no perfect pitch, but Sidda did find a rotting stump. Not five feet from where she had been squatting. She looked into the center of it, and there was the resiny part, the last part to rot. Reaching into the trunk, she broke off several pieces and returned to her erstwhile fire site.

"Separate your sticks, Siddalee," she heard her mother (or Caro) say. "Start with a tiny teepee, with the littlest twigs over some shavings. Good. Now use some slightly larger sticks for your next layer. Just keep building it like that, easy does it, while your fire builds."

Sidda did exactly as her mother had taught her. But the fire would not catch. Everything was simply too wet. It was dark, only the tiny lights on the other side of the lake were visible. Still a thick cloud cover, no stars visible. And this was supposed to be the time of meteors. May had told her the Olympic Peninsula was known for shooting stars in late summer. Just Sidda's luck to show up the one summer when clouds refused to budge. All this quiet dampness was somewhat spiritual. And somewhat depressing.

Returning to the cabin, Sidda slipped into a pair of dry, warm sweatpants, and lit a fire in the fireplace. She put on a Rickie Lee Jones CD of songs from the forties, poured herself a glass of brandy, sat down, and tried to make herself read a Jungian book on marriage. Three pages in, she closed the book.

Lying down in front of the fire, she stroked Hueylene. She could smell the alder logs as their burning warmed the room. Through the glass doors she could see nothing but gray and rain. This is cozy, all right, Sidda thought, but if it's like this in August, I hate to think what December looks like.

She pulled Hueylene's travel bed in front of the fireplace. She stared into the flames for a moment, then reached for the book of "Divine Secrets." It fell open to a florist card that read, "Happy Anniversary, Ya-Yas! Love from the Ya-Ya Husbands." Wild. But that's the way it was: every year the Ya-Yas threw themselves a party to celebrate another anniversary of their friendship. And the husbands actually brought gifts! Sidda remembered more about Ya-Ya anniversaries than she did about Vivi and Shep's.

A flier from the grand opening of the Southgate Shopping Center in Thornton was tucked in next to a handwritten recipe for a cheese soufflé. The recipe had been crossed out, and a note to the side read: "Forget it! Fix a drink and go out for hamburgers!"

Next she ran across a photo of a younger Caro holding an infant in her arms. Caro was making the A-OK sign with her fingers, and wore a jaunty little beret. The infant was tucked in the crook of her arms, and they seemed to be standing in front of a statue. Which one of us wild children was that? Sidda wondered.

As she turned to the next page, what looked like pieces of walnut shell fell out of the book. Sidda imagined her mother years ago snacking on the nuts while pasting things into the scrapbook. Sidda thought about throwing the remnants away, but changed her mind. Gathering the shards up off the floor, she tucked them back into the book where they had been for God knows how long.

Sidda thought about nuts, how they are food and seed at once. How they hold fertility magic in one tight, tiny space. Her mind ran to rich symbolic imaginings, but still she could not guess the enchantment those particular walnut shells contained.

As the smells of sweet woodruff and alder burning and lake water wafted about her, so did the essences of her mother's stories. Not in the way Sidda wanted, but in the way of hidden things that mysteriously reveal worlds unsuspected and longed for.

Vivi, 1937

Mother won't let Caro and me play in the new hammock until we rub the face off the Blessed Virgin statue Father brought back from the island of Cuba.

"This turpentine stinks," Caro says. "I don't see why we have to do this."

"Rub hard," I say. "Then Mama will let us try out the hammock."

The statue is sitting on our front porch, right where it got delivered in a wooden box, alongside Father's luggage. Father is just back from Cuba, where he went to the Tennessee walking-horse show with his rich friends. He stayed in a big hacienda with servants. Cuba is paradise, Father says, with white beaches and orange flowers growing everywhere and wild parrots and all the people happy. His rich friends run the whole island, and Father said he will take me with him next time. He said Mother dresses too much like hired help to take her. If Mother would take the kerchief off her head and the dust rags out of her pockets, I just know she'd be beautiful.

Father bought the Cuban Blessed Virgin for Mother. The statue was gorgeous, with brown skin! She had earrings and a necklace, and the brightest colors of any Mother Mary I had ever seen. Big red lips and a violet color on her eyelids like she was ready for a fiesta. Mother just hated her.

The first thing Mother did after Father left for the office this morning was to unscrew the gold hoop earrings and take all those pretty red and yellow necklaces off the Virgin's neck and drop them in a pile over by the hen-and-chicken planter. The whole time she was doing it, she shook her head like that statue had gone and done something bad.

"The Blessed Virgin is not a Negro," Mother said. "It is just like foreigners to try to turn the Mother of God into a gaudy tart. That statue needs to be cleaned up! Imagine what Father Coughlin would say if he could see this statue."

Mother listens to Father Coughlin on the radio. If Father Coughlin says something, then it's like Moses brought it down from the mountain.

"You listen to that radio priest more than you do your own husband," Father tells her.

She says, "If Demon Rum wasn't stalking your soul, then I might listen to you more."

Mother says that Father spends too much time with his horse friends, and he has turned his back on God. Mother will not go to any horse shows with him, so I get to take her place. I love all the ladies in their jodhpurs and boots, and the picnics with vodka gimlets for the grown-ups and pink lemonade for me, and everyone all dressed up. Father's Tennessee walking horses, Passing Fancy and Rabelais's Dream, take prizes right and left. Every time those horse people get together, it's a party.

"Take your fingers and rub every bit of that color off the Virgin's cheeks," Mother says.

I pour a little more turpentine on my rag and rub in circles to get the rouge off the Virgin's cheeks.

After Mama goes inside, we can finally talk about our secret plans. Today is the day leading up to the night of our Divine Ritual Ceremony, which Caro and Teensy and Necie and I have been planning and planning.

"Do you think Necie will chicken out?" I ask Caro.

"She thinks we'll get kidnapped like the Lindbergh baby," Caro says. "She is scared to go out in the woods at night."

"I go out in the woods by myself at night all the time."

"You do not!"

"Oh, yes I do. I go out there all the time. I'm brave as Amelia Earhart. Sometimes I sleep out there by myself."

"Vivi, you lie lie lie," Caro tells me.

I just smile.

Mother comes out to inspect our work on the Virgin. "Now," Mother says, "now she looks more like Mary Most Pure. Well done, girls, the Blessed Virgin is proud of you."

"We've turned her into a white lady," Caro says, examining the statue.

Mother smiles. "The Blessed Virgin is not a colored person. She is the Mother of God. She is above even white people."

"Then how come we had to rub all her brown skin off?" Caro asks. Caro doesn't believe everything grown-ups tell her. Caro makes up her own thoughts.

"Little girls shouldn't ask so many questions, Carolina," my mother tells my friend.

"*Bonjour!*" Teensy calls out, walking up our path, wearing a little sunsuit Genevieve's cousin on the bayou made her, all out of dishcloths. Necie is with her, and they're holding hands, coming to play.

"Hey! Pals!" Caro calls out.

"Hello, girls," Mother says when they reach the porch. She

reaches out to pat Teensy's pretty black curls, but Teensy pulls away. She doesn't like my mother ever since Mother spanked Teensy's bottom for taking all her clothes off at my sixth birthday party and dancing around buck naked singing to me.

"Ooh, who is she?" Teensy asks, pointing to the statue.

"That is the Blessed Virgin that these good little daughters of Mary have reclaimed. She was a tacky colored Cuban with rouge like a harpy, but we took care of that, didn't we, girls?"

"Yes, ma'am," Caro and I say.

"She used to be a gorgeous brown lady," I say.

"Well, she sure looks like a spook now," Teensy says. "How come yall rub off her mouth?"

"What do you think, Denise?" Mother asks Necie.

"Did yall use an eraser?" Necie asks.

My mother laughs. "No, dear. We started with Clorox and switched to turpentine."

"Can we go play in the hammock now, please, ma'am?" I ask.

"Yes, you may," Mother answers, "but first come and genuflect in front of Our Holy Mother."

And so we all genuflect in front of the statue that looks like she saw something scary and lost all her color. Then Teensy spots the jewelry Mother took off the Virgin. She snatches it up so fast that Mother doesn't see her do it. That Teensy has quick hands, and she loves jewels.

So now it is me and Caro and Teensy and Necie out on the side porch. Harrison, who works for us, just hung the big hammock Father brought me. It's hanging from the blue ceiling of the porch, just outside the windows of Father's study.

"None of yall have a hammock like this. This one is *Cuban*." I climb into the hammock and lay back facing the street.

Caro says, "Okay, you ready for me?"

"I most certainly am," I tell her, and she scrambles into the hammock.

"Okay, Necie, now you."

Necie starts to climb in. She holds her dress so we can't see her panties.

"Necie, who do you think is going to look up your dress?" Teensy says."

"I don't know," she says, and rolls her eyes.

Then Teensy turns away from us, and lifts up her dress so we can all see her underwear. She shakes her butt in the direction of the street; she doesn't care who sees her.

"Panties on the porch!" Teensy sings. "Panties on the porch!" And Necie is blushing. We love to embarrass her.

She's squenched in between Caro and me with her head at my end. I give her a little kiss on the cheek.

"Good Necie, perfect fit," I tell her.

"Now, Teensy, you climb in and just get wherever you can fit."

Teensy gets in the hammock and just lays on top of us like we are her pillows.

"Hey! Get off me!" I yell.

"Well, you said 'wherever,'" she laughs, and I push her and she pushes back. Teensy always pushes back. If you push Necie, she just says, I'm sorry. She is a relief sometimes after the rest of us.

"Yall cut it out," Necie says.

"Teensy," Caro says, "scooch up here by my arm and put your legs over the side."

Teensy obeys her, snuggling in, and we are lying there like sardines in a mesh can. Through the spaces in hammock netting you can see the porch floor, and through the porch floor you can see slats of sunlight hitting the ground underneath the porch. I pull on the rope that Harrison has rigged so we can swing ourselves without getting up.

"Oh, this is great!" Caro says.

And it is great, like we are in a big cradle together.

"I want a hammock like this," Teensy says.

"Well, then tell your daddy to go to Cuba and get you one," I say.

"I will, I'll tell him this evening. I'll tell him to get me a Cuban Blessed Virgin too. And I won't rub her face off either. I'll glue a pair of *Maman*'s false eyelashes on her."

It is around ten in the morning and things are already hot. You can smell the morning sun hitting the grass and bringing up smells like lemon. I lean my head back and smell things, wherever I am. To me, smells are like an invisible person that a lot of people forget is even there. I would rather lose my eyes than my sense of smell.

"I can't wait till we have our Indian names," Teensy says.

"Tonight is the night," Caro says, and she closes her eyes and leans her head back in the hammock.

"Ooooh," Necie says, "I hope it's not too dark in the woods."

"*Of course* it'll be dark," Teensy says.

"It will be dark as *velvet*," I say.

Necie's eyes grow big. Caro reaches out and grabs her like a monster out of nowhere, and she lets out a squeal.

I can smell all Mother's flowers, and I can hear everything from my spot in the hammock. Someone beating rugs a few doors down, lots and lots of birds, a fly buzzing, and Mr. Barnage's truck rattling down the street. I know the sound of all the automobiles and trucks in our neighborhood.

Mother's honeysuckle mixes in with the smell of her gardenia and butterfly ginger, and makes it smell so sweet out here on the porch. The Rose of Montana vine that Mother has trained to climb across the porch ceiling is just dripping with flowers. She takes cuttings other people throw away and puts them into old coffee cans, and pretty soon they take over our porch and yard with blossoms. My mother can grow any flower in the world, and she knows all their names too. Our whole yard is full of camellias, Mother's pride and joy. And she's got all kinds of roses and white and purple periwinkles and a potted kumquat that she brings inside during the winter so it won't freeze. If there is one thing my mama loves to do it is work in the garden. Father and my grandmother Delia make fun of her. They call her a field hand. Necie's mama always asks Mother to join the Garden Club, but Mother won't. She says her club is the Altar Society. Most of her flowers end up on the altar at Divine Compassion, not in our house.

In the spring and summer, I live out on this porch that's surrounded by flowers. Come the warm weather, Mother and Delia's maid, Ginger, set up two beds at the end of the side porch with the mosquito netting that drops from the ceiling, then Mother sets up a little night table and a boudoir lamp and we all take turns sleeping out here. When my girlfriends come over to spend the night, Mother makes Pete and his pals move back to his room and lets us sleep out here. My favorite nights in the world are the nights I have my girlfriends over. That is when I sleep my best, hardly a nightmare at all when my buddies are with me.

Sleeping on the porch is the best thing in the world. You fall asleep with the sound of crickets, and you wake up with the sound of birds chirping. When you're still half-asleep, they sound like a waterfall. If Huey Long himself came to visit, the porch is where

I'd put him. We don't have servants fanning us here in Thornton, although sometimes we try to get Ginger, my grandmother's maid, to fan us with Delia's vetiver hand fans. But she says, "Go soak your head, that cool you off."

It is evening and we all play cards after supper out on the porch with Pete and Mother. Father has business tonight, and so he didn't come home for supper again.

My brother, Pete, teases us all the time. He keeps making up names for us. He calls Teensy "Tinky," and calls me "Stinky." Caro he calls "Karo Syrup." And Necie he calls "Knee-sie" and points to his knee and then his eyes like he's playing charades. Pete is two years older than us and big and strong, and has foxtails that fly from his bicycle.

After four hands of Crazy Eights, Mother says it's time for bed. We all say goodnight and put on our gowns and Mother comes out to make sure the mosquito netting is draped around our beds on the porch. She puts out a little *pissoir* so we won't have to troop all the way inside and up the stairs to powder our noses.

We act so good and quiet that Mother thinks she has saints on her hands.

"Did yall thank the Holy Lady for helping you through the day?" she asks.

"Yes, ma'am," we all call out from our beds.

Mother is standing there on the other side of the mosquito net, already fingering her evening rosary. "Well, then tell your guardian angels goodnight."

"Goodnight, angels," we say.

"Goodnight, little girls," Mother says.

We lie silently and watch her cross the gray planks of the porch and head back into the house.

When she is out of sight, Caro says, "We're not little girls, we are Royal Indian Maidens."

"Maybe instead of thanking the Holy Lady, yall should apologize for wiping her face off," Teensy says.

That makes us giggle.

"Yall scrubbed off her lips and turpentined her skin," Teensy says. "*Imbecile.* I bet those Cubans would have never sold that statue to your father if they knew yall were going to ruin her looks."

"Shhh!" I say. "Mother might be in the living room listening. If we're quiet, then she'll think we're sound asleep and go on upstairs."

We get quiet and just lie there for a moment, with our bundles of supplies stashed beneath the beds.

"Now are we going into the dark woods?" Necie murmurs.

"No," I whisper, "we have to wait till the whole house is asleep."

"How will we know?" she asks.

"I can tell," I say. "Houses sleep like people sleep. I can tell."

After a while, I climb out of bed to check. "The coast is clear!"

We pull out our stash from under the beds, lift up our night-gowns, and take turns rubbing a raw onion all over our bodies so the mosquitoes won't carry us away. We're lucky it's been a dry summer so far or we'd never be able to go into the woods at night without getting bitten to death.

Then we sneak off the porch and into the backyard.

"*Stealthily!*" Caro says.

We cut across the Munsen's alley, walk a few hundred yards, take a deep breath, and then slip into the woods.

We have Pete's flashlight and a half-moon for light. I finger the piece of paper in the pocket of my nightgown. It holds our tribal story. I am the Mistress of Legend tonight.

"What if we run into a camp of hobos?" Necie asks.

Caro is holding the light since she's the tallest. She also carries a rucksack with some pieces of wood in it. She's the Mistress of Fire.

"The hobos are closer to the railroad tracks," I say.

"Father says his friends at the police station have already run all the hobos out of Thornton," says Teensy. "*Maman* and he got in a big fight about it."

"Mama fed some hobos a few days ago, right on our back steps," Necie says. "But I am not supposed to talk to hobos, just feed them."

"Hobos keep coming round your house because your mother won't erase the hobo mark, even though the Mayor told everyone they should," I say. "Mother only feeds them once a week now, or else she says we'll end up joining them, as much as Pete eats."

Necie is the only one of us who knows how to cook, so she has brought fudge in a paper sack. She is the Mistress of Refreshment. Teensy, the Mistress of Dance, has got four empty oatmeal boxes in her sack for our drums. And I've got the needle.

We keep walking until we are on the edge of the little bayou that runs back behind Teensy's house. We all help Caro build a small fire. Caro is a swell fire builder, good as a boy. Mr. Bob taught her and she taught me.

When our fire gets going, we all sit around it.

I gaze into its flames and begin my telling the story of the Divine Tribe of Louisiana Ya-Yas.

THE SECRET HISTORY OF THE LOUISIANA YA-YAS

Long before the white man showed up, the Mighty Tribe of Ya-Yas, a band of women strong and true and beautiful, roamed the great state of Louisiana. Leopards slept with us and bears fed us honey from their paws and fish jumped up into our hands because they wanted to be our food. The trees were so thick that we could travel from New Orleans to Shreveport on treetop, and we did, hundreds of Ya-Ya Indians traveling on the tops of trees.

Our mother was a black she-ape named Lola, who found us in a cave at the beginning of time and raised us like her very own children. We loved her like a mother. People didn't mess with the tribal Ya-Ya sisters.

But then Hurricane Zandra, the hugest hurricane known to man, came and ripped all the trees out by their roots and turned all the streams into rivers and killed everybody, including our mother, Lola. Only four of us survived. Everywhere we turned, evil alligators tried to eat us. There was nowhere to hide because those alligators could crawl from water to land and be just as mean in either place. We were starving so bad that our bones were sticking out, and we didn't sleep for forty days. Finally we were so weak we just gave up.

The alligators rejoiced and crawled up to where we lay helpless. They crawled so close that we looked right into their ugly old eyes and saw the light of the moon reflected. We tried everything we knew, but our strength was gone. Then from behind the moon came a gorgeous lady. We could see her from where we lay on our deathbeds. She looked down and saw we were hanging by an eyelash over the canyon of doom! And the Moon Lady shot silver rays from her eyes so hot and mighty that those alligators were burned to a crisp right in their sleazy tracks! Fried those ugly critters sunny side up, right there on the road. We could hear them sizzling.

And the Moon Lady said, "You are my daughters in whom I am well pleased. I will always keep my Divine Eyes peeled for you."

We, the Ya-Yas, had lost our jungle home, and our town does not realize we are royal, but secretly we all know our history and we will be loyal to our tribe forever and ever, in sickness and in health. As it was in the beginning, is now, and ever shall be. The End.

Then I look at everyone in the eyes and say: "Now it is official: we are from here on out to be known as Ya-Yas!" And everybody starts clapping.

"Some of that kind of sounds like it came from the Bible," Necie says.

"Do not question the Mistress of Legend," I say.

"Yeah," Teensy chimed in. "The Bible doesn't *own* those words."

"Never mind," Necie says. "Would yall care for some fudge?"

"Why, thank you, Mistress of Refreshment," I say.

And we all bite into big chunks of chocolate pecan fudge.

"I hate those old alligators," Caro says, then looks in the direction of the bayou.

"Uh," Necie says. "Yall don't think there are any alligators in this bayou, do you?"

"*Maman* put a *gris-gris* on all the alligators behind our house," Teensy says. "We don't have to worry. *Maman* is the one who gave us our name! She's the one always saying, 'Gumbo Ya-Ya, gumbo ya-ya!'"

"That's us," Necie says.

"*Exactement!*" Teensy says. "From here on out to the end of time, we will be known as The Ya-Yas! Nobody can take our name away!"

Then Teensy whips the empty oatmeal boxes out of her paper sack, and we all beat on them. And while we drum, we yell out to the night and the woods and the fire that we are now The Ya-Yas. Then Necie, the Mistress of Names, formally gives all of us our Ya-Ya Indian names that we have chosen ourselves. Mine is Queen Dancing Creek. Caro's is Duchess Soaring Hawk, and Necie's is Countess Singing Cloud. Each time Necie pronounces our new names, she sprinkles us with water from an old RC bottle with a hole punched in the top that she borrowed from her Mama's ironing board.

Teensy has been keeping her Indian name a secret from us for weeks. Finally when it's her turn, she hands Necie an envelope, all secret-like. Necie opens the envelope, looking for Teensy's name, and when she sees it, her eyes get big as Popeye's and she starts blushing from head to foot. For a minute Necie doesn't say a word. You can hear a whippoorwill calling from far away somewhere, and little crackling sounds from Caro's fire.

Then Necie turns back to Teensy, who is grinning even bigger than ever. "I now name you Princess Naked-as-a-Jaybird."

The Princess goes wild.

"Hot-cha-cha!" Teensy screams, and starts spinning around in circles. She rips off her nightgown and makes us take off ours too. Necie tries to chicken out, so Teensy and I have to take off her gown for her.

"This might be a mortal sin, yall," she says.

"Yeah!" I tell her. "A Royal Ya-Ya Mortal Sin!"

"Everybody ready for ceremonial paint?" Teensy asks, with one of her bad looks.

"What?" we all say. This is not in the program, but the Ya-Ya tribe plays things by ear.

Teensy reaches into her sack and pulls out a bunch of Genevieve's Max Factor of Hollywood tubes and pots of color, and pencils and lipsticks, and oh all kinds of lovely little items that Mother thinks are vulgar.

Teensy hands me a pot of red rouge. Caro gets a pot of brown color, Necie gets lipstick, and Teensy has the pencils. We take turns drawing on each other until we could pass for full-blooded Injuns. Red and brown streaks across our foreheads and black stars on our cheeks, and then Teensy has the idea of painting our stomachs and chests too. I draw a black line down the center of my body, and I rub lipstick all over one side and leave the other side regular skin color. Teensy draws lipstick in circles around her titties!

"Necie," Teensy says, "take your hands away from your titties. We've all seen them before. They are nothing new."

If that isn't enough, old Teensy pulls out the necklaces and earrings that Mother made us take off the Negro Cuban Virgin.

"Ah!" I call out. "*The Secret Ya-Ya Jewels,* lost all these centuries, and only recently found by Princess Naked-as-a-Jaybird, world-famous lady archeologist!"

We all scramble to put on the jewels, and pretty soon we are following Teensy, all slapping our thighs and running and whooping, "Hi-ho, Silver!"

Then we stop dancing to prick our thumbs with the sewing needle. The Mistress of Fire holds the needle under the flame of a match, and then we each take turns letting Caro draw a tiny bead of blood.

Raising our hands above our heads, we rub our thumbs together and recite our oath: "I am a member of the royal and true tribe of Ya-Yas. No one can come between us and no one can break away, because now we have the same blood. I do solemnly swear to be loyal to my sister Ya-Yas, and to love and look out for them, and never forsake them through thick and thin, until I take my last human breath—"

But of course, instead of "breath," Teensy goes and says "breast."

She says, "Until I take my last human *breast*." And she says it loud just to be bad.

My heart is beating so hard I can see it move my chest up and down. And I can see the same thing in Teensy's and Caro's chests. All our eyes are shining.

"Now," Teensy instructs us, *"everybody lick the blood off your thumbs."*

I look at her. This wasn't in the plan.

Teensy goes ahead and licks, though, and so I do too. I flick my tongue lightly over the dot of blood on my thumb.

"Now, swallow!" I tell everybody, the words just flying out of my mouth without me even thinking them.

And we all swallow the tiny drops of each other's blood. Like Holy Communion, but it's *our* blood, not Jesus Christ's.

When I have babies, they'll have Caro and Teensy's and Necie's blood! That will make us all related. And when I get old and die, as long as the heart of one Ya-Ya is still pumping blood, I'll still be alive! Our blood is all mixed into one.

Then Necie says, real soft, "Can I do my closing Divine Walnut Ceremony?"

I had forgotten all about the surprise Necie said she had for the ending.

We follow her to the edge of the bayou, and out of her bag she pulls four walnut halves and hands one to each of us. Then she gives us candle stubs and has us light them.

"Now, drip a little bitty wax inside the shell," she tells us, "and stick your candle stub in there."

We are all surprised at Necie coming up with this. Every time I think I know my friends, they surprise me. They are full of secrets I will never know.

You can hear the scratch of the kitchen match against the box and the little *poof* sound it makes when it ignites. We each light our candles and watch Necie. She bends down and gently lowers her walnut shell with its lit candle until it rests on top of the water. She gives the shell a tiny little push, and we all watch it float a little ways onto the dark water of the bayou.

Then we each do the same thing, until there are four walnut halves bearing tiny lights out on the water that look like little fairy boats. The beauty of it makes me want to cry. We are holding hands, and we are high and mighty Ya-Yas, descendants of royal blood, which we will pass on down through many generations.

Back at my house, the white statue of the Cuban Virgin is still sitting on the porch. The porch light is shining down on her, and June bugs flicker around the bulb, making little crackling sounds. The four of us stop dead in our tracks. We kneel down in front of Mary, and Teensy hands us items from her bag. Caro, Teensy, and I take the very same brand of Dark Beauty Contouring Makeup that Carole Lombard and Norma Shearer use, and begin to smear it on the face, hands, and feet of the turpentined Holy Lady. The makeup feels waxy and it smells like Genevieve's dressing room. Under my fingers I can feel the smooth wood of the Virgin.

After we color her skin brown again, we dip into the rouge pots and color her cheeks. We apply blue eye shadow to her eyelids and to the folds of her gown, and then line her lips with lipstick that reads "Harem Red" on the bottom of the tube. After that, we remove her jewels from our royal selves and put them back on the Virgin.

When we're done, we stand back in silence to admire our handiwork. Necie, who has still not touched the Virgin, steps forward and kneels at the foot of the statue. At first we thought she was going to pray. But she reaches over and takes the tube of lipstick away from Teensy, and at the last minute dots little flecks of red on the Virgin's toes where they show under her gown. She paints the Blessed Virgin's toenails red, something even the Cubans hadn't thought of!

I lean over and give Necie a kiss on the cheek. Caro kisses her other cheek. Then Teensy gives our Necie a big fat smack right on the lips.

Back in bed, I can feel Caro's body next to mine. I hear her breathing and feel her heart beating. I smell her Caro smell that's like rice cooking and fresh-cut hay.

Moonlight shines down on my friends and me. The smell of sweet olive hangs in the air like someone is breathing it out of her mouth. I look at my three friends sleeping. They still have traces of makeup on their faces, even though we tried our best to wipe it off with the sheets so Mother wouldn't see it. The Ya-Yas are my real family. I am Queen Dancing Creek, a mighty warrior. I am of the great and royal tribe of Ya-Yas, and no white man will every conquer me. The Moon Lady is my mother.

The next morning we strip the beds before Mother even comes out on the porch to wake us. We have been up since sunrise, when the colors of the day came alive and we threw back our mosquito nets. Our first morning as full-fledged Ya-Yas.

"Girls," Mother is saying, "yall didn't have to remove the linens. There's no need for you to wash those sheets. Give me that bundle. I can't have your mothers think I make yall work like laundresses when you spend the night with Vivi."

We're trying to hide our sheets from her because they're covered in makeup.

"Mrs. Abbott," Necie says, all smiles. "*Please* let me take them home and wash them. I am doing it as a special penance."

What a smooth talker that Necie can be.

"Why, Denise, that is wonderful," Mother says. "I only wish Viviane would follow your example more. You are making the Blessed Virgin very happy this morning."

Necie smiles at Mother and blinks her eyes like a true daughter of Mary, a credit to our tribe.

"Well, come on in for some breakfast," Mother says. "I've got fresh Ruston peaches that Mr. Barnage brought for us."

We follow Mother around the porch. "Just a minute, girls, I want to see if there are any new blossoms on the gardenia."

And Mother rounds the porch to where the statue is.

"Jesus, Mary, and Joseph!" We're right on her heels. Mother

covers her mouth with one hand and makes the Sign of the Cross with the other. Then her body starts shaking inside her housedress. "Who could have done this?" she calls out. "Who in the world?!"

Teensy steps right up, looks straight into my mother's eyes, and says, "Mrs. Abbott, this could be a *miracle*."

"*A miracle*," Mother whispers, like the statue has wept or bled from her palms.

Mother freezes like a statue herself for a moment, then she begins plucking off honeysuckle blossoms, Rose of Montana flowers, sweet olive branches—any bloom she can get her hands on—and showering them upon the Cuban Virgin. She runs out into the side yard and snaps off whole big magnolia branches, she snaps off the heads of tuberoses and hibiscus flowers, and gathers them into her apron. I have never seen her move like this, like she is possessed. When she flies back onto the porch, she drops the blossoms at the statue's painted feet, then reaches up to shake the Rose of Montana vine so that its flowers fall from the porch ceiling onto the statue's head. Never has our porch been so filled with my mother's blossoms. She has turned our front porch into an altar to the gorgeous colored Virgin.

"Holy Mother of Christ!" she murmurs. "Kneel, girls! Kneel and pray."

So me and Caro and Teensy and Necie all fall to our knees with my mother, who has pulled her rosary out of her apron pocket. She is praying:

> *Hail, bright Star of all the oceans,*
> *Hail, Mother of the Flowers,*
> *Shower us with the sweet fragrance*
> *Of your love and compassion,*
> *You who carried in your womb*
> *Him who heaven could not contain!*

My girlfriends and I kneel beside my mother. We have been saved by grace from the devil alligators, from the raging storm. We alone of all have been spared. The High and Mighty Almost Lost But Miraculously Found Tribe of Ya-Yas is just wrapped up in miracles.

9

*I*t was drizzling the next day when Sidda and Hueylene set out
for the Quinault post office. Not raining, not showering, not
sprinkling. Drizzling. If Sidda could have thought of a word for precipi-
tation that was more passive-aggressive than "drizzle," she would have
used it. For the first time she began to understand what May Sorenson
meant when she said the Northwest could mildew a person's soul.

She used the pay phone outside the post office to check in with
her agent. He reassured Sidda that she was not flushing her career
down the toilet by taking this time away, and that the world had not
ended in the last week.

Waiting for her in the general-delivery basket was a card from
Connor made from a recycled watercolor sketch of one of his set
designs. On the back he'd written:

Dear Sidda,

The bed is too big now that you're away. I can't sleep
when I have more than the 1/16 of the mattress you
leave me to sprawl on. Finished the designs for the

second act, and the Seattle team is good. There are
about a million trumpet lilies coming up in our temporary backyard here. Did you find the box I put in
the car? Give Governor Hueylene a belly rub for me.

I love you.
Connor

Back at the cabin Sidda dried Hueylene's long ears, which resembled curly flaps. She made herself a cup of tea, and changed into dry,
warm socks. Sorting through the CDs she'd brought, she once again
chose Rickie Lee Jones singing the old standards from Vivi's era. She
walked to the windows and looked out at the lake, humming along
with "Spring Can Really Hang You Up the Most."

Picking up a postcard with a picture of a gigantic geoduck, Sidda
drew a set of wings on the giant clam, so that the unseemly
Northwest shellfish resembled a penis about to take flight. On the
back, she wrote to Connor:

Baby-cakes,

Don't exaggerate. I always allow you at least *one-fourth*
of any bed we've ever slept in. I miss you too. Yes,
Mama's box is in hand. Well, not in hand—let's just
say it's here. And there. And everywhere. More on
that later. I love you.

Sidda

After she stamped Connor's card, she reached for the scrapbook. She
puzzled at four narrow strips of leather that had been tied together with
a piece of twine. A 1941 penny was slipped into a slot on each band of
leather. Leaning her head back and staring at the ceiling, Sidda let out a
muffled little laugh. Four penny-loafer cutouts! She could picture her
mother and the three other Ya-Yas wearing out their loafers, then ritual-
istically carving the penny slots out of them. Was this a fad that was
popular with all the kids back then, or something peculiar to the Ya-Yas?

On the same page was a photo of the four girlfriends, taken on the
side porch of the Abbott home on Compton Street, from the same era
as the penny loafers. After glancing at the photo for a moment, Sidda

put the album down and went into the kitchen. She checked all the drawers before returning to the big room. There, in the second drawer of an old pie chest that held playing cards, a Monopoly game, and a collection of moon snails, she found what she was looking for.

Returning to the scrapbook, Sidda blew on the magnifying glass, then wiped it clean with her sweatshirt, and began to examine the photograph. She'd looked at it before, but she wanted to really study it. In the photograph, a Rose of Montana vine wound up and across a porch railing so thick with blossoms that the light must have glowed pink. On an oversized rattan sofa with wide, curved arms and chintz-covered cushions lay Vivi, Necie, Caro, and Teensy, two by two, head to foot, with their legs in such a tangle that Sidda could not tell whose painted toenails were whose. Vivi wore a striped halter top and shorts, and her hair was pulled up off her neck, with little blond tendrils falling loose in the moist heat. A wrought-iron table was to the side of the sofa and held a black rotary fan. Four tall tea glasses sat on the floor with long spoons in them.

Sidda studied every detail. Who had taken this picture? What was happening just outside the frame? What happened the moment before this image had been captured?

Setting the magnifying glass aside for a moment, Sidda relaxed her eyes so that the photo was only vaguely in focus. An afternoon of iced tea and idleness. Those Ya-Yas aren't going anywhere. They're lying low on the side porch shaded by live oaks. The Germans are about to reach Stalingrad, and the gas chambers are heating up, but the Ya-Yas are still in high school, and the life of the porch surrounds them. They are lazy together. This is comfort. This is joy. Just look at these four. Not one wears a watch. This porch time is not planned. Not penciled into a DayRunner.

Those porch girls had no idea they were going to sprawl on that couch until the weight of their adolescent bodies sank down into the pillows. They have no idea when they will get up off that couch. They have no plans for what will happen next. They only know their bodies touching as they try to keep cool. They only know that the coolest spot they can find is in front of that rotary fan.

I want to lay up like that, to float unstructured, without ambition or anxiety. I want to inhabit my life like a porch.

People took porches and porch time for granted back then. Everybody had porches; they were nothing special. An outdoor room halfway between the world of the street and the world of the home. If the porch wrapped around the house as the Abbotts' did, there were different worlds on the front, side, and back porch. If you were laid up on the side porch the way the Ya-Yas were in the picture, you were private, comfortably cloistered. The side porch—that's where the Ya-Yas went if their hair was in pin curls, when they didn't want to wave and chat to passersby. This is where they sighed, this is where they dreamed. This is where they lay for hours, contemplating their navels, sweating, dozing, swatting flies, trading secrets there on the porch in a hot, humid girl soup. And in the evening when the sun went down, the fireflies would light up over by the camellias, and that little nimbus of light would lull the Ya-Yas even deeper into porch reveries. Reveries that would linger in their bodies even as they aged.

When people encountered them years later with babies on their hips; or, still later, with hands shaking from some deep-six sadness nobody could name, there was an aura about them. You could not put your finger on it, but you knew these women shared secret lagoons of knowledge. Secret codes and lore and lingo stretching back into that fluid time before air conditioning dried up the rich, heavy humidity that used to hang over the porches of Louisiana, drenching cotton blouses, beads of sweat tickling the skin, slowing people down so the world entered them in an unhurried way. A thick stew of life that seeped into the very blood of people, so that eccentric, languid thoughts simmered inside. Thoughts that would not come again after porches were enclosed, after the climate was controlled, after all windows were shut tight, and the sounds of the neighborhood were drowned out by the noise of the television set.

Viz'tin. That's what the Ya-Yas called their impromptu get-togethers when Sidda was a girl. The four Walker kids crammed into the T-Bird with Vivi, bombing into town to Caro's or Teensy's or Necie's, pulling into the driveway, madly blowing the horn, shouting out, "Yall *better* be home!" Then a batch of Bloody Marys appeared, and cream cheese with Pickapeppa and crackers, a gallon of lemonade and Oreos for the kids, Sarah Vaughan on the stereo, and a party. No planning, no calls in advance.

On such outings, Sidda might dress up in one of the Ya-Yas' trousseau peignoirs and let Vivi coach her in reckless, delicious Isadora Duncan–inspired interpretive dancing. Waving a yardstick magic wand with a tinfoil star, Sidda might gyrate wildly across whomever's porch they happened to be on. What heaven it was when Vivi's light shined on her! Afternoon would pass into evening and evening into night, and before you knew it, the day was gone, and Vivi and the kids were weaving their way back home to Pecan Grove, windows rolled down to a cool breeze.

"Ain't we got fun, Little Buddies?!" she'd call out to the kids.

And they'd call back, "Oh, yes, Mama, we do got fun!"

Sidda picked the magnifying glass back up and studied her mother's eyes in the photograph. When did things go bad? What created the paradox of Vivi full of light, Vivi full of dark?

For every such scene of magic, there were an equal number of terrifying cocktail hours when Vivi's bourbon and branch water took her far away from her children, although she might never leave the house.

On those evenings, when Vivi stepped out of her bedroom to freshen her drink, she would say, "Get away from me; I cannot stand to look at you."

Sidda learned to stay on the ball, she learned to walk the tightrope. She perfected the ability to walk into a room and instantly divine each person's mood, need, desire. She developed the capacity to take the temperature of a scene, a character, a conversation, a single gesture, and to gauge just what was needed and when and how much. Vivi swung wide in her waltzes with angels, in her jousting with demons, and her daughter learned to choreograph drama from these fluctuations. Her daughter learned the subtle, wobbly, inspired emotional patois that a good theater director needs to speak fluently in her art.

But Sidda was tired of being vigilant, alert, sharp. She longed for porch friendship, for the sticky, hot sensation of familiar female legs thrown over hers in companionship. She pined for the *girlness* of it all, the unplanned, improvisational laziness. She wanted to soak the words "time management" out of her lexicon. She wanted to hand over, to yield, to let herself float down into the uncharted beautiful fertile musky swamp of life, where creativity and eroticism and deep intelligence dwell.

As Sidda set down the magnifying glass and closed the book of "Divine Secrets," something caught her eye. An adult and an adolescent eagle took off from the uppermost perch of an old cedar near the cabin. As the adult swept from her spot in the tree, her wings beat so loudly it almost sounded amplified. When Sidda heard the clamor, her head tilted to one side. Those eagles, like angels, don't distinguish between work and play. To them, it is all one and the same.

10

*F*rom May's cabin Sidda struck out in the rain along the lake trail, then deep into the rain forest, where the canopy of trees was so thick she could not feel the rain. The darkness and quietness both comforted her and frightened her. She felt like a child might feel in a dim, silent cathedral.

When she arrived at the Quinault post office, she found a postal worker behind the counter watching soap operas on a tiny television. The woman glanced up at Sidda.

"You general delivery?" she asked.

"Yes, Sidda Walker, please. Anything for me?"

Trying not to take her eyes off the TV, the woman reached over to a shelf and pulled down a small package.

"From Louisiana," the postal worker said. "Certified."

"Goody-goody!" Sidda said, then felt slightly embarrassed.

"Forest Service says we got sun coming this week," the postal worker said as she handed the package to Sidda.

Sidda said, "That would be lovely, wouldn't it?"

"One thing you got enough of in a rain forest, and that's moisture."

"Oh, well," Sidda said, turning to the door. "Makes for smooth complexions."

"That's what I tell my girlfriends," the woman said.

This comment struck Sidda, and she turned back to look at the woman once more before leaving. *My girlfriends.* Said so casually. Sidda almost felt a twinge of envy.

Standing under the covered walkway in front of the little post office, Sidda examined the package. A certified package from Mrs. George E. Ogden, or as she was better known to Sidda: Necie. Sidda wanted to rip the package open right away, but decided to wait until she was back at the cabin. She tucked it under her Gore-Tex parka, and walked back to the cabin.

As soon as she'd entered the cabin and removed her wet parka, Sidda opened the package. She had not expected to hear from any of the Ya-Yas. Not one of them had contacted her since *The New York Times* piece had come out.

Written on engraved stationery, blue with a gold rim, with Necie's monogram on the top, was the following letter:

August 16, 1993

Dear Siddalee,

I am sending you all my best wishes for your upcoming wedding—whenever it takes place. You just take your time, Honey. I'm just so sorry yall aren't going to tie the knot down here, so I can see you and meet your Mr. Right—and see your dress and all.

Many congratulations on your big theater hit! I am so sorry George and I couldn't get up to see it. Frank and his wife and the other Petites Ya-Yas who saw it just raved—and they loved seeing you. Even though I couldn't come, I want you to know that my brood reported back. I am so proud, Sidda. I always knew you had greatness.

Honey, I personally think it is marvelous that you are even interested in our lives as Ya-Yas. I told Liza, Joannie, and Rose, and they all thought it was quaint.

My daughters have very little interest in the past, but
then they did not choose a life in the theater either.
They all send kisses, by the way. Malissa said again how
much she loved seeing you last year when she flew to
New York with Stephen for that convention. I swear, he
is one of the nicest husbands she has ever had.

I hope the Ya-Ya-rabilia your mama sent is helpful.
The New York Times upset your mother terribly.
I'm sure you know that. Newspapers have exaggerated
since the beginning of time, but still that's no excuse.

Your mother gave me full permission to send you
anything I thought you might be interested in, so I'm
sending you some of her letters that I've saved.

I have started a novena to St. Francis Patrizi,
Patron Saint of Reconciliation, for you and your
mama, Siddalee. We all love you, Honey, and are praying for you all the time.

Hugs and Kisses,
Necie

P.S. I swore to your mama that I would make you
promise to return these letters to her when you return
the scrapbook. I know you'll take good care of them.

Necie's letters were in a Ziploc bag, and as Sidda opened it, she
gave a little prayer that her intentions be true. She didn't pray that
they be pure—that was asking too much.

Handwritten in Vivi's girlish hand, on sheets of unlined writing
paper, was the following account:

December 12, 1939
11:15 in the morning
On the Southern Crescent, heading to Atlanta

Dear Necie,

Gosh, Sugar-Roo, you can't imagine how much we
miss you! I'm not kidding either. The Ya-Yas just aren't
the same without you along. You asked me to write

you about every little thing, and that is just what I'm
going to do. I'll save everything and we can paste it
into my Divine Secrets album when we get home!
Even though your mama wouldn't let you come
because she thinks Ginger isn't a proper chaperone, I
am going to make you feel like you are right here with
us. We are all mad at your mama. After all, we *are
thirteen years old.* Juliet Capulet was only fourteen, for
heaven's sake. And Ginger is so too a real chaperone,
even though she is a maid.

Oh, I love being on a train, girl! When we pulled
out from Thornton waving to you, I was so sad to
leave you behind.

Once the Southern Crescent got going, oh, it was
just wonderful! You just feel like you can go anywhere
when you're on a train. Like Thornton isn't the only place
anymore but just one of a whole lot of towns all over the
world. This is my first time on a train without Mama or
Papa, and I look at everything. At the backs of the
houses and the ladies out there hanging clothes on the
line, and the little bitty towns we pass. You just wonder
and wonder what the people are doing in those places. I'd
like to get off the train at one of these little old stops and
just go into the town and tell them I was somebody else
and try out living a whole other life! You could be
anybody you wanted and no one would ever know.

Honey, we have four seats all to ourselves facing
each other. You were the sweetest thing in the world
to make us these cookies. We have got two shoe boxes
of fried chicken and biscuits that Ginger made. There
is a whole car just for colored people, and that's where
Ginger is. She was worried as can be that she had to
leave us. She even tried to talk the porter into letting
her stay because we are her responsibility, but he told
her, "I wish I could, but it be against the law, and the
boss would have my hide." Then Ginger said, "Yeah,
well, Miz Delia gon have *my* hide if anything happen
to these here white girls."

I have never gone on a trip with a colored person,
so I didn't know they had a separate car so they

wouldn't break the law. Anyway, that is where Ginger is, so we are on our own! It's like we don't even have any kind of chaperone at all.

You should see people look at Ginger. They can't believe a colored woman with red hair, just like everybody in Thornton.

Let me tell you, sweet patootie, we have got a deluxe *compartment*. It has two pull-down berths, which make four beds altogether, and that is what breaks our hearts because there is an empty bunk which would have been yours, Countess Singing Cloud. Tonight before we go to sleep, we are going to fold down the covers and pretend you are there.

Teensy brought the latest *Modern Screen* with her, so we're reading all about *Gone With the Wind*. Miss Yankee Vivien Leigh's picture is all over it, which just breaks our hearts. We have still not forgiven them for not casting Tallulah. Vivien Leigh is not only not a Southerner, she isn't even an American!

Oh, all those hats! They have pictures of Scarlett's outfits and hats in *Modern Screen,* and it is enough to make you wet your pants just waiting to see them for real on the screen. We are so so so lucky to go to the *premiere*!

Teensy's Aunt Louise and Uncle James in Atlanta are just rich as sin. He was a friend of Hoover's, and he just about owns the Coca-Cola Bottling Company! In Atlanta, he just runs the show! Teensy's father asked her to have us up there.

My secret dream is to meet Margaret Mitchell. Don't tell anybody, but it is my plan to get her autograph at the ball. I will just slip away and find her and tell her how much I love her book and ask for her autograph. What do you think of that?

Countess, I have to go now because Duchess and Princess Jaybird want me to play cards with them. They all say kiss kiss kiss and we love you to death and miss you every single minute.

I'll write you again later today.

XXXXX Viviane

Tingling with excitement, Sidda put down the letter and walked into the big room. She picked up the scrapbook and began to search through it. She felt sure she'd seen something about Atlanta some-where among her mother's souvenirs. She flipped through page after page until she found what she was looking for. It was a clipping from *The Atlanta Journal* dated December 15, 1939. The headline read: "Junior League's Ball By Far Most Brilliant in History of Atlanta."

The article read:

> Social brilliance without compare in Atlanta's romantic history wrote a glorious chapter of accomplishment for the Junior League's *Gone With the Wind* costume ball at City Auditorium Thursday night. New highs were recorded for elegance of setting, quality of program, and importance of those in attendance. It was an epochal occasion from any standpoint—one not remotely approx-imated by anything that had ever happened before.
>
> Clark Gable, Vivien Leigh, Olivia De Havilland, Claudette Colbert, Carole Lombard, and dozens of gov-ernors, capitalists, socialites from Maine to California, and magnates whose genius has created a mighty indus-try in motion pictures, statesmen, and writers and actors, all richly garbed, were serenaded with spirituals by a group of Negroes in plantation costume from the Ebenezer Baptist Church. Fifty members of the Junior League then promenaded through the curtain one by one, each attired in a gorgeous party frock of Scarlett O'Hara's day.

The piece went on from there, but Sidda's eye was drawn to a paragraph further on in the article. It was circled and had an arrow pointed to it. In the margin were the handwritten words "Guess who?"

The circled paragraph read:

> Dancing on a floor with around 3,000 other people, the feminine guests found their hoop skirts were apt to be up in the back or out on the side. One young girl in a navy bengaline and green taffeta hooped skirt getting

up to dance tried to pass in front of a couple in the
dress circle, and her skirt, much to her confusion, went
entirely over the head of the person sitting in the seat in
front of her.

Sidda laughed out loud. Hungrily, she went back to her mother's
letters.

Later
11 o'clock at night
In our berth!

Necie-o,

I am in my top berth with Caro and Teensy up here
with me. The curtains are open and we can see fields
passing by with moonlight shining down on them. We
have on our nightgowns and we've got your cookies
right up here with us. And as I promised, we folded
down the covers on your bed just like you were going
to lay your sweet little head on the pillow. Oh, Necie, I
wish you were here! You should be here.
     You won't believe what happened only about a half
hour ago! We were singing and getting loud, but no
louder than usual, and then out of nowhere there was
a knock on our door! We didn't know who in the
world it was and we had on our nightgowns already,
and we started giggling and then Caro whispered that
it was Clark Gable. And we started rolling around on
the bunk kissing the pillows, moaning, "Rhett, oh,
Rhett!" And then the knock came again and we just
almost wet our pants. So Caro jumped down from the
bunk and cracked open the door and said, "What do
you want?" And me and Teensy were leaning down,
peeking, and we saw the conductor. Oh now! I
thought he is going to tell us we're making too much
noise! But all he said was, "Just checking to see if you
young ladies are doing all right. Your father asked me
to keep an eye out for you." And we all told him we

were doing just fine. But then Teensy said, "Do you think we could please get some cold milk to go with our cookies?" You know Teensy, she will ask for anything, anywhere. And the conductor told us he'd see what he could do.

And Caro climbed back up in the bunk, and she said since she was the one to answer the door that I had to pretend to be Rhett. "Kiss me, Rhett," she said, and I gave her a kiss, and she said "Rhett, oh Rhett," and then I put my finger back up above my lip the way we do to pretend we have Clark Gable's mustache. And then there was another knock on the door!

And we all thought it was the conductor again, and so I climbed down and opened the door. It was a colored porter with three glasses of milk on a platter for us. I thanked him and he asked if we wanted our shoes polished. We all said, "Yes, thank you." And I got our shoes and handed them to him. Then he said in a whisper, "Ginger want to know if yall be doing all right. She say run two cars down if you in trouble and she take care of you." We were all surprised that he knew Ginger, but Ginger gets around you know she does. I thanked him, and he said, "My name is Mobley if yall need anything."

And so Mobley has just taken off with our shoes and he better bring them back or we'll have to go sock-footed to the diner in the morning!

Riding a train is a wonderful thing. I have decided that I just want to live on a train. Oh, you should just see the way the world looks as we roll along. I don't know exactly where we are right now. Just somewhere in the countryside I guess, heading up to the Gate City of the South.

We all say goodnight, sleep tight, and don't let the bedbugs bite.

XXXXX
Vivi

࿇

December 13, 1939
Atlanta, Georgia
3 o'clock in the afternoon

Dear Dear Necie-cakes,

We pulled into the Atlanta depot at 9:17 this morning. The station is huge. You could fit maybe three of
our Thornton depot into this one and still have room
left for a small dance party.

Teensy's Aunt Louise met us at the station. She was
wearing a big fur coat with a matching hat and muff,
and she had Teensy's cousin James Junior alongside of
her. She greeted us all very politely, but right off the bat
I could tell she was a snob. She is a nicer snob than her
son, but still a snob. That James Junior is a snob without even the decency to try and hide it. He said something ugly about my luggage before we even got out of
the station, and when he saw Ginger he acted like it
was illegal that she was not wearing a maid's uniform.
Teensy told him that not all maids wore uniforms in
Thornton. And he looked at her, his very own cousin,
like she had head lice. Well, Necie, I have decided to
overlook the way they act because we are their guests.

Let me tell you, girl, this whole city is on fire with
excitement! You can feel it crackling through the air.
There are movie displays in every single store window,
and it's like all of Atlanta is one giant movie advertisement.

I hear that Miss Mitchell has been staying inside
her apartment ever since October because the swirl is
just too much for her. She's just been having to rest and
take aspirin every half hour. I can imagine how she
feels after all she has been through to write the best
book in the world, and then to have the movie opening
and all. Oh, I wish I could get to know Miss Mitchell.
I would give anything in the world. I feel like I already

do know her, but I want to know her better.

Well, when we got to Aunt Louise's house we all had to pick our jaws up off the sidewalk. It is a mansion. Teensy said Genevieve secretly calls it the "Coca-Cola Palace." I mean, it's like nothing we have in Thornton. Big circular drive and a porch that is so dressy you feel like you're in a dining room. And inside, oh, Necie, it's like something out of the movies! They are so rich that all their colored help wears crisp uniforms and act English. Not at all like at home, where we play cards in the kitchen with Ginger or Shirley or whoever.

The very minute we got here, Aunt Louise said to one of their maids, "Go and outfit this maid from Louisiana right away."

It was like she didn't know Ginger's name, although I had introduced them when we got off the train. Aunt Louise looked at Ginger's clothes like they were full of fleas and bugs or something. Which you know isn't true because Delia would not have it.

Well, then the next time we saw Ginger she was tugging at this black starched uniform and white ruffled apron. And she had this little maid's cap on her head! I teased her and said, "Ginger, I'm gonna take a picture of you so everyone at home can see you all dressed up." And she acted real funny, like she didn't know me. Delia would just fall over laughing at the sight of Ginger in that Frenchy uniform.

The three of us are staying in a gorgeous big room here in the mansion with its own huge bathroom and a fireplace and a bay window looking out over the backyard. Our antebellum hoop dresses had already been hung in the armoire. I just can't wait to wear my navy bengaline! This is all real different from at home, Necie. It is way fancier than Teensy's house. There are tiny little bars of soap in the shape of tennis rackets in a silver dish in the bathroom, that is how rich they are.

Caro and I are sleeping in the big bed and Teensy's going to take the day bed that has a jade satin comforter on it. The butler or whatever he is brought our bags up here and that's where I am now, writing this all down to you so you'll feel like you're here with us. I like having to write everything down because then I know I will remember it. There is so much to see and do and take in that my head is spinning!

Oh, well, we are in Rome and I reckon we'll do like the Romans.

More later.

XXXXX
Vivi

                              ❧

Later
10:30 at night

Necie, girl—

We had this formal sit-down dinner and met Uncle James. Finger bowls and silver napkin rings with their high-hat monograms on them. That awful James Junior sneered at me the whole meal. I don't even see how that boy could be related to Teensy and Jack.

Teensy has taken off all her clothes and you should see her. She's stretched out on the bed with her legs crossed and her head thrown back and she's saying, "Peel me a grape, Beulah!" You know how she is. She made all three of us climb into that big claw-foot bathtub and bathe together when we got upstairs! She dumped the whole bottle of French bath salts into the water! The whole bottle. We just laid up in that tub and soaked ourselves silly. I know I shouldn't be telling you this because your face is probably all red by now, Necie-pooh-bear. You are so much more modest than we are. (But we love you anyway.)

XOX
Vivi

P.S. Our beds were turned down for us when we came upstairs. It made me miss Mother. She always turns my pillow over to the cool side when she comes in to say goodnight.

P.P.S. Gee whiz, I almost forgot to tell you! In *The Atlanta Constitution* tonight they described what Miss Mitchell is going to wear to the premiere: "a pink tulle dress with layers and layers over pink crepe, over a tight-fitting bodice with a sweetheart neckline." I can't send you the paper because Aunt Louise is keeping it for her *Gone With the Wind* scrapbook. But I copied this down for you before I gave her back the paper: "Rose-colored camellias, those flowers so redolent of the Old South, will form her floral adornment, and tiny silver slippers will peek beneath the folds of the bouffant skirt." Since I plan to meet Miss Mitchell personally, I will tell you more about her outfit after I see it for myself!

∞

December 14—no! December 15, 1939
2 o'clock in the morning!

Dear Necie,

Girl, girl, girl! We have just gotten home after the most exciting day that I have ever had in my life. Ginger was waiting for us, all upset because she didn't get to come with us for everything, and almost in tears because she thinks she's not doing her job as chaperone. We have hardly laid eyes on Ginger since we got to the Coca-Cola Palace. She says Delia is going to kill her when we all get home. I said, "Ginger, I don't even want to think about going home! Now, will you please go downstairs and make me some coffee-milk because I have to stay awake to write Miss Necie."

So here I am writing you from the big bed where

Caro is sound asleep and Teensy is snoring as usual
from her bed. I am always the last one to go to sleep,
no matter where I am. But, honey, I have got to tell
you everything.

First of all this morning, we had breakfast and do
you know that Aunt Louise was already dressed up in
a gorgeous antebellum dress?! Yes, right there at the
breakfast table. And that little weasel James Junior
had on a tattered Civil War uniform that Aunt
Louise had got her hands on. Uncle James had
already gone off to Coca-Cola, and I don't know
what he was wearing. All I know is that Aunt Louise
revealed that her dress came from the actual movie!
A whole bunch of her friends from the Junior
League were extras for the bazaar scene (remember
from the book?) and got to be in the picture. Can
you imagine?

That goon James Junior took off with some of his
twelve-year-old goon friends, and Aunt Louise said
she was spending the day going to the events with her
friends before they had to go over and check the
Municipal Auditorium where the ball was. So that
meant that Ginger and one of Aunt Louise's maids
came with us when William, the driver, took us out
and about.

Girl, there were already people on the streets of
Atlanta out walking around in their Civil War finery
and antebellum dresses! We had on the car radio and
they were reporting everything like it was FDR himself coming to town. A whole bunch of stars were
arriving at the train station, including Claudette
Colbert, but we missed a lot of news because at 10:15
we were at the corner of Whitehall and Alabama
streets for the big lamp-lighting ceremony. I never
knew it before but that very lamppost managed to
remain standing after Sherman's siege of Atlanta. And
that very lamppost was relit to show that the
Confederate spirit has not died. The three of us just
cried and cried, thinking about the Confederacy. And
then the Governor gave everyone the rest of the day

off because Premiere Day had been declared a state
holiday.

So then old William drives us to Peachtree Street
and he finds us a good place and we sit on the roof of
the car to watch the parade. Oh, it was so crowded, I
mean people were eight and ten deep. And then the
parade started. Necie, there must have been fifty or
sixty cars, with stars sitting in the back of convertibles,
looking like royalty. Clark Gable himself was there!
Honey, I am not kidding! I saw him with my own two
eyes. And he is just as wonderful as I thought he
would be. Carole Lombard was with him and they
waved and smiled at us, and I swear to you, Necie, *he
looked right at me.* Teensy and Caro are still trying to
act like this did not happen, but they are just jealous.
I'm telling you the truth: *Clark Gable looked right at me
and smiled.*

But back to the parade. I saw more stars in ritzy
cars than you ever imagined existed. You just forget you
ever heard of a Depression when you see something like
this. After the parade was over, William took back
streets to get us to the Georgian Terrace Hotel. At the
hotel, would you believe that there were governors from
five Southern states up there giving speeches? We had
to wait until all those old men were through, and then
Clark Gable himself got up! Everyone was yelling and
screaming and clapping and giving the rebel yell. So the
three of us did our rebel yell, you know how we do, and
I gave some of my famous whistles. You would have just
fainted from all the hoorah.

We were just exhausted by the time we got back
home, and we had some fruitcake and Cokes in our
room and took a nap. We pretended that we were the
Southern belles at Twelve Oaks during their nap
scene. We said, "Ginger, why don't you find a fan and
fan us like at Twelve Oaks?"

And that Ginger said, "It's December. Yall don't
need no fan. Hush up and go to sleep."

Teensy whispered, "Delia lets Ginger get away
with murder!"

But Ginger heard her (she can hear a cat tiptoe across a carpet), and Ginger said, "Miss Teensy, you better nod off or you gonna find out what murder mean."

We didn't get to sleep for long because Aunt Louise's maid came in and woke us up to start getting ready for the ball. Aunt Louise's dressmaker was here, and we had to try on our antebellum dresses for her because Aunt Louise wanted to see if they needed any adjustments. My navy bengaline and green taffeta is the cat's pajamas, *as you know.* But I tell you, those hoop skirts are hard to get around in. Just turning around, I knocked a fussy little knickknack off a prissy table in the Coca-Cola Palace. Thank goodness it didn't break!

And so we were all dressed to the nines in our Civil War getups and William drove us over in the Packard, and another car carried Aunt Louise and Uncle James to City Auditorium for the costume ball, Dixie's greatest social function. That skunk James Junior came with us and drove us crazy. He is only a year or so younger than us but he acts like he is a big fat baby. I started making faces at him before he had a chance to make faces at me. He told Teensy she looked stupid in her white taffeta ruffles, and so she pretended to wipe a booger on his goofy-looking Confederate uniform. We started laughing so hard that I busted some little hooks in the back of my dress. I don't see how Scarlett and them ever managed a good laugh in these things.

Well, I forgot about everything when we got to the ball!

There were thousands of people lined up in a little park in front of the auditorium. Uncle James said they were the people who didn't have tickets, and that they should have stayed away like Mayor Hartsfield requested. But they were standing out there in the cold, looking like the folks who live at Ollie Trott's Trailer Paradise at home, with bad teeth and all. When the police gave them orders to move back, they did.

We just walked right by them, Necie. Aunt Louise tried to make us hurry, but we all had trouble walking in those hoop skirts. You might look like a lady in those things, but you get nowhere fast, let me tell you.

Oh, my God! Inside was all done up like the Old South! The stars sat up in their own boxes by themselves. Gable the King and Vivien Leigh wearing this black velvet gown with eighty-four thousand ermine tails on the sleeves. And Carole Lombard with her hair under a black snood. And Olivia De Havilland arrived late and she had to be lifted up into her box! Teensy and Caro and I fought over the opera glasses just to see it all!

Oh, all the stars were there! But not Prissy or Pork or Big Jim, or even Mammy. They couldn't come to Georgia because they are colored.

Aunt Louise told us exactly what all the stars' outfits were made of and she could also tell you whether the outfits were designed by the guy who designed the movie costumes or not. Aunt Louise knows all these kinds of things because *Gone With the Wind* has been her personal project for two whole years. She is actually friends with the actress who plays India Wilkes in the movie because that lady is from Atlanta herself. Aunt Louise says that she doesn't think her friend is all that good of an actress, but at least she represents the South.

Finally I asked Aunt Louise if she had any idea where Miss Mitchell was. And do you know that Aunt Louise (the witch) looked right at me and said, "Don't worry yourself over that ungrateful hack, Vivi. She has not shown up."

I said, "What?! What do you mean, Miss Mitchell hasn't shown up?! This party is hers! She is as big a star as Vivien Leigh!"

But Aunt Louise just gave this little laugh like she knew better.

All the way back home and getting out of our costumes, all I could think of was Miss Mitchell. (I did pop the hooks, and I also tore my costume under the arms, and sweated a lot. I guess you are not supposed to move

or breathe when you wear those outfits.) I can't get Miss
Mitchell off my mind. I asked Caro and Teensy, "Why!?
Why didn't she come? Why in the world didn't she
show up?" Teensy said, "Maybe she was sick."

But I think there is something more to this. A
great writer like Miss Mitchell has a reason for the
things she does. I'm going to find out why if it
kills me.

So that is our day, Countess Singing Cloud. And
every single word is true. And when we get home, we
will act things out for you—like the way Gable and
Lombard turned and talked to each other while they
walked arm in arm, and how the actor that plays
Scarlett's father kind of dances like your Uncle Collie.
But for now, it's sleepytime.

Scarlett-ly Yours,
Viviane

❧

December 15
3 o'clock in the afternoon

Dear Denesie-oh,

Caro and Teensy asked me this morning, "Vivi-cakes,
what all are you writing to Necie?"

And I said, "I'm recording all our divine secrets for
when it is time to write our memoirs!"

Because, Necie, I just know that somehow everything the four of us do is *important*. I believe that years
from now people are going to want to *know* about us.

Well, we all slept real late, especially me who was a
real lazyhead after staying up all night writing to you.
When I woke up, Aunt Louise was already back from
the Press Club luncheon and she was stirred up to beat
the band. We all went downstairs where she was on the
phone to about a hundred of her friends. We tried not

to listen in, but really we had no choice. Because we
had to stand near the phone because it was cold in the
house and the heating duct by the telephone was the
warmest and also because we were looking for a button
that Caro said she lost right around in that area. (Hah,
just kidding. I *had* to listen in, in case she was talking
about Miss Mitchell.) Well, Aunt Louise kept on giving us looks, but we just kept ignoring her and listening. Just before it sounded like she was about to finish
a conversation, we ran into the kitchen and started
looking in the icebox for something to eat.

The maid had left us some roast-beef sandwiches
and a cheese and fruit platter, and we were opening
some Cokes when Aunt Louise walked in.

She said, "Well, I don't suppose I need to tell you
what I'm so upset about."

We acted like we didn't know what in the world she
was talking about, like we had not listened to her rant
and rave over the telephone to everybody in Atlanta.

Teensy acted all concerned and said, "Auntie Lou,
what is wrong?"

And then Aunt Louise reached into the back of
the pantry, pulled out a cracker tin, and lifted a bottle
of brandy out.

She poured herself a glass, and said, "Do not ever
call me Lou. My name is Louise. I believe I've made
that clear in the past, Aimee."

Well, our Teensy smiled at her aunt and said,
"Please, ma'am, do not call me Aimee. My name is
Teensy."

That Teensy is so sly.

Aunt Louise ignored Teensy, and sat down at the
kitchen table, and told us that Miss Mitchell, according
to her, had just slapped the Junior League right in the
face by not showing up last night for the costume ball,
which was sponsored by them. After all they had done
for her and her book. And it was all because back in the
early twenties when Miss Mitchell was a debutante, she
went to a charity ball and just went wild and performed
this wild and risqué Apache dance, and shocked all the

Atlanta Junior League ladies so horribly that there was nothing they could do but punish her by never inviting her to be a member of the Junior League. So Miss Mitchell was trying to get back at them by not showing up at the ball, even though she was a guest of honor.

"What is an Apache dance?" I asked. I just had to know. I am a reporter here, Necie. I need details.

"I see no reason to expose you girls to the lurid details," she said, which made me want to know all the more.

"Was she *naked* like a savage?" Teensy asked.

"Well, no, Margaret was not exactly unclothed," Aunt Louise said, putting her hand to her head.

"Well, then," Caro said, "what was all the big fuss about?"

"I can only tell you that Miss Margaret Mitchell performed what she later described as an 'Indian mating dance.' The whole thing was utterly unacceptable for any lady to do. No matter how firmly ensconced her family was in this town, they could not protect her from the consequences of such an act. The Junior League has its standards, something I hope you girls will never forget."

"Oh, no, ma'am, we won't forget," Caro said, then turned her back to Aunt Louise and made like she was going to throw up.

Then we all got the giggles and Aunt Louise told us to run on upstairs and amuse ourselves.

Well, Necie, I think it is marvelous that Miss Mitchell tweaked their noses, don't you? Still, I am *sick* that I did not get to meet her last night, and I am going to do everything I can to meet her tonight at the premiere.

I have got to close now because the three of us are going for a walk to look at the Christmas decorations in the neighborhood before we come back and get ready for the premiere.

XXXX
V.A.

Later
10:45 P.M.

Dear Countess Singing Cloud,

I don't know how to put it all into words, but I will
try. We have just come from the premiere of the greatest movie ever made. I take back every single thing I
ever said against Vivien Leigh. I love her. I adore her.
Vivien Leigh *is* Scarlett. I went in thinking I would
not ever let myself like her, that I would never forgive
them for not casting our Tallulah Dahlin in the best
role ever written. But all of that is gone. The minute I
saw Miss Leigh there on the steps of the porch at Tara
with the Tarleton twins at her side and she said,
"Melanie Wilkes, that goody-goody," well, I was a
goner. Oh, gee, honey, I don't know how to tell you
about the movie. You are just going to have to see it
for yourself. I didn't know that it could ever ever be so
romantic. Oh, when they kiss! Oh, when she pretends
she doesn't know which way the hat goes! Oh, when
he picks her up and carries her up the stairs (he was so
much nicer than in the book when he does that). Oh,
when she gets the idea to take down the curtains and
make that dress! Vivien Leigh's right eyebrow shoots
up and you can just see the thoughts shooting through
her head. And all the times the Ya-Yas have said
"fiddle-dee-dee" and how we said it made us sick to
think that an English person was going to be the one
to say those words. We were wrong, Necie. We were
wrong wrong wrong and I don't mind admitting it.
    I want to live in this movie, Necie! This is the kind
of drama I was born for.
    Let me tell you as much as I can get down. I am
still so excited and so tired from crying and clapping.
But don't worry. It is worth it to get everything
down.
    I forgot to tell you about the theater! The
Hollywood people made it so the front of the Loew's
Grand looks exactly like the front of Tara. And there

somehow was a whole lawn they grew across
Peachtree Street for all the stars to walk on. They
walked on this new grass the whole way. Mr. Gable
was so chivalrous, Necie. He said exactly what I would
have wanted him to say. He said that the night wasn't
his night but that the night *belonged to Miss Mitchell.*
Oh, that really showed me what Mr. Gable is made of.
That made me fall in love with him to the point that I
will just never get over it.

He was so handsome, oh, girl, he had on this black
overcoat and a white scarf wrapped around his neck
and Miss Lombard was wearing this gold lamé gown
that just about blinded your eyes out.

Then—the moment I have been waiting for all my
life. A limousine long as a city block pulled up, and
Miss Mitchell got out. Oh, Necie, she is so tee-ninecy.
She makes our Teensy look like a giant. And she gave
a short little speech, mainly thanking everybody, and
then she walked into the theater. To tell you the truth,
I think she was nervous. I wanted to run up to her and
get her to sign her name for me, but it was not the
thing to do, even if I could have gotten through the
crowd. Just seeing her was a thrill.

So we went into the theater, which was packed to
the gills. You could smell the men's hair tonics and the
ladies' perfumes, and hear the shiny dresses rustling.
Caro and Teensy and I all held hands. I guess I was
holding my breath too because when the curtains
opened I felt like I was going to pop.

Oh! These huge titles crossed the screen like the
wind was blowing them, and there was this music that
had me crying even before the credits stopped rolling.
And after that I don't think I breathed for hours until
Scarlett was out in the field with that turnip swearing
she would never go hungry again as God was her witness! And the music got louder, and pretty soon the
intermission lights came up and everybody was clapping like crazy and the movie was only half over! At
intermission, the three of us just held hands in the
lobby and could hardly talk. We had trouble getting

down the refreshments that Uncle James handed us because we were still back at Tara. How could we drink punch when Scarlett was starving?

And then all the sadness. Oh, Necie, it just broke my heart into a million pieces all over the floor of the Loew's Theater. I cried and cried, and so did Teensy and Caro. We used up all our hankies, and all I could think of was how much I am like Scarlett, never having a handkerchief when I need one. Honey, why did she treat him so bad? Why? Rhett loved her. Couldn't she see that? Why couldn't she see that? I am never, never going to let something like that happen to me. When I meet my own Rhett I am going to love him back if it just kills me.

Oh, Necie, I just can't write any more. I'm so tired and I start crying all over again when I start thinking about it all. I am going to sleep now after the most exciting day in my life. (I was wrong: I had thought yesterday was the most exciting day in my life, but today is. I can't ever imagine having a more exciting day as long as I live.)

Fiddle-dee-dee and a kiss,
Vivian

(I have decided I will drop the "e" in my name so it will be more like *hers.*)

⊗

3 o'clock in the morning in the Coca-Cola Palace
December 16, 1939

Necie—

This house is too big, and it has scary sounds too. I had a bad dream, I think it was about Scarlett. I was running through the fog with her. I woke in a sweat and at first I didn't know where I was. The others were

all asleep, so I got out of bed and went looking for
Ginger. To see if maybe I could wake her up and make
her play some cards with me like we always do at
Delia's.

It took me forever to find her room. Well, it's not
really her own room, but a maid's room that she is
sharing. I knocked and when nobody answered, I
pushed the door open and saw Ginger lying on a little
cot.

And, Necie, she was *crying*. Ginger was crying.

Necie, I don't think I've ever seen a colored person
cry before.

She startled when she saw me, and she said, "Miz
Vivi what you want coming in here?"

"I can't sleep, Ginger," I told her. And I sat down
on the floor by the cot.

Ginger looked so different than in the daytime.
She had on an old flannel gown of Delia's, like the
ones Mama uses for dishrags.

"Why are you crying, Ginger?" I asked her.

"I be cryin cause I misses my family."

"You miss Delia?" I asked her.

And she looked at me like I had hit her or something.

"Your grandmother ain't my family," Ginger said.
"I got me my husband, and two daughters. They a lot
you don't know."

And then she started crying again.

"Stop crying, Ginger," I said. It made me too
afraid to see her cry, Necie. She is supposed to be our
chaperone. She's not supposed to be crying. She cried
like she was choking, like somebody was choking her.
I hated seeing her cry.

"Ginger," I said, "we're leaving tomorrow. We'll be
back in Thornton before you know it."

She didn't say anything, just kept on crying there
all wadded up in the covers.

"Get up, Ginger," I told her. "Let's play cards, like
at home. Come on, I want to play cards."

Then she stopped crying and just laid there.

"I want some hot chocolate, Ginger. Will you get up and make me some? You can have some too. I want some hot chocolate like you always make me at home."

And Necie, she looked at me like no colored has ever looked at me in my life, and she said, "*Go fix it yourself.*"

And she went back to crying, and wiping her eyes with the bed sheet.

So I got up and came back here to our room. But everyone's sound asleep. I am so scared, Necie, and I don't know why.

Your Vivi

&

December 16
8 o'clock at night
On the train, we're coming home.

Dear Necie,

We are back on the train, and I am worn out. This trip has changed. I hate to tell you how it ended, but I vowed I would tell you everything and so I will.

This morning we woke up and packed all our things and went down to breakfast. The back of my eyes hurt, the way they do when we stay up all night talking when I spend the night at your house. Breakfast was in the dining room, and there was Aunt Louise reading *The Atlanta Constitution* oohing and aahing over all the pictures, and there was James Junior, the snooty stupe-nagel.

Teensy said, "We really do thank you for letting us stay here and go to all the events, Aunt Louise. Everybody will be so jealous at home!"

And I chimed in and said, "We just can't wait to get back and tell our good friend, Necie."

And Caro thanked her too.

And I started to say something else, and then that little worm James Junior started repeating every word that came out of my mouth!

I said, "Pardon me, Blaine, but what are you doing?"

"I'm trying to learn to talk like a hick before yall leave," he said.

I looked over at Aunt Louise to see how she'd correct him, and she did not say a word. She just took a bite of her biscuit.

I tried to keep talking, but James Junior wouldn't stop. He kept on and on.

And then Ginger came in out of the kitchen. Which surprised me because we had not seen her in the dining room during the entire visit. Necie, she had a cup of hot chocolate on a tray. She had made it just for me. She was walking over to where I was sitting, and I was just about to thank her.

And that is when James Junior opened his trap.

"Nigger," he said, "who told you you could walk your black Louisiana ass into our dining room? Get on out of here!"

Ginger froze in her tracks, right there on the Persian rug. She didn't move, she just looked straight ahead like she was alone in the room, like none of us were even there. I looked at Aunt Louise to see if she was going to knock that James Junior upside the head, but that woman did nothing but stir her coffee.

I could hear the hot chocolate cup rattle against its saucer while Ginger stood there. All of this happened in an instant. And before I knew it, I picked up my plate and threw it at James Junior. That Limoges china plate with my eggs and grits and bacon and biscuits and fig preserves flew across the table and splattered all over that little two-legged rodent.

"Shut your ugly little snobby mouth, you long-nosed weenie-faced mama's boy!" I screamed. "Didn't your mother teach you good *manners*?!"

And for a split second before Ginger got out of the

room, I thought I saw her look at me and wink, but I'm not sure if it really happened or if I imagined it.

Nobody could believe it. Aunt Louise was screaming, and the other maid came in and James Junior started crying. He actually started crying, Necie. It's not like the plate cut him or anything. I mean he wasn't bleeding or anything.

Then Aunt Louise snatched me up from my seat and shook me so hard I thought my teeth were going to fall out of my mouth and shoot across the floor like someone just threw a hand of jacks. And Necie, the way she shook me, I could tell that she had always *wanted* to shake me like that, that she had just been waiting to do it ever since she laid eyes on me. She had only been holding back because she was in the Junior League.

Then she caught herself and let me go. "You are never welcome in this house again, Viviane Abbott! Nor in any of the homes of my friends here in Atlanta!! After all that I have done for the three of you! I have done my best to expose you all to the way civilized people live. All because my brother asked me to. All because Teensy is being culturally crippled by that tasteless Genevieve! I have bent over backwards trying to *work* with you little bumpkins so you would not be the laughingstock of Atlanta. Well, I wash my hands! Go back to your tacky little hick town and grow up without a shred of gentility or breeding. The four of you are a quartet of embarrassments! Aimee, I'm wiring your father that I am done with you! You and your little heathen pack of hussies."

"We are not hussies, Aunt Lou," Teensy said. "*We're Ya-Yas.*" Teensy said it with such piss and vinegar that Caro started applauding.

Aunt Louise acted like she hadn't even heard Teensy, and said, "I told you: my name is *Louise.*"

Your name is asshole, is what I thought. But I didn't say it because I was her guest.

Aunt Louise had William take us to the station early, just to get us out of her house. Well, Necie, I cried and cried. I felt so bad. Caro and Teensy just held me and held me. As we pulled out of the depot, we were so upset, and when we looked out at Atlanta, all we kept seeing was the way it looked with those dying Confederate soldiers stretched out for miles, and I kept thinking how tired and hungry Scarlett was and how she just wanted her mother. I cried and cried until something came into my mind: Necie, I am like Miss Mitchell who they kicked off the Junior League roster because of her Indian love dance. And I started thinking, Well, maybe Miss Mitchell knew exactly what she was doing when she danced that dance. Maybe she *wanted* to be X-ed out of the club so she could be free to go and write the greatest book of all time.

Yes, I have decided that I am like Scarlett and I am like Miss Mitchell. None of us like pale-faced, mealy-mouthed ninnies, and if that bothers the Junior League, well, that is just too bad.

Love,
Vivian (remember: Drop the "e"!)

Later
12:07 in the morning

Necie-oh,

We are rolling through the state of Alabama. I went back to the colored car to see what Ginger was doing, and bring her a Coca-Cola. And do you know she was having the time of her life. She was back there smoking cigarettes and chewing gum and nipping on a bottle that was being passed around four or five other coloreds while they played cards. She was laughing and laughing, and when she saw me, she smiled and said, "We goin home, baby chile! Ain't that good news?"

"It's real good news," I said, and handed her the Coca-Cola.

"Thank you, baby," she said, and took a sip of the Coke and then a swig off the bottle.

"Ginger," I said, "you know a lady doesn't smoke and drink and chew gum with strangers."

And Ginger looked at the others, and they all started to laugh like they were old friends.

"Miz Vivi," she told me, "Old Ginger ain't got to worry about being no lady. That yo' problem, baby. That yo' problem."

Necie, I have had enough traveling. I can't wait to get home. I love you. We all love you. We are lonesome for you. Tonight Caro said you were a little like Melanie. Well, I don't think that's true, but all I have to say is that I love you, like Scarlett realized she loved Melanie right as Melanie lay in the bed there dying. You are our blood sister, remember, and blood sisters can never really go away from each other, no matter how lonesome train whistles sound in the night air.

Love forever and ever,
Vivi

11

*S*idda carefully folded the letters and slipped them back into their Ziploc bag. As she stood up from the easy chair, she felt disoriented, the way one feels upon emerging from a movie theater in the middle of a sunny day. As she looked around the cabin, with its comfortable furniture, Northwest touches, and photographs on the walls, everything seemed suddenly alien. A wave of homesickness swept over her like she hadn't experienced in years. She bent down to Hueylene, who was lying on the sofa, and rubbed the dog's belly. Hueylene moaned and rolled over, wanting more. Sidda moaned in response to Hueylene's sounds, then rubbed the dog on the ears. How was it that this cocker remained so perpetually cheerful? So willing to love and be loved?

"Come on, Buddy," Sidda said. "Let's go for a walk."

They walked into the forest, thick and old. It was only four in the afternoon, but the day was so overcast it felt like twilight. Sidda marveled that some of the logs she passed by had actually toppled to the forest floor several *centuries* ago.

She paused at one of the National Park Service signs. It read:

Very little light reaches the forest floor in the deep temperate rain forest. The only way young seedlings can survive until they reach the light of the upper canopy is to grow on the nutrient-rich decaying logs. These logs are called *nurse logs*.

People can be nurse logs, too, she thought. Rich, generous, deeply well-mannered.

After her walk, Sidda stepped into the Quinault Mercantile, the general store that served the area. She was surprised to discover that they had a rental videotape of *Gone With the Wind*.

As she pulled cash from the pocket of her jacket, the fellow at the cash register said, "You carry any videos at all, then you got to have old Scarlett and Rhett. Even the Japanese want to see them."

Back at the cabin, Sidda laid a fire in the fireplace. With rain falling outside, a bowl of popcorn, and a Diet Coke on the table in front of her, she leaned forward from her spot on the sofa, and, with the remote control held tightly in her hand, screened *Gone With the Wind*.

As she watched, she rewound the tape again and again, playing certain scenes over and over. She anticipated certain moments and fast forwarded to them, pausing the tape to analyze dialogue, lighting, pacing, scenery. Then, rewinding, she studied the buildup. From there, she'd rewind to find certain touches, details she thought she might have missed; she'd turn off the volume during certain scenes just to observe the visuals.

By the time she was done, almost six hours had passed. Her hand was cramped from her vise grip on the remote control. She flicked off the TV, stretched, and let Hueylene out. Glancing at her watch, Sidda wondered how it could possibly have grown so late. She thought about Connor, and pictured his body the way it looked when he was asleep. Does he turn in his sleep, she wondered, like I do, here alone, ready to spoon, belly to back?

She lifted Hueylene up onto the sofa with her and the two of them lay staring at the dying fire. Although this was the first time she'd seen *Gone With the Wind* in years, it was as if she had been watching the film every day of her life in some hidden screening room of her own.

Sidda remembered how as a teenager she used to worry constantly whether the boy she was in love with at the time was a Rhett or an Ashley. If he was an Ashley, she'd want a Rhett. If he was a Rhett, she'd long for an Ashley. Every girl she met she'd subject to a "Scarlett/Melanie" rating. If the girl weighed in as a Melanie, she was to be pitied. If the meter leaned toward Scarlett, the girl wasn't to be trusted.

How different her own first viewing of the movie was from her mother's experience. She had seen the epic upon its rerelease in 1967. Her date was some boy whose name she now could not recall. Sidda remembered how the boy held her hand, how his sweaty palm had distracted her. How she'd pulled away during the most intense scenes because she'd wanted to concentrate on the drama alone.

As Sidda lay on the sofa, she envisioned Vivi as a girl, holding hands with her girlfriends, enfolded in the dark womb of Loew's Theater. She imagined Vivi's reddish-brown eyes grow wide as the Technicolor burst across the screen, ushering in "A time of Ladies and Knights, the last ones." She felt her mother's goose bumps when Big Jim opened the movie by reprimanding the other slaves: "I'm de foreman. I says when it's quittin time."

Sidda stroked Hueylene's chin. Vivien Leigh and Victor Fleming and David Selznick and Clark Gable grabbed Mama, she thought. And didn't let her go for three hours and forty-eight minutes, with the exception of an intermission when she was too dazed to go get refreshments. Mama was thirteen years old and she didn't know that part of what she was feeling was the confusion that comes from three, four different male directors biting into Margaret Mitchell's romance. Mama didn't know how close the emotional bones of the story were to Miss Mitchell's own life. Mama didn't know that she was being fed a regurgitation of the mythic South.

Mama did not think; Mama just felt. Her palms sweated in the palms of her girlfriends. Her eyes moistened, her heart beat fast, her eyes tracked Vivien Leigh. Unconsciously, Mama began to raise her own right eyebrow and believe that every man in the world adored her. Without knowing, Mama stepped into the tiny tight boots of Scarlett O'Hara. And Mama would do anything for the rest of her life to keep that drama going.

I want to live in this movie, Necie! This is the kind of drama I was born for.

There, with Gable's lips two feet tall, Mama couldn't pause, rewind, or fast forward. She was at the mercy of the myth.

But not completely. Mama hurled that plate. She might not have been able to explain why, but she hauled off and hurled that plate at James Junior, that bratty little white-racist-society ninny baby.

Oh, Mama, you are the star of your own movie, Sidda thought. You are waving from the back of the convertible. As much as I want to, I cannot direct the scene.

Sidda thought about Ginger. She remembered the birthday parties Buggy gave for Ginger, a tradition started by Delia. When Delia was alive, those parties were something everybody looked forward to. When Delia died, Vivi and Jack, the various cousins, uncles, and aunts, gathered at Buggy's for the celebration. Ginger was always the only black person present.

Sidda remembered Ginger as a strong-willed woman who got a kick out of Vivi. Like Delia, Ginger did not care much for Buggy. At the parties, Vivi and Ginger would sit and smoke cigarettes together, and Ginger would tell wild stories about trips she'd taken with Delia all over the country after Sidda's great-grandfather died.

Sidda remembered how resentful Buggy was about the way Vivi and Ginger carried on. The way Vivi and Ginger would spike their cups of birthday punch with gin and grin and wink, just to drive Buggy crazy.

"Miz Vivi," Ginger used to say to Sidda, "done got Miz Delia's high spirits. High spirits done skipped Miz Buggy, gone straight to you mama."

Sidda roused herself from the sofa. Was there a photo of Ginger anywhere in the scrapbook?

She combed the album, but could not locate one. What she did find was a photo of herself as an infant. Sidda knew it was herself because underneath was written "Baby Sidda w/ Melinda." Melinda, a heavy black woman dressed in the starched uniform of a practical nurse, held Sidda in the crook of her arm. Melinda did not smile, but stared straight into the camera as though on watch.

Black women, Sidda thought. They changed my diapers, fed me, bathed me, and dressed me. They helped me learn to crawl, talk, walk, and get out of harm's way, even when the harm was my mother. They hand-washed my underwear, and in turn were given my old dresses to take home to their daughters. They did the same for Mama, and now they're doing the same thing for my nieces.

Sidda thought of Willetta, the black woman who helped raise her during most of her childhood. Willetta, over six feet tall, a face that looked part Choctaw, a smile that revealed crooked teeth and a forgiving heart.

Willetta, you risked your job and the roof over your head to come to the big house and protect us from Mama that Sunday afternoon. You are the one who put salve on my body where the belt had struck. When Mama went beyond control. Did Mama, in some secret place, hate the four of us?

Willetta, now almost eighty, still cleaned Vivi and Shep's house. Sidda and Willetta still exchanged letters. Vivi's jealousy of their affection did not keep Willetta and Sidda from loving each other.

Is jealousy a gene passed down like blonde hair or brown eyes?

Sidda cannot think about her mother without thinking about Willetta. And yet she can barely unravel her relationship with her white mother, let alone her black one.

What is my civil war about? Is it the fear of being held in the warmth of familiar love versus the fear of running through the fog, searching for love? Each holds its own terrors, extracts its own pound of flesh.

Flesh. Now we draw closer. The question is: can I love Connor, who will die someday, any day, the smell of his shoulders becoming only a memory. Can I soften to love, with full knowledge of the suffering I welcome in? Thomas Merton said the love we most cherish will, of necessity, bring us pain. Because that love is like the setting of a body with broken bones.

But I want to stage the setting; I want to direct all scenes.

Sidda crawled back onto the sofa, lay back, and invited Hueylene to curl up close. As she drifted off, she imagined the Ya-Yas in the Coca-Cola Palace. Teensy commands them to climb into the big claw-footed bathtub filled with hot water. She extravagantly pours in French bath salts that rich Aunt Louise ("Do Not Call Me Lou") has left for guests. Their bodies are young and smooth, buds of breasts scarcely announcing themselves, pubic hair barely filling in. Their legs remain unshaved, not yet enveloped in the brand-new nylon stockings introduced only months before. One girl is propped against the back of the tub. Another leans into her, her body fitting between the first one's legs. And yet another girl leans against that girl, and they float in a tub in a neutral nation while Hitler penetrates countries in a world far away. They soak in a country newly pulled out of depression by the European orders for guns and tanks and weapons of war that the Ya-Yas do not yet know about. The war they are concerned about happened eighty years before. And they agree with Scarlett that all this talk of war can ruin a party.

This is my mother in the bath with her sister-friends. Her skin is pink from the hot water. Her hair is wet in curls around her forehead. Long before her body held mine inside. When her pubic bones stuck out and her belly was still concave. Before her body, in its search for peace, discovered bourbon and its comfort and its prison.

Sidda wants some of that Ya-Ya innocence. She wants girlfriends to hold her hands.

At four o'clock in the morning, Sidda woke up on the sofa. She lay there and remembered how, throughout her childhood, Vivi made fun of the term Junior League. Until Sidda was eight years old, she thought the name Junior League was one word: "juneyaleeg." And she thought it meant the same thing as "idiotic" or "disgusting."

This belief was not challenged until one night at her girlfriend M'lain Chauvin's house. They were sitting at the dining-room table when one of the young Chauvin boys pulled a garter snake out of his shirt pocket and upset the whole room. Everyone was shocked, and to express her repugnance, Sidda loudly exclaimed, "Oh, how juneyaleeg!"

Their maid immediately removed the critter, and Mrs. Chauvin nailed Sidda with a frown.

"What in the world did you just say, Siddalee?"

"'Juneyaleeg,'" Sidda explained. "It means something terrible."

Mrs. Chauvin raised an eyebrow and shot her husband a look.

Later, after Sidda's own breasts bloomed, and boys pinned orchids on her prom gowns and what to wear to Cotillion became a pressing concern, she came to realize just what power the Junior League had in the social world of Thornton, Louisiana—and precisely where Mrs. Abby Chauvin, *née* Barbour, fit in.

Tonight, though, in a cabin twenty-five hundred miles from Thornton, Sidda decided to return to her original understanding of the term.

Def. juneyaleeg: Ya-Ya term for phonus-balonus. *or.* 1939.

Sidda got up off the sofa, brushed her teeth, and got into bed.

I must sleep now, she told herself. I must climb into my berth and dream while the train rolls on. Angels of the Southern Crescent, fluff my pillows, please. Let moonlight bathe me in my slumber. I'm a second-generation Ya-Ya on a long, long trip.

12

$\mathcal{T}$he next day around noon, Sidda woke to the sound of really loud, really bad singing. Wade Coenen and May Sorenson stood on the deck of the cabin and belted old disco tunes at the top of their voices until Sidda got up out of bed to open the door to the deck.

"I love the night life! I got to boogie!" they belted as Sidda sleepily stared at the two of them. May's inch-long black hair stood up in little tufts, and Wade's long blond tresses flowed down his shoulders and onto his cotton tank top. May wore a baggy little pair of Hawaiian print shorts and a T-shirt with a picture of a woman looking shocked, a bubble of thought drifting up from her head, which read, "Oh, no! I forgot to have children!"

They each held bags of groceries.

"Hey, girlfriend," Wade said. "You said Connor couldn't come visit, but you didn't say a word about us."

Sidda gave them each kisses. "You brought the sun. I don't believe it! It's been Gore-Tex weather for days."

"We specialize in psychic weather control," May said.

"Come on in," Sidda said.

Wade led the way into the cabin with a flourish. "How positively Northwest Native!" he said.

"Yah, you betcha," May said. "Das the Sorensons."

"The place is great, May," Sidda said, peeking into the grocery bag. "Yum. Goodies."

"We only hope and pray that we aren't interrupting a deep existential soul search," Wade said, walking toward the kitchen.

"From Connor," May said, pulling out an envelope and two bottles of Veuve Cliquot from the bag. "He told us to leave you alone, that you only wanted to communicate by mail, but when we refused to obey, he sent this."

Sidda studied the envelope, which was hand-decorated with Connor's calligraphy and little drawings of flowers. She suppressed a little shiver of excitement at the sight of his handwriting and tucked the envelope away to read later.

"Thank you," Sidda said, "Here, I'll put the bubbles in the fridge."

"Oh, Madame Voilanska," Wade said. "How unspeakably rude! Your paramour sends the elixir of the gods, and you dare to hide it away in the cold darkness of the Frigidare?! *Au contraire!* We must drink this now. Champagne goes bad very quickly when you're near a rain forest. Isn't that true, Bitch Goddess of the May?"

"Absolutely," May said.

"You two sound like my mother," Sidda said, shaking her head.

"Your mother?" May said. "I never knew your mother was so—"

"So 'alcoholic'?" Sidda asked.

"No!" Wade said. "So bewitched by the bubbles!"

Wade launched into a campy Billie Holiday version of "Bewitched, Bothered, and Bewildered."

"Hueylene," Sidda said, "our ascetic seclusion has been breached."

"Goodness," May said, heading to the deck where Hueylene lay in the sun. "I forgot to greet Huella."

May pulled a dog bone out of her pocket and presented it to Hueylene.

They made a pitcher of mimosas and a platter of prosciutto and cantaloupe, and sat out on the deck. The sun warmed Sidda's legs, which she propped up on the railing.

"So," Wade said, "the previously planned wedding bacchanalia has now been derailed?" He lowered his head, and cocked his eyebrow at Sidda.

"Wade," Sidda said, "you make it sound like *you* were the one I had wedding plans with."

"But, Darlingissima, you *did.* You had wedding plans with me; and with May and Louise; and that eternally irrepressible ninety-year-old acting teacher of yours, Maurine. You had plans with Gervais and Lindsay; with Jason if he is well enough; and the Baileys and their brood of no-neck monsters with their nanny and her mustache. You had plans with Alain, who was actually planning to come from *England,* assuming she was still at liberty; you had plans with Ruthie Mueller *and* Stephan, even though they aren't speaking. Not to mention the entire cast and crew of *Cusp,* and regional theater directors from at least three theaters, who were planning to fly in for the nuptials and turn it into a New York theater trip. I am not even going to bother *listing* the countless other friends who adore you and who are now *desolate* over this heartbreaking news."

Wade took a breath before sipping his mimosa.

"When you plan a wedding," he said, "you plan it with an *orgy* of people, Sidda. *What,* pray tell, is going on?"

If Sidda had not known how Wade was devoted to her, she would have taken this tirade as intrusive. They had been friends for almost fifteen years. She had helped him nurse a dying lover; he had picked her up off the floor countless times, personally and professionally.

She got up and knelt on the floor beside Wade's chair, and began to bow. "Forgive me, Baba Wade, forgive me. I know not what I do."

"Oh, yes, you do. You know exactly what you do. Now please get up off your knees. You know that stuff doesn't turn me on when girls do it."

Sidda stood up and brushed off her knees. "May, when will he stop calling us girls?"

"I've given up," May said.

"Is that what *you've* done, dear heart?" Wade said to Sidda. "Have you given up on love?"

"No," Sidda said. "That is not it. That is not it at all."

"Well," Wade said, "then what?"

"Wade," May said, "lighten up. Maybe Sidda doesn't want to talk to us about it."

"Thank you, May," Sidda said.

"The playwright, Ms. Sorenson, may have sensitivity to these issues," Wade said, "but as a lowly costume designer, who will even stoop so low as to design for *Las Vegas* between legitimate shows, I must be crass and ask: *Have you lost your mind?!*"

"Well," Sidda said, "I have considered that."

"See," May said, "I told you she would have already taken that into consideration."

"Because," Wade said, "temporary insanity is the *only* reason my feeble brain can come up with for you to '*postpone*'—whatever the hell that means—your wedding to Connor McGill. In case you have forgotten, my little bonbon, we are talking about a man who is your equal in every area—psychologically, professionally, spiritually, and—*if* my memory serves me correctly, and I believe it does—*sexually*. I seem to recall the way you *trembled* in his presence for an entire six months before you would admit you even liked him. But old Uncle Wade was not fooled. Why? Because Uncle Wade has known you for a long time, and has witnessed you go through enough men to make up not one but *two* rugby teams. I wrung out your hankies when you ended up in tears over at least a third of those characters, some of whom I would describe as, if not completely Neanderthal, then at least lacking in, shall we say, a certain *sangfroid.* I do not think it is open for debate when I observe that not one of those men treated you with one ounce of the love and respect Connor does."

Sidda slapped her forehead. "I completely forgot you were a traveling preacher-therapist as well as a costume designer! How could that have slipped my mind, Reverend Doctor Coenen?"

Wade put his glass down.

May cleared her throat.

Sidda looked at Wade, then at May. "Is this visit a mission or something?"

"No," May said, quietly. She thought for a moment, then continued. "You know how some people, when they're together, they somehow make you feel more hopeful? Make you feel like the world is not the insane place it really is?"

"Like when you see a couple on the dance floor who really know how to waltz," Wade said. "You want to wait till the music stops, and then run up and congratulate them."

May touched Sidda's hair lightly. "We were all looking forward to the wedding. I mean, we've all watched you and Connor fall in love after all these years of us working together."

"Yeah," Wade said. "We feel like you just broke up with *us.*"

Sidda reached up to touch May's hand. "Oh, I'm really sorry. I didn't even think about you guys. But I haven't broken up with anybody. I just need some *time*. Getting married is treacherous." She stood up and walked to the edge of the deck. "I mean, I don't see either of *you* getting married."

Wade came over to Sidda and put his arm around her. May did the same. Someone passing on the trail below might have looked up and mistaken them for two sisters and a brother; or, missing certain clues, a *ménage à trois*.

"Ah well," Wade sighed. "I suppose Gertrude Stein, the mother of us all, is right: 'Nothing is really so very frightening when everything is so very dangerous.'"

For the rest of the afternoon, the three friends did not discuss marriage. They pumped air into three plastic floats and took them down to the lake. The day was a hot one, with brilliant blue skies, all signs of Northwest gray vanished. They laughed and talked and stared up into the sky, occasionally paddling back to the dock, where their cooler and snacks were set up. It was a scene that could have taken place thirty years earlier, on a Southern creek, only the water was colder.

Toward the end of the day, they gathered back on the deck to grill salmon. As the sun set, they hungrily dove into plates of salmon, pasta, and fresh sourdough bread. May regaled them with stories of her childhood summers on Lake Quinault with her four brothers. Sidda smiled. She liked this woman. Sidda's professional life had crowded out most of her girlfriends, but as she looked at May, she recognized an equal, a sister, and she was thankful.

Later, Sidda brought out her mother's scrapbook.

"'Divine Secrets of the Ya-Ya Sisterhood!'" May exclaimed. "I'd give anything to have thought up that title. How old was Vivi Dahlin when she wrote that?"

"Young," Sidda said. "Mama has always been imaginative."

"This is *fabulous*, Sidda!" Wade said, turning the pages of the album. "God, it almost makes up for the *fatwa* Vivi Dahlin put out on you."

All Sidda's friends referred to her mother as "Vivi Dahlin" because that is what Sidda called her when she told Garnet Parish stories. Feeling both proud and protective of her mother's book, Sidda announced, "You can each look at one item."

Then Sidda blushed when she realized how childish she sounded.

"What grade are you in right now, little girl?" Wade asked her.

"Second," Sidda said. "Maybe third?"

May opened up to a photo of Vivi, surrounded by Sidda, Little Shep, Lulu, and Baylor on a blanket spread in the yard at Pecan Grove, sometime in the early sixties. Sidda glanced over her shoulder as May studied it silently.

"I wonder who took this picture," May said.

"I really don't remember," Sidda said.

"I wonder where I can get a pair of those sunglasses like your mother is wearing," Wade said.

"You were an intense little kid, weren't you?" May said.

"Rumor has it," Sidda said.

Wade then carefully turned to a page at random and plucked out a clip from *The Thornton Town Monitor*.

"Adults Crash Cotillion," the caption read.

Wade scanned the piece and roared with laughter.

"Is this *true?*" he asked, turning the paper over to examine it. "Or is it one of those made-up newspaper headlines?"

"I beg your pardon," Sidda said, taking the clip from him. "This is *The Thornton Town Monitor*, which has been monitoring every citizen in Cenla for over a hundred years. As God is my witness, Mama and the Ya-Yas and the Ya-Ya husbands crashed the Cotillion ball my junior year in high school. They had been forbidden to come after several years of misbehaving."

She paused.

"Am I boring yall? Mama sent me this album, and I happen to be quite interested in it, but really—"

"Sidda," May said, "come on. A lead-in like that? Of course, we're interested."

"Well," Sidda continued, "It was a Cotillion rule that no alcohol was to be served. Of course, everybody always brought their own little flasks and mixed drinks in the bathroom. But when the Ya-Yas chaperoned, they had a tendency to turn the whole event into their *own* party. Of course, they refused to hide their own booze, and would pour drinks for any kid who wanted a drink or two or five. They did that for two years, the second year resulting in a little problem with the boys hoisting us girls in our formals up onto their shoulders so we could burst the papier mâché piñatas. However, once we were up that high off the ground, we found it rather appealing to begin trying to knock other girls off their dates' shoulders. Oh, it got rowdy, honey. Yards of tulle were torn and taffeta ripped. A few femme fatales knocked to the floor, a couple of chipped teeth. That sort of thing.

"After that, the Cotillion Committee pointedly did not ask Mama, Teensy, Caro, and Necie and their husbands to chaperone. In fact, they were sort of forbidden to show up. Granted, they had their rules, but these committee women were the worst—Miss Alma Assholes. That's Ya-Ya-ese for stuffy, officious people."

"You need not explain to me, Preciosa," Wade said. "The International Society of Miss Alma Assholes had a very active chapter in my own hometown of Kansas City. In fact, there was also the brother society: The International Association of Mister Albert Assholes."

"Don't keep us hanging by an eyelash, Miss Walker," May said. "What happened?"

"You would have thought people in my hometown would have known *better* than to forbid the Ya-Yas to do anything. The next year they showed up in their evening gowns, and, with the husbands in dinner jackets, they walked straight past a receiving line of Cotillion Committee members, who were too shocked to stop them. Once they got inside, they commandeered a big table, set up bar, and of course became the center of attention. I was horrified."

"Was there a scene?" Wade asked.

"Not until the police arrived. As they were escorted out, flashbulbs were popping all over the Theodore Hotel ballroom," Sidda explained. "This was 1969, and in the tone of the times, Mother began referring to her crowd as 'The Cotillion Eight.'"

"You are making this up," May said.

"There are a million stories in the Naked City," Sidda said. "This is only one."

Before Sidda could close the album, Wade leaned down to examine yet another photograph.

"Ah, the teenage Vivi Dahlin," Wade said. "And is this your father?"

As Sidda bent down to study the photograph, she was startled to see a beautiful young man who was playing a fiddle. Lanky and graceful, he was leaning back against a large tree trunk. His eyes were large and dark, and he had the most sensual lips Sidda had ever seen on a man. He wore a white shirt with the sleeves rolled up, a pair of khakis, and the expression on his face was one of happy concentration. To his left was a low branch, the kind that old live oaks in the South are known to grow. On the branch sat Vivi at age sixteen. She wore a white peasant blouse, a full skirt, and sandals. Instead of looking at the fiddle player, her head was tilted to the side and slightly down. Her eyes were closed and she was smiling, lost in the music. Whoever had taken the picture had captured a very private moment, and Sidda felt as though she should have asked permission to behold the image.

"No, that's not my father," she said, "that's Jack Whitman. My father has never played the fiddle."

"Don't you think he looks rather like—" Wade said before May interrupted.

"I don't know who was behind the camera on this one, but you can tell she loved her subjects," May said.

Sidda looked at May, then back at the photo. She longed to breathe herself back in time, to hover invisibly near the young woman in the picture, to hear the fiddle music, to witness up close her mother's fledgling joy.

In spite of Sidda's invitation to spend the night, Wade and May left after dinner, protesting they'd already made reservations at Kalaloch Resort, on the coast. Sidda walked them to May's vintage convertible Mustang, and the two women hugged.

"Take care of yourself in the former Czech Republic," Sidda said.

"And Greece and Turkey, and wherever else she decides to light," Wade said.

"Your mom can't stay enraged forever, Sid," May said. "God, I wish she could simply *see* the play. Keep the door open, girlfriend. As long as you're both still breathing, there's a chance."

"Thanks, May," Sidda said.

"You take care of yourself," May said. "Fax any brainstorms about *The Women*—which we did not discuss at all!—to Jeremy. He'll know where to reach me."

Wade hugged Sidda. "Sorry if I was a bitch. I just want all my children to be happy. And Connor McGill is such a stud-muffin—oops! I mean genius designer."

"Love you, Wadey," Sidda said.

"Love you, Siddkins," Wade said.

Sidda was surprised how sad she was to see them leave. She was relieved to still have Hueylene for companionship. For the first night since she'd arrived, it was warm enough to sleep with the windows flung open, wearing only a T-shirt. She pulled the sheet up as she propped up in bed, eager to open Connor's envelope.

He had written her name beautifully, but what she had not noticed earlier was that he'd drawn flowers into the letters of her name. In his exquisite hand, he had drawn sweet peas to form the "d's" in her name. A soul from another age. When she opened the envelope, she found a seed catalog from a firm that identified itself as "The Sweet Pea Specialists, Birdbrook, Halstead, Essex." A corner of one page was turned down, and when Sidda opened to that spot, she found the following item circled:

"LOVEJOY. One of the best Sweet Peas of recent years, strong and unrivaled. A very vigorous grower and sound in constitution; the crowning glory being its colour of salmon pink enhanced with a soft orange overlay, giving a clear brightness and purity. This is a colour that will neither bleach nor scorch in the hottest of sunshine. It is tip-top for both garden and exhibition, giving well-balanced flowers on long graceful stems. (Sweetly scented.)"

Folded into the catalog was a single sheet of drafting paper. On it Connor had written: "Sounds like you."

Sidda closed her eyes and leaned back into her pillows, astounded at how aroused she was. Connor knew *just* how to get to her. She saw the incredible roof garden Connor had cultivated at his loft in Tribeca. She remembered the first time she stepped into his loft. A Sunday morning in February, 1987. A wood stove burning, a hand-made quilt hanging on an exposed brick wall. A brunch of fresh oysters and cold beer. The sudden shift in her body that day as she admitted she had never, ever, felt so at home on the island of Manhattan.

She switched off the lamp and slipped the seed catalog under her pillow. Maybe a giant stalk will grow during the night, and I can climb my way out of indecision. I *must*, I *must* figure out what I'm doing.

But, as she settled into the darkness, her angels lit near her feet. *First*, they whispered, love your salmon pink and soft orange overlay; let it glow with clear, bright purity. So Sidda touched herself. She touched her blossom until, out of self-love, it swelled and quivered. Then she nodded off.

13

*M*ay was correct: the person who snapped the photo of Vivi and Jack on that day in 1941 had indeed loved them. Genevieve St. Clair Whitman had captured the image without disturbing the two adolescents. She had snapped it fast and true, and when she advanced the film, she uttered a silent prayer for her son and Vivi Abbott. She did not doubt that the two of them were meant for each other. She had not questioned this since the afternoon she witnessed the two of them sitting in a swing together sometime late in 1938, holding hands, not speaking, swinging in an easy rhythm. She knew her son was born with a well of tenderness that was a curse in his father's world. Genevieve could not imagine a stronger, more vital girl than Vivi to receive and embrace Jack's tenderness. Not a woman to second-guess her intuition, Genevieve accepted the fact of Jack and Vivi, and she did not stand in their way.

Oh, she had to keep an eye out every now and then. With Vivi constantly at the house, as close to Teensy as any sister, Genevieve had developed a graceful chaperoning—a kind of trust coupled with a few well-timed distractions. Both of them were so busy—Jack with basketball and track, Vivi with tennis, cheerleading, and the school paper—that she usually didn't worry. In her prayers, she thanked the Virgin for granting her son love at such an early age.

Sidda could not know this. As she returned to the photograph on the next evening, she studied the image, transfixed by her mother's expression. Sidda could not know the autumn afternoon in the early forties on Bayou Saint Jacques, Genevieve's country. She could not know the pungent aroma of the *cochon de lait,* or the sight of that pig roasting over the slow fire, or the huge vats of boiling water for the corn. The raw-boned jubilance of Genevieve's and Jack's and Teensy's *cousins* and *cousines* and *tantes* and *oncles* and all the other Cajuns on that Saturday evening over a half century ago. The crispness in the autumn air. The easy joking. The little girls dancing with their grandfathers, the older girls, dark like Genevieve and Teensy, in their full skirts and peasant tops. The presence of the bayou, the feel of liquid Louisiana land, the language of these people who staged a *fais do-do* at the mere mention of Genevieve and her two children coming back to visit.

On these visits to the bayou with the Whitmans, Vivi felt a sense of having escaped, of entering another world. And she was terribly afraid that somehow her joy would be found out and snatched away from her.

That day on the bayou, Vivi's head tilted back as Jack kissed her lightly on the neck as they waltzed to "Little Black Eyes."

"I will always love you, Vivi," he said. "There is nothing you could ever do that would make me stop loving you."

The words shot through Vivi's bones and blood and muscle, and her body relaxed, so that when her feet touched the ground they met the earth differently, as though they had found roots that reached deep down and anchored to something tender and undamaged.

On that late afternoon in 1941, Vivi believed for the first time: *There is more that is right with me than there is wrong with me. Jack loves me. He will always love me.* To look at Vivi Abbott spinning and smiling, no one on the bayou would have perceived that she had stumbled into love's seductive offer of bedrock, or how desperate she was to seize it, or how completely she believed that Jack Whitman himself was her terra firma.

With Jack's love, everything Vivi had not been given could now be made up for. Every reflection of herself that was not mirrored in her mother's eyes, every curious question her father had not asked, every visitation of the belt on her true-blonde skin could be redeemed. Vivi did not think of these promises on that afternoon with her skirt swirling and her hair swinging, but they curled inside her and attached themselves.

To look at Vivi, it would be difficult to spot the tectonic shift that took place in her that afternoon. But it would render her more vulnerable than a person wants to be. It would create infinitesimal fault lines, perhaps profound enough to be passed on, like brown eyes or a proclivity for mathematics.

But Siddalee could not know any of this. She could only study the photo and wonder.

Putting the scrapbook aside, she took out a piece of paper and wrote Connor a note. It read:

> Connor, unequaled—
>
> You know I'm no gardener, but the fragrance of those
> sweet peas wafted into my dreams. I was preparing
> soil in my sleep last night (something you know I
> know nothing about), and kept encountering masses
> of thick, dense roots. Did *not* (this will come as no
> surprise) like getting my hands dirty, but found myself
> bent on disentangling the roots and shaking the soil
> off them. This would have seemed a chore, but it was
> actually rather pleasant, because I could smell the
> sweet peas the whole time.
>> How is it you know just how to delight me?
>> May and Wade made me laugh. They also made
> me look at my rather embarrassing tendencies toward
> bull manure.
>
> XX
> Sidda
>
>
> P.S. My, but you gardeners know how to romance a
> blossom. Take my breath away, why don't you?

14

$\mathcal{T}$he wrinkled page looked like it had been torn out of a comb-bound book. On it was the following entry:

MISS ALMA ANSELL'S ACADEMY OF
CHARM AND BEAUTY
HOW TO BE SMART AND CHARMING COURSE
WINTER SESSION, 1940

LESSON 4: DO NOT CRY!

Tears will do you no good. No one will want you with dark, lifeless, dingy, lusterless, sparkleless eyes in a setting of bags and puffs. Gentlemen prefer eyes brilliant and alive and glowing, without benefit of satchels, grief, and blackness. If you must insist on crying, use a boracic-solution eye bath immediately afterward, then put cotton pads soaked in warm water and the essence of rose petals over the eyes. Next, pat very, very gently a little rich lubricating vitamin cream around the eyes. Then take a

warm bath, followed by a nice nap with eye pads soaked
in half-and-half witch hazel and ice water. Leave those
pads on for twenty minutes, and remember that *plenty of
sleep is essential and it is vitally important NEVER TO CRY.*
A girl has enough handicaps in the campaign for love.
Do not add to them with tears.

Sidda didn't know whether to laugh or cry. She was lying on the
sofa, facing out toward the lake, with a fan blowing on her, munching
on Jonagold apples and hunks of Stilton cheese, which lay on a plate
that sat on her stomach. All her life she thought her mother had made
up the name "Miss Alma Asshole" out of whole cloth. But the name
must have come from this Miss Alma Ansell and her Academy of
Charm and Beauty.

Winter Session, 1940, Sidda thought. Mama was fourteen years
old. Just after the gang had attended the *Gone With the Wind* premiere. Interesting.

Tears will do you no good.

Although Sidda was not one to quote the Bible, there was a quote
from Luke she'd always loved. "Blessed are ye that weep now: for ye
shall laugh." Sidda thought the quote was lovely and was impressed by
its light touch. Luke—or whoever really wrote it—didn't promise
you'd prosper or be saved. He promised that if you wept, sooner or
later you'd *laugh.*

She folded Miss Alma's lesson back into the scrapbook, and let
her mind wander. As she lay on the sofa in the cabin on the lake,
where she had come to decide her future, Sidda thought about tears.

Sidda remembered the first time Lizzie Mitchell came into her
life. It was an Indian-summer afternoon in 1961 and Vivi had not left
her room in almost two weeks. Sidda was relieved just to have her
mother back home after a long unexplained absence, an absence that
left them all dizzy with abandonment and confusion.

The golden afternoon light hit the fields where Chaney and Shep
and a host of others worked to harvest cotton. The afternoon air was
warm and cool all at once. If things had been normal, Sidda would
have been in the backyard, picking up pecans, singing to the dog,
dreaming about becoming a missionary in Africa or an actress on the
London stage. But she was inside, sitting on the floor outside Vivi's

door with a Nancy Drew book in her lap, one ear cocked for any sounds or requests that might issue from the room. She had been doing this for weeks; she considered it her job.

Lizzie Mitchell pulled into the driveway at Pecan Grove driving a black 1949 Ford with a cracked window on the front passenger side. When Sidda heard the front doorbell ring, she jumped up from her position outside Vivi's door, and ran to see who it was. Vivi didn't want to see anyone, and Sidda was standing sentry. Only the Ya-Yas were allowed into Vivi's room, and sometimes Vivi didn't even feel up to seeing them.

Lizzie Mitchell stood in front of Sidda wearing a blue shirtwaist dress with a gray sweater draped over her shoulders. Painfully thin, with sad blue eyes, she had a frail kind of beauty. Her face, her whole body appeared tired. In her early twenties, she had beautiful skin, but her teeth were bad, and even Sidda could see she wore the wrong shade of lipstick. She carried a suitcase, and for a moment Sidda thought the woman was a traveler who had stopped to ask for directions.

At the sight of Sidda, she gave a quick forced smile and said, "Good afternoon, is the lady of the house at home?"

Sidda just stared at the woman. Finally she said, "Yes, my mother is home. But she's busy."

"Would you tell her that a representative of the most advanced line of beauty products available in the world today is calling, please?"

"Just a minute, please," Sidda said, and left the woman standing at the door.

She knocked softly on Vivi's door.

"Mama?" she asked in a soft voice. "You asleep?"

When she got no response, she opened the bedroom door and walked in. Vivi was curled in the bed. The Snickers bar and club sandwich and Coke that Sidda had made for her when she got home from school was still untouched on the TV table.

"There's a lady at the door asking for you, Mama," Sidda said.

"I don't want to see anybody," Vivi said, without moving. "Who is she, anyway?"

"She is a representative of the most advanced line of beauty products available in the world today," Sidda said.

"What?" Vivi asked.

"That's what she said. And she has a suitcase."

Vivi slowly propped herself up in the bed, bunching her old feather pillow behind her head.

"She probably just wants to sell me something. Can't you get rid of her?"

Sidda looked at her mother. Her face was pale, had been since she'd gotten home. For the most part, she stayed in her nightgown. She hadn't even worn any of her fabulous hats because she had hardly left the house.

"No, ma'am," Sidda said. "I can't get rid of her."

"Why not?"

Sidda thought for a moment. She glanced down at the cover of her book.

"Because," Sidda said, "she's got on the wrong color lipstick."

"She's selling beauty products and she's wearing the wrong shade of lipstick?"

"I think you need to talk to her, Mama."

"Oh, all right," Vivi said. "Ask her to come in for a minute."

When Vivi walked into the kitchen, Lizzie Mitchell was sitting at the kitchen counter with Sidda. The minute Vivi walked into the room, Lizzie jumped up from the stool.

"Good afternoon," Lizzie said. "Are you the lady of the house?"

Vivi had pulled her green-striped silk bathrobe over her night-gown and stood barefoot. She put her hand on the counter as if to steady herself.

"May I help you?" Vivi asked.

"Yes, ma'am," Lizzie said in a soft voice. Her eyes went blank for a second, and then she reached into the pocket of her dress and pulled out some scraps of paper that had notes scribbled on them. Attempting to hide the fact that she was reading the notes, Lizzie began her spiel.

"I am here," she said, in a terrified voice, "to offer you the golden opportunity to discover the finest line of cosmetics ever made for a woman's skin. The Beautiere Line is a elite line of beauty products designed for the discriminating lady whose first concern is her looks."

"*An* elite line," Vivi said.

"Yes, ma'am," Lizzie repeated, her hands quivering, "it is a elite line."

"The correct grammar would be *an* elite line," Vivi explained automatically.

"Pardon me?" Lizzie asked, her voice quivering. Lizzie's scraps of paper fluttered out of her hand onto the floor. Embarrassed, she bent to pick them up. Sidda watched as the woman seemed almost unable to stand back up. When Lizzie did finally right herself, she was in tears.

Sidda wanted to hit her. The last thing she needed was for this woman to upset her mother. Just the week before, Vivi had sort of capsized at the A & P, and Sidda had had to call Caro to come and get them. Vivi moved like someone who was still getting over the flu, tired and uncertain, guarding her energy instead of flinging it around like she used to. Both her father and her grandmother had told Sidda that it was up to her, the oldest, to make sure that nothing upset her mother.

To her surprise, Sidda saw her mother touch the woman's elbow gently.

"Please," Vivi said, "excuse my rudeness. I'm Vivi Abbott Walker, and this is my oldest daughter, Siddalee. Won't you sit down please?"

Unable to meet Vivi's eyes, the woman sat back down at the counter.

"Would you care for a cup of coffee? I personally do not *touch* coffee after ten in the morning. I think I'll have a light cocktail. Shall I make you one as well? Something light?"

Lizzie continued to cry and said, "Coffee, please, if it's not too much trouble."

"No trouble at all," Vivi said. She took ice cubes out of the freezer.

"Sidda Dahlin, do you feel like making some coffee?"

"Yes, ma'am," Sidda said, relieved to be given a task.

Vivi filled the crystal ice bucket with ice cubes, then dropped a couple into a glass. Into the glass she poured orange juice and a half jigger of vodka.

Sidda put water on to boil and measured Community Coffee Dark Roast with chicory into the filter of the Chemex coffeepot. She tried not to look at her mother's bare feet. The toenail polish was chipped, something that Vivi would never have allowed when she was well.

"I'm sorry," Vivi said, "I didn't catch your name."

"Oh, no! I'm so sorry," Lizzie said, covering her face with her hands. "The first thing you're supposed to do," she mumbled "is introduce yourself to your customer."

"Well, give it a try," Vivi said as she stirred her drink. Sidda could see that her hands were still shaky. Vivi reached into the pocket of her bathrobe and swallowed a huge B–12 vitamin.

Taking her hands down from her face, the woman said softly, "Allow me to introduce myself. My name is Lizzie Mitchell and I'm your Beautiere lady."

"Pleased to meet you, Lizzie Mitchell," Vivi said, and sat down at the counter with the woman.

"I'm pleased to meet you, Mrs. Walker," Lizzie said. "You too, Siddalee."

"Would you like cream and sugar?" Sidda asked.

"Yes, please," Lizzie said. "If it's not too much trouble."

Sidda started to get out the blue coffee mugs, but Vivi said, "Dahlin, let's use china, shall we?"

Sidda poured coffee into a china cup and set it out on the counter with sugar, cream, and a spoon. Then she warmed milk on the stove in a little saucepan and made herself a mug of coffee-milk. She pulled a stool up to one of the upper cabinets and pulled down the bag of Oreos she'd been hiding from the other kids. She laid cookies out on a plate and joined the woman at the kitchen counter.

"Tell me, Mrs. Mitchell," Vivi said, "how did you come to be a cosmetics saleslady?"

Lizzie Mitchell, who was raising the coffee cup to her mouth, set it back in its saucer. She tried to speak, but when she did, she began to cry again.

"I'm sorry," she said, breathing in short, ragged little breaths. "I just started up with the Beautiere business. Sam—that's my husband—Sam died four months ago last week. In a accident at the Tullos Lumber Company. I got me two little boys and no insurance."

Lizzie Mitchell stared at her coffee cup and blinked. She seemed shocked that she had just blurted this out to Vivi. As if to try once again to establish herself as a real saleslady, she glanced desperately down at her notes and lapsed back into her rehearsed spiel.

"The Beautiere Line is something I feel honored to be able to represent. If I did not believe in the products one hundred percent, I would not sell them. Now, if—"

"Oh, my God," Mama interrupted. "What you have been through! How old are your boys?"

"Sam Junior is four and my Jed is two going on three."

Sidda looked at her mother's fingers as they held her drink glass. She was embarrassed at how unkempt her mother's nails looked. Vivi's hands, her nails, everything about Vivi used to be so cared for, so beautiful. Sidda could not understand what had happened to her mother.

"Mama," Sidda asked, "you want a cookie?"

"No, Dahlin, thank you," Vivi said.

Then, training her eyes on Lizzie, Vivi asked, "Where are your boys now? Who is taking care of them?"

"They're at my sister-in-law's, Bobbie's. Her girlfriend Lurleen got me hooked up with the Beautiere Line. Lurleen has got a savings account of her own and she done so good with her sales they awarded her The Pink Chrysler."

"She *did* so good," Sidda said.

Vivi shook her head at Sidda.

"Yes, ma'am," Lizzie said, "Lurleen done real good."

"I see," Vivi said.

"They make pink Chryslers?" Sidda asked.

"The Beautiere men gets the cars and has them painted pink for the top sellers. Beautiere is your most scientific line of beauty products."

Lizzie took a sip of her coffee.

"Scientific," Vivi repeated, and took a sip of her drink.

"Oh, yes, ma'am," Lizzie said. "It is important to be scientific in today's world."

Then, as if the coffee had picked her up, Lizzie Mitchell seemed to draw herself together. Sidda could see the woman's notes tucked in the left sleeve of her sweater. Trying her best to appear natural, Lizzie started her sales pitch again.

"The Beautiere Line costs far less than your Avon products, and yet the quality of these beauty aids has pleased thousands of women throughout Mississippi, Arkansas, and now—Louisiana," Lizzie Mitchell continued, like a trembling windup doll.

Vivi lit a cigarette. Sidda climbed down from her stool and crossed to the bar to bring her an ashtray. Sitting back down, Sidda alternated between watching Lizzie Mitchell and watching her mother. This was the most interest her mother had shown in anyone in a long time.

"Ma'am," Lizzie said, "if I can just take a minute out of your busy day to show you some of the most modern and scientific beauty boosts available, I can promise you, you won't regret it."

Lizzie Mitchell waited a beat, then reached down for her sales kit. The kit itself looked like a regular train case, but there was a silhouette of two women's heads facing each other emblazoned on the front in a Pepto-Bismol pink. Moving her coffee cup aside, she set the kit on the counter, flicked its openers, and lifted the lid. Then, as if she saw something terrible inside the suitcase, something no one else could see, Lizzie dropped her head and began to sob deeply. Her bony shoulders bobbed up and down, and her crying sounded almost like that of a small dog.

Slowly Vivi put her cigarette in the ashtray. Leaning in slowly to the woman, she gently lifted Lizzie Mitchell's chin with her hand.

"Dahlin girl," she said, "are you all right?"

Lizzie Mitchell looked up at Vivi. "It's my oldest," she said, barely audible. "Sam Junior. He's the one taking it the worst. He wants to be up close to me all the time, can't stand me to leave."

Sidda watched as her mother closed her eyes and listened.

"When I left him at Bobbie's this afternoon he started up crying and hollering, wrapped hisself around my legs, and wouldn't let go. I walked all the way to the door with him hanging off me. Me and Bobbie had to peel him off for me to leave on my sales rounds."

Without thinking, Lizzie Mitchell grabbed onto her Beautiere notes and wadded them up in a ball so that she could no longer see them.

"He's thinking you're going to leave and never come back, like his daddy did," Vivi said softly.

Lizzie Mitchell nodded her head up and down. "Uh-huh, that's it. My boy Sam he is just wired up delicate," she said.

Then Lizzie took a great gulp of air, which caused her whole body to shudder.

"I know how that can be," Vivi whispered. By this time she was crying too.

Sidda was crying as well, but not just over Sam Junior.

Using her fist to wipe back tears, Vivi said, "Sidda, precious one, would you please go find us some Kleenex?"

When Sidda got back to the table, Vivi was pressing the palms of her hands against her cheeks, and it looked to Sidda like she was trying to hold her face together. Sidda held the box of Kleenex out to Lizzie Mitchell. Even though the woman's face was wet with tears, she took only one Kleenex, like she thought that was the polite thing to do.

"You can take as many as you want," Sidda said. "We have lots."

"Thank you," she said, taking a few more tissues and wiping her eyes.

Then Sidda offered the box of Kleenex to Vivi, who grabbed a handful.

Vivi wiped her eyes, which were ringed with eye makeup.

Although Vivi had let herself go since returning home, the one thing she remained religious about was her mascara and light-brown eyebrow pencil. Without it her own blonde lashes were so light that she claimed they made her look like an albino.

Vivi frowned at the tissues, now spotted with mascara she'd cried off. Then she glanced at Lizzie Mitchell's used Kleenex.

Holding up her tissues covered in slashes of mascara, Vivi said, "Will you look at this? Will you just simply *look* at this!"

Lizzie Mitchell and Sidda stared at the tissues Vivi was holding up as evidence.

"Every single bit of mascara I put on this morning has ended up on this tissue. Cheap, cheap, cheap! All that mascara I paid good money for has ended up on a Kleenex. And here I am left looking like a hairless dog! And this is not the first time this has happened, let me tell you."

She gestured to her eyes, and indeed her lashes and eyebrows had all but disappeared.

"It should be illegal to sell eye makeup that rubs off with the merest provocation."

Vivi paused and pulled another Lucky Strike out of the pack. She tapped it on the table several times. She took her time lighting it, examining the sterling-silver lighter that sat on the table as though seeing it for the first time.

"I don't imagine you carry a Beautiere mascara line, do you?" she said.

Lizzie examined her wadded-up Kleenex. It was moist with her tears, but held no signs of rubbed-off eye makeup. Sidda watched as she reached into her purse and pulled out a cheap plastic compact. Holding it up, she examined her reflection in the small mirror.

When she looked up, Sidda saw something in Lizzie's eyes that made her think of a gate opening. Sidda's head tilted slightly to the side, her lips parted slightly, and she thought: My mother is a kind person.

Lizzie Mitchell closed her compact, took a deep breath, and opened her sales kit again. She pulled her stool over closer to Vivi's, and spoke in the voice of a woman who was coming back to life.

"Yes, ma'am," Lizzie Mitchell said. "Beautiere has a fine—*an* elite—line of mascara. We call it our Wand of Beauty. I would be pleased to show it to you. I think you'll find it a bargain at any price if you purchase it as part of one of Beautiere's Mixed Gift Packs."

Shortly after that first visit by Lizzie Mitchell, Vivi began to get dressed in the mornings. After a week or so, she was still shaky, but she'd agreed to a small dinner party at Teensy's. When Sidda and the other kids came home from school in the afternoons, they no longer found her still in bed with the door closed. They found her making phone calls to friends and acquaintances, talking up the Beautiere Line, especially the Wand of Beauty—which, when Vivi said it, sounded somewhat like a woman's name: Wanda Beauty.

On those fall afternoons when Sidda was still keeping a close eye on her mother, she would sit at the counter and listen as Vivi talked on the phone.

"You *must* let Lizzie Mitchell come show you her Beautiere Line. It's *miraculous*," Vivi would say. "I can shower in it, swim in it, go to a sad movie. You can cry all you want and never, *never* does it smudge."

It seemed that no matter how many times Vivi repeated these lines, they made her feel better. It was like she'd found a cure for a disease.

At Vivi's invitation, Lizzie began coming out two or three afternoons a week, bringing along her little boys. While the boys crawfished or rode Shetland ponies with Little Shep and Baylor, Vivi coached Lizzie on her presentation skills.

"Lizzie Dahlin," Sidda would hear her mother say, "if you want to feed those boys, then you have got to stop using the word 'ain't.'"

Vivi helped Lizzie come up with a kicky sales pitch that she was comfortable with, so she no longer sounded like she'd memorized it.

"You are terrific," she'd tell Lizzie. "Every one of your customers will be delighted to see you at the door."

The names of Lizzie's other products cracked up Sidda and Lulu. Estra-Glo was supposedly packed with estrogen. Skin Sublime was packaged in a decorator bottle that was lip-shaped. Beautiere's Hair Magic smelled a little like Evening in Paris. Each of the Ya-Yas bought Lizzie's Mixed Gift Pack—they wouldn't have dared say no. But Vivi was more successful in finding customers for Lizzie among the country women who were married to the cotton farmers who ginned at the same place as Sidda's father.

Sidda and Lulu took to calling the skin cream "Lizzie Lotion," but when Vivi heard, she fussed at them.

"Don't yall dare make fun of that young woman," Vivi told them. *"She is trying to make something of herself."*

With each visit, Vivi herself seemed to be getting her own

strength back. By the middle of November, Caro had even been able to talk her into a game of tennis at the country club. Although Sidda could not have put it into words, it seemed that the Beautiere Line was not only a cosmetics line, but also a lifeline. Not only for Lizzie Mitchell but also for her mother.

One afternoon Sidda came home to find Lizzie's car in the drive-way. She expected to find Vivi and Lizzie at the kitchen counter as usual, but instead found the house so quiet she thought nobody was home. It took her a moment to realize that they were out in the den. But when Sidda stepped into the room, she took one look and was filled with terror.

Her mother was lying back in Shep's La-Z-Boy recliner. She was covered with sheets and Lizzie stood behind her, with her hands around Vivi's neck. Vivi lay perfectly still, with cotton pads over her eyes, her hands crossed over her chest. The two women were perfectly quiet, so concentrated, so unaware of Sidda's presence. For one horri-ble moment Sidda thought her mother was dead.

Sidda held her breath and stepped closer, her stomach clenched, her heart hammering. It was not until she saw her mother's hand move that Sidda began to breathe again. Then she noticed that Lizzie's hands were gently massaging something pink onto her mother's neck. With small circular movements, Lizzie stroked the pink concoction up Vivi's neck, then carefully around her temples.

Sidda had never seen her mother be touched so tenderly.

As Lizzie's customer list grew, and as Vivi resumed her life, their visits grew less frequent. A couple of years had passed when Sidda arrived home one afternoon to see an almost-new bright pink Chrysler in the drive at Pecan Grove.

Lizzie was wearing a little two-piece suit and a Jackie Kennedy hairdo.

"Will you look at this!" Vivi announced to her children, "Lizzie has won The Pink Chrysler!"

Lizzie then flung her arms wide like a lady on a TV game show.

"I am a Beautiere Top Ten Saleslady!" she announced. "And I could not have done it—never, ever—without your mother."

"We're off for a spin," Vivi announced, climbing into the car.

Sidda watched as Lizzie backed the big Chrysler out of the drive. She stood at the end of the driveway as the two women rolled down the long gravel road that led away from Pecan Grove in the direction of town. As she watched, she could see her mother's and Lizzie's heads silhouetted against the green fields filled with her father's cotton. For a moment Sidda thought they looked like sisters.

Sidda took a bite of cheese and got up from the sofa. She walked out onto the deck of the cabin and did a few stretches. Rolling her neck in small circles to relax, she remembered once, many years after Lizzie Mitchell, when she had returned home from LSU for holiday break. She had gone up into the attic looking for extra boxes to wrap gifts in. In the corner of the freezing cold attic was a large cardboard box. She opened it to find that it held many boxes in quite good shape. "Perfect," she thought, "just what I need."

But when she reached down to pick up a few of them, she found that they were not empty. She picked up one of the boxes and examined it. It took a moment for her to recognize the gray-and-pink packaging, the silhouettes of the two ladies' heads facing each other. But once she opened it, everything came back.

It was one of the Mixed Gift Packs from the Beautiere Line. There must have been thirty of them stacked in the larger box, unopened. Another cardboard box stood next to it, and Sidda peeked into it as well. More Mixed Gift Packs.

Dear Lizzie Mitchell, Sidda thought. You came into my mother's life on an afternoon as she hid in her bedroom, trying to nurse some long-seated sadness that flows beneath her vivaciousness like a secret river. Mama looked at you, grieving the loss of your husband, struggling to keep your boys alive by selling cheap beauty products with glamorous names to women who could never be perfect enough. As the unsightly tears flowed from your eyes, Lizzie, my mother's eyes watered too.

Over a Wand of Beauty, the scientific mascara that still allowed you to cry, my mother taught me something about what it is to be feminine.

Mama taught me a lot of other lessons about femininity too. Some of them carry marks that no cosmetic can erase. My mother lifted Lizzie Mitchell's chin and said, "Dahlin girl, are you all right?" My mother slapped my cheek, where sometimes it still stings. My mother also laid her Beautiered soft palm on my girlish face and just cupped it there, for love.

I climb to the attic and discover my mother. She is a mixed gift pack.

15

$\mathcal{J}$t was Friday afternoon and Sidda was speed-walking on the lake path when she saw the gang of little girls on the beach at the bottom of the Quinault Lodge lawn. The volume on her Walkman was turned up loud, the metronomic beat of her "Advanced Classical Beat Walking" driving her relentlessly forward. She exercised like this for an hour and a half a day. In New York, she walked in Central Park; in Seattle, along Lake Washington. Only a blizzard could force her indoors to a treadmill.

She passed the scene twice before stopping. Positioning her baseball cap so they could not tell she was staring, Sidda observed the scene as she pretended to stretch. Five little girls, ranging in age from five to eight, were running and playing. Two of them wore shorts with no blouses, one of them wore a swimsuit with a little skirt on it. Another girl with pigtails wore a short little dress that was soaking wet, and the other, the oldest, wore a pair of jeans rolled up at the cuffs and a little bikini top.

Some distance away, a woman about Sidda's age sat on a blanket, under an umbrella, leaning back against an ice chest, painting with watercolors in a large sketch book. Every once in a while, she glanced up to check on the girls.

"Look!" one of the girls yelled out. "There it is!"

With that, the five of them ran headlong into the lake and began dragging out a large piece of driftwood. Working together, they pulled the log onto the beach and balanced it on a large rock. This took quite some time, and as Sidda watched, they gave each other directions and encouragement. When the piece of wood was finally on the rock, the girls stood back and admired their work.

"A seesaw!" the girl with the pigtails called out.

"A seesaw by the seashore!" one of the bare-chested girls said.

Then, bolting in the direction of the blanket, the other bare-chested girl ran to the woman and announced, "We built a seesaw!"

"That's great!" the woman said. "That is terrific!"

Then the little girl sped back to the others. Without warning, they abandoned their creation, and the five of them all ran screaming into the lake water.

Before long, Sidda heard a voice call out, "Ahoy there!"

She turned to see a group of two women and three men walking down the path that led to the beach from the lodge. Pointing to an older couple who stood on the lawn waving, one of the newly arrived women began to gather the girls.

They came down to the woman on the blanket, and immediately the scene shifted. In a moment, the blanket, ice chest, sandals, towels, and sunscreen were pulled together, and the group started in the direction of the stairs.

As they were leaving, Sidda heard one of the women say, "Oatmeal cookies for the wild girls."

She watched as the woman reached into a bag and handed each of the girls a cookie. As the group climbed the stairs, the older couple who were waiting for them hugged each girl in turn, and the whole group disappeared in the direction of one of the cottages.

Sidda stood and stared, as if waiting for the entourage to reappear. When they didn't, she went to sit near the seesaw the girls had created. Staring out into the lake, she hugged her arms around her chest.

She craved the warm Southern waters of her childhood. She was overcome with longing for the loud messiness of summers at Spring Creek. For the kids and the moms and the mismatched pajamas and

Noxema on her nose at night. She wanted to be part of an entourage like the one she had just witnessed. She wanted to be part of a family. How was it that she was forty years old and she had created no family of her own?

Her life suddenly seemed ridiculous: her career, her apartment, her creation of worlds on stage. It all seemed beside the point. How was it that she had spent the last twenty years bringing fictional characters to life rather than all-too-real children who screamed and flew across the sand and hugged you when you handed them oatmeal cookies? How was it she was here at the edge of the continent alone, while these other women had already made families, surrounded by friends who'd done the same? What was wrong with her?

She felt ashamed of her insularity. She longed for rambunctiousness, for the communal craziness in which she'd been raised. She felt sick at the thought of her constant questioning, her constant self-examination.

Perhaps I should just finish directing May's new play, leave New York, move to Seattle, and start a family.

The wildness of that thought so rocked her that Sidda removed her Walkman, stripped out of her shorts and T-shirt, down to her swimsuit. She walked out on the dock that stretched into the lake, and dove straight into the freezing Northwest water. The first contact numbed her skin. As she burst back to the surface, she felt painfully alive, charged with energy. She could see the deep blue of the sky, and the endless green of the trees that rimmed the lake. Lying on her back in the water, she began to kick hard, stretching her arms out wide. No matter how hard she kicked, she could still hear the laughter of those little girls.

Letting herself sink beneath the surface, Sidda closed her eyes and swam down in the direction of the bottom. The icy fluid world felt cleansing. Would that these clean waters could wash away all confusion, all doubt, all sins.

She stayed down as long as she could, then broke the surface again, gulping air. Then she began to swim the crawl. Rolling her head from side to side to breathe, barely lifting her face out of the water, hands tilted at just the right angle to break the water. She swam like her mother had taught her.

I have already come to terms with all this, she thought. I never wanted kids, not as a girl, not as a young woman in my twenties, not now—not really. It's fine with Connor, he made that clear early on. Why do I resent the little families I just witnessed? Why do I fantasize kidnapping those wild little girls, at least for a weekend?

℘

Friday afternoons always got to Sidda. If anything made her want a family, it was Friday afternoons. She was always shocked by this longing, but it blindsided her time and again. Friday afternoons. That school-is-out-a-whole-sweet-weekend-in-front-of-you feeling. Even in Manhattan, when she saw moms walking their kids home on the Upper West Side from the Montessori school, it hit her.

She still longed for those countless Friday afternoons at Pecan Grove. Pecan Grove was a sort of destination house for kids. Nine hundred acres, and all the room in the world to scream and run and ride Shetland ponies and crayfish in the bayou and play with the puppies in the huge barn and climb on the old live oak tree. A backyard filled with rope swings hung in the trees, where you could swing out over the bayou. An old golf cart her daddy had given the kids to drive all over the plantation when they weren't in the mood to ride horses. A big house filled with toys and musical instruments and tons of food from Vivi's end-of-the-week trip to the A & P.

And Vivi herself, who on happy weekends waited for them with open arms in the backyard, excited at the prospect of kids and making fudge and *Saturday Night at the Movies* and card games where she, and maybe one or two of the Ya-Yas, would gamble with the boys, happy to take their nickels.

It was nothing for five or six little friends to end up at Pecan Grove for the weekend. It was open house, and Sidda's little girlfriends loved it. Plenty of fried shrimp for Friday-night supper, as many cold Cokes as you could grab, and, if it was wintertime, hours in front of the fire in the den, playing the Ouija board with Vivi, as she sipped her bourbon. Kids would show up at Pecan Grove without even an overnight bag, because they knew Vivi Dahlin could supply what they needed.

"I've got *84,000* extra p.j.s and 64,000 guest toothbrushes. Just don't bring any head lice," Vivi would say.

How could Sidda Walker *not* think about family on Friday afternoons?

As she swam, Sidda calculated ages and stages if she started a family that very day. When my kids start having spend-the-night company, I'll be forty-seven. Okay. When they start dating, I'll be fifty-five. Charming. When they start college, I'll be pushing sixty. And when they have their own kids, I'll be out of my mind.

She switched to the breast stroke and concentrated on her kick.

She told herself: I am only experiencing the last gasps of a completely normal and inescapable biological urge. I have had these spasms before, and they always pass. My life is not one colossal mistake. Angels of the Evening Sky, something wants to be born, I'm just not sure what.

When she returned to the cabin, Sidda ate standing up, listening to Bonnie Raitt on the CD. She stared at a photo she'd come across when Wade and May were there: the one of Vivi in the backyard, surrounded by the four kids. Was this taken on a Friday? No. If it were a Friday, there would've been twice as many kids, spend-the-night company for all four Walker kids. It must have been a school day.

Late September, 1962. Her mother is sitting on the pink-checked picnic blanket. There in the big yard that slopes down to the bayou. Sidda is in fourth grade, Little Shep in third, Lulu in second, and Baylor in first. If Vivi is on the picnic blanket, Sidda knows she's in a good mood. If Vivi is in her room with the door shut, then you have to leave her alone or else get lucky and find just the right thing to break the spell. You never know exactly what will work. It is magic what makes or breaks Vivi's moods.

"What on earth did yall do at Divine Compassion today?!" Vivi asks, all eager like the kids might have big news. "Drop those book sacks and gather round."

The four Walker kids kneel and flop beside her on the blanket.

"Our Lady of Malnutrition!" Vivi says. "Yall look absolutely *famished.*"

"Famished" is one of Vivi's words that Sidda loves to roll around in her mouth like candy.

"Are yall really hungry as you look?" Vivi says. "What did they feed yall for lunch? It wasn't those big, fat, ugly green peas, was it? Oh, I bet it was awful, whatever it was. I don't know what those nuns do with the money we pay them."

"Here, Little Shep," Vivi says, starting to hand out sandwiches. "You're my peanut-butter man. Sidd-o: heavy on the strawberry jelly. Lulu, you like lots of everything, so this one's for you, but you can only have *one*, do you hear me? Hand me those Dixie cups, will you, Dahlin? Bay, sweetie, yours is the one cut in fourths. Don't worry, I've cut the crust off all of them, you slave drivers you. Lulu, do not grab. There's enough for everybody."

Vivi pours lemonade out of the cooler. The children hold their sandwiches on little gold cocktail napkins with "Happy 10th Anniversary, Vivi and Shep!" printed on them. Vivi freshens her drink from a separate cooler, the thermos that holds her "cough medicine."

Sidda leans back on the blanket and eats her sandwich. She's been waiting for this moment all day. The taste of the jelly and the soft fresh white bread make her happy. She watches as Vivi leans back against a stack of pillows. She watches Vivi smoke and stare up at the sky. Smoking and looking up at the sky are some of her mother's favorite things. Along with matinees, good hamburgers, Spring Creek, lying in the bed reading a good book, and getting dressed up and having fun.

Sidda loves her mother's hands. She loves her fingernails. Pretty rounded nails that Vivi buffs while she talks on the telephone.

After Sidda finishes her sandwich, she turns over on her stomach. Vivi reaches over and tickles Sidda's back under her uniform blouse.

Vivi has the perfect fingernails for tickling Sidda's back. Nobody can tickle her back like her mother. You have to have nails just like Vivi's to make Sidda feel this good.

Sidda put the photo down and closed the album. She walked into the bedroom and took off her clothes. Lying down on the bed, she looked at her stomach. Even after her sandwich, her belly was still flat. She could see where her pubic bones stuck up on either side. God knows, she worked to keep her belly that flat. Reaching down, she ran her hand slowly from one side of her stomach to the other. For the first time in her adult life, the sight of her concave belly did not please her. Instead, it made her feel alone, unused, as though she were the kind of woman who enjoyed packing for a trip more than the trip itself.

She thought of the backyard photo again. It had been taken around the time that her mother had sent Baylor to school with one of her garter belts for first-grade Show and Tell. As a result, the school had called and demanded that Vivi come in to meet with Baylor's teacher. Evidently Vivi had gotten in a fight with the nun and ended up sideswiping the Infant Jesus of Prague statue that stood not far from the church parking lot.

Sidda remembered ending up at Caro's that night. Vivi had been upset, but Caro kept the bourbon flowing and fed them big bowls of chili. In front of the fire, as Vivi told the story, she switched from tears to laughter under Caro's accepting gaze. The night ended with the women teaching the kids how to cha-cha with a how-to record on the stereo. Sidda remembered dancing, breathless, in Caro's modern living room with the kidney-shaped coffee table and fireplace shaped like a black funnel.

"Listen up, kids," Vivi said. "I sideswiped the Infant Jesus of Prague today. *And no one must ever know but us. It's a secret.*"

One-two-three, cha-cha-cha. That's not the only secret we kept, Sidda thought. They could bribe us and torture us, and we would not betray your secrets, Mama. There are some things you never show and tell.

16

The two clippings from *The Thornton Town Monitor* were sta-
pled together, with numerous arrows and exclamation points
marked in the margins. Sidda shook her head in amazement. She
would have given anything if Wade and May were still at the cabin
with her. It would have been great to share with them the news of her
mother's entry into a life of crime.

The first clipping read:

THURSDAY, AUGUST 3, 1942.
DAUGHTER OF PROMINENT CITIZENS ARRESTED FOR
DISORDERLY CONDUCT.

Viviane Joan Abbott, age 15, daughter of Mr. and Mrs.
Taylor C. Abbott; Caroline Eliza Bennett, 16, daughter
of Mr. and Mrs. Robert L. "Bob" Bennett; Aimee
Malissa Whitman, 15, daughter of Mr. and Mrs. Newton
S. Whitman III; and Denise Rose Kelleher, 15, daugh-
ter of Mr. and Mrs. Francis P. Kelleher, were arrested

last night and taken to city jail for disorderly public conduct. Charged with violating Municipal Statute 106: the willful soiling of public property and indecent exposure, the girls gave no explanation for their actions.

Sidda had always heard rumors of the Ya-Yas' being arrested while they were in high school, but she'd never known the details. Oh, how she'd love to transport herself back a half century and just be a fly on the wall.

The second clipping read:

TUESDAY, AUGUST 9, 1942
SHOOTING THE BREEZE
ALICE ANNE SIBLEY'S SOCIAL COLUMN

A little bird has it that Mrs. Newton L. Whitman III (the former Genevieve Aimee St. Clair, daughter of Mr. and Mrs. Etienne St. Clair of Marksville) hosted an impromptu patio party for her daughter "Teensy" this past Saturday afternoon, from 4–7 in the evening at the Whitman home on Willow Street. Present were Teensy's close friends, Vivi Abbott, Caro Bennett, and Necie Kelleher, known locally as "The Ya-Yas." The girls have made news of late with a particularly high-spirited escapade, even by Ya-Ya standards.

Among those in attendance at the evening fête were Mary Gray Benjamin, Daisy Farrar, and Sally Soniat. Among the high school boys attending were Dicky Wheeler, John Pritchard, and Wyatt Bell, along with Lane Parker, of St. Petersburg, Florida. Mr. Parker is in town visiting his aunt and uncle, Mr. and Mrs. Charles Simcoe.

Served were cold fresh shrimp, cold corn on the cob, tomatoes with dilled onions, and French bread. Jack Whitman, Thornton High's prize basketball player, entertained by playing tunes on the violin in the French Louisiana tradition. Mrs. Whitman went on to explain that she was throwing the spur-of-the-moment party to celebrate the installation of a new fountain that she has acquired. The fetching fountain, composed of two lovely mermaids who spurt water, is to be ensconced on her patio next to her prize-winning American Beauty roses.

Mr. Whitman was not in attendance, having left on Thursday for his camp at Dolphin Island, Alabama. Wonder why he'd ever want to miss such a soirée.

It was too rich. Give me more, give me more, give more more, Sidda thought. It was just killing her not to have the whole story. It made her itch. It made her salivate. And it made her wish, not for the first time, that she was part of a girl gang that got its name in the paper.

∝

The night of August 3, 1942, not five hours after Jack Whitman announced he was joining the Army Air Corps, an embarrassed policeman locked Vivi Abbott and the Ya-Yas into a cell in the Thornton jail.

A month or so earlier, American torpedo bombers had swept down over Midway, only to be killed by flak, their young bodies sacrificed as surely as any kamikaze. Lights were dimmed in cities and towns on both coasts, and many inland cities as well. The Pacific seemed far away from Central Louisiana, and nobody knew how to pronounce the funny-sounding names of the islands. But Nazi submarines had landed spies on the Florida shore, and although nobody in Washington would admit it, folks in Thornton heard endless stories about the U-boats cruising the Gulf of Mexico.

Vivi dreamed of Roosevelt and Rommel and Robert Taylor. On the tennis court she lobbed bombs across the net to kill Hitler. When she lay in bed at night, after long walks with Jack, her panties moist with arousal, she prayed to the Queen of Peace for all the scared boys in faraway foxholes and on trains crisscrossing the country. She ate little butter, less beef, no bacon, and when she stepped out, she painted "bottled stockings" on her legs. She gave blood every Friday; Saturdays, she collected newspapers; and on Wednesdays, scrap metal.

Daily, she listened to the news. While the war reports were bleak, the fashion magazines reported that the new uniforms of the Women's Army Corps would add to the prestige of the foundation industry because girdles and brassieres were included in the ensemble. The Catholic *Commonweal* opposed the recruiting of women. One article Buggy made Vivi read claimed that "removing ladies from the heart and home would turn them into pagan female goddesses of lustful sterility."

Vivi believed in war bonds and victory gardens. She believed that Nazis and Japs were evil. She believed in democracy at all costs. But what she wanted was tenderness and passion, so she did not believe Jack Whitman should go to war.

The August night was hot and humid. It was almost eight o'clock in the evening, and the temperature had not begun to drop. The moon was almost full, and everywhere there was the smell of grass and river water and high summer in the Deep South. In the South Pacific, Marines were preparing to land on Guadalcanal; in Europe, bombers were getting ready for the first all-American air raid.

In Thornton, Louisiana, Vivi and Jack were sitting in Jack's 1940 blue-green Buick at LeMoyne's Hamburger Drive-In. Vivi was leaning against the inside of the passenger door with her feet in Jack's lap, holding a Dr Pepper bottle in her shaking hand.

After he announced he had enlisted, the first thing she said was, "Why are you leaving me?"

"It's my responsibility," he said. "Besides, I want to fly."

"You're lying," she said. "I've never even heard you talk about flying."

Then she sat up straight and hit him hard with her fist. She sucked in her breath and tried to keep from crying. "You don't want to be a pilot. You just want to impress your father."

At first Jack did not speak. When he did, he could not look at her. "*Mais oui.*"

Vivi and Jack had known each other since she was four and he was seven. She had spent at least two nights a week at his family's home for the past eight years. There was not a lot he could hide from her about his family, even if he'd wanted to. On the other hand, he also knew her well. Knew the unseen marks her mother's blaming, jealous silence left on her, especially after her sister, Jezie, was born. And he knew the not-so-hidden marks her father's belt left on her skin.

He looked at her, hoping he could make her understand. "Got to do one thing right for the old fellow, you know?"

Vivi did know, but she didn't like it, had never liked it. She had always disliked Jack's father. He was arrogant; he made fun of Genevieve's accent—he forbade "bayou French" to even be spoken in his home. He refused to let Jack be called by his French name, let alone play the Acadian fiddle in his presence. She had not forgotten Mr. Whitman's condescension (although she did not know to call it that at the time) when, after their return from Atlanta, he forced the Ya-Yas to spend tortured Saturday afternoons in training with Miss Alma Ansell, whose job it was to mold them into alluring, well-behaved young women.

"There's one thing right you could do, Jack." She spoke in a near whisper. "Stay home and *love me.*"

The back of Jack's neck was magnificent to her. She had lived her life flirting with hundreds of boys, and prided herself on having as many dates as she had the stamina for. But the thought of losing Jack made her ache.

"I'm sorry, *Bébé*," he said. "It's already done."

Vivi closed her eyes, and when she opened them, she could not regain her equilibrium. The dashboard in front of her seemed to undulate slightly; she could not make the objects around her stop moving. It was as if the sliver of fine wire on which her inner balance rested had just been imperceptibly bent. The sensation was vaguely familiar. She closed her eyes again and shook her head in tight, quick, hard, little shakes.

"Vivi," Jack said, reaching for her foot, pulling it slowly back into his lap. "You okay?"

She glanced at him briefly with a look of pure hatred, then turned away.

He began to rub her foot with his hand, a slow, stroking motion. Although she turned away, she could see his hands in her mind. The long, tapered fingers, the short, square nails. Large, graceful hands that knew how to handle a basketball, a fiddle, and her awakening body with gentleness and easy confidence.

"Will you come back?" she asked.

"Are you kidding?! You think I could stay away from you? Of course, I'll come back."

"Do you swear to me you will come back?"

He reached over to touch her cheek, but she did not respond. "I promise, Vivi."

She sat soundless for a moment, perfectly still, staring out. When she turned back to him, she was smiling, her mouth open wide.

"I think I could learn to love a man in uniform," she said and winked, working hard to sound flirtatious. But there was something in her gaze that was slightly off, as though she had seen something in the brief time she had been turned away from him and could not shake it.

Jack bent down and kissed her foot. He kissed her painted toenails. His black hair fell slightly over his eyes as he leaned over her feet, and when he raised his head, his eyes were wet. He turned his body, so his legs stretched out on the seat, then pulled her into his lap. They sat like that without talking for a while. The strains of Ginny Simms singing "Deep Purple" drifted over from someone's car radio. A flat-bed cotton truck with a red cab passed by on the street. The aroma of hamburgers and barbecue sauce wafted through the thick, humid air.

"When you come back, it'll all be fabulous again, right?" she asked.

"*Ma Petite Chou,* Uncle Sam's the boss for a little while, but when I come home, *you* write the ticket."

"I might be a newspaperwoman by then, Jack."

"We could live in New York, how bout that?"

"I like that," she said. "Or maybe Paris, after the war is over. Or I might be a tennis star, live in Rio de Janeiro."

"There'll be pictures of you in all the papers."

"Or I might be in college studying I don't know what."

"You could go to Newcomb, and I'll go to Tulane. Rent an apartment in the French Quarter. We'll head to the bayou on the weekends, how's that sound?"

"I wish I knew how long this war will last."

"When this war is over," Jack said, stroking her face, "well, would you have me, Vivi?"

This question did not surprise her, and she answered almost casually, sounding utterly sure of herself.

"You are the only man in the world I would ever want to be married to," she said. "If I can't marry you, then I'm going to marry the Ya-Yas."

Jack laughed. He looked into her eyes.

"You could do anything, Vivi Abbott," Jack said. "You could be anything. Anything you want."

"Will we have kids?" she asked. "Loud, good-looking ones?"

"You want them, you got them. You don't, we won't. Like *Maman* says, 'Nowhere in the Bible does it say every Catholic woman has to have a *ripopée*."

"What's '*ripopée*' mean?"

"Gang of obnoxious children," Jack explained.

Vivi laughed.

"I can have as many as I want, right?" Vivi said. "Or none at all."

"Roger wilco," Jack said.

"Maybe a dozen."

"Okay, cheaper by the dozen."

"We'll put them all in pirogues and row up and down the bayous, teach them the fiddle and squeeze box—"

"*Maman* will spoil them rotten. We could name one for her."

"Oh, hell, let's name *two* for her! Teensy and I will be real sisters. We'll have a three-story house and raise collies, okay? Tennis court, can we have a tennis court?"

Jack stopped Vivi with a kiss.

My father, Jack thought. My father will see what kind of man I am, and he will be very, very proud.

"Because," Teensy said, as she poured rum into a tumbler filled with Coca-Cola and handed it to Vivi, "Jack made me *swear* not to say a word until *he* told you himself."

The Ya-Yas, having returned from their respective dates later that night, sat in their panties, smoking cigarettes and talking, on the upstairs sleeping porch of the Whitman home.

"There's not a Goddamn breeze in the state of Louisiana," Caro said, slumped down into the cushions of a rattan chair, her feet propped on the screen, smoking a cigarette.

"He only told *Maman* and Father and me this morning," Teensy continued. "Father came home from the bank this afternoon with a bottle of French champagne to celebrate. Can you imagine—*French champagne*?"

"Leave it to your father to lay his hands on something like that in the middle of the war," Caro said.

"I've never seen Father make over Jack like this before. Not when he was elected class president or captain of the basketball team. Papa said he's going to organize a black-tie scrap-metal drive in honor of Jack's signing up, and we're all supposed to put on the dog."

"What did Genevieve say?" Vivi asked. She sat next to Necie on the glider, holding her drink against her left temple.

"*Maman* asked if it was too late to change his mind!" Teensy said. "Father called her unpatriotic. 'My God, woman,'" Papa said. "'This is France, this is the free world we're talking about!'" You know how he gets. Made a little speech and gave a toast to Jack. *Maman* wouldn't even touch the champagne—and yall know how she adores it. She went upstairs, and after a few minutes, Jack went up to see about her."

Fanning herself with one of Genevieve's fans made of vetiver root, Teensy lay across one of the beds. "It's really rather momentous, yall," she said. "The first one of our crowd to join up."

The other three didn't respond.

"Well, isn't it?" Teensy repeated. "Isn't it marvelous?"

"Oh, it's marvelous; it's thrilling; it's Jimmy Stewart," Vivi said. "Only it means Jack has to go far away for a long time. It means he will sit suspended in the air miles above the earth in a small metal cigar while Germans try to kill him."

"Goodness," Necie said, "I never thought of it like that."

"Of course, you didn't, Pal," Caro said. "Miss Apple Blossom Time."

"Jack went out to Spring Creek after he dropped me off," Vivi said.

"Father gave him a whole book of gas stamps," Teensy said.

"Our Mother of Pearl," Caro said. "Is your father the *president* of the black market? The guy can get his hands on anything."

"I don't know," Teensy said. "I never ask."

"Bunch of the guys are going with him," Vivi continued, taking a drag off her Lucky. "A stag party to celebrate, I guess. They're spending the night out at the creek."

"Well, they should have taken us with them," Teensy said. "It's always cooler at Spring Creek. I'm about to *die* from all this humidity. I wish somebody would just *wring me out!*"

"He should have at least taken Vivi," Caro said, standing, walking the length of the porch, her bare feet slapping the boards. Turning and walking back, she picked up a cushion and began to fan Vivi with it. "When's he leave?" she asked. "Where's he go? What's the skinny?"

"I do think the Air Corps has the cutest uniforms, don't yall?" Necie asked.

"My brother doesn't need a uniform to be handsome," Teensy said.

"More hooch, please," Vivi said, holding out her glass.

Teensy splashed more of Mr. Whitman's black-market rum into

Vivi's glass, and a full moon shimmered over Central Louisiana. This was no rinky-dink moon. This was a moon you had to curtsy to. A big, heavy, mysterious, beautiful, bossy moon. The kind you want to serve things to on a silver platter. The noise of the crickets and cicadas and the clinking of ice against the girls' glasses mingled with their voices and sighs. From their spot on the porch, they could see a paradise of stars holding their own with the moon.

Taking turns, they stood in front of the fan with wet washcloths held in front of their bodies. They tried lying in bed, but even the sheets felt soggy. When nothing else worked, Teensy started moaning.

"Come on, yall," Teensy said, "moan with me. You'll feel better, I guarantee, *mes chères!*"

And so they moaned until a dog started howling somewhere, which made them laugh, because it sounded like he was trying to communicate with their pack.

"Would Tallulah stay here and boil to death?!" Teensy asked.

"Look, Pal," Caro said, "Eleanor Roosevelt herself wouldn't *languish* here like this, and she's one tough trooper."

Wearing nothing but their fathers' old seersucker pajama tops over their panties, the four girls pushed Genevieve's convertible to the end of the long drive before Vivi climbed behind the wheel and started it. There was only a dollop of gas in the tank so they couldn't get far.

"I just know we shouldn't be doing this," Necie said as they journeyed into the night. "We should have at *least* put on pajama bottoms."

"Necie, this is not a mortal sin, you know," said Teensy.

"I do not recall it being listed in the Baltimore Catechism," Vivi said.

"Moses didn't utter one word about pajama bottoms when he came down from the mountain," said Caro.

"Well," Necie said, "I guess these tops do cover more of our bodies than our swimsuits do."

As Vivi drove, it seemed that not only the Ya-Yas' bodies but the earth and sky were sweating. The very air they breathed was almost a juice. Moonlight spilled down into the convertible, onto the four friends' shoulders and knees and on the tops of their heads, so that their hair seemed to have little sparks shooting off it. "Bewitched, Bothered, and Bewildered" played on the radio. Vivi had no idea at all where she was headed, but she knew that whatever direction she went, her friends would go with her.

She stopped the car at City Park, near a clump of trees, not far from where the water holding tank for the city of Thornton sat atop a raised tower. Turning off the ignition, Vivi dimmed the lights and turned to the others. "Climb to the heavens, anybody?"

"Top-notch notion," Caro said, jumping out of the convertible, without bothering to open the car door.

"Oooh, yes!" Teensy said.

"They don't like you to go up there," Necie said.

"That's one of the reasons we want to do it, Countess," Caro said.

"Only the men from the Parks Department are supposed to be up there, yall," Necie said. "Really."

"Necie, Baby Doll," said Vivi, getting out of the car, "can it, *s'il vous plaît.*"

"Yall," Necie continued. "We *can't* climb up there. It is against the *law.*"

"We know," Teensy smiled. "It's *forbidden.*"

Necie stared at the other three for a moment before she finally opened the car door and joined them.

"I don't even want to think about what could happen to us," she said.

"Then don't, Sweetie Pie," Caro said, putting her arm around Necie.

"I'm just going to think me some pretty pink and blue thoughts," Necie said.

They made their way to the back of the platform, where a crude ladder stopped six feet or so above the ground. They took turns giving each other boosts, with Caro, the tallest, going last. As Vivi scrambled up, her heart beat rapidly and sweat ran down the back of her neck. If the sultry heat, the rum, and the late hour were not enough to put her in a trance, the magnitude of the moonlight was.

At the top of the ladder, Vivi stepped onto a narrow catwalk that encircled the tank. It was an old wooden water-holding tank, once used by the railroads, but now pushed into service by the city, since nearby England Air Force Base and Camp Livingston had swelled its population. From her spot twenty or so feet above the ground, she looked down on the town of Thornton.

She thought of her mother and father, and Pete, and the baby Jezie, and the wobbly life they lived there. Of the way Buggy stiffened when her husband stepped near; of the way she said, "Here's your supper, Mr. Abbott," her lips thin and tight. She thought of the way her father laughed at her mother's housedresses, dirty fingernails from gardening, and sanctuary candles. She thought about the faint smell of Scotch, not quite disguised with Dr. Tichenor's Antiseptic Tincture, on her father's breath; she thought of the clinking sound of his belt buckle when it dangled from the strap.

Her mother's discontent lay coiled inside her own body. Ever since Vivi's little sister Jezie was born, Buggy had slept in the nursery, on a daybed against the wall. Although Vivi could not have put it into words, she felt her own exhaustion at constantly attempting to hold back part of her vitality so she would not cause her mother more sadness. At fifteen, Vivi Abbott was more masterful than most at rationing parts of herself without appearing anything but exuberant.

She did not know that the holding back did no good. Nor did she have any understanding of the inner rationing her mother had learned herself at a tender age. There was a lot Vivi did not know about her mother.

She did not know about the old nightmare that haunted Buggy. The dream that came from something that had happened when her mother was twelve years old. At that age, Buggy had kept a journal, filled with her secret feelings and little rhyming sentimental poems. She wrote about anger toward her sister, Virginia, and her mother, Delia. She wrote romantic girlish poems about fairies, love, the Virgin Mary, and her love for horses (which Buggy was too afraid to ride).

In Buggy's nightmare, it happened just the way it had happened in 1912. Delia found her journal, became infuriated by what Buggy had written in secret. Forced Buggy to follow her and Virginia to the backyard. There Delia ripped the pages from the journal and one by one handed them to Virginia, who fed them into a fire.

"Buggy," Delia had told her, "you are not a writer. There is nothing in your pitiful little life to write about. If anyone is a writer, it is Virginia."

As Buggy watched her secrets go up in smoke, she vowed to get back at her sister. And she did. When she was nineteen, she managed, through painstaking calculation, to steal Taylor Abbott from Virginia and get him to marry her. He told her she was the sweetest little thing in Garnet Parish and that he wanted her to be his little girl forever.

Buggy's victory was a dubious one, however. She was left with a husband who ran around on her for the duration of their marriage.

From the top of the water tower, Vivi felt a relief spread through her. What a sweet small-town thrill this was, like the delight of watching a parade from the top of a tall building. She could see the tangled Spanish moss hanging off the oaks in City Park. She could make out the camellia bushes and azaleas, the salvias; she could smell the night-blooming jasmine. Closing her eyes, she imagined she could look down into her house, into her bedroom and everything in it. The four-poster bed with the silk canopy Delia had bought for her in New Orleans; the new vanity her father bought for her fifteenth birthday, on top of which sat a photo of Jack clad in his basketball uniform, fiddle in hand; the tall armoire crammed with loafers and sweater sets; the ceiling fan; the tennis racket propped against the night stand; her tennis trophies; countless photos of the Ya-Yas, and one of Jimmy Stewart.

Looking away from her parents' house, Vivi imagined she could see the block she lived on, and then her whole neighborhood. She conjured up all the people she knew and the few she didn't. She saw them tossing and turning in their beds, too hot to sleep. She saw lights burning on front porches; slivers of light where icebox doors were open, someone standing there, reaching for a bottle of milk, just an excuse to feel the cool air of the icebox. She saw night lights in the rooms of the babies who dreamed soft seersucker dreams, drugged happy with the heat, their pink baby bodies curled against worn cotton, not fearing Hitler yet, their strong, tiny hearts beating in unison with the trees and the creeks and the bayous.

Vivi saw the flicker of candles burning at Divine Compassion for the souls of the dead; she spotted tiny fiery red tips of cigarettes dangling from the lips of sleep-starved souls seeking the faintest of breezes in backyards; she caught the soft glow from radio dials left on all night, in case a warning was broadcast, in case the Nazis or Japs invaded on this feverish night, executing the horrors that lived in the town's heart even as the bank opened for business, as the milk was delivered, as the wafer changed to body and blood.

Winging higher still, Vivi left her town, went up so high she could no longer see the trees or the boulevard or the faces in ecstasy or worry. She flew above all the forgotten things hanging in the air between people. She lifted above her town until she could see Bunkie and Natchitoches and how the Cane River was more like a lake, and how the Garnet River fed into the Mississippi; she soared over Spring Creek, with its cool shade trees and pine-needle paths leading to the cabin where Jack lay sleeping that night. She flew over the German irises with their pale gray-green spikes, above the brown waters of the bayous with their silent cypress trees; over the swamps; over the cotton; over the shotgun houses, where the tired black men and women who stooped to pick the cotton slept; over the rice and sugar cane; over the swamp myrtles; over the millions of tiny estuaries; over the crayfish in their beds of mud.

Then she left it all, and ascended even higher to banks of clouds, perfect clouds cool with mist and closer to heaven. She could see the whole little Earth, blue and white, spinning around in terrifying magnificent space. No people, only hearts, hearts beating, countless hearts; and the sound of breathing.

This is how it was for Vivi Abbott, age fifteen, labile, in every sense of the word. Such were the places she could travel when a tiny gate opened inside her and her mind went loose-jointed. Such holy and terrible suppleness is not always safe, and never without trade-offs.

For a moment Vivi stopped feeling solid. And then she began a fast free-fall, which carried a shock of impermanence, a panicky jolt of her own *temporariness.* She clawed to hold on to the moist clouds, to the grand view. She did not want to return to earth.

Back on the water-tower platform in City Park, in the heart of the state of Louisiana, Vivi thought: With Jack Whitman, my life will be different. *You can be anything you want, Vivi,* he said. Anything at all.

And then Vivi thought: *If Jack disappears into the sky, I will shrivel up and die.*

Caro was the one who figured out how to pry the lid of the water tower open. It was tricky and required some work, but the Ya-Yas were wily and hot.

Even Necie, the careful Ya-Ya, was captured by the vision of the moonlight in the water. They flung off their pajama tops. Seersucker fluttered through the still air to the parched ground below. The Ya-Yas stepped out of their panties and forgot about collecting scrap metal. They didn't talk much, and they thought even less. They slid into the cool, clear liquid caress of the city water supply.

A bold kind of holiness hung in the air as the Ya-Yas leaned their heads back in the water, their hair floating out around their shoulders. They stared up into the bright sky, where there wasn't any war. They counted stars, thought they found Pegasus, and were sure they spotted Venus. They touched their toes to one another's and kicked their legs to the heavens like Esther Williams.

Vivi completely gave herself over to the water. A black stone that lived inside her chest was temporarily lifted out, and she breathed deeply, and then released her breath like she was blowing out a candle. Her stomach softened, her shoulders released, her dizziness went away. Then she started to cry.

After a few moments, and with no explanation, Teensy's tears joined Vivi's. Then Necie's, and, a few of Caro's. Their tears rolled down their faces and into their community's water. They cried because Jack's enlistment had cracked open their tight universe to the suffering world. They cried because in their highly resonant Ya-Ya bones, they knew that they would never be the same.

Through her tears, Vivi gazed at the moon. A silent prayer for Jack issued from her body.

> *Moonlight in the summer sky, look down on my love from*
> *up on high. Shine on him now while he is safe and shine*
> *on him when he flies through enemy skies. Let his journeys*
> *into the sky bring him closer to you, so that while he is*
> *away from me, he will be safe. Tell him I love him, tell*
> *him I am longing for him, tell him I will always wait for*
> *him. Your milky brilliance can protect him from all ene-*
> *mies. He is a tender boy, do not let him suffer. Moonlight*
> *over the only town I know, bring my love back home so we*
> *can live and be happy.*

Turning her head to look at each of her friends, Vivi saw Teensy and Caro and Necie as she had never seen them before. They seemed to glow from within, like there were lanterns inside their bodies. They looked very old to her, and very young all at once. They looked both invincible and utterly, utterly fragile. Their bodies were the density and weight that anchored her, that made her more real. She looked at them and loved them and was flooded with gratitude.

Officer Roscoe Jenkins didn't know what to think when he saw the four pajama tops lying on the ground. He'd been making his regular rounds when he spotted the convertible at the side of the lane, and had wondered if someone had run out of gas. The night was so bright he hardly needed his flashlight, but when he shone it on the pajama tops he saw monograms and grew more perplexed. When he spied the panties, he became alarmed. Holding the shirts in his hand, he looked around, but saw nothing out of the ordinary. Then he heard the faint sound of splashing water. He swung his flashlight up in the direction of the water tower, and that's when he thought he saw a naked woman.

Once the Ya-Yas agreed to come down from the tower, Officer Roscoe Jenkins was every inch a gentleman. Averting his eyes, he handed each one of them a pajama top before climbing up to the tower himself to make sure they had indeed closed the lid back tightly over the water. He knew these young ladies. He'd known the Whitman girl ever since she managed to get a pecan stuck up her nose when she wasn't but four or five. Blowing out the side of his lips and shaking his head, he was more embarrassed than angry. The fact that he let the gang follow him to the station in the convertible rather than shuffling them into his squad car was not a sign of trust. Actually, he was a little nervous about sharing a car with the four of them.

In Genevieve's convertible, there was some controversy about whether they should actually follow him, or gun it and head for the hills (of course, there were no hills).

Teensy finally prevailed. "Come on," she said, "I've never been in a lockup before!"

When their fathers arrived at the station, rumpled and hot, they conferred among themselves.

"Too bad we can't harness their energy. It'd be an asset to the Allies," Caro's father said.

"It's their utter lack of regard for appearances that astounds me," Teensy's father said. "My son has done something praiseworthy, and now my daughter turns into a common criminal. Those four have been a quartet of embarrassments ever since they humiliated my family in Atlanta."

"I wonder how the water department might go about purifying that holding tank," Necie's father said.

"Cool em off in a cell for a night," Mr. Abbott said. "Maybe that'll clip their wings."

"*Book them?*" Roscoe said, not believing.

"Book them," the fathers agreed. Then they turned and left.

"*Book them!*" Teensy said, her hands dramatically clenching the bars of the cell. "Aren't those *marvelous* words!"

"The *pokey!*" Caro said.

"Jailed for our convictions," Vivi said.

"Oh, my," Necie said.

The cell the girls were escorted to was possibly one of the coolest spots to sleep in all of Thornton. At basement level, with windows on both sides and a side door propped open (not to mention the fan that Officer Roscoe Jenkins moved from his desk to a card table just outside the cell), the space was downright pleasant. Their hair was still wet, their bodies still cool from the water, and Roscoe brought them sodas from the station's icebox, for which they thanked him politely.

"Roscoe," Vivi told him, "when I write my memoirs, you will be *much* more than a marginal character."

The Ya-Yas drank their sodas and lay on the bunks.

"My *Père*," Teensy said, "hasn't a shred, not even a *shred,* of human understanding. Jack is lucky to get away from him."

"We are *not* common criminals," Caro said.

"There is nothing common about us," Necie said.

Vivi stared up at the low ceiling of the cell. Sometimes higher laws than Thornton's must be obeyed, she thought. Too many people hide in their rooms when the light of the moon is strongest, when she's bouncing light back to us whether we want it or not.

As the Ya-Yas slept that night in the Thornton City Jail, the moon loved them. Not because they were beautiful, or because they were perfect, or because they were perky, but because they were her darling daughters.

17

*I*f Sidda Walker had been able to witness Vivi and the Ya-Yas in the light of that summer moon in 1942, their young bodies touching, their nipples luminous in the light, she would have known she came from goddess stock. She would have known that a primal, sweet strength flowed in her mother like an underground stream, and that the same stream flowed in her. Whatever scars Vivi had inflicted with her unhinged swings between creation and devouring, she had also passed on a mighty capacity for rapture.

Anxiety high-jacked Sidda as she walked down the steps to Lake Quinault. Even as the moon strutted, prissed, and swelled into a gorgeous globe, Sidda was aware only of her own confusion and rattled determination to get to the bottom of things. But a summer moon will put up with inattention for just so long. Just as Sidda was about to place her foot down onto the step in front of her, moonlight tapped her on the shoulder and forced her gaze skyward. She took a long, deep breath, and when she exhaled, she felt a spaciousness that had not been there before.

Beholding the moon in its chalky wonder, Sidda thought, Our

Lady of Pearl! That moon is why the word "comely" was invented.

Sitting down on the wooden steps, she reached her hand down to Hueylene's long, curly ears and began to rub gently. Sidda rubbed and the dog sighed, producing funny little off-key sounds, like the cock-eyed music a child might blow on a harmonica. Sidda could feel her heart beating and could hear crickets around the lake's edge.

Crickets, she thought. They've serenaded me since the day I was born. Breathe in, breathe out. Right now I am sitting in the light of the moon. Right now my dog is beside me and we are taking a moon bath.

Softly, unexpectedly, she began to sing. Something she had not done by herself in a long time. First off, she launched into "Blue Moon," singing the alto part that her Aunt Jezie had taught her many years ago. When she finished that, she moved on to "Shine on, Harvest Moon," accompanying her singing with light foot tapping when she came to the line, "I ain't had no lovin' since January, February, June, or July."

Lightly thumping her tail against the wooden steps, Hueylene watched her mistress. Sidda might as well have been singing dog lullabies. In fact, Sidda was singing a sort of lullaby, songs to calm the baby girl who'd lived inside herself for forty years. Sidda rubbed the crown of the dog's head, where tufts of white fur sprouted like feathers against the otherwise buff-colored coat. As Sidda stroked, she began to roll her own head around in gentle circles, feeling the tightness in her neck and shoulders. How much does a human head weigh? Twenty, twenty-five pounds? She considered the tender stem that connected her head to her heart, and for a moment she experienced a trickle of gratitude. She wondered if it was possible for gratitude to replace anxiety.

From Sidda's pondering grew a hum. It drifted along until it blossomed into the song "Moon River." She sang the words, remembering how for a period in the early sixties, after *Breakfast at Tiffany's* came out, that song had been her parents' favorite. She remembered how it was to step into Chastain's Restaurant with Vivi and Shep, and blush with delight as the piano player would stop whatever he was playing, and switch to "Moon River" in honor of her parents. How royal it made her whole family seem. Say it was a Saturday evening in what— 1964—say it was end of summer, say they all wore a summer glow on their faces. Say Vivi wore a beige linen sheath; Shep wore a sports coat over a pair of khakis; Sidda and Lulu wore new sundresses, Little

Shep and Baylor wore crisp polo shirts. Say the meal was lobster; all went well. Say they used finger bowls, Shep gave his old saw: "Lovely meal. I'm *elephantly* sufficed."

"Two drifters," Sidda sang as she sat on the dock, "off to see the world. There's such a lot of world to see." She continued singing all the verses of the song, which Vivi had taught her.

"My huckleberry friend," she whispered in Hueylene's ear when the last verse was finished. This made the cocker spaniel lay her blonde furry head on Sidda's lap and give a great sigh. Sidda's chest was opened, her head felt tingly and good. The singing had given the inside of her body a little massage.

I learned to love singing from Mama, she thought. These days nobody sings the way Mama and the four of us used to do.

What Sidda did not know was how much more singing there was when Vivi was growing up. That's the kind of thing the history books don't tell. How people sang outdoors all the time. How it was impossible to walk down the street in Thornton, Louisiana, in the thirties and forties and *not* hear somebody singing. Singing or whistling. Housewives singing while they hung out the clothes; old codgers whistling while they sat in front of the courthouse on River Street; gardeners humming while they weeded and hoed; children lilting and yodeling while they tore through the neighborhoods on their Schwinns and Radio Flyers. Even serious businessmen whistled on their way in and out of the bank. These were people with pianos, not TVs, in their living rooms. Their singing didn't always mean they were happy; sometimes the tunes were dirges or the old hymns. Often the music flowed from black people whose songs touched a sadness inside Vivi that she herself had no words for. In those days, it seemed, everybody sang.

When Sidda was growing up, Vivi led her four kids in song as she drove them to school on mornings they missed the bus. She taught each of them to whistle before they could spell, and she made sure they knew all her old camp songs and chosen favorites from the forties. Sidda and her siblings knew all the verses to "Pennsylvania 6–5000," "Can't Help Lovin' That Man of Mine," and "Chattanooga Choo-Choo" before they knew how to tie their shoes by themselves.

On good days, Vivi would sit at the baby grand that Buggy had given her, and pretend their living room was a piano bar. Sometimes even Shep joined in on tunes like "You Are My Sunshine" or "Yellow Rose of Texas."

At those times, Vivi would turn to him and say, "Great Scott! You have a *marvelous* voice. You should sing more often! Don't hide your light under a bushel!"

That would embarrass Shep, who would mumble, "You're the performer in this family, Viviane," and wander off to the kitchen to freshen his drink.

Sidda loved the moments when her father joined in the free-for-all rambunctiousness her mother encouraged. These occasions were rare, as were any moments with him. Shep loved his children; he loved his wife. But he knew a lot more about farming and duck hunting than he did about being part of a family. Mostly he stuck to what he was good at. Sidda can count the number of times she was ever alone with her father, and most of those were after she was grown. He was a man with his own brand of rural poetry, but its expression was gruff with bourbon and unarticulated melancholy.

Shep Walker did not fly as high as Vivi, but every so often, unpredictably, he was capable of unbounded whimsy. Like the Christmas Eve he came home with cowgirl and cowboy outfits, complete with hats and boots, for each member of the family, including a ridiculous little bitty cowboy hat for their cocker spaniel. He was so delighted with himself that he managed to charm Vivi into allowing all of them (except the dog) to wear the getups to Christmas Mass. After Mass, as friends gathered round the Walkers, who looked like a wild offshoot Western singing group gone wrong, Vivi laughed and said, "Saint Shep the Baptist thought Our Lady of Divine Compassion Parish needed a kick in the butt."

As a young man, Shep Walker had been a good-looking lady-killing sleeper of a gentleman farmer who married Vivi Abbott because he coveted her irrepressible vitality. He never stopped to consider why he needed such vigor. Nor did he suspect that Vivi's animation had a dark side. It never crossed young Shep Walker's mind that Vivi might, as the years passed, wear him out. The physical attraction they shared when they were courting was almost overpowering, and it had a way of resurfacing over the years, unbidden and sometimes unwanted, after long droughts of blame and abstinence.

For her part, Vivi married Shep Walker because she adored the sound of his voice; because she loved how he looked so confident after she kissed him; and because—at first—he made her feel like a star. And because she no longer believed, at age twenty-four, that it mattered all that much whom she married.

Vivi once told Sidda, "I meant to marry Paul Newman, but Joanne Woodward got him first. After that, I didn't give a damn."

It was this devil dance between Shep's quiet melancholy and Vivi's frenzied charm—all of it oiled with an endless stream of Jack Daniel's—that sculpted Sidda's impression of marriage.

Later, back inside the cabin, Sidda made a glass of Earl Grey iced tea, and pulled a floor lamp and chair out onto the deck so she wouldn't lose sight of the moon. The minute she sat down with her mother's scrapbook, Hueylene flopped a cloth toy against Sidda's leg, announcing that it was time for a game of tug-of-war. Looking at the dog, Sidda had to laugh. The dog's huge eyes, slightly elongated nose, and curly flaps of ears were so familiar and lovable. Sidda got down on her knees and pulled on the toy and growled. The dog was delighted, and they played till Sidda gave up and let Hueylene win.

Picking the scrapbook back up, Sidda took a deep breath and closed her eyes for a moment before she opened it again. Unfold to me. Let me unfold.

When she opened her eyes, she beheld an invitation. Engraved in script on a card of white bristol board, the invitation read:

> Mr. Taylor Charles Abbott
> requests the pleasure of your
> company at a dance in honor of his daughter
> Miss Viviane Abbott
> Friday the eighteenth of December
> One thousand nine hundred and forty-two
> at eight o'clock
> Theodore Hotel Ballroom
> Thornton, Louisiana

December, 1942. It must have been some sort of sweet-sixteen ball. Had they really carried on with such grand events even during the war? Sidda turned the card over. Where in the hell was her grandmother's name? The omission took her breath away. Was it an oversight? If this blackballing of her grandmother was intentional, then what did it mean?

Once again, she longed to be able to pick up the telephone and simply ask her mother. But Vivi had made her feelings clear: do not call.

Sidda looked at her watch. Nine o'clock. Eleven o'clock Louisiana time. Caro would still be awake. She'd just be gearing up, downing the thick black Community coffee she adored. The one true Ya-Ya night owl would still be receiving phone calls, unless her life had radically changed. Up until *The New York Times* interview, Caro still called Sidda every couple of months and always after midnight. But they had not spoken since the offending article. Not since Vivi had handed down the *fatwa*.

Grabbing a flashlight and Hueylene's leash, Sidda and her cocker spaniel struck out for the phone booth at the Quinault Merc. The road was deserted, all the happy campers bedded down for the night. When Sidda passed the Quinault Lodge, she saw the warm lights in the lobby still burning, and felt a little comfort knowing that she could wander in there anytime she wanted, if she grew tired of being alone. She liked the late-night buzz she felt; she liked the *frisson* she experienced as she set forth to sleuth out information about Vivi Abbott, age sixteen.

"Eatin' cheese biscuits and playing with the damn-fool CD-ROM, that's what I'm doing," Caro said, drawing in a ragged emphysemic breath. "How about you, Pal?"

"Caro," Sidda said, "I'm out here on the edge of the United States, trying to figure out what to do with the rest of my life."

"That is a filthy habit for such a lovely girl," Caro said in a near-perfect Groucho Marx voice.

Sidda laughed, picturing the way Caro's shoulders shrugged when she tossed off a comment like that. "I can't help it, I'm an addict."

Sidda sat on the narrow shelf of a bench inside one of the few 1950s vintage public phone booths left in North America. She unhooked Hueylene's leash, and gave her a command to sit.

"Don't corrupt that word 'addict,' Goddamnit," Caro said. "I'm fed up with everybody claiming they're addicted. You're just a *ponderer*, Sidda, that's all. Have been since you were four. It's your nature. What else is new?"

"You don't sound very surprised to hear from me."

"Should I be?"

"After—well, all the mess with—"

"With that fat-ass New York reporter? Come on, what do you take me for?"

"My mother's best friend."

"That's true," Caro said, then paused. "I'm also your godmother."

"You're not upset with me?"

"No, I'm not."

"Then why didn't you call? Why didn't you write?"

"Well, to quote that pointy-head idiot, George Bush, it wouldn't have been prudent."

"Caro, when have you ever been prudent?"

"When it comes to my friends, I have been known on occasion to be prudent."

There was a silence while Sidda thought of how to respond.

"I sent Blaine and Richard up to see your play," Caro said. "You know that, don't you? I sent my ex-husband and his boyfriend up there to see your *tour de force* and report back to me."

Sidda never stopped marveling at Caro. Growing up, Caro's husband, Blaine, had always turned heads in the French Quarter. But when he finally left Caro for the man he'd been secretly seeing in New Orleans, it had rocked the whole Ya-Ya universe. That was eight or nine years ago. After threatening Blaine with an unloaded gun and tearing up an entire portfolio of architectural drawings for a house he was designing, Caro had finally forgiven him.

As she had explained things the last time Sidda had been home two years earlier, "It's a shock, but it's not a surprise. And the fact is, I really *like* Richard. The man can *cook*, for God's sake. Nobody has cooked for me since Mama died."

Blaine moved to New Orleans to live with Richard, but they were always driving up to Thornton to stay with Caro, especially since she'd been diagnosed with emphysema.

"I know Blaine and Richard saw the show," Sidda said. "I mean, Connor and I took them out while they were in New York. But what do you mean you *sent* them?"

"I mean," Caro said, "*I* bought the Goddamn tickets for the play and *I* instructed the lovebirds that if they didn't come back with a detailed description of *Women on the Cusp*, and graphic particulars on how you looked, sounded, and behaved, that I would turn them over to the Divine Compassion vice squad."

"And?"

"The boyfriends told me not to worry. Said you were gracious, good-looking, if a little thin; sad about your mama, but proud of your success. And that they—and I quote: '*adored*' Connor McGill. If I recall correctly, Richard said, 'He's Liam Neeson crossed with a young Hank Fonda, who's spent a few sessions on the couch.'"

"Jesus!" Sidda said. "How do you put up with those two?! Scuse me a second, please, Caro—Hueylene, get back over here!" Sidda called out to the spaniel, who was starting a slow lumbering across the road in the direction of the lake.

"Sorry, the dog was wandering off," she apologized.

"Is that code language for something?" Caro asked.

"No!" Sidda laughed, realizing she had just uttered the kind of phrase the Ya-Yas would use to convey a piece of information they didn't want anyone else to understand. "It's Hueylene, the theater dog."

"Are you still carrying that dog around with you everywhere you go?"

"Yes," Sidda said. "She has this thing like epilepsy, you know. I don't like to kennel her. Connor calls it 'puppylepsy.' She's on downers."

"Don't tell me you've turned into a nut," Caro said.

"You should talk, Caro!" Sidda said. "You're the woman who once raised a litter of *four* beagles, if I recall."

"Now, what about this hunk, Connor? What about—"

"You still haven't answered my question," Sidda said, changing the subject. She did not want to discuss her postponement of the wedding with Caro. "How do you put up with Blaine and Richard?"

"I not only put up with them, I *relish* them. Blaine's ten times more fun. Every time Blaine and Richard come to visit, they cook, redecorate, and throw me a party. How could I *not* enjoy the hell out of them?"

Caro then began to cough. It was a horrible, ragged cough that hurt Sidda's chest to hear. She pictured the Caro she grew up knowing: tall, tanned, athletic, emerging from swimming laps in Teensy's pool, reaching for a cigarette before she'd even dried off. Baylor had told her that Caro's battle with emphysema was up and down.

"I'm sorry I didn't call, Pal," Caro said softly. "It was just too Goddamn touchy down here with Vivi. She made us swear not to talk to you. Your mama's terrified of betrayal. By the way, don't let the coughing bother you. It sounds worse than it is—always flares up at night."

Sidda was quiet for a moment. "Do *you* feel I betrayed her?"

"No, I don't. I think *The New York Times*, and every other woman-hating publication in this country, would like to siphon the milk out of every single mother's tits, and then blame them for being dry. But no, I do not think you meant to hurt your mother."

"Thank you."

"Don't thank me, Sidda."

"May I ask you a question?"

Caro coughed again before she responded. Sidda winced.

When Caro spoke, she sounded wary. "Depends on what it is."

"I found this invitation in Mama's scrapbook. To a dance thrown on her sixteenth birthday. My grandmother's name is missing from the invitation. It reads like Buggy wasn't even alive."

"You ask Vivi about it?"

"She doesn't want to talk about the scrapbook. In fact, Mama doesn't want to talk to me at all. She says she sent 'The Divine Secrets' and that's enough."

"Isn't it?"

"Isn't what?" Sidda said.

"Isn't the scrapbook enough?" Caro said.

"No, it's not enough!" Sidda said. "It irritates me, it frustrates me to look through that scrapbook and only get inklings, only tiny *slivers* of information. No explanations for anything, no dramatic structure! When I *know* there must be stories, narratives that could solve—maybe not solve—but *account for* . . . Mama *owes* me some pointers, for God's sake."

Sidda cleared her throat, embarrassed at her outburst. Caro didn't speak for a moment.

"You think your mama has something to do with your cold feet about Connor McGill?"

"I don't know," Sidda said. "I'm a little shocked at my vehemence about all this, to tell you the truth."

"I'm not. You and your mama have broken each other's hearts. But while you're slinging arrows, let me remind you that you *did—do*— have a father, Sidda. Understandable that you should overlook him, vanishing act that he is. Not that that distinguishes him from any other Ya-Ya husband."

"Yeah, but Mama was always the star. Daddy was a bit player."

"How many years of therapy did you say you've had?"

"Put it this way: with the money I've spent trying to deal with the ways Mama fucked me up, I could have retired at the age of thirty."

"Let me tell you something, Pal: your mother doesn't *owe* you any-thing. You're a *grown-up*. She fed you and clothed you and held you, even if she did have a drink in her hand while she was doing it. And however she fucked you up—and I'm sure she did—every mother fucks every kid up—she did it with style, you hear me?"

Sidda reached down to pull Hueylene closer to her. Therapy *has* done *some* good. Five years ago I would have gone catatonic if some-one spoke such blunt crazy wisdom to me.

"You still breathing?" Caro asked, softly.

"Yep."

"I think about breathing a whole lot these days," Caro said. "Uncountable the number of breaths I've taken for granted in my life."

Caro's words swept into Sidda with the air she was breathing, and caused her to notice her breath. For a moment, Sidda said nothing. She simply rode with her breath, like a surfer on an afternoon wave. At opposite ends of the country, she and Caro breathed into their telephones, neither of them speaking.

Eventually Caro said, "Okay: about that sweet-sixteen business: it was ugly."

"What do you mean?" Sidda asked.

"You really want to talk about this?"

"Are you tired?" Sidda asked.

Caro breathed raggedly. If Sidda hadn't known better, she would have thought the breath was stagy.

"The man had settled some big case, what have you, wanted to strut his money. Your grandmother Buggy didn't want to have that dance. Your grandfather did it to spite her. Goddamnit, Taylor Abbott treated your grandmother like a piece of shit. Weird as she was, she didn't deserve it. Ran around on her for years. Every maid in the parish knew about it. He treated his horses better than he did his wife. Hell, I don't know. Your mama got caught in the middle of all their shit."

Caro was silent for a moment before she continued.

"That dance. Taylor Abbott gave Vivi this drop-dead diamond ring. It was the last big party before we lost Jack. Not a birthday you'd want to remember."

Sidda waited for Caro to say more, but she didn't.

"Is that all, Caro?" Sidda asked. "What happened? How did all this affect Mama?"

"Your mama's next birthday is going to be grand, I can tell you that," Caro said, ignoring Sidda's probing. "We're planning the party for October rather than December. Vivi announced she wanted an outdoor party this year, so we need to have it before it gets cold. I'm doing the invitations on my Macintosh."

Caro began to cough.

"Queen of Evasion," Sidda said.

"Godmother of Evasion," Caro said in a weary voice.

"You're tired. I've kept you too long."

"Yes, I am tired, Pal."

"Thank you for answering my question."

"I didn't answer your question."

"No, you didn't."

"'There is no answer,'" Caro said. "'There never has been an answer. There never will be an answer. That's the answer.'—Gertrude Stein."

"You're the second person to quote Gertrude Stein to me this week."

"Life ain't no Baltimore Catechism, Pal—Caro Bennett Brewer."

Sidda laughed. From where she stood, she could see part of the moon through the tall, inky-black silhouettes of the old Douglas firs that lined the lake.

"Caro," Sidda said, tentative. "There's one more thing."

"What's that?"

"There's this photo—looks like it's from the early sixties. It's a group photo at an Easter-egg hunt, looks like it might be at Teensy's. We're all lined up holding baskets, dressed to the nines. Everyone's there—you, Blaine, the boys, Teensy, Necie, all the Petites Ya-Yas. Chick's dressed up in this crazy bunny outfit—with a cigarette in his hand! All of Necie's brood, except for Frank, who was probably taking the picture. Daddy and the four of us are there. Baylor looks like he's screaming bloody murder, and I'm wearing this Alice in Wonderland organdy affair, complete with hat. My arms are around Little Shep and Lulu, and we all look slightly tortured. The curious thing is that Mama's not there. She was gone that Easter, wasn't she? Where was she, Caro?"

Caro was silent.

"Oh, boy," she finally said, dodging. "Back in the days of the smoking bunnies."

"That picture makes me sad," Sidda said. "I think it was after we drove Mama away."

"What?" Caro said.

"When we got to be too much for Mama. When she went away."

"Haven't you and Vivi ever talked about this, Sidda?"

"No," Sidda said. "We haven't."

Caro was silent.

"She went away because of me, didn't she, Caro?"

Caro began to cough then, and Sidda felt guilty.

"No, Pal," Caro said. "She didn't go away because of you. Life is more complex than that."

"What are you saying, Caro?"

"There's a lot more than you're going to find in a scrapbook. Now go do something sweet for yourself. Like Necie says, go and think you—"

"Go and think me some pretty pink and blue thoughts."

There was a pause.

"That means: I love you, Siddalee."

"I know, Caro," Sidda said. "I love you too."

A spasm of coughing followed. Then Caro said, "Sleep tight. Don't worry bout the boogeymen; I've fumigated under the bed."

There is the truth of history, and there is the truth of what a person remembers. As Sidda sat at the edge of Lake Quinault, memory blossoms floated unbounded, as though breathed, no words spoken. Like birds that fly across national borders, between countries at war with each other.

18

*S*idda sat in the phone booth and practiced breathing.
   You are a grown-up.
   Do I expect Mama to be responsible for my life?
   Because she gave me physical birth, do I expect her to give me
spiritual birth as well? Have I not forgiven her for being ripped from
the womb of innocence and flung screaming into the raw, cruel, glorious demands of this world? Do I expect Connor to do what Mama
couldn't or wouldn't? Am I afraid that I don't deserve him? Am I
afraid he will leave me if I'm not good enough?
   She punched in Connor's number. She heard the phone ring five
times, and then his voice on the answering machine.
   "Hi. Connor McGill and Sidda Walker aren't in now, but we'd like
to know you called."
   The sound of his voice aroused her.
   "Hey, Dreamboat," Sidda said softly into the phone. "Hueylene,
the Canine Governor, misses you. It's late. It smells like pine pitch
and wild roses out here. Still no meteors. Is that starry starry sky stuff
all fiction?"
   She made a little kiss-kiss sound into the receiver and hung up.

Was Connor still at the theater, or the opera house? Or was he out having a glorious time at some groovy place without her? *Fool.* What are you doing, leaving him like this?

As she and Hueylene walked along the lake path in the direction of the cabin, Sidda found herself thinking about her own birthdays. She remembered how it was to awake back then, midwinter, at Pecan Grove.

The first sound she'd hear on those mornings was the mingling of Vivi's, Little Shep's, Lulu's, and Baylor's voices as they sang "Happy Birthday" to her.

It was so early on those mornings that the fields and the bayou were still shrouded in darkness. Baylor and Lulu were still half asleep, rubbing their eyes, their young voices husky with sleep, pajamas all whompa-sided. Little Shep, wired from the instant he woke up, was jumping around in the doorway of her bedroom. Sidda would open her eyes to see four people she loved most in the world, their faces lit by the glow of birthday candles on the cake Vivi was holding. She'd gaze up at her mother, still clad in her pink Barbizon nightgown, face gleaming with Beautiere overnight cream. Sidda would smell the scent of the candles burning, feel the soft cotton sheets, the weight of the covers just right on her body. Sitting up in bed, she'd sense the just-waked-up scent of her family. She would not smell her father because he was not there. Where was he? Already out in the fields? Still sleeping? Away at the duck camp, his second home?

Sidda would sit up in bed on those mornings, mouth wide open at the beauty of the tiny birthday candles glowing in her dark bedroom. After they finished singing, Vivi would bend down to kiss Sidda. *"I'm so glad I had you,"* she would whisper into her daughter's ear.

Some birthdays Vivi's voice might be hoarse from smoke or tears, or both. Sometimes the tension in her mother's voice was so high it resonated in her daughter's just-waking body. Some birthdays Vivi was so hung-over, she'd wince even as she sang. The year after Vivi got sick and went away, her eyes were so red and puffy, her voice so weak, her panic so close to the surface. Even as a child, Sidda sensed how much it cost her mother to sing, to hold out a rose-bedecked cake at dawn, and to whisper, "Siddalee Walker, I'm so glad I had you."

As Sidda remembered the singing of her siblings, she wondered how it was they'd grown so far apart. With the exception of Baylor, none of them kept in touch.

Little Shep, Lulu, and Baylor would climb on her bed as Sidda blew out the candles and made her wish. Then Vivi would relight the candles, and Sidda would blow them out all over again, this time with help from the others. Vivi would leave the room and reappear with a tray set with good china dessert saucers, forks, and four tall crystal glasses of milk. They'd switch the bedside lamp back on, and Sidda would reach greedily for the biggest rose on the cake and plop it into her mouth. After that, she'd royally decide which remaining flowers would go to whom. Vivi encouraged total self-indulgence on their birthdays, and the mere knowledge that on her birthday Sidda didn't *have* to share made her want to. As they licked sugar roses Vivi would make them promise not to tell their father. Big Shep claimed eating cake like that so early in the morning was a "whore's breakfast." The rest of them didn't care. They were happy little whores who didn't worry about saving a morsel. They knew that Vivi ordered not one but *two* birthday cakes from the bakery for birthdays. One for their morning orgy, and another for the birthday party later in the day.

Vivi worked hard to make every birthday a good one. It was as though she had made a covenant with herself that she would do anything within her power not to let a birthday go bad.

As Sidda walked along the lake, she occasionally stumbled over the thick, knotted tree roots that crisscrossed the path. Although she carried a small flashlight, and the light of the moon was strong, if she wasn't careful, the very vividness of her memories caused her to lose her footing.

She felt safe here on the Olympic Peninsula. It had been too long since she felt so protected. As a girl, she'd walked like this at night at Spring Creek, guarded by the creeks and the pine trees and the cicadas. After all her years of living in the city, it was a relief to feel her shoulders relax. It was a relief not to have to glance behind her every few steps to see if she was about to be mugged.

She remembered a dramatic-theory seminar she'd taken in graduate school in which *liminal* moments on stage were discussed. Liminal moments, those moments apart from time, when you are gripped, taken, when you are so fully absorbed in what you are doing that time ceases to exist.

Those early-morning birthday moments were liminal, Sidda thought. Mama knew how to embrace liminality. In spite of—or maybe because of—her emotional acrobatics, Mama taught me rapture.

What were Mama's birthdays like when she was a girl? What was that sixteenth birthday like? Did Buggy bring her a cake in bed? Hard to imagine. What happened? Was there a viscous glue of jealousy passed down from mother to daughter in our lineage, invisible and life-threatening as cancer?

Sidda didn't want to think about jealousy and Vivi. Not that it hadn't been suggested to her by her therapist, by her friends. Sidda didn't even like the word "jealousy"; she was superstitious about using it.

The harder Sidda tried to block certain thoughts from her mind, the less aware she grew of the sweet summer air that surrounded her along the lake. As she walked, she tried to think pretty pink and blue thoughts. But old gray thoughts walked behind her, quacking and biting at her heels.

You are not a child anymore.

The first time Sidda was socked in the stomach with the full impact of the word "jealousy" was on the opening night of the first professional play she directed. It was a production of *Death of a Salesman* at the Portland Stage Company in Maine, in the dead of winter. It also happened to be her twenty-fourth birthday.

Vivi had flown to Boston, and a friend of Sidda's had driven her up to Portland. Sidda had overrehearsed her cast up to the last minute and didn't see Vivi until an hour or so before the opening. All had seemed fine. Vivi had borrowed one of Teensy's furs and was having fun pulling it up to her neck, and asking in a Dietrich voice, "What Becomes a Legend Most?"

The opening went well enough, although Sidda made copious notes and called a rehearsal for the next day to try several adjustments in blocking. She had not yet begun to understand how to step aside and let a production stand on its feet.

One of the board members of the theater, who owned a huge Victorian home overlooking the harbor, hosted the opening-night party. Mediocre wine and lots of finger food. The actors were happy, and there was a cozy feeling, a fire in the fireplace, a classical guitarist in the parlor. Cast and crew, theater subscribers, and the board of directors were pleased with the production, and Sidda felt relieved and proud and nervous.

Vivi had packed three bottles of Jack Daniel's in her suitcase, as she always did when she traveled. At the opening-night party, she carried a sterling-silver flask. It was the first thing Sidda noticed. That and the fact that her mother refused to take off the fur.

Sidda watched her mother out of the corner of her eye, wondering how long before things got crazy. Big Shep had been the one who'd arranged the visit, having called Sidda and told her how much Vivi wanted to come. Sidda had been doubtful, but had agreed. After all, it was her directing debut, even if it was in the far North, and she wanted to have her mother there, to make her proud.

When Sidda was a girl at Ya-Ya parties she used to witness the women perform their "numbers"—whimsical, lightly choreographed renditions of songs they loved, done in an ever-so-slightly off-key, but invigorating, Andrews Sisters style. Vivi would take the Patty Andrews role, making faces, rolling her eyes, goofing around while she sang. Sidda would lean against the closet door in her mother's dressing room and watch the Ya-Yas as they polished their routines.

"How do we look, Dahlin?" Vivi would ask. "Any directorial tips?"

Sidda would always offer a suggestion, and sometimes the ladies would take her up on it. Then a surge of delight, of power, of delicious authority would sweep over her. Later, in the smoky living room, surrounded by grown-ups and the tinkling of ice against crystal cocktail glasses, Sidda would witness the small bit of business she'd suggested, and the thrill it gave her was beyond words. It is something she still doesn't know how to explain. Sidda's passion for theater and her tangled relationship with her mother intersect at a place in Sidda that does not respond to direction.

As Sidda worked the opening-night party in Portland, she took care to introduce Vivi whenever possible. But the gathering was large, and it was inevitable that they become separated. When the managing director of the theater proposed a toast to Sidda, and the host brought out a birthday cake with the twin masks of tragedy and comedy done in icing, Sidda blushed with excitement. She said a few words, thanking her cast and crew, made a joke about the challenge of directing the great Arthur Miller, and proclaimed the evening the most lovely birthday she could imagine. She forgot to mention Vivi.

Afterward, standing next to the fireplace talking with the lighting designer, a young British man, she noticed a crowd gathering over by the windows.

Wade Coenen, who had designed the costumes for the production, eased over to Sidda. "Mama likes her drink?"

Sidda blushed.

Wade was blond and funny and did fabulous Diana Ross imitations. He'd been trying to get Sidda to lift weights at the local gym with him, telling her it was important for directors to be muscular. Sidda hoped they'd have the chance to work together again, hoped they'd become pals.

"Her poison of choice?" he asked.

"Bourbon," Sidda replied. "Good bourbon."

"My old man did himself in on good Scotch."

"The smell of bourbon makes me ill," Sidda said.

"I'll go see if I can get Mama a piece of cake," Wade said. "In the meantime, try some of the spanakopita, and remember—it's your birthday."

"Thanks, Wade," she said, kissing him on the cheek. "And thanks for your extra work on the costumes. I'll never forget the scavenging we did to come in on budget. You're amazing."

"You ain't seen nothing till you see my Salvation Army evening-gown collection, honey."

Sidda was chatting with a husband and wife who were asking questions about being a "woman in the theater," when she heard the unmistakable sound of her mother's voice. She closed her eyes and listened. She knew that sound: the cacophony of five jiggers of bourbon.

In front of the fireplace, center stage, Vivi was staging an elaborate promenade in which she dragged Teensy's fur on the floor behind her. Her head was thrown back in a grotesque exaggeration of a diva, and she was talking loudly in a Tallulah voice.

"They should not allow *children* to direct," she was saying. "They should not allow *children* to touch an American classic like Arthur Miller!"

Flipping the fur up and over her head and so near the fireplace the coat almost caught on fire, Vivi stared out into the crowd. She impaled Sidda with her drunken gaze. "Who gave you *permission* to direct a play, anyway?"

The gathering grew deathly quiet.

Sidda bit her lip. She took a step toward her mother.

"I *asked* you a Goddamn question, Siddalee Walker," Vivi said, her voice slurring.

Sidda felt every eye in the room on her. The space felt suddenly hot and airless. As though all life had stopped.

"Nobody gave me permission, Mama," Sidda said softly. "I was hired."

"Oh, excuse me!" Vivi said loudly. "You were *hired*?"

Then, gesturing wildly to the room, Vivi announced loudly, "She was *hired*."

Sidda could feel the tears in her eyes, but she would be damned if she would break down. Taking a deep breath, she turned to leave.

At that moment, Wade Coenen appeared with a plate of food. "You know," he said to Vivi, "I have been *dying* to get you alone. I have something I absolutely *must* tell you, and there is not one single other person in this room I could possibly reveal it to."

Caught off guard, Vivi looked at him with childlike astonishment.

"What?" she asked. "What could you not possibly reveal to anyone else?"

"You must follow me," Wade whispered dramatically, taking her by the arm. "This is strictly *entre nous*. And *do* try some of the spanakopita," he said as he led her out of the room. "It is positively divine."

Sidda's mouth hung open as she watched her mother follow Wade, seemingly delighted to be at his side, and seemingly oblivious of her daughter.

That night the camaraderie of her colleagues held Sidda up. The moment Vivi and Wade disappeared from the room, the actress who played Linda Loman broke spontaneously into an Irish tune she claimed she had learned from an acting teacher who once had met James Joyce.

Then Shawn Kavanaugh, the aging ex-TV star, himself a part-time lush, who'd created a haunting and somehow heroic Willy Loman, put his arm around Sidda.

"Oh, Doll," he said, "the Church is wrong. Despair is not the worst of the cardinal sins. Jealousy is. It's more complex."

Then he bowed his head to Sidda, as though he were recognizing royalty. "Terrific opening, Ms. Walker," he said. "Thank you for your keen direction. Looks like you have a fine background for drama. Just remember: keep your elbows out."

That night, Sidda walked by herself back to the old salt-box house she was sharing temporarily with Wade Coenen and the other designers. The night had grown bitterly cold.

When she got to the theater house, she found Wade Coenen sitting at the kitchen table talking on the phone. He smiled, threw her a kiss, and gestured upstairs to Sidda's bedroom. When Sidda went up, she found Vivi already asleep. She was lying in bed with her night-gown on. She had removed all her makeup, and her face was moistur-ized.

Sidda looked down at her sleeping mother. You always take care of your complexion, no matter what. Holy Mary, Mother of God, pray for us sinners.

Back downstairs, the kitchen was warm, and an old Stevie Wonder tune was playing on the radio.

"Thank you," Sidda said simply, touching Wade on the shoulder.

"*Use it,*" Wade said.

"Right," Sidda said, thinking how many times she'd repeated the same Stanislavsky axiom to actors. *Use everything in your life to create your art.*

She sat down at the wooden kitchen table. She wanted to remain calm in front of her costume designer. She wanted to make a cynical joke or a Shakespearean reference. Instead, she burst into tears.

Wade Coenen poured her a glass of brandy. "Theater," he said. "Glorious theater. It creates family for all kinds of orphans."

19

*C*aro lay back in her recliner and let her mind drift back to an earlier time, when the world was different and her breathing was easier.

That whole birthday ball had been odd from the beginning. It was out of character for the Abbotts to stage something so extravagant.

She'd never liked Taylor Abbott, never really liked Buggy. Didn't hate her like Teensy did, just didn't like her. Or trust her. Buggy acted like a maid. Housework, digging in the yard, and going to Mass, that's all the woman did. No luncheons with friends; she didn't even go to movies. Always said she had too much work to do.

And Taylor Abbott. When that man came home from work, the whole household had to stop breathing, stop living. If Vivi and the Ya-Yas walked into the living room when he was home—laughing like they always were—he wouldn't even look up at them. He'd just say, "Viviane, keep it down." And Vivi would clam up and they'd have to tiptoe across the room and up the stairs, not breathing a sound until they were in Vivi's bedroom with the door shut. Taylor Abbott wanted his home to be a library or a museum where he could read his newspaper.

The girls could make all the noise they wanted, do anything they felt like, until he got home. Buggy would just go on working. That woman did tolerate umpteen kids running in and out of her house, from the time the Ya-Yas were four until they got married. During high school, they'd roll up the rugs in the afternoons, push the furniture back, and practice the latest dance steps for hours. Buggy always had plenty of food, no matter how many of them trooped in.

But Buggy Abbott did it as her *job*. She wasn't sour with the food or anything, but the way she set it out, the way she opened her kitchen, it felt like she *worked there*, like she was hired help, not the lady of the house, as women were called back then.

The night of Vivi's birthday ball was cold and clear. Cold enough for Vivi to wear the sable stole that Genevieve had loaned her. Jack had arrived the afternoon before, home on leave, handsome and tall in his Air Corps uniform, a miracle that he'd been able to come home early for Christmas to celebrate Vivi's birthday.

The Theodore Hotel ballroom had been decorated with poinsettias and sparkling lights. Stan Lemoine and His Rhythm Kings, cool cats in sharp jackets, had a terrific horn player who blew "Happy Birthday" in swing tempo. Vivi stood next to the gift table, piled high with parcels, a birthday cake, and glasses filled with mysteriously acquired liquor. She wore a stunning off-the-shoulder midnight-blue velvet and organdy gown that she'd had made just for that evening. While the guests sang to her, she smiled wide, eyes glistening, with her father on one side and Jack Whitman on the other. Photos snapped at that moment would not have shown Buggy in the frame. (They would not have shown Vivi's grandmother, Delia, either. But then Delia, cigarette holder and drink in hand, was busy flirting with two men thirty years her junior.)

Vivi had decided that the ball was worth all the fights her parents had had over the event. ("I'll throw my own daughter a ball if I want to, harpy!" Mr. Abbott had said to Buggy at the dinner table one night.) Longing for rare, unexpected recognition from her father, Vivi had flushed with guilt. When she swallowed, the food had caught in her throat. Vivi had never received this much notice from her father. It came out of nowhere, as though Taylor Abbott were driven to spotlight his daughter's move into womanhood, as though the sixteen years Vivi had spent trying to get his attention were finally paying off. In this one splendid event the attention had come so suddenly, though, that Vivi did not trust it. She feared that she might disappoint her father, without knowing why or how. She was almost nauseated with the sheer richness of it all.

The perfect moment of the birthday dance had come just before the band took its first break. To end the set, they played "Deep Purple," a song both Vivi and Jack loved. In Jack's embrace, Vivi danced, floating, held safely in the frame of his arms. Her eyes half closed, a tiny smile on her slightly opened mouth, she felt royal. For a moment, the craving to hold on to the moment gave way to simple joy. A ballroom full of people celebrated her birth. It was like a fairy tale. A tiny kingdom for Vivi Abbott in Thornton, Louisiana.

After the guests finished singing "Happy Birthday," the Ya-Yas and their dates flocked around Vivi. They watched as Mr. Abbott, standing perfectly erect in his tuxedo, reached into his pocket and retrieved a small gift-wrapped package. With a little flourish, he handed it to his daughter, and gave her a kiss on the cheek.

Caro surveyed the scene with a cool eye. Standing next to her date, Red Beaumont, who was at least four inches shorter than she was, she thought how she'd never in her life seen Mr. Abbott kiss Vivi. She'd seen him knock Vivi upside the head, but she'd never seen him kiss her. In fact, she'd never seen either of Vivi's parents kiss her.

As the band played "White Christmas," Caro watched Vivi unwrap the package. She studied her friend's face as Vivi snapped open the lid of a velvet ring box.

"Our Mother of Pearl!" Vivi uttered, holding up a diamond ring. Vivi reached out and hugged her father. "Is this really for me?"

Mr. Abbott readjusted his cummerbund as though the hug made him uncomfortable. Caro punched Red Beaumont. "Cig, please," she said, without taking her eyes off Vivi.

Red lit two cigarettes and handed her one. Caro took the cigarette, broke away from her date, and edged closer to the Abbott family. Pete was laughing with his date and a circle of buddies. Ginger, Delia's maid, stood just outside the circle of family, holding Jezie Abbott, age three, in her arms.

Buggy wore a gray lace and tulle dress. Her hair was swept up, and for once she wore lipstick. But with her arms crossed at her chest and the frown on her face, she looked uneasy, as though embarrassed to be caught looking pretty.

"Mother!" Vivi said, hugging her mother, then holding out her hand. "Look! Isn't it *gorgeous*? Did you help pick it out?"

The ring was beautiful. Five diamonds in a round setting, twenty-four karat. It sparkled tastefully, if a bit grandly.

For a moment, it looked like Buggy might slap Vivi. She grabbed Vivi's hand, regarded the ring for a moment, then flung her daughter's hand away as though it were disgusting.

"Mister Abbott," Buggy said, "that is not a proper gift for a *girl*."

Taylor Abbott regarded his wife for a moment, and then, as though he had not heard her, turned away and began to chat with guests. Buggy struggled to compose herself as Delia grabbed her arm.

"Don't make a damn fool of yourself," Delia hissed to Buggy. "If you didn't carry on like such a sanctimonious hag, your husband might give *you* diamonds!"

Buggy Abbott's head dropped. She looked as though Delia had just slapped her. Staring out into the large room filled with tulle and satin and dancing young people, she had to hold on to the edge of the table to keep her balance.

She turned back to her daughter, who was encircled by the Ya-Yas. Reaching out for Vivi's hand again, she said, without expression, "Aren't you just the luckiest little girl God ever made?"

Then, abruptly, Buggy walked over to Ginger and jerked Jezie from the maid's arms. The roughness of the gesture made Jezie cry, and Buggy began to comfort her. She whispered something to Ginger, and the three of them walked away, Buggy cooing to little Jezie.

Caro did not see Buggy for the rest of the dance.

Rousing herself from the recliner, Caro walked slowly into her kitchen. Reaching into the refrigerator, she took out a bottle of cold St. Pauli Girl, and brought it back to the bedroom. She adjusted the volume on the CD player, and sat back in the recliner. She took a sip of the beer and thought that life was not so bad if she could still enjoy the taste of a cold beer out of a bottle.

Thinking back to that night, she felt the pinch of old sadness. The memory of Jack could still hit her square in the chest. She could see him as he'd stood next to Vivi that night. Young, handsome in his uniform, in love with her best friend. If the loss could hit her this way, she could only imagine the way it still snuck up on Vivi.

Caro could still see Vivi's bedroom on Compton Street, with its tall ceilings and floor-to-ceiling windows. There was an old live oak tree outside the window, and Caro remembered how the branches of that tree brushed against the windowpanes that night as the wind blew. The night of the birthday dance had turned quite cold, and the four girlfriends were all piled in Vivi's mahogany four-poster bed, their bodies warming each other.

The Ya-Yas had planned for weeks to spend the night together at Vivi's the night of the dance. They'd looked forward to staying up late, munching ham sandwiches, downing tall glasses of cold milk, and rehashing the details of what everyone wore, said, did, and who danced with whom.

Caro remembered how it was to lie so unself-consciously next to her best friends. Her aging body recalled the singular comfort of just being in bed next to Vivi's and Teensy's and Necie's bodies. It had been like no comfort she had ever taken from a man, not from her husband, or from the two lovers she'd had during her marriage. As she thought of her friends, she wished they could sprawl like that once more, their old-lady bodies touching, their varicosed legs thrown over one another's, toes touching, their scents mingling. The tribe, together again.

We had probably been talking about Jack that night. How thrilled we all were to see him again. How excited we were to have him home, with the Christmas holidays to look forward to.

Caro could once again hear the door being flung open as Buggy entered Vivi's bedroom, ripping wide the cocoon the four girlfriends had settled into. Their conversation stopped; they put their laughter on hold.

Wearing her bathrobe, a rosary dangling from her hand, Buggy crossed to the bed where the four girls lay.

"Viviane, give me your hand," she said.

Vivi looked up at her, confused.

"It's beautiful, isn't it, Mother?" Vivi said, holding out her hand, still hoping to win Buggy's approval.

Instead of admiring the ring, Buggy slid it off Vivi's finger. She looked at the Ya-Yas snuggled in bed together. Turning her gaze only on Vivi, she said, "Whatever you did to make your father give you this ring is a mortal sin. May God forgive you."

Then she turned and stomped out of the room.

Vivi's body started to shake. Caro could feel it quiver against her own. Tucking her head down, Vivi crawled underneath the covers.

The friends did not know what to say.

"I didn't do anything wrong," Vivi whispered. "That diamond was from my daddy. He gave me that ring."

More than fifty years later, Caro remembered how she wanted to burst out of the room, run down the hall, and grab Buggy Abbott. She wanted to shake that woman, retrieve the ring, and tell her you do not treat people like that. As Caro sipped her beer, she thought: My friend Vivi never knew how much her mother hated her. If she had, I don't think she could have stood it.

"She's a witch," Caro had said that night.

But Vivi stayed under the covers, pulled into herself.

Teensy tried to take them back to the fun of the party.

"Remember," she said, "when they started 'Begin the Beguine'? Remember how you and Jack started that dance?"

"Vivi," Necie asked, "can I get you something, honey? Anything?"

But Vivi still did not respond. She lay there and shook. And so the friends lay there with her and tried to hold her. They tried to tuck the covers in around her the way you do a baby who is upset by something she doesn't understand.

When they first heard the yelling and screaming from down the hall, they assumed that it was Vivi's brother Pete, roughhousing with buddies. They were surprised to hear such a ruckus this late at night, but Pete always had three or four pals sleeping over, and they were known to get rowdy. Taylor Abbott had a lot more tolerance for loud boys than for loud girls.

It was not Pete. There was silence for a moment and then the fighting started up again. The Ya-Yas could hear Mr. Abbott's loud, deep voice, and then the sound of Buggy's crying. They heard a crash, then silence again. Then, "God*damn* you!"

Vivi lay almost preternaturally still, listening with her whole body.

Caro was afraid. Her own Poppo and Mom fought, but not like this. They had disagreements, but they were out in the open, never lasted for long, and always ended with her father lifting her mother up off the floor with a hug, proclaiming, "You're a hot tamale, yes, ma'am, you're a hot tamale!"

The Abbotts' fighting was different. It made Caro feel that she was not safe in their home.

Before long, the door to Vivi's bedroom burst open, no knock, no anything.

Mr. Abbott roughly pushed his wife into the room. His face was red and his breathing was heavy. Buggy's nightgown was ripped at the shoulder, and Caro could see the shape of her bosoms underneath the cotton.

"Do it, Buggy," Mr. Abbott said. "Give her back the ring."

Buggy stood there, not moving, staring at her bare feet on the floor.

"I said, give the girl the Goddamn ring, you pathetic Catholic idiot!"

Then Mr. Abbott shoved his wife so that she stood, shaking, next to the bed. Caro could feel Vivi's body shaking, and now she could feel Buggy's body shaking. As though a trembling passed between mother and daughter that even the Ya-Yas could not block.

Mr. Abbott took his wife's hand and pried open her clenched hand, finger by finger, until the ring dropped to the floor. Then Taylor Abbott slapped his wife once, hard, across the face.

"Pick it up," he commanded. "Bend down and pick the ring up."

As if in a trance, Buggy Abbott bent down and picked up the ring. Then she flung it onto the bed so that it landed in the folds of the winter quilts.

Vivi, who had been watching in silence, her head peeking out from the side of the covers, now pulled the covers up around her face completely so that she could not see or be seen. Caro was afraid Mr. Abbott would strike Vivi too. It would not have been the first time.

Mr. Abbott took a step toward the bed. He was a tall man, just as threatening in pajamas as in pin stripes. Caro's body tensed, ready to protect her friend.

Caro thought that he might hit her, might hit any one of them. Instead, he fumbled among the quilts for a moment until he found the ring. Then he slipped the ring under the covers where Vivi lay.

"Here, Viviane," he said. "I gave this ring to you. It's yours. It's from me to you. Do you understand?"

He sounded almost desperate.

Vivi didn't respond.

"Answer me, Viviane," he said.

"Yes, sir," Vivi said from under the covers. "I understand."

Looking as close as he ever came to being embarrassed, Mr. Abbott glanced briefly at Necie, Caro, and Teensy, who cowered in the bed.

Then, sneering at his wife, he said, "What do you have to say, making a fool of yourself in front of Viviane's friends?"

Buggy did not answer. Caro could see her lips moving the way they often did, mumbling silent prayers to the Virgin.

Suddenly Buggy reached down and threw back the covers off of

Vivi. She was curled into a tight ball, her toes barely sticking out from under her flannel nightgown. The sight of Vivi broke Caro's heart.

Without speaking, Buggy picked up the ring and jammed it onto her daughter's finger. Vivi cried out in pain. Instinctively Caro reached out to grab Buggy's hand, but before she could, Buggy turned quickly around and walked out of the room.

Mr. Abbott followed. "Go to sleep, girls," was all the man said.

"Burn in hell," Caro said when the door had closed. "Rot and burn in hell."

If she could, Caro would have taken her friend Vivi away from that house. She would have spirited Vivi away from that house of hate to the Gulf Coast, where her parents had a cabin. She would have taken care of Vivi because she loved her. She would have cared for Queen Dancing Creek, who had so much life in her tightly coiled body.

The three girlfriends curled in the bed with Vivi. Caro pulled Vivi close and held her. Necie began to cry and Teensy began to curse.

"*Diablesse!*" Teensy said. "*Fils de garce!* Both of them, sons of bitches."

Necie climbed out of bed and returned with a handkerchief. Wiping Vivi's cheeks, she said, "Vivi, Honey, we love you. We love you so much."

Vivi did not speak. Caro could feel the pounding of her friend's heart. She cupped her hands around Vivi's cheeks.

"Oh, Pal," she said.

Then Caro got up and lit them each a cigarette.

Necie, still crying, cracked open the window.

"Come on, Vivi," Caro said, "let's smoke a cig and talk."

Vivi smoked the Lucky Strike that Caro handed her. She stared at her dresser, which was laden with corsages and notes, and a photo of her with Jack and the Ya-Yas together on the beach at the Gulf.

"Are you okay, sweetie-poo?" Necie asked.

"You shouldn't have to live here," Teensy told Vivi. "Come live with us. Genevieve would love it. And you *know* Jack would."

Vivi didn't say anything.

"Vivi," Caro said, "your mother is crazy and your father is crazy."

"She's not crazy," Teensy said. "She is a jealous bitch."

"My mother loves me," Vivi said.

"Well, let her *act* like she loves you, then!" Caro said. "You're her daughter."

"That ring is worth a whole lot of money," Teensy said, gently touching Vivi's hand.

"Father bought it for me," Vivi said. "He picked it out himself."

Something almost mechanical-sounding about Vivi's voice scared Caro.

"You can do whatever you want to with that ring," Teensy said. "You could sell it if you want."

Caro and Necie looked at Teensy.

"That ring is all yours," Caro said.

"It's like money in the bank," said Teensy.

Vivi nodded, and looked at her three friends. "How about that?" she said finally. "I'm rich, huh?"

"Yes," Caro said. "You are rich."

Vivi's midnight-blue velvet dress lay draped on the end of the window seat. The branches of the oak tree brushed against the windowpane. It was mid-December. The whole world was at war, and it was growing cold in Vivi's bedroom. The cigarette smoke drifted out the window into the night air.

If Mr. or Mrs. Abbott had stepped back in the room at that point, Caro would have jumped up and punched them, she would have knocked them down the stairs.

That night before she finally fell asleep next to Vivi, Caro swore she would wake in the middle of the night, sneak down the hall to the Abbotts' rooms, and do something horrible to them. She'd hurt them somehow, for hurting her friend.

But she slept though the night.

When Caro woke, Vivi had been up for hours. She already wore her tennis clothes. She was smiling. She was jumping around the room like she was already on the court. She was acting like nothing had happened. She was sixteen and a day.

Pushing herself up from the recliner, Caro walked into the bathroom, filled a glass with water, and swallowed a handful of vitamins. She poured a bit of sweet almond oil into her hand and smoothed it onto her deeply wrinkled face. As she slipped on her pajamas, she thought, I don't like to remember this stuff, Goddamn it. It makes me angry all over again. She pulled a cover from the end of her bed and spread it over her as she lay back in the recliner. Turning off the light, she checked one final time to make sure her inhaler was nearby.

Now Buggy and Taylor Abbott are gone, Caro thought, and the

Ya-Yas are old. When we die, will our children wish they could still get us back, the way I wish I'd had revenge on the Abbotts? Or will they have forgiven us all the tiny murders? When Siddalee wrote, asking Vivi for information on our lives together, I said: Vivi Dahlin, send it! What are you going to do with that scrapbook of old memories? I know you want to kill Sidda *and The New York Times*. But send it! Life is short, Pal. Life is so short.

20

For a week after Vivi's birthday ball, Buggy Abbott woke every morning in tears. When her youngest child, Jezie, with whom she shared a room, asked, "Mama got bo-bo?" Buggy could not answer.

Finally, Taylor Abbott told his wife, "If you're going to continue to behave like this, you will have to do it somewhere other than my house."

After that, she cried only in private, and made sure that her husband could not hear. Buggy Abbott cried alone, and prayed to the Virgin for an answer to the problem with her daughter.

Buggy was sure she received her answer in the form of a suggestion from one of the Altar Society women. One morning as they were starching the altar cloths, Buggy said: "I tell you, Mrs. Rabelais, I live in mortal fear for my daughter's soul."

"You ought to send her right up to Saint Augustine's in Alabama," Mrs. Rabelais said. "Those Saint Augustine nuns know how to straighten a girl out. They don't put up with foolishness. I send them money every year to keep up their work of purification."

An old Catholic boarding school in Spring Hill, Alabama, dating back to just after the Civil War, Saint Augustine's Academy was five hours from Thornton. It was known in four states as the place to enroll pious Catholic girls who were serious about doing penance. It was also the place to incarcerate girls whose parents thought needed a lesson in piety. And discipline.

Buggy waited until the house was empty. With Jezie down for a nap, she sat at the kitchen table and took a piece of stationery. She sipped on a cup of coffee and took pleasure at putting pen to paper. It had been a long time since she'd written anything other than grocery lists.

In a careful longhand, on plain white paper, after starting over four different times, Buggy completed the following letter. She mailed it as soon as Jezie woke from her nap:

December 31, 1942
322 Compton Street
Thornton, Louisiana

Mother Superior
Saint Augustine Academy
Spring Hill, Alabama

Dear Mother Superior:

I want to write a mother's letter to you about why you must take my daughter, Viviane Joan Abbott, into the academy at midterm. I am not a writer, Sister, but with God's and our Blessed Mother's help, I will do my best.

My daughter has gotten in with a fast crowd of hooligans. The pack of girlfriends she runs with just encourage her vanity. She pays no attention to me, her mother. Vivi and these girls are thick as thieves, Mother Superior, and bad influences on each other. They smoke and curse and flaunt themselves and have no shame. And the public high school treats them like pagan princesses. These girls put their friendship before their love for God the Father. I fear for the loss of my daughter's soul with all this popularity that has been heaped on her at the high school.

They build her up too much, Sister. They made Viviane Joan a cheerleader and Most Popular and Cutest and on the tennis team and the school newspaper. It is too much for such a young girl. Thornton High School is not a bad school. My boy does just fine there. But my daughter is in great danger. They encourage vanity in her to the point where she thinks she does not need to prostrate herself at the feet of the Mother of Mercy, Advocate and Refuge of Sinners.

There is not a sign of God in my daughter's bedroom. Everywhere I turn there is nothing but pom-poms, tennis rackets, and pictures of movie stars. And photographs of the boy she thinks she's in love with, everywhere. She worships false gods, Sister. She is running out of grace.

My husband, Mr. Taylor Abbott, Attorney-at-Law and a non-Catholic, has spoilt Viviane rotten since she was old enough to pout. Ever since I had Jezie, my late-in-life baby, Mr. Abbott has gotten worse. He gave Viviane a diamond ring, Sister, when she is only sixteen years old. He should have never done that. A diamond ring is for your wife in Holy Matrimony, not for your young daughter.

She is too much under Mr. Abbott's influence. He is an Episcopal, Sister, and he is nothing but a socializer. He drinks rum and runs with the crowd that raises the Tennessee Walking Horses. He is not the man I thought he was when we were young.

I had to go against him to even have my baby Jezie. It is not my fault that I cannot propagate the faith as I promised I would when I married. I do penance every day for only offering God three children.

Sister, I do not know the exact sins my daughter has committed. My husband has forbidden me to talk about it. Sister, a mother can only imagine the worst kind of impurities. Mr. Abbott tells me to stop dwelling on it; he says a wife should obey her husband. But I can't help it. I have a dwelling kind of mind.

Mother Superior, it is not what my daughter has done to *me*. It is what she has done to Holy Mother Church, to the Blessed Virgin Herself, that pains me so. If Viviane had only hurt me, I would not be writing to you as I am doing now.

Viviane needs to learn self-sacrifice, she needs to be near others who are chaste and pure in body and soul. She needs the discipline only the nuns of Saint Augustine's can give her.

Your academy must take my daughter. I give thanks to the Queen of Heaven that such a place as Saint Augustine's Academy exists.

I beg you, Mother Superior, in your wisdom, please allow my daughter to enter the academy as soon as possible. Do not hesitate, but act fast in Our Lady's name so that we may save my daughter. She is a flower made by God, but she is wilting. And if I do not remove her from the temptations of the world, she will die before she has had the chance to bloom in the spirit.

Yours in the name of Christ through
the intercession of the Blessed Virgin,
Mrs. Taylor C. Abbott

P.S. My husband and I understand that you are in the process of expanding the living quarters of the teaching sisters. We look forward to mailing a donation to the Saint Augustine's Building Fund as soon as Viviane is situated in her classes.

21

When Sidda found two packets of letters in the scrapbook addressed to her mother at Saint Augustine's, she experienced something akin to what an archeologist feels when she stumbles onto an important find. The first letter was from Necie, and on the back of the envelope there were the faint imprints of three pairs of lips.

When Sidda opened the envelope, the words on the page flew out at her like angry, mixed-up birds. There were smears at the edges of the paper, and, where the writer had borne down hard on the page, there were splotches of ink. Sidda began to read.

January 21, 1943

Dearest Darling Vivi,

Oh, Honey, I never thought my first letter of 1943
would be so sad. I thought this was going to be the
year we won the war and instead it's the year we lose
you. It breaks my heart into a million pieces on the
kitchen floor to think that you left town on that train

like you aren't even loved, *which you are.* We're over
here at Caro's now. Mr. Bob tried to cheer us up with
three free passes to see *To Be or Not to Be*, but we can't
be cheered up.

Your big brother was so blue himself. I have never
seen Pete so low. When he and Caro came by the
house this morning, I just burst into tears and climbed
into the car—in my pajamas—and went with them
over to Teensy's. Pete apologized over and over that he
had to be the one who drove you to the train station
with none of your thousands of friends to see you off!
When he told me about it, he was almost crying himself. Oh, Vivi, Sweetie-poo, we would have all been
there at the station to see you off. We had all kinds of
things planned. There is a shoe box full of pralines and
sour-cream cookies that I baked for you sitting on the
counter right now. I had it all wrapped and everything, and now you are on your way to the nuns with
no sign of our love. Oh, I am crying all over again.

We all went by your house at a little before noon,
to the kitchen door like always. We were going to tell
your mother where to get off. But the door was *locked.*
We knocked and hollered until Buggy finally came
downstairs, and when she came to the door, she was
crying. That made us think twice about cussing her
out. She told us she was sick.

"*Mais oui,*" Teensy said. "We are all sick. We are
sick in our hearts at losing Vivi." And then your
mother said she had to get back in bed because she
thought she might faint. Caro started to say something, but I stopped her, and then we left.

Oh, Vivi, we are so torn up, like part of our own
body just got ripped away.

Please don't think for one second that we wouldn't
have been there kissing you and holding you and begging for you to stay home with us where you belong.

Love and kisses and prayers,
Necie

P.S. I am running to the post office with this. Caro
and Teensy are going to write their letters after they
calm down some. They have been sitting on your back
porch with your brother, Pete, smoking cigarettes in
the freezing cold and crying. Caro wants to go back
and let your mother have it, whether she's sick or not.
Oh, Honey, we love you so much.

Sidda felt like she'd stepped into another world. Carrying the letters with her to the sofa, she sat down, taking great pains to unfold
each page with care. She read on.

January 21, 1943

Stinky—

Sis, I'm sorry. I woulda just about rather driven into a
nest of Japs than drive you to the station this morning.
  You make them treat you good up there, you hear.
Stick em with my pocketknife if they give you any
trouble.

Love from your brother,
Pete

P.S. Caro told Mother if the sisters of Saint Goddamn
Augustine mess around with you, they'll have the
Sisters of Saint Ya-Ya to deal with. Mother just ran
back to bed and didn't say a word.

Finally, Sidda opened a Western Union envelope to find the following telegram:

JANUARY 22 1943.

MISS VIVI ABBOTT-SAINT AUGUSTINE'S ACADEMY
SPRING HILL ALABAMA-CHER-WE LOVE YOU-CALL IF
YOU NEED ANYTHING AT ALL-QUE LE BON DIEU VOUS
BENIT REAL GOOD-GENEVIEVE ST. CLAIR WHITMAN.

Sidda set the first packet of letters down and stood up to stretch. Hueylene sat staring out the glass doors, her gaze trained on a pair of noisy Northwest crows that were fighting over some imagined slight. Turning back to the letters, Sidda picked up a larger stack of envelopes that was bound by a piece of faded blue ribbon.

April 22, 1943

Dear Vivi,

We haven't heard from you in ten days. Are you all right? I have written you four letters. Haven't you gotten them? Pal, we are worried.

Damn your parents for doing this. Your mother should be shot.

Make contact, Queen Dancing Creek.

XXX
We love you.
Caro

❧

April 24, 1943

Vivi Cher,

I think maybe my last two letters didn't reach you because I refused to put "Joan" on the envelope. But this time I did, even though I hate to. But I want to make sure that you get this. Baby doll, I had a scary dream about you last night and I woke up crying. I told *Maman* about it, and she said to try and call you up. So we tried to call you first thing this morning and the nun wouldn't put us through. She said students were only allowed calls from their family, and then only on Sundays. What *is* this place that they won't let you talk to the people who love you? *Maman* got on the phone and tried to talk some sense into that nun, but she wouldn't listen. *Maman* is worried. You know, she went to the nuns too when she was a girl, but it was never like this. She says you must have some bad ones up there. Jack says your letters still sound cheery, but I know that's just because you're putting on a good face for him. We think *you're* the one that needs cheering up, *Bébé*.

Maman wants to know how she can help. Should she try to talk to your parents? Please let us know.

Mais oui, Vivi, we miss you so much you can't imagine. There has been a big hole cut out of us. Our whole *communauté des soeurs* is suffering. And it's not just the Ya-Yas who feel this way. Our whole class is not the same without you. School spirit has gone straight down the toilet. Even Anne Snobby-Butt McWaters and her crowd ask about you all the time.

I don't know who I miss more, you or my brother off in uniform. I can tell you this, with the two of you gone and this war raging all over my head, I am one blue girl. Write back right away.

XXXOOO
Teensy

P.S. Did you receive the package with the *Silver Screens*? I'm so so sorry I haven't been able to get my hands on more hooch to send. I'll keep trying.

Sidda frowned as she pictured the young Vivi wrenched from her tender sisterhood and deposited like damaged freight at a convent school. As she carefully folded the letters back into their envelopes, she longed to fold the sixteen-year-old Vivi into her arms and comfort her. She longed to hold her mother, full-bloom flower ripped by the roots and thrown onto unfriendly soil. She longed to hold her mother and call her by her true name.

If Caro, Teensy, and Necie were this shook up by Vivi's departure, what must Vivi herself have been feeling? Sidda wondered. What were her mother's letters like? If only she could hear her mother's side of the story. Sidda stood up from her place at the table in the big room where she had been reading.

Her neck was tense, and she rubbed it and shook her shoulders. All life, all history happens in the body. *I am learning about the woman who carried me inside of hers.*

Sidda needed to move. She snapped the leash onto Hueylene and headed out for a walk along the lake, then into the forest, where the midmorning sunlight filtered down through the thick canopy.

With each step Sidda took, she thought of her mother. What had happened? Why was Vivi shipped off in the first place? What could she possibly have done that would have merited this punishment? She held deep reservoirs of anger toward her mother, not just because of her latest withdrawal of love, but for earlier, older hurts. Yet, as she walked, Sidda experienced her anger dissolve into grief and anger *for* her mother. Then, just as soon, the emotion switched back into anger toward Vivi.

She concentrated on putting one foot in front of the other. She thought about her mother's body and about her own body, and how they were so much alike. She thought about her legs as they strode forward. She thought about how her legs connected to her trunk. She thought that she was not a person with a body; she *was* her body, a body that had spent nine months inside Vivi's body. And as she walked, feeling the ground beneath her feet, and hearing the happy breathing of her dog alongside her, Sidda wondered about the subliminal knowledge that passes between a mother and a daughter. The preverbal knowledge, the stories told without words, flowing like blood, like rich oxygen, into the placenta of the baby girl as she grows in dark containment. Sidda wondered if, forty years later, she was not still receiving information from her mother through some psychic cord that linked them, thousands of miles, and countless misunderstandings apart from each other.

It was a cool, rainy day, with mist rising among the towering hulks of evergreen trees. As she stepped forward, her eye caught an intricate, lacy dead hemlock branch that hung in front of her. Each tip on every one of its tiny, feathery branches ended in a droplet of water, as if set with diamonds, like the delicate fabric of a party dress suspended in air. The exposed roots of a tree that ran across the trail, purple-black in their wetness, looked like the raised veins on an old woman's hands. Or like the tributaries and meanderings of the Garnet River as seen from a crop duster high above the delta farms. As she walked over Mother Earth, Sidda prayed: *Stretch me wide so that the divine secrets that lay inside my mother, inside myself, inside the earth itself will find room enough in me to bear fruit.*

∝

Buggy had woken Vivi in the morning when it was still dark.
"Viviane Joan," she said, flicking on the overhead light, "wake up.
Wake up this instant."

The light hurt Vivi's eyes, and the sound of her mother's hard
voice made her stomach tighten. She hugged her pillow and tried to
hold on to sleep. She had been dreaming about dancing with Jack in
Marksville. It was green summer and she was wearing a white dress.
She could feel his palm against the small of her back and smell his
breath as their cheeks touched.

"Viviane Joan," Buggy said, flinging Vivi's full name out like an
accusation. "Get up and get dressed." Buggy bent down to pick up
some of Vivi's clothes from the floor. "Your father has decided you
need to take the early train."

"What?" Vivi asked, bolting up in bed, shocked.

This can't be, she thought.

"But, Mother," she said, "everything is planned for the afternoon
train. That's when everybody's seeing me off. I'm supposed to take the
2:56. We have it all *planned*."

"You heard me," Buggy said, sighing as she reached under the bed
and pulled out one of Vivi's saddle shoes.

"Father decided this?" Vivi asked. She could hardly breathe. How
could her father have betrayed her like this?

"Yes," Buggy said, without looking at Vivi. "Get up. I need to strip
your bed."

Vivi got out of bed and stood beside it, her feet cold against the
floor, her body longing for the warm covers. There was something different about Buggy this morning, something in her voice, an excitement. Buggy was already dressed in her clothes for Mass, and the
chapel veil was on her head.

Buggy flung back the covers, then the sheets. Efficient as a hospital nurse, she whipped the pillows out of their cases, and peeled back
the cotton mattress pad.

With each gesture, Buggy signaled the overwhelming rage she felt
toward her daughter. Silently, and with every flick of the linens,
Buggy rejected Vivi's firm, flowering adolescent body, which had,
until moments before, warmed the bed.

Although no words were spoken, Vivi felt all this as she stood
watching her mother. Instinctively, she crossed her hands over her

breasts, as though she needed an armor stronger than her flannel nightgown to safeguard herself from Buggy.

"When did Father decide this?" Vivi asked. "He didn't say anything about it to me last night."

"Your father does not have to tell you everything," Buggy said. "You are not his wife. He told me just before he went to bed. He wants you on the 5:03 this morning."

Buggy gathered the pillows underneath her arms, raising her chin slightly, as though she were waiting to see how her daughter would take this. At first Vivi said nothing. Mother and daughter stood glaring at each other, muscles tensed for action in a battle neither understood.

For a fleeting moment, it occurred to Vivi that her mother might be lying. But the thought was so horrible she could not make an accusation.

Instead, she said, "I want to take that little pillow with me, please," and pointed to a small goose-down pillow that Delia had made with Ginger's help. Delia had given it to Vivi, along with a silk pillowcase, before the war made such luxuries as silk *verboten*.

"You don't need this," Buggy said, squeezing the pillow tightly to her chest. "They'll have pillows at Saint Augustine's."

"I want that pillow," Vivi said. "It was a gift from Delia."

As Vivi said this, she would have given anything if her grandmother had been in the room at that moment. She had written Delia as soon as Buggy had started up about Saint Augustine's, but Delia was visiting with Miss Lee Beaufort at her ranch in Texas, and she had not responded. Vivi imagined that if Delia had only been there she would have protected her. But Delia was never there. Vivi wanted to turn on her mother, slap her, kick her, denounce her for her cruelty and unfairness.

"Is Father downstairs?" Vivi asked.

"No, he is not," Buggy answered. "Your father is still sleeping. He is exhausted, Viviane Joan. You have worn him out."

Taylor Abbott had spoken very little since the night of Vivi's birthday. When Buggy first brought up the idea of Saint Augustine's, he had tried only once to veto the idea.

"We can clip Vivi's wings just as well here at home as they can in Alabama," Vivi's father had said. "Girls' schools are strange breeding grounds."

Buggy refused to be silenced. She didn't back down to him as she usually did. Taylor Abbott didn't so much agree to Saint Augustine's as finally turn around, walk into his study, and close the door on the subject.

Just the night before, Vivi had gone to her father in the living room, where he sat in his chair listening to the war news on the radio.

She waited until a radio advertisement came on before she spoke. "Father, may I interrupt you?"

Everyone in the Abbott household always had to ask permission before speaking to Taylor Abbott.

"Yes, Viviane, you may," he said, still half listening to the radio.

Vivi had meant to be controlled, present her case logically, in a way that would please her father the lawyer. Instead, she blurted it out, her voice quivering.

"Must I really go, Father? Do I have to? Must I get on that train tomorrow afternoon? Please, Father. You could stop this from happening. You know Mother has to do what you say."

He looked at her for a moment, and Vivi felt some hope.

"It's already arranged, Viviane," he said. "You are going to Saint Augustine's."

Immediately Vivi adjusted her body so that she stood more erect. She grabbed control of her voice.

I have to compose myself, she thought, or he will not listen. If only I could be poised, if only I can smile in that way he likes, if only I can speak in the unruffled tone he admires, then Father might see me. One true glimpse is all I need. One true glimpse and he will understand that he cannot ship me away.

But when she opened her mouth, the words tumbled out in a desperate gush.

"Father, please, please," she said, on the verge of tears. "I will do anything you want. Just please don't make me leave."

Taylor Abbott looked at his daughter as she stood in front of him, her blonde hair pulled back in a scarf, her pajama top slightly askew so that one freckled shoulder was partly revealed. Her lips quivered, her eyes brimmed with tears that had not yet spilled over. Her skin looked sallow, almost blue around the eyes; her sweet paleness now looked anemic to him, a gardenia bruised around the edges. He could not bear such raw emotion; it made him physically ill. It was what he hated about his wife, along with the sweat, the smell, the blood every month.

"Vivi," Taylor Abbott said, "never beg."

Then he reached to the radio and turned the volume up. Leaning back in his chair, he closed his eyes and resumed listening to the war news, as though his daughter were no longer in the room.

Vivi continued to stand there, studying the patterns of the living-room rug. She listened to all the news of the British and Indian troops in Burma. Finally, Taylor Abbott opened his eyes and trained them on his daughter.

In a confident voice, he said, "You'll do fine, Viviane. I don't worry about you. Don't have to. You take after the Abbotts."

Then he stood up, turned off the radio, and started up the stairs. All Vivi could see was his back. All she could see was a pair of suspenders and a white shirt.

"Hurry up and get dressed," Buggy said as she stood at Vivi's bedroom door. "You have just enough time to make the train. Pete is taking you to the station."

"What about Father?" Vivi asked. "Isn't he coming? I want to tell him goodbye."

"Your father asked not to be awakened, Viviane Joan. Please. Do not cause any more trouble than you already have."

"But I won't be able to see the Ya-Yas, Mother. I *can't* leave without telling them goodbye. We had our goodbye all *planned*."

"The four of you have been saying goodbye for a week now."

"The Ya-Yas are my best friends, Mother. I *have* to see them."

Suddenly, as though she could not contain her rage any longer, Buggy took the pillows and bedding she'd just stripped from the bed and flung them at Vivi.

"Stop it!" Buggy said, vehement, resentful. "I won't hear one more word about the all-precious Ya-Yas! Are they all you think about?!"

"Mama," Vivi said, dropping the more formal way she usually addressed her mother. "Don't do this, please. They're my best friends. I can't just leave them like this!"

Buggy straightened the waist of her dress, then adjusted her sweater. "Haven't you caused enough suffering in this house? Enough is enough."

As her mother left the doorway Vivi thought, *Enough is not enough, Mother: And it never will be.*

The Buick was warm when Pete opened the car door for Vivi.

"Warmed her up so you wouldn't freeze," he said. "Buggy the Bitch still inside?"

"Checking on Jezie," Vivi replied. "Maybe we'll miss the train."

Pete checked his wristwatch, then went around to get in on the driver's side. He looked serious, his usual athletic swagger replaced by a heaviness.

He pulled the car door tight, then turned to his sister. "Want a smoke?"

"Yeah," Vivi said. She watched as her brother lit two Luckies off a kitchen match, which he struck on his thumbnail.

"Sorry I'm the one that has to drive you, Buddy," he said as he handed over a cigarette to his sister.

"Not your fault," Vivi said, taking a deep drag.

Pete picked a speck of tobacco off his tongue. "Not *your* fault any of this shit is happening."

"What do you mean?" Vivi asked.

"I mean nothing you ever did deserves getting crated off to the penguins like Goddamn freight, Vivi."

Vivi tried to smile. "Mother ever knew we called nuns 'penguins,' she'd croak."

"Nah," Pete said. "She'd do penance for us. Shit, that woman loves doing penance."

Pete patted his jacket as though he were checking for something. Then he inspected the rearview mirror, nervous. "She's been wanting to punish you for years."

Vivi counted the pieces of luggage that were in the backseat. She looked out at the yard, Buggy's garden almost dead in winter. The Rose of Montana and clematis vines on the porch were shriveled and brown.

"What're you saying, Pete?" Vivi asked.

"Sis, I'm your bud, you know that, don't you?"

"Yeah, I know that."

"Trust me, then. Look out for Mother. She's gunnin' for you. Keep your elbows out."

She is my mother, Vivi thought. *She loves me. Doesn't she?*

Pete reached over and took Vivi's hand, squeezing it tightly. He looked at her with sad eyes and shrugged his shoulders. "Gonna miss you, Stinky."

Then, pulling his hand away, he reached under his jacket and pulled out a flask. "For the trip. Swiped expressly for you from Father's liquor cabinet."

Vivi received the flask like a sign of love. She tucked it into her purse. "I'll carry it with me like a friend."

As she kissed Pete on the cheek, she could see her mother in her gray coat making her way toward the car.

"I will say nothing about the smoking," Buggy accused her children, as she positioned herself in the backseat.

"Good, Mother," Pete said. "Don't."

Once settled, Buggy began to hum softly. Vivi thought the tune sounded like "Salve Regina." Pete began to whistle, to drown out the sound. As they rode, Vivi pulled down the vanity mirror, as if to see if there was something in her eye. But it was not her own face she wanted to see. She wanted to see the face of her mother as she sat silent in the backseat. Vivi did not know what she was looking for, but she thought that if the right expression passed over her mother's face, then she would know the right thing to say, the right thing to do, the right way to *be* in order to sidestep this banishment.

I want to tell her to shut up her crazy humming, Vivi thought. I want to bash her in the head with one of my suitcases. I want to truss her up with ropes like a cow, and drop her in a ditch on the side of the road. Then seize the wheel myself, whip this car around, blast the horn up and down the streets of my town, declaring my freedom from that woman in the backseat who thinks she's a modern martyr.

But Vivi could not move. She was too sad.

It required all the strength she had to ask, "Can we just stop by Caro's? They wake up early. Or could we swing by Teensy's real quick? It's on the way. Sometimes Genevieve reads all night long when she can't sleep."

"You do not barge into someone's house at this time of day," Buggy said. "Your father gave specific instructions that we were to go straight to the station."

You are lying, Vivi longed to say, but she could not. To say it out loud would be to admit her mother's cruelty.

Vivi glanced down at her gold Gruen wristwatch, with its green dots glowing with poison. Four-fifteen in the morning. Nothing will ever be the same.

She studied her mother sitting in the high, rounded backseat of the Buick, fingering her rosary beads.

She is lying through her teeth, Vivi thought. She is lying and she is happy. Why is she so serene?

∾

It was still dark when they reached the train station at Jefferson and Eighth streets. Pete climbed out of the car and went around to open Vivi's door.

As she stood on the curb by the car Vivi could see her breath in the early-morning air. Watching as Pete ferried her luggage into the lobby, she pressed her purse to her side and thought of the flask of bourbon. The anticipation of its comfort kept her from crumbling to the ground.

Rolling down the window, Buggy said, "Aren't you going to tell me goodbye?"

"Goodbye," Vivi said.

Then Buggy opened the backdoor. She turned her body slightly, as though she might climb out of the car and go to her daughter.

Vivi longed to run to her mother and bury her head in Buggy's lap. She longed to hold on to her mother and not let go. Leaning into the car, touching her mother's hand, she asked, "Mama, what are you praying for?"

Buggy placed her hand on Vivi's cheek. In a gentle voice, she said, "I'm praying for you, Viviane. I'm praying for you because you've run out of grace."

Then Pete's hand was under Vivi's elbow, pulling her upright, all but tucking her under his shoulder.

"Ma," he said, "get the hell off my sister's back."

Then he slammed the car door, leaving his mother in the backseat with her rosary.

Inside, the lobby was empty except for four sleeping soldiers, their feet propped on duffel bags. The sight of them made Vivi think of Jack.

After buying her ticket, she and Pete sat on one of the long wooden benches. Vivi tried to imagine she was in a movie. *The beautiful young girl misses her lover,* she thought. *The camera comes closer. She sits in a train station with her brother, waiting for the war to end. Heartsick and lonely, she reaches for the only comfort she has.*

Checking the door to make sure her mother had not decided to come in, Vivi took out the flask and offered it to Pete.

"You first, Buddy-o," he said, and Vivi took a swig.

The bourbon went down smoothly. She waited a moment, then took another swig, feeling the warmth spread through her body, associating the taste of the whiskey with good times, with being desired, with what little she knew about sex. At her third sip, Vivi was wishing she had yet another flask—no, a bottle or two—tucked into her luggage.

She passed the flask to Pete, who took a sip and handed it back to her.

"Gimme your hand," he said.

Vivi put out her palm. Into it Pete slapped a compact, weighty little object. Vivi looked down to see his pocketknife, a prized possession of his she'd always admired. She could feel the knife's red-and-silver heft. She held it to her nose and smelled the handle. It smelled like Pete. It smelled like *boy*.

"A buddy should never be without a pocketknife, Viv-o. It can get you out of all kind of jams. If one of those penguins sits on you, stick her in the battookus with your pocketknife, and run like hell!"

Vivi tried to smile. "Thanks, Pete-o."

Then, with the time she had left, Vivi carved her name into the wooden bench where they sat.

"V-I-V-I A-B-B-O-T-T," she gouged into the wood.

"The Vivi Abbott Memorial Bench," Pete said.

"Now nobody can forget me," Vivi said.

Pete boarded the train with her, carrying her train case. When Vivi was settled into her seat, he gave her a rough hug. "Love you, Stinky," he said.

"Love you, Pete."

Pete turned to the black porter who was squeezing by at that moment. "Yall take care of my little sister, you hear? You're traveling with precious cargo."

"Yassir," the porter said, giving Vivi a smile.

After Pete climbed down from the train, Vivi reached for the flask, took two swallows of bourbon, then began to cry.

Viviane Joan Abbott, age sixteen, sat on the Southern Crescent wearing a baby-blue angora sweater over a cream-colored pleated skirt. She pulled her navy wool coat with the lovely fox collar tight around her body. She tried to believe that her own arms were Jack's holding her close. She tried hard to believe that everyone adored her.

January 26, 1943

Dear Caro,

Every single girl at this school is ugly. I do not mean plain, I do not mean homely. I mean *ugly*. This is one of those schools where there are two types of girls: (1) the daughters of Catholic nuts; and (2) bad girls who they want to punish. I guess I fit in both categories.

They're all ugly and they stink. The whole joint reeks like sauerkraut and old men's socks. The odor alone is enough penance for eighty-four thousand mortal sins. Obey the Church, confess your sins, and die, that's the plan. It all comes down from the Mother Superior, the Boris Karloff of the nun world.

My room here is not a room. It's not even a cubby-hole. It's a pen, a hole, a cell. It has a cot, a chair, and a water basin on top of a small chest of drawers. Hooks on the wall, no closet.

I asked the nun who brought me here where my closet was. She said, "You have no closet." Like I had asked for a suite at the Grand Hotel.

"I *need* to hang my dresses," I said, pointing to my suitcases and footlocker.

She looked at me like I had a harelip.

"That luggage is your cross to bear," she said.

Caro, I do not know whether I am in purgatory or just plain hell.

Love,
Vivi

It took Vivi a week at Saint Augustine's to realize the girls hated her. It took her a week and a half to realize the nuns did, too.

She tried smiling at first, but it was a waste of face muscles. Nobody, not one person, would smile back. They looked her up and down and whispered malicious things she couldn't quite make out. Vivi's hair was too blonde for them, her eyes too bright, her language too jazzy, and above all, they hated the clothes she'd brought. She tried, but Vivi could not locate any other bad girls to become buddies with.

The hallways smelled like oatmeal with Lysol stirred in. The very air made Vivi cringe. Vivi lived by her sense of smell. She could tell when people were scared, or if they had eaten peaches, just by their scent. She could sniff and tell whether a person had gotten enough sleep the night before by breathing them in. She could smell the scent of tuberoses in a person's hair days after they had been near those flowers. There weren't any tuberoses at Saint Augustine's.

Sister Fermin, who taught Religion, delighted in introducing lessons by looking at Vivi and saying: "For those of you girls who have been sent here because of sinful behavior, pay special attention. You do not deserve God's love after the pain you have caused your families, but if you study hard and keep ever present in your heart the shame you carry, in time you may be welcomed back into the light of God the Father's love."

Then the other girls would turn around and gawk at Vivi like she was a child murderer or a Nazi. Vivi wanted to tell them all to go straight to hell, but it was not worth the effort.

Vivi set her footlocker up in her cell, and on top of it she placed the photograph of Jack and her at the Thornton High Mardi Gras Ball. Next to that, she arranged photos of the Ya-Yas at Spring Creek and at the Gulf Coast. The little basket of dried rose petals from the roses Jack sent her the day he left for boot camp sat in front of the picture of her family.

Lifting her blue velvet birthday gown from the trunk, she pinned it up on the wall of her cell, where it bloomed like a huge flower above the crucifix that was standard issue in every Saint Augustine room. She had to have something colorful in there or she would die. When she came back to her cell after the chalk dust and freezing cold class-rooms and the cafeteria that smelled like green peas covered in mold, Vivi took little nips from Pete's flask, and stared at that wall, trying to make a party.

Thank God she'd snuck Delia's feather pillow from home. *They do not sleep on pillows here. Pillows are against the rules.* This scared Vivi more than the puke-green color all the walls were painted. Every morning she woke in that penitentiary, she had to actually hide her pillow so the proctor nun would not take it away from her.

Screw them, Vivi prayed. Screw them and the horse they rode in on. Don't let them get me. I am Vivi Abbott. I am a member of the Royal Tribe of Ya-Yas. I am a cheerleader. I am going to play at Wimbledon someday. I have a perfectly wonderful boy who loves me. Where I come from, I am popular.

> *Holy Mother, full of gracious virtues, patient and well taught, give me strength against my enemies. Make these headaches go away. Send me a touch, a smoke, a kiss, a hug. Help me not to shrivel up and die.*

March 1, 1943

Dear Caro, Teensy, and Necie:

It's been five weeks and three days. I am entombed here. I cannot breathe. They wake us by pounding on the door of our cell at five in the morning. I am supposed to splash cold water on my face, take off my gown, put on my gray scratchy wool uniform, pull on the gray knee socks and the oxfords, tie my chapel veil on my head, and walk straight to the chapel without saying a word. A priest with bulging eyes says Mass and hears Confession. No singing, no music, no dancing at all. This is the longest I have gone without dancing since I was born. Even Mother never minded our dancing. When I take Communion, the host sticks to the roof of my dry mouth.

They only allow you to use *two squares of toilet paper* in this place because *waste is a sin.* They monitor you in the john. There are girls here who beg to be bathroom monitors. They think it is something great, like being elected class president. That's how sick this place is.

No such thing as a bath here, only showers that feel like someone spitting on you. No Ya-Yas. No Jack. I would commit murder for the café au lait that Shirley brings us in bed at Teensy's in the big bowls, sweetened with honey. I would commit double murder to see the three of you and Jack.

No one laughs here.

I am parched. I am drying up.

Please ask Pete to talk to Father about me. I've written to Mother, but have received no response.

I shouldn't complain like this with a war going on. I don't know why they want me so miserable.

Your Vivi,

P.S. Get your hands on hooch and send it soon.

Then she wrote her mother a variation of the same letter she had written several times since she arrived at Saint Augustine's:

March 1, 1943

Dear Mother,

Please forgive me. I am not sure what I have done wrong, but I am sorry. I never meant to hurt you. If you let me come home, I will not disappoint you. Please, Mother. Please let me come home. I miss you, I miss everyone so very much.

Love,
Vivi

After she'd been at Saint Augustine's a little over a month, food began to repulse Vivi. Everything tasted too salty. For four days straight, she became nauseated after eating the oatmeal served at breakfast, and after that she simply sat and pushed the oats around in the stained bowl. She sipped her juice and pushed the oats around.

At lunch, the soup was as salty as the oatmeal, so she stopped eating that as well. In the evenings, the limp cabbage smelled like her baby sister Jezie's diapers. The only food Vivi ate with relish was the apple they were given with supper. She took it back to her cubicle, opened the window, and set the fruit on the windowsill until it grew chilled with the night air. Then she took out Pete's pocketknife and divided the fruit into tiny slivers, placing them in her mouth one at a time. She'd have given anything for a full flask of bourbon.

After she ate the apple, Vivi lay on the hard bed, with the core of the apple on Delia's feather pillow, next to her head, so she could smell it while she slept.

She ached for her girlfriends, for Jack, Genevieve, Cokes and po-boys, and Gene Krupa drum solos. She missed the sweet strains of Harry James and talking every day with the Ya-Yas and lying next to them on the rug in front of the fireplace or out on the porch. She missed attention and music and laughter and gossip. She missed playing cards with Pete in the kitchen at night. She even missed her mother and father. She missed home so deeply that she finally began to give up.

She stopped writing letters, and when letters came, she dreaded reading them because they reminded her of what she was missing. The war news only made her sadder, made her worry about Jack. She felt like she was slipping away, but trying to hold on wore her out. As the weeks passed, she grew exhausted just walking up a flight of stairs.

One afternoon in April she received the only letter her mother wrote her at Saint Augustine's. It read:

April 24, 1943

Dear Joan,

I am glad to hear they now call you by your saint's name. It was your father and Delia who named you Viviane, not me.

Mother Superior wrote me about her session with you last week. Because she is concerned with your spiritual welfare, she has decided it is God's will that from this day forward you will be known only by your saint name: Joan. The other girls have been instructed to use only that name. You will only answer to Joan. Any mail sent to Viviane or Vivi will be returned, unopened, to the sender.

It is hoped that by invoking the name of Joan of Arc you may be more successful in battling the demon that plagues your soul.

Mother Superior also reported how you defied her, how you tried to joke and say you were relieved your saint name was not Hedwig. She also told me that you referred to her as a "warthog." I can only say that I agree wholeheartedly with Mother Superior that public school has damaged your respect for sanctity and for authority. You are in grave need of discipline.

No, I cannot let you come home. You will get used to Saint Augustine's. It will simply take time. You must offer up any discomforts to Our Holy Savior, who died for our sins.

You wrote that you are sorry for hurting me. You need to understand that nothing you do can hurt me. It is the Blessed Virgin and the Baby Jesus who you hurt. They are the ones you should get down on your knees to and beg forgiveness from. May the Lord our God bless you and may the Virgin Mary guide you in everything you do.

Love,
Mother

That afternoon Vivi fainted during gym class. Her legs buckled underneath her and she drifted to the ground, her knees hitting the old varnished floor. It felt almost pleasant to simply let go like that.

The nun who taught physical education was terse, businesslike about the event, seeming almost to blame Vivi for such weakness.

Vivi was allowed to return to her room for the rest of the day, where she plunged into a feverish sleep. When she woke, she was sweating so profusely that her sheets were wet against her skin. The headache that had been circling for weeks settled in like a conquering enemy. She tried to get out of bed, but the room and its sparse furnishings were reeling. She could not make anything stay solid or still. Not inside or out.

Alternating waves of hot and cold washed over her, and she knew she needed to get herself to the bathroom. Vivi forced herself to get out of the bed, but her legs would not hold. Remaining on her knees, she crawled to the door. Shaking violently, she tried once again to stand. This time her legs stayed under her, but she could not get her equilibrium. She felt as though some central ball bearing inside her that made balance possible had been knocked loose.

Vivi slowly made her way down the hall by leaning against the wall, the door knobs to the other girls' rooms jabbing into her side. It took all she had to make it to the bathroom stall. Never had she been this sick before. Kneeling with her head over the commode, she was so violently ill that the contractions sent pain into her neck and back. Her head throbbed so that she no longer saw shapes, only patches of gray and black. She felt as if she were being turned inside out, as if she were being scoured.

At some point, the stall door opened, and Vivi almost cried with relief. Someone is coming to help me! she thought. Someone kind is coming to pull my hair out of my face, and lay a cool cloth on my forehead like Mother does when I am sick.

"You have been in there for too long," the voice said. "I am going to report you to Mother Superior for being wasteful with toilet paper, Joan Abbott."

Vivi lay on the floor and could not respond.

When she first began to stir, it was to the sound of tree branches scratching lightly against a window. It sounded like her bedroom at home, and the belief that she was back in her own bed rushed through her sore body. For an instant Vivi felt like laughing out loud. The bed was soft, and she lay back on not one but two pillows. For some reason she felt utterly convinced that if she didn't jump up immediately she'd be late for a tennis game with Caro.

When she opened her eyes, Vivi expected to see the armoire and dresser that sat in her bedroom at home. She expected to see the chintz curtains with the roses and green trailing leaves. Instead, what she glimpsed was a white curtain stretched along one side of the bed in which she found herself. On the other side was a bank of windows with shutters closed tight.

For a moment, she felt dazed. And then it struck her: she was not at home at all. She did not know where she was, but she knew it wasn't home.

She began to cry until tears soaked her face, her hair, her gown. She did not remember putting on the gown she wore, did not recognize it. She needed terribly to blow her nose, but she did not have a handkerchief. She could not bear the thought, but she decided she was going to have to blow her nose on the sheets.

God, she sighed. I do not want to lie in a bed of snot. I want to die. I want to fall back asleep and never wake up.

Then the white curtain that ran alongside the bed was pulled back, and Vivi looked up to see a round, smiling face, young and almost pretty. A pair of rimless glasses sat on a small, upturned nose. The gray-blue eyes were slightly almond-shaped, with the lightest lashes and brows. Around the edges of the veil, Vivi thought she could see a light dusting of the same light hair.

"How are you feeling, Viviane Joan?" the nun asked, smiling.

It was the first time anyone had called her by her real name in over a month. It was the first smile anyone had given her since the porter when she'd got off the train.

"Are you a Saint Augustine's nun?" Vivi asked, her voice hoarse. Her habit and veil were different from the rest of the sisters at the school, and the fact that she was smiling was something of a shock.

"I'm from a different order—a nursing order," the nun replied. "My name is Sister Solange."

A French name, Vivi thought. The small interaction had already tired her. She closed her eyes.

"Are you ready for a little nourishment?" Sister Solange asked.

The nun's kind voice astounded Vivi. *It has been so long since anyone treated me with kindness. In my old life, I had so much kindness. I took it for granted, like sugar before the war.*

Trying to hold back tears, Vivi sniffled loudly.

"Forgive me, please," Sister Solange said. "The first thing you need is a clean handkerchief."

The nun disappeared for a moment, and when she returned, it was with two white cotton handkerchiefs that had been pressed and neatly folded. She placed them on the bed next to Vivi's right hand.

Vivi grasped a handkerchief and brought it to her nose. It smelled just laundered, with a lingering smell of flowers. It was the first lovely fragrance she had smelled since she left home. Slowly, she unfolded it and wiped her eyes. Then she wiped her face and blew her nose. She started to reach for the second one, but pulled her hand back, as though afraid.

"May I use the second one, Sister?" Vivi asked, cautiously.

"Of course you may," the nun said. "Perhaps you need a whole stack of handkerchiefs."

When Sister Solange disappeared again, Vivi did her best to clean her face. Her skin felt sticky, unattractive. She could feel the residue of old tears, along with the wetness of new ones.

Back at her side, Sister Solange placed a stack of freshly laundered handkerchiefs on the bed. There was a time when such a gesture would have gone unnoticed by Vivi. But the presence of those cotton cloths folded at her side, ready for her to use, seemed so extravagant that her first instinct was to hide them before they were snatched away.

As the nun turned away from the bed again, Vivi thought, *She does not hate me.*

When she returned this time, Sister Solange carried a large white bowl filled with hot water. Setting it on the table beside the bed, she dipped in a washcloth, wrung it out, and then leaned over Vivi. "Close your eyes, please," the nun said. Then she laid the warm wet cloth over Vivi's eyes. Vivi took a deep breath that filled her whole body. She could feel the warmth entering the space behind her eyes. She could feel the kindness entering the bruised space around her heart. She drifted back to sleep.

When she woke again, Sister Solange stood next to her, bearing a tray of food. The plain, pleasing smell of potatoes, carrots, and onions cooked in a clear soup wafted up to Vivi's nose. When she looked into the steaming bowl, Vivi could see the orange color of carrots and the green of celery. A hunk of homemade bread lay on a plate next to the soup, and next to that was a small glass of apple juice.

"Here you are," Sister Solange said, "your first infirmary meal."

The nun did not order Vivi to eat. Rather, she set the tray down on the table where Vivi could regard it warily. She slowly sat up, and allowed the nun to place the tray in front of her. Staring at the bowl, she almost gagged at the memory of the saltiness of Saint Augustine food. Slowly, Vivi brought the spoon to her lips. What she tasted was clean and good. The old familiar taste of cooked potatoes and onions and the almost-sweet flavor of cooked carrots soothed her. Vivi ate almost half the bowl of soup before she stopped, exhausted.

Sister Solange removed the tray and then, like magic, pulled out of her pocket three apples.

Setting them on the bedside table, she said, "In case you become hungry later."

Vivi floated back into another deep sleep, and when she woke again, she had no idea how long it had been. Sleepily, she spotted the three apples as they sat on the table next to her. In her haze, she imagined that the apples were watching her, calling her up out of her dark slumber.

Sister Solange appeared again, and Vivi wondered if she had been sitting just on the other side of the curtain the whole time she had been sleeping.

"Good morning, Viviane Joan," she said. "May I show you to the bathroom?"

"Yes, sister," Vivi said.

As she sat up and swung her legs down out of the bed, the dizziness returned and Vivi lost her balance. Catching her, Sister Solange placed an arm around Vivi's waist, and leaned the girl against her. Slowly, she led Vivi to a bathroom, which was not a series of stalls as in the dorm, but a real room with a door that closed.

"I will be just outside if you need help," Sister Solange said as she pulled the door shut.

When Vivi finished, she tried to stand up, but grew dizzy, and sat back down immediately. "Sister," she called softly. But she got no response. Maybe the nun had left her alone to be dizzy and sick and attacked by another bathroom monitor. This time she would curl up in a ball and die.

"Sister," Vivi called out once more, a little louder. "Will you help me, please?"

The door opened, and Sister Solange stepped forward, keeping her eyes down so that she did not embarrass Vivi. Putting her arm around the girl, the nun led her gently back down the hall.

"You are weak as a kitten, Viviane Joan," the nun said. "Weak as one of God's little kittens."

Vivi thought she could detect the faintest scent of lavender about Sister Solange. That's what it is, Vivi decided. Lavender. That's what the handkerchiefs smelled like too. How could that be? I haven't seen any lavender bushes growing at Saint Augustine's. Vivi loved smelling Sister Solange. It was a tiny pleasure that made her feel so grateful.

"Do you think you might be ready for a bath?" Sister Solange asked when they got back to Vivi's bed.

A bath, Vivi thought. Our Lady of Mercy. *A bath*. "Do you mean a real bath? Or a shower?"

"A real bath," the nun said. "That's all we have here in the infirmary. One old bathtub."

The very word "bath" sounded beautiful, almost too luxurious to bear.

"Yes, Sister," Vivi said. "Yes, I think I'm ready for a bath."

"Very good," she said. "We'll make an agreement, then. You eat a meal, I mean a sizable portion of a real meal, and then you will have a real bath."

This nun is bargaining with me, Vivi thought. I have never had anybody bribe me with a bath to make me eat.

Slowly, chewing every bite, Vivi Abbott ate almost all of a baked potato. Her sixteen-year-old body, long unstroked, long unheld, craved the sensation of hot water against her naked skin, of steam rising, of her body sinking back into the arms of another element. There was almost nothing she would not do to earn such an indulgence.

Sister Solange left her alone in the tub for a moment while she left to get towels. Vivi lay back in the water, letting her head submerge, feeling the warm water cover her chin, then her nose, then her forehead.

When she came up for air, she felt cold, naked. So she let herself slip back under the water. She lay back like the Ya-Yas would do at Spring Creek when the sun went down, casting swimsuits aside to bathe with Ivory soap, creek water flowing between their legs. Vivi went underwater to another world. She could see light filtering in from the high casement windows; she could hear nothing. She thought she would just stay down there. No reason to rush back up. Just sink back down into a liquid life with no sharp edges. Glorious.

"Viviane Joan!" the nun called out loudly, leaning down over the tub.

Vivi emerged. She resented being called back to the surface. "What?!" she said, sharply.

"I've brought you a surprise," the nun replied.

"A surprise?" Vivi repeated, unbelieving. She had had enough surprises.

"Indeed," Sister Solange said. "Only you mustn't tell anybody. This must be our secret."

"Yes, Sister," Vivi said, interested in spite of herself.

From the folds of her gown, Sister Solange pulled out a small cheesecloth sack about the size of a ripe fig. *"Voilà!"* she said, and plopped the little sack into Vivi's bath.

"What *is* it?!" Vivi asked, amazed.

"Close your eyes and breathe in," the nun said.

Vivi took a long, slow breath. As she did, the fragrance of lavender rose up and met her nose, joining with the steam from the bathwater.

Lavender in my bathwater. How divine, Vivi thought. *This person knows who I am.* "Lavender," was all she could say. "Oh, my."

"I grow it," Sister Solange confided as she sat down on a stool near the tub. "I have three fat lavender bushes growing back behind the laundry."

"Why can't I tell anybody?" Vivi asked.

"Well," the nun said, "all God's children have different ideas about healing. The other sisters might think I was being old-fashioned. Or . . . indulgent."

This Sister Solange is full of surprises, Vivi thought. Every time I want to go under, she pulls something else out of her cloak.

"Well, thank you," Vivi said. "I love lavender."

"Indeed," Sister Solange nodded. "I saw the way you smelled the handkerchiefs."

A little smile crept over Vivi's face.

"Well, Viviane Joan," Sister Solange said, her mouth wide open in mock surprise. "That is the first smile you have given me in three days."

"Three days?" Vivi asked. "I've been here *three days*?"

"Three, going on four," the nun replied. "You were brought to me late Friday afternoon. This is Tuesday morning. You have been my only patient for the past week. Sometimes it gets slow around here. But I expect business will pick up in a couple of weeks when the next rash of colds goes around."

Sister Solange shifted the stack of fresh towels in her lap.

"Aren't you embarrassed, Sister?" Vivi asked. "I mean, with me naked?"

"For heaven's sake," Sister Solange said, rolling back the sleeves of her habit. "Why should I be embarrassed?! I am a nurse, Viviane Joan. I have seen people's naked bodies—boys, girls, men, women of all shapes—all of them God's creatures. The soul needs the body. It is nothing to be ashamed of."

Vivi closed her eyes again. This nun was not what Vivi had expected.

"Besides," Sister Solange said, "I come from a family of five sisters. We always bathed together when I was young."

"*Five?*" Vivi asked. "I only have one sister. She's really little. But I have three best friends. They're like my sisters."

"I bet you have a lot of friends, Viviane," Sister Solange said, standing. "It's probably best if you don't stay in there too terribly long. You don't want to end up a stewed prune. Besides, you're still weak. Want to climb out now?"

"I'm fine to get out by myself," Vivi said. She was not too thrilled at the thought of anyone, even a nun, seeing her body at this point. She was embarrassed at how skinny she was.

"No, Viviane Joan," Sister Solange said, firm. "I am responsible for you. You will let me help you."

Giving up, Vivi allowed Sister Solange to help her out of the tub. Steadying her, the nun helped Vivi pat herself dry, and soon Vivi was dressed in a plain, clean gown.

Exhausted, she slept for the rest of the day, waking only when the nun brought her a bit of rice and vegetables for supper. Vivi ate a small portion of it, and then ate an apple in large bites, rather than her customary small slivers.

That night she dreamed she saw her mother's face. Buggy was

leaning close enough for Vivi to touch her cheek, but Buggy did not see Vivi. She looked straight past her daughter like she was searching for something she had lost.

"Mama!" Vivi called out in her sleep. "It's *me*, Mama! Look! Mama!"

Vivi twisted in the sheets, sweating and crying. Trembling, her body jerked sharply when Sister Solange turned on the light, but she was still not fully awake. The nun wore a white cotton gown and her head was unveiled. Her hair, closely cropped and blonde, resembled a scruffy canary, and she had about her an unself-conscious beauty and grace.

"Viviane Joan," she said, putting her hand on the girl's forehead. "Blessed child."

The words were spoken with great compassion, and they helped Vivi wake from the nightmare. But it was her mother's voice she wanted, no one else's.

"What is troubling you?" the nun whispered.

"I want to go home," Vivi said. "I want my mother."

The next afternoon, Vivi woke from a nap to hear Mother Superior's voice. She opened her eyes and began counting the strips of light that fell through the shutters that she had opened slightly. It was around noon, she could tell by the quality of light.

A short while later, Sister Solange helped Vivi get out of bed and get dressed. She slipped a lavender sachet into Vivi's hand and curled her hand over Vivi's when she said goodbye. She did not want to let her go.

Sister Solange has taken a vow of obedience, Vivi told herself. That is why she is doing this. That is why she is seeing me to the door, that is why she is making me leave her.

At Mother Superior's instruction, Vivi went immediately back to her classes that afternoon. Afterward, she skipped supper and lay on the bed in her dorm room. She held the sachet in her hand. The halls were quiet, with the other girls away at supper. Vivi felt like she was on a huge ship, alone.

After she slipped out of her gray wool school uniform, Vivi took down her blue velvet gown from the wall. She longed for a mirror, but there were none at Saint Augustine's. Reaching into her trunk, she lifted out the silver compact, a gift from Genevieve before she left. A single rose was engraved on the lid, and inside the powder smelled sweet, like Genevieve's dressing room. Opening the compact, Vivi looked at her face. She studied her eyes, her nose, her mouth. She longed to see her whole body reflected. She pulled the straight-back chair on top of the cot. Holding her dress, she climbed up onto the chair in front of the high window. Darkness had fallen, and with the light on in her room, Vivi could see her naked body mirrored in the windowpane. She pulled the dress over her head. Strapless, with tiny hooks that fastened up the side, the dress was now far too big for Vivi's emaciated body.

Jack could not keep his hands off me in this dress, she thought. He would rub the velvet lightly when we danced; his tender touch made me shiver with excitement.

Letting the dress fall, Vivi looked at her breasts reflected in the window. She cupped her hands under her bosoms. Then she dropped her hands to her side and stared at her own image until the room started spinning.

Climbing down carefully from the chair, Vivi put it back in its place, and turned off the light. Then she opened the windows wide, and lay down on top of the wool blanket that covered the cot. It scratched her back. She could feel her eye sockets burning. She wished she had some bourbon. Soon she fell into a deep sleep.

She dreamed of Jack lying next to her on a pink-and-white-checkered blanket at Spring Creek. They were holding hands, staring into a bonfire. In the dream, she was achingly hungry for the kind of food they usually cooked out at the creek. Suddenly the flames of the bonfire leapt toward the two of them. Flames hot and furious, ready to devour them. When she reached for Jack, he was already on fire.

She woke screaming, the smell of burning fabric assaulting her nostrils. It took a moment before she realized the flames at the foot of her bed were real. Her midnight-blue velvet dress was on fire and the flames had leapt to the sheets.

Vivi flew from the bed, careening in dizziness and fear. She clutched Delia's pillow tightly to her chest, but her feet felt shackled to the floor. She could not make herself move. As the fire crept further up the bedclothes, Vivi could not take her eyes off her party dress, now being released from its solid material into air. She watched the flames in horror, but the warmth felt good against her naked body. She felt like she was witnessing a demonic, lovely ballet.

Although she didn't see or hear anyone in the room with her, it felt like a pair of strong hands grabbed her from behind and pulled her out of the room. The next thing she knew, she was standing alone in the cold, dark hallway, naked. The door to the burning bed was closed. She heard the sound of feet running down the hall and a door slamming. She heard her own breathing.

She began to scream, and she did not stop. Not when the other students ran into the hall to see what was wrong. Not when a flock of nuns arrived in a panic. Not after the fire was put out. Not when Mother Superior threw a blanket over Vivi's bare body, saying, "Cover your naked self!"

They have incinerated my birthday dress, Vivi thought. *They want to burn me alive.*

Jerking Vivi by the arm, Mother Superior shoved her into her office. Once inside, she took Vivi by the shoulders and shook her. The wool blanket scratched Vivi's skin. Every part of her body itched.

"Stop shrieking this moment," Mother Superior said. "Get control of yourself, Joan."

Terrified, Mother Superior slapped Vivi across the face. She was determined to get the girl under control in the only way she knew how.

But Vivi could not stop screaming.

Sister Solange arrived in Mother Superior's office without her veil, her hooded cloak hastily thrown over her nightgown. Ignoring her superior's frown, she crossed to Vivi and took the girl in her arms.

"You must see to this student," Mother Superior said, the light from the desk lamp reflecting in her glasses. "The girl is seriously disturbed."

Behind Mother Superior's desk was a painting of the Sacred Heart of Jesus, bleeding. A crucifix hung to the right. Under the crucifix was the phrase "The Immaculate Victim."

"Of course she's upset, Mother!" Sister Solange said. "Her bed was set on fire with her in it."

Mother Superior rubbed her fingers against the rosary beads that hung at her waist. "Joan could have set the fire herself. We will have to look into it."

Vivi half heard their conversation. She had stopped screaming and now could only shake. Nuns came and went out of the room, but she could not follow it all. There was discussion about calling in Father

O'Donagan, the priest who came to say Mass and hear confessions at the academy.

"Mother," Sister Solange said, "do you think it might be prudent to call her parents?"

"I do not think it wise to worry her parents about this," Mother Superior said. "This is better handled here at Saint Augustine's."

"With all respect," Sister Solange said, "as a nurse, I think it advisable to contact her family. Viviane Joan has been ill, and the shock of the fire may have her more troubled than we realize."

"Sister Solange," Mother Superior said, "I have made up my mind. Her parents will not be called."

"Yes, Mother," Sister Solange said, looking from Vivi to the image of the Bleeding Heart, then down at the floor. Her vow of obedience was a sacred one.

Sister Solange said, "Perhaps Mother might agree to letting Vivi spend the night in the infirmary so that I might observe her medically."

Mother Superior crossed back behind her desk, folding her hands into the sleeves of her gown. "It is agreed. You may have the girl tonight."

Then, raising the small crucifix of her rosary, Mother Superior kissed it. "Now, we have all had quite enough excitement for one night. It is time to return to bed. Pray, sisters, for the soul of this daughter of Mary."

They only pray for your soul around here, Vivi thought. Your body could burn up, for all they care.

At the infirmary, Sister Solange dressed Vivi in a long oversized flannel gown. The sleeves were full and poufy and sat like clouds over her skinny arms. She arranged a cotton throw over Vivi's shoulders, and placed a hot water bottle at her feet and one in her lap. Together, they sat in the small infirmary office, their chairs almost touching. A vase of roses sat on the desk, and to either side there were glass-fronted cabinets containing various pills and tonics.

On the desk, the nun had placed a cup of tea and a small plate of ginger cookies. She observed Vivi closely. "Please have some, Viviane Joan."

When Vivi raised the cup to her mouth, her hands shook so that she spilled tea onto her gown. She did not seem to notice. She stared at a few tiny yellow-gold chamomile flowers that floated in the cup.

After Vivi took a sip, Sister Solange said, "Good, now have a cookie, please."

Sister watched Vivi as she stared at the cookie without taking a bite. "Now you must talk to me, Viviane."

Hearing her true name caught Vivi the way sun unexpectedly glinting off a buckle or a piece of tinfoil might catch the eye. She looked at the nun, unsure.

"What name do they call you at home?" Sister Solange asked.

Vivi thought the nun looked tired. She stared at the nun's blonde hair, and looked down at Sister's hands. The nun was squeezing her fingers tightly together and then releasing them. When Sister saw Vivi notice this, she folded her hands underneath her cloak.

"At home," Vivi said, "at home they call me Vivi."

"Vivi," Sister Solange repeated, "what a lively name."

The nun lowered her head for a moment, in prayer or deliberation. When she lifted it, her eyes looked even more tired. "Vivi, I want you to try to pay attention to what I'm saying, please."

Vivi was listening to the tones of Sister Solange's voice. It was a mossy, quiet sound, the perfect green-blue.

The nun took Vivi's hands in hers. She watched Vivi closely.

"Vivi?" Sister Solange said. "Squeeze my hand."

Vivi looked up at Sister Solange, but she did not appear to have heard her. She began to shake violently. The nun took the teacup from the girl's hands. She did not want Vivi to hurt herself.

Sister Solange stood, took out a key from her desk, and opened one of the cabinets against the wall. She chose a bottle of tablets and shook two of them into her palm.

"Will you swallow these, please, Vivi?" she said. She had wondered earlier if the girl needed something stronger than tea to help her shock, but she dared not suggest it to Mother Superior. But Vivi was in *her* office now.

Vivi swallowed the pills as she was told. The nun knelt back down at Vivi's side. "Vivi," she said softly, "tell me who I can call at home to come and help you."

At first Vivi thought she might have dreamed the words. So many times in the past four months she had imagined someone saying these very words to her. She studied the nun's face. Was this some kind of trick? Was she about to be trapped and then punished?

Sister Solange waited patiently for a response. Slowly she lifted her hand and placed her palm tenderly against Vivi's cheek. "Vivi, dear, tell me who to call."

The touch of Sister Solange's hand against her skin revived Vivi.

"Call Genevieve Whitman at Highland 4270 in Thornton, Louisiana," she said. "Don't talk to Mr. Whitman, only talk to Genevieve."

"Is she a relative?" the nun asked.

Terrified that the nun might not call, Vivi lied and said, "Yes, she is my godmother."

"Thank you, Vivi," the nun said. "You are a dear girl, a blessed girl."

Vivi slept again that night in her old infirmary bed. She dreamed that she and Teensy and Jack were sitting on the sea wall at Biloxi, the sun caressing their faces.

The next day, Sister Solange helped Vivi dress in an outfit that she scrounged together with bit and pieces from the Lost and Found. The ensemble was mismatched, ugly, and scratchy, and the nun apologized as she handed the items to Vivi. "These garments are those of a match girl," she said, laughing, "not a tennis player."

Vivi buttoned an off-white blouse with stains under the arms. Over that she pulled a nondescript brown jumper that hung loosely on her thin frame. Wool socks and a pair of uniform oxfords were on her feet.

"How did you know I was a tennis player?" Vivi asked Sister Solange.

"Oh," the nun said, "you spoke of tennis many times in your sleep. Tennis and someone named Jack Ya-Ya."

Vivi gave a tentative laugh that turned into a cough.

"Anyway," Sister Solange said, "there is no reason for such a pretty girl to look like a penitent. But this clothing is the best I can do."

"What about my own clothes?" Vivi asked.

The nun bit her lip before she spoke. "Vivi, they are all too damaged."

"All of them?" Vivi asked.

"Yes," the nun said. "What wasn't burned was ruined by smoke."

"Except my pillow," Vivi said.

"Except your pillow," Sister Solange replied. "Your pillow survived, and so will you."

The sight of Genevieve and Teensy standing in Mother Superior's office was almost more than Vivi could bear. She longed to run to them, to hold them and smell them, to soak in all of the life that they carried. But she could not make herself take a step forward. She stood frozen, clutching Delia's feather pillow in her hand, looking far younger than her sixteen years.

Rushing to her side, Teensy and Genevieve enveloped Vivi in hugs. The suddenness of it disoriented Vivi, and she could not respond. She felt as though they were onlookers and she was a wreck on the side of the road.

"Mrs. Whitman," Mother Superior said, "I cannot release this child to you. You are not her mother."

"You are not her mother either, *cher*," Genevieve shot back.

"Do not speak to me in disrespect," the nun said.

"*Cher* is not a sign of disrespect," Genevieve said, changing her tone so that she might charm the nun. "It's French for 'dear.'"

"Then do not call me 'dear,'" Mother Superior said.

Leaving Vivi's side, Genevieve stepped in closer to Mother Superior's desk. Teensy gave Vivi's hand a squeeze, then let it go as she stepped close to her *maman*.

The light coming in through the windows seemed extraordinarily bright to Vivi. From where she stood, she could see Genevieve's Packard parked outside near the curb. The car seemed like a car in a dream, and Vivi thought that at any moment it might shift shape into a boat or a bird.

"If you continue to disregard my wishes, I will have to call Father O'Donagan," Mother Superior told Genevieve, as though the arrival of the priest were a deadly threat.

"Call anybody you like, Sister," Genevieve said, taking Vivi's hand. "But, Vivi, she comin home with me."

"Drop that child's hand," Mother Superior commanded.

Ignoring the nun, Genevieve walked Vivi out of the office.

"Let go of Joan!" the nun said, following them.

"Her name isn't Joan," Teensy said. "Her name is Vivi."

Genevieve led the girls down the long, dark hall. Vivi could hear Mother Superior's footsteps as she followed them; she could hear the rustling of the nun's gown. The footsteps sped up, and then the nun was upon them, her bone-dry hand reaching down to pry Vivi's hand away from Genevieve's. Vivi's fear was so strong she could taste it in the back of her throat. So strong it caused her to pee ever so slightly in the borrowed boxy panties she wore.

Genevieve flung Mother Superior's hand away. The nun stumbled backward, so that when Vivi looked at her it seemed a wind had lifted her black veil and spread it out in all directions. The nun was no longer Mother Superior, but a shuffling black vulture.

"I am responsible for saving this girl's *soul!*" the nun shouted.

"You'll be lucky if you can save your own!" Genevieve said. "Now, get out of here! Go on! Get!"

Genevieve put one arm around Vivi and one arm around her daughter, and the three of them walked fast, but did not run, out of the building. They walked down the stone steps and into the waiting Packard. Genevieve climbed behind the wheel, and Teensy shoved Vivi into the front seat and then climbed in herself. As the car sped out of the grounds of Saint Augustine's, not one of them looked back.

Still clutching Delia's feather pillow, Vivi thought she could detect the scents of oranges and pine needles and shrimp boiling in a big iron pot. She thought she could smell October in Louisiana during cotton harvest on crisp Friday nights. She thought she could smell life.

She looked at the dress Teensy wore underneath her plum jacket. It was the garnet wool jersey with the peplum waist they'd picked out together at Godchaux's on a trip to New Orleans with Genevieve. Reaching down, Vivi rubbed her fingers across the fabric. The material seemed to come up and meet the flesh of her fingertips.

Teensy placed her hand over Vivi's. "*Bébé,* that outfit you're wearing has *got to go.*"

"*Got to go,*" Vivi repeated after her, trying for the old Ya-Ya tone.

"Got to," Genevieve said, and lit a cigarette, tears in the corners of her eyes.

They rode along in silence for a mile or so before Genevieve spoke again.

"*Ecouté, femmes,*" she said, her voice like the slow-moving rich bayou itself, her tone wavering somewhere between tears and ferocity. "God don't like ugly, *mes petites choux. Ça va?* No matter what they'll try to tell you, *Bébés!* God don't make ugly, and God don't like ugly. *Le Bon Dieu* is a god of loveliness, and don't yall forget it!"

"Yes, *Maman,*" Teensy said.

"Yes, *Maman,*" Vivi said.

"And, Vivi, *ma petite chou, écouté voir ici:* life is short, but it is wide. This too shall pass."

With those catechism lessons, Genevieve drove Vivi, mile by mile, all the way back home.

22

The girl in the photo on the front page of *The Thornton High Tattler*, from May 21, 1943, was so thin and drawn-looking that at first Sidda did not recognize her mother. My God, Sidda thought, she looks like a war orphan.

Accompanying the photo was the following item:

THORNTON FAVORITE RETURNS HOME

Vivi Abbott, sophomore cheerleader, beauty, and varsity tennis player, has returned from Saint Augustine's Academy in Spring Hill, Alabama, were she spent almost all of the past semester. Sorely missed by the entire student body, Vivi is welcomed back by everyone, from the football team to the Red Cross Canteen. Have a great summer, Vivi! Even with Jack gone, we know you and the Ya-Yas will be in high form!

Sidda ached for more information. Searching the scrapbook, she examined each pressed corsage, each ticket stub, *willing* there to be more information about her mother's departure and return from Saint Augustine's. She tried to imagine what her mother's life had been like during the summer of 1943. Shoes were rationed, along with meat and cheese, but what else was rationed? Was her return difficult, or did Vivi "rise above it" as she'd always told her children to do?

When she could find no other information, Sidda began to make it up. Say Mama flourished that summer. Say she was safe and loved. Say the newspaper clipping tells the whole story: golden girl, universally welcomed home. Say Mama watched *Casablanca* when it first came out, and necked with whatever boy she was with. Say she was beautiful and blonde and more popular than I ever was. Say Mama did not know what lay in store for her and woke every morning grinning. Say there is no truth. Say there are only scraps that we feebly try to sew together.

Vivi Abbott Walker lay on the table in the small rose-colored room with the piped-in music at Chez Health, ready to let Torie, the massage therapist, touch her body. Necie had been the first to discover Torie, and now all the Ya-Yas made appointments to lay their aging bodies on her table, and indulge in a sensual pampering that the Church they grew up in would have labeled a sin of indulgence, if not a near occasion of sin.

Once a week, Vivi took off her clothes, lay down, and babbled nervously for ten minutes. Then, as her breathing grew deeper, she gave over to the stroking she craved. Never in her life had Vivi been showered with such physical attention, no strings attached.

"A bargain at *any* price, Torie Dahlin," she said at the end of each session as she handed a check, complete with generous tip, to the massage therapist.

Now, as Torie massaged her feet and toes, Vivi felt herself sink down into the table. She found herself, as she had many times in the past week or so, thinking about Jack.

Vivi had done her best to reclaim her old life when she returned from Saint Augustine's. She had tiptoed back onto the tennis court, where her weight loss and exhaustion embarrassed her no end. She had hung out at Bordelon's Drugs and drunk Coca-Colas with peanuts plunked into the bottles. She wrote Jack cheery letters at least every other day, and she tried to stay out of her mother's way. Buggy had refused even to speak to her for the first month Vivi was back home, but as the summer passed, things began to return to what passed for normal life in the Abbott house.

Vivi said regular novenas for Jack, and tried to get excited about the other boys she still dated. But even after she began to eat again, to rediscover some of the energy she'd lost, there was something about her that hesitated, that held back, that hedged her bets. Now she did not know who she was or what she was supposed to do. And she did not know exactly when she had stepped away from herself. She did not know if she would ever stop feeling tired. She learned to camouflage her exhaustion with a slightly forced vitality. She became a high priestess of self-presentation, and was rewarded for it at every turn. The town of Thornton, Louisiana, extolled self-presentation. It was a sort of religion.

It had been a Sunday afternoon, the third week of June, 1943, not long after she'd returned from Saint Augustine's. Jack was home for a visit before departing for a bomber base somewhere in Europe. Buggy had suggested that the gang come back to the Abbott home that afternoon for some homemade ice cream.

All week long, there had been swimming parties, barbecues, and get-togethers to celebrate Jack's visit. Vivi, Jack, Caro, Necie, and Teensy had just walked over from the Whitman house, where Genevieve had prepared a meal that included every one of her son's favorite foods—from Saint Landry crayfish bisque to mayhaw jelly rolls.

It was early summer, not yet unbearably hot. The clematis vine was in full bloom, and blackberries trailed along the fence in wild profusion. Some of the berries, picked and washed by Buggy, were already gathered in a big yellow bowl that sat on the steps.

Vivi's baby sister Jezie, quiet for once, leaned against her mother's leg as Buggy stood cranking the ice-cream freezer. Buggy wore the lilac-and-gray housedress she changed into every Sunday after Mass. Her hair was caught up in two combs at the side of her face, and her cheeks were slightly flushed from the exertion of the cranking. Pete was draped over the porch railing with a couple of his buddies.

Vivi sat on the swing, between Teensy and Necie. Caro leaned against a column, her feet kicked out in front of her, crossed at the ankles.

Jack sat in a straight-back chair in the middle of all of them, his fiddle in his lap. Not just any fiddle, but the handmade Cajun fiddle his Uncle LeBlanc had made for him when he was nine years old. The fiddle his father forbade him to play inside the house because it smacked of the bayou, of a world unacceptable to the prosperous banker.

But, oh, Jack played on every single visit to Genevieve's people in Marksville, on the bayou. And he played it at all his friends' houses. And he played in the middle of fields when Genevieve loaned them the Packard and they'd head out to Spring Creek with picnic blankets and a couple of six packs.

Jack's French fiddle joined with the music of Harry James to break Vivi's heart in those days. Once, after she'd sprained her ankle on the tennis court and was laid up in bed in the foulest mood, Jack had played under her bedroom window, making her feel like Juliet. Another time, she put him up to playing during a basketball game half-time in the Thornton High gymnasium. There Jack Whitman stood, waving that bow across the strings, his long legs flowing out of his gold-and-blue-satin basketball uniform, his head tossed back with the music, a wide grin sweeping across his face.

And now he was home again, his father's pride. Never had Vivi seen Jack so contented. His father had bragged about him all week long. Mr. Whitman, in fact, had been the one to arrange several of the parties. His son was going to fly bombing raids over France. Jack was proud that his father was proud.

Vivi was delighted that her mother was making ice cream. It was the first outwardly kind gesture Buggy had made toward her daughter since Genevieve had talked Mr. Abbott into not sending her back to Saint Augustine's. As Buggy cranked the ice-cream freezer, Vivi hoped this was a sign things would get better between them.

The sunlight hit Jack's jet-black hair. His skin was tanned, and he was thinner than usual. Chiseled down to his essence. He tucked his fiddle under his chin and raised his bow. But before beginning to play, he paused. He glanced at Vivi and smiled. Then, for some sweet Jack reason, he looked over at Buggy.

"Madame Abbott," he said, "how bout I play this little waltz for you?"

It was the most gentlemanly thing Vivi had ever witnessed. As she watched her mother's face, she understood for the first time that no one—ever—had dedicated a song to Buggy Abbott. She watched as her mother raised her hand to her mouth, shy, embarrassed, and utterly delighted. Buggy let go of the ice-cream crank, and the grinding sound of ice against wood gave way to silence.

Then Jack began to play.

He struck up "Little Black Eyes," a waltz he knew Vivi loved.

There was no war on the Abbott front porch that afternoon. Just an overflowing of Cajun fiddle music, sweet, plaintive, from the heart. The notes danced through the June air; Vivi could feel them dust her hair and shoulders. She could feel the notes enter her and settle deep into her bones. Jack's notes tumbled over all of them that afternoon, as if there were an endless supply of music somewhere, waiting to be called forth.

As Vivi listened to the music, she glanced at Buggy, and she noticed a smile she had never before seen on her mother's face. It was the smile of a girl with her own longings, her own pleasures. It was a smile smiled for no one else. It was a smile that forgot about motherhood and the Catholic Church and the child clutching at her leg. For that one moment, Vivi saw Buggy as a person. The music and the fading afternoon light and the berries in the yellow bowl and the sun on Jack's face, Vivi's own bony body sitting in the swing surrounded by her friends and family, and the expression on her mother's face—all of this seared Vivi's heart for an instant, and she was filled with love.

She credited it all to Jack. That is what Jack could do: he could crack her wide open to more love; he could transform the face of her mother.

When the tune ended, everybody clapped. Jezie, who had been mesmerized, called out, "Do again, do again!" Pete and his buddies whistled and cheered. But it was Buggy who surprised Vivi most.

She stepped over to Jack and gave him a kiss on the cheek, something she never did, not even with her own children. "Thank you, Jacques," she said.

Then she took the corner of her apron, wiped her eyes, and resumed cranking the ice-cream freezer.

It was a small thing. Nobody noticed it but Vivi. Even if they had, they might not have thought it special. But Vivi loved her mother for it. On the day Buggy died, almost forty years later, Vivi remembered the kiss her mother had given her beloved on that day and the tear she had wiped away, and she loved her mother for it. She didn't forgive her mother for never loving her the way she needed, but she loved Buggy for that one kiss.

In late October of 1943, Vivi Abbott was playing a mean game of singles against Anne McWaters. Back in shape but still not at the top of her form, Vivi was to have played Caro that afternoon, but Caro had had to stay late at a yearbook meeting.

Anne McWaters, Vivi's old rival, was beating her three to two, and it was driving Vivi crazy. Ever since coming home from Saint Augustine's, she had devoted herself to tennis, and even though she was still a bit underweight, she'd picked up a lot of her old strength. But Anne McWaters could always throw her. The girl had a killer serve, and she knew how to keep her opponent running.

Vivi was determined to close in on her, and thought she saw her chance, when she noticed Pete ride up on his bicycle. Usually the arrival of a spectator wouldn't faze Vivi—on the contrary, she pre- ferred to play most any game in front of an audience. But Pete's show- ing up anywhere without two or three buddies tailing along was unusual.

"Viv-o," Pete called out, his voice sounding strained.

When Vivi didn't respond, Pete came closer to the fence that sur- rounded the city-park courts. He was wearing a brown baseball cap over his auburn hair, and his nose was sunburned. It was October 19, 1943, around five in the evening. Teensy and Vivi had a double date planned that night to see Orson Welles's *Jane Eyre*. A green parks- department truck with a bad muffler passed by. Vivi's body was per- fectly poised, ready for her opponent.

Anne McWaters served hard and Vivi returned it down the line. She'd worked extra hard at her backhand since coming home, and she knew how to keep her eye on the ball. She was training herself, once she stepped onto the court, to think of nothing but that ball. In the past few months, with Jack away, she'd devoted even more time to her tennis. She still dated, of course, still had at least three boys at any one time who claimed to be in love with her, but Vivi never gave them a thought unless they were standing right in front of her. She thought more about Pauline Betz winning the U.S. Singles than she did about any of those boys. Vivi thought about tennis, the war, and Jack Whitman.

As Anne McWaters lobbed a high return, Vivi's mind was with the ball. Her body responded easily as she stepped back to get under it, in perfect position to take the point.

At that moment, though, a bird flew close to the ball. It seemed to come out of nowhere, and it stole Vivi's attention. Never in her life had she seen a bird fly quite so close to a tennis ball. The bird mesmerized her for a second, causing her to forget about the ball, forget about the game, forget about everything but the bird's gray-blue wings against the October sky.

Signaling a time-out, Vivi strode off the court to Pete. "Darn you, Pete! What do you want?"

Pete looked at his sister for a moment, then turned away.

"What do you want?" she asked again.

"Why don't yall call it a game, Viv-o?" Pete said.

"With McWaters leading? You gotta be kiddin.'"

"Yoo-hoo!" Anne called out, twirling her racket.

"Just a minute," Vivi called back. "I'm in the *middle* of a game, Pete. Either tell me what you want, or let me get back on the court."

She waited for Pete to respond. When he didn't, she started back toward the court.

As though it were easier to speak now that Vivi's back was to him, Pete said, "Teensy asked me to come get you. She wants you over at their house."

"Great," Vivi said, bouncing the ball with her racket, smiling at her opponent. "Tell her I'll be there soon as I beat McWaters."

"I think you better come right now, Stinky," Pete said. He shook a cigarette out of a Lucky pack, and lit it, his face pale in the fading light.

"Is something wrong?" Vivi asked, turning back to him.

Unable to meet her gaze, Pete said, "Why don't you just come on with me? You can ride on the handlebars."

"No," Vivi said. "I don't *want* to come now. I want to finish this game."

Focusing her attention, Vivi resumed the game, smashing the ball hard. In the few minutes it took for her to win the game, each sensation was heightened for Vivi.

She shook hands with Anne McWaters, then took her time gathering her racket press, the extra can of balls, her jacket. Stalling, she took a long drink of water, and ignored Pete, who stood waiting, watching her every move.

Finally, Pete rolled his bike to where Vivi stood, pulling on a sweatshirt over her blouse. "Will you come on with me now, Viv-o? Please, Baby-cakes."

"You're being too nice to me," she said. "What the hell's going on?"

"Come on," he said, pointing to the bicycle handlebars. "Hop on."

Carrying her tennis racket, Vivi climbed onto the handlebars and balanced herself. As Pete pedaled, she looked straight ahead, and they did not speak. When they reached the bottom of the circular drive that led to Teensy's house, Vivi felt dizzy.

"Turn around," she said.

"What?" Pete said, continuing to pedal.

"I said turn around, Pete. I don't want to go in there."

Pete stopped pedaling.

Vivi jumped down from the handlebars, her breath coming fast. She could feel herself begin to sweat as though she had been the one pumping the pedals for eight blocks.

"What did you bring me here for?" she asked him, accusing.

"Cause Teensy wants you."

"I want to know *why*. Tell me this instant."

Pete set his bike down on its side. It seemed to Vivi that it took him an inordinately long time to do it, like everything was happening in slow motion. She watched as he walked over and put his hands on her shoulders. She could smell spearmint gum over the scent of tobacco on his breath.

"It's Jack," he said, the weight of his hands heavy on her shoulders.

Vivi appeared not to have heard. "What did you say?" she asked.

Pete pulled her to him. She could smell the healthy smell of sweat, and did not know whether it was her brother's or her own.

"It's Jack, little sister," Pete said.

Vivi jerked away.

"Genevieve got a telegram," he said, choking up.

"You're crazy," Vivi said, giving a small laugh. "You're joking."

"I wish to God I was," Pete said.

"You're messin with me," Vivi said. She shoved him on the arm as if to say the joke was over. "Shake your head and say you're messin with me."

"I'm not messing with you, Vivi," Pete said, wiping the sleeve of his jacket across his face.

"Shake your Goddamn head, Pete."

"Vivi—"

Taking her brother's head in her hands, Vivi shook it from side to side. Pete let her do this for a moment, and when she did not stop, he reached up and took her hands in his. Lowering both their hands to his chest, he looked at her.

Tears rolled down onto Pete's cheeks. "You got to listen to me, baby sister. I am not making this up. This is real."

Vivi stared at their hands. She stared at her tennis racket, which lay on the ground where she had dropped it. She thought of home-made blackberry ice cream and the way Jack's face looked when he played music. She thought of the touch of his hand on her shoulder when they danced. A long thread of pain entered her through her feet, and worked its way up into her heart, where it knotted, twisting so tightly that Vivi had to drop Pete's hands and rub her throat in order to continue breathing.

Shirley, the Whitmans' maid, sat on the bottom step of the wind-ing staircase. Her head was in her hands, and when she looked up at Vivi and Pete, her black face was streaked with tears that shone silver in the fading light.

"I knowed something bad was comin. Jes yestiddy I done heard the screech owl. Oh, I helt that baby boy in my arm when he was born, I done blessed him wit magnolia leaves like Miz Genevieve want. Poor Miss Vivi, you done lost yo sweetheart. I done tried to get Miz Genevieve to drink her nerve tea, but she won't take it. *Ça, c'est dommage!*"

Vivi could hear Genevieve's screams coming from the master bed-room. She ran past Shirley and up the stairs. When she stepped into the bedroom, Genevieve was slapping Mr. Whitman on his face, his neck, his arm, whatever she could reach. Teensy stood by herself, near the bay window, her hands covering her face.

"Mon fils de grâce!" Genevieve screamed as she slapped her hus-band. "You killed my *bébé*. You and your *patriotisme!*" Her reaction was so strong that it seemed to push the very air out of the room, leaving little space for anything else.

Vivi wanted to hold Genevieve, she wanted to hold Teensy. She wanted them to hold her.

"Oh, man," Vivi heard Pete whisper as the two of them watched Genevieve claw at Mr. Whitman, dragging her nails along the side of his face. Mr. Whitman did not attempt to stop her as she began to kick at him and punch him, pummeling him wherever she could reach. The man stood there motionless in his gray pin-stripes.

Pete took Vivi's hand, and the two of them stood at the door. Everything seemed to be happening in slow motion.

There was a lull, a drawing-in of breath from Genevieve. Mr. Whitman slowly reached into his pocket and drew out a mono-grammed handkerchief. Without speaking, he wiped his tears with the cloth, and then cleaned the blood off his lips. Only when he was done with the handkerchief did he offer it to his wife. But she took no notice.

Jack would have offered the handkerchief to Genevieve first, Vivi thought. He would have shown good manners.

Genevieve turned to look at her daughter, then at Vivi. Both girls took steps toward her. Genevieve will hug us now, Vivi thought. She will take us into her arms and tell us everything is all right.

But Genevieve took no one into her arms. Instead, she let out a low keening sound, then pulled the skirt of her dress up over her head, revealing a beige slip and bare legs. It was the gesture of a small girl, hiding her face. It was the gesture of a woman whose grief was too much to bear.

The longer Genevieve stood there with her skirt above her head, the more Vivi's grief compounded. This was the woman she looked to when her own mother was absent. Now this mother, too, was turning away.

"Son," Vivi heard Mr. Whitman say.

Stepping forward, Pete answered, "Sir?"

Pete did not know Mr. Whitman well, only to be polite to him at the bank or on the street. Mr. Whitman did not know Pete well either, only enough to nod if he passed him, perhaps note the touch-down he'd made the Friday night before.

But on that day, as Pete stepped forward, Mr. Whitman reached out his arms and the man and boy fell into an embrace. Vivi would never again witness anything like it between two men. Often, later in her life, she would long to have her own sons and husband share such a moment, but that afternoon in the Whitman home what she felt was envy. Envy that she herself was not encircled in the arms of a mother or a father.

Finally, Vivi stopped waiting for Genevieve to lower her dress and hug her. She crossed the room to Teensy and took her into her arms. The two girls began to sob.

Torie was working points from the base of Vivi's skull down into her shoulder blades when Vivi began to sob. Torie was not alarmed; it was not the first time that a client had cried in her massage room.

Vivi took a deep breath as she lay, face down, on the massage table. Her body shuddered. I lost all my patriotism that day, she thought. I lost my cheerleading self. From that day forward, when I jumped up and down for the team, I was an actress. A damn good actress, only nobody gave out Oscars.

"Forgive me," she muttered to Torie. "I've got to get a grip."

Torie began to work Vivi's shoulders. The touch was so sure, so utterly *free* that it released even more tears. Vivi's body shook, and the massage therapist stopped briefly to hand her a Kleenex.

Vivi propped herself up on her elbows and blew her nose.

"Do you want to talk?" Torie asked.

"No," Vivi said, reaching for more tissues.

"Okay," Torie said.

I will not ruin this massage by crying, Vivi thought. But the more she strained not to cry, the more tense her body became. When Torie began to knead her shoulders, Vivi began to weep again.

"Let's just call it a day, shall we?" Vivi said, lifting her head. "I cannot seem to stop crying, I'm terribly sorry."

"Well," Torie said, pumping more lotion into her palm from a small plastic bottle she wore strapped to her waist. "Don't call it a day on my account. You can cry and get massaged at the same time. Why don't you trying picturing your tears like soft rain?"

Vivi lowered her head back into the padded face cradle.

Torie began to lightly stroke Vivi's back, and to rock her ever so slightly. Her hands were warm against Vivi's skin, and as Torie stroked, Vivi could feel her own breathing start to steady. Sometimes she could not believe that anyone could touch her body like this, with such acceptance, such loving detachment, asking for nothing in return. There were places she still could not bear to be touched. Her belly, for one. Her belly stuck out too much, she was ashamed of it, could not accept the idea that it was anything but hideous. There were other spots, though—her legs, her neck, her head—which luxuriated in being massaged. There were moments during her sessions with Torie that Vivi could only describe as religious. Moments when she came home to her body in ways she never had before—moments when she felt its aches, varicose veins, and wrinkles so intimately and gently that she groaned with a happiness she could never describe. Fleeting seconds when Vivi knew that her body, in all its imperfections, was her own lived-in work of art. She lived there and she'd die there. Her body had borne four children. Five, if you counted Sidda's twin, which Vivi always did.

"I do want to talk," Vivi said softly.

And so Vivi opened up to the massage therapist. She murmured her words in between sighs and tears, haltingly, but with an ease she had never known in a confessional.

"I try to believe," she said, "that God doesn't give you more than one little piece of the story at once. You know, the story of your life. Otherwise your heart would crack wider than you could handle. He only cracks it enough so you can still walk, like someone wearing a cast. But you've still got a crack running up your side, big enough for a sapling to grow out of. Only no one sees it. *Nobody sees it.* Everybody thinks you're one whole piece, and so they treat you maybe not so gentle as they would if they could see that crack."

Vivi sobbed. Torie placed one palm at the base of her spine and one at the base of her neck, and pressed lightly. Vivi felt as though the massage therapist were touching her actual spinal cord, sending it messages to calm down.

"I'm thinking," Vivi said, "about an afternoon in my life when all the cracks were clear. Like a pile of broken crockery."

Torie moved her hands to Vivi's shoulders. Vivi gave a little jump, as though from pain.

"It is not in my personality to talk like this," she said.

Another sob escaped from her body.

"But one of these days I might trade in my personality for a new one. I might say: 'To hell with being popular. Yall don't think I'm fun enough, then go screw yourselves.'"

Then Vivi forced a little laugh and started to sit up. "My God, I'm starting to sound like Blanche DuBois: '*I have always depended on the kindness of strangers.*'"

"Maybe I'm not a stranger," Torie said, pressing into Vivi's shoulder blades with her thumb.

"Ouch!" Vivi said. "That hurts."

"Why do you think your shoulders are so sore?" Torie asked.

"Oh, I carry a lot of heavy luggage with me, Dahlin," Vivi answered. "I carry footlockers."

"Well, put them down for a few minutes while we work on this kink," Torie said. "Okay?"

"Okay," Vivi said, and sank down into the massage table. This table, she told herself, is held up by the floor, which is held up by the building, which is sunk deep into the earth, which is my home.

23

*V*ivi put on her sunglasses before stepping out of the massage room. She did not want to talk to any of her health-club pals. Not the young men who always flirted with her, and not the young women who worked for the cable TV station.

Once in her little convertible Miata, a "surprise" from Shep that she had broadly hinted for, she slipped the Barbra Streisand CD out of the player. She could not bear anything else that might make her cry. It was almost evening, but she didn't feel like going home. Instead, she drove toward Teensy's house.

Vivi and Teensy had not just lost Jack. They lost Genevieve too. For weeks after the telegram arrived, Genevieve saw no one, and when she did, it was to announce her belief that her son was not dead. According to Genevieve, Jack had survived his plane crash, and with the help of the French Resistance was being cared for by village people in southern France. From that day forward, she refused to use her son's anglicized name, which her husband had always insisted on. "Our Jacques is alive," Genevieve said. "Without a doubt." All she had to do was find him.

In the few first months after Jack's death, Genevieve's fantasy impeded Vivi's own mourning. It was easy, with Vivi's imagination, to enter into the sad deception Genevieve offered. Falling asleep at night, Vivi would envision her sweetheart under the same moon she could see from her bedroom window. Together with Teensy and Genevieve, she spent countless hours studying maps of France. She devoured every shred of news she could find about the French Resistance. She helped compose countless letters to the Army Air Corps, which Genevieve instructed Mr. Whitman's secretary to type. Wanting so hard to believe, for a while Vivi did believe. Joining in Genevieve's tireless conversations about how Jack was doing, what food he was eating, what sort of bed he was sleeping in, Vivi sometimes grew giddy with the fiction they were creating. She agreed with Genevieve that yes, of course, Jack was learning French folk songs on his fiddle. He was playing music and thinking of the time when he could come home.

Each time Vivi began to cry, she felt guilty for giving up hope. She and Teensy would stand together in the hall by their lockers at school after lunch. Some afternoons they could not bear to walk into history class because the tears were falling too fast. Instead, they sat outside on the grass, and cried. They didn't want any more history, they'd had *enough* history for a while. Vivi did not want Jack to be a part of history. She wanted him to eat hamburgers with her at LeMoyne's Drive-In, she wanted to see him round the corner as she sat in a booth at Bordelon's drugstore, she wanted to see his eyes light up when she entered the room, she wanted him to hold her and give her back her life.

For months, Vivi spent Friday and Saturday nights with Teensy, forsaking all offers of dates. Side by side, they would lie in bed and drink Cokes, and, if Genevieve was not near, they would cry. Later, on those evenings, Caro and Necie would drop by, and often, Chick, Teensy's boyfriend, whose devotion to the Ya-Yas never wavered. No one thought it odd in those days for two young women to lie in bed like that, holding each other in their flannel nightgowns. Holding each other until they could stand up again and walk and talk and maybe start to pretend that their lives had not had a hole blown out of them.

It was Buggy Abbott who had stepped in to crush the fantasy about Jack, a move that made Vivi at once thankful and resentful for the rest of her life.

One Saturday night a little over three months after the news of Jack's death, Buggy had knocked before entering Vivi's bedroom door. Vivi and Teensy were sprawled on the bed, surrounded by newspapers. It had become a weekend ritual for them to scour not only the Thornton paper but also *The Baton Rouge Daily Advocate* and *The New Orleans Times-Picayune* for news of the French Resistance.

Buggy wore a high-necked gown with a robe tied around it. In her hand was an unlit sanctuary candle. Vivi was surprised to see her. Buggy had rarely entered her daughter's bedroom.

"Vivi?" Buggy said.

"Yes, ma'am?"

"Yall doing okay in here?"

Vivi nodded. "Yes, ma'am, we're fine."

"Yall want anything? I saved some peanut-butter fudge for you."

"No thank you," Vivi said. "We just had a Coke."

"Look, Vivi," Teensy said, holding up a page from one of the newspapers. "Here's something about a railway line being blown up outside Lyon, France. That's them, Vivi. I know it."

Vivi began to read the clipping, concentrating intently.

"The Lyon French Resistance group is the one that first found Jack," Teensy explained to Buggy.

"Shhh—" Vivi said, trying to silence Teensy, who, like Genevieve, did not attempt to hide her beliefs about Jack's "rescue."

Buggy Abbott hesitated in the doorway for a moment before she crossed to the bed and sat on the edge. "Yall keeping real busy with your research, aren't you?" she asked, awkward.

"We make headway every day," Vivi said.

"There's a lot to do," Teensy explained. "*Maman* says we should put in at least four hours a day on our research."

Buggy nodded. She was afraid of what was happening to her daughter, but she did not know what to do. She watched as Vivi studied the article in front of her, marking it with a red pencil, then clipping it out of the newspaper with a pair of manicure scissors.

"Hand me the Lyon file," Vivi said to Teensy.

Teensy reached for a manila envelope, one of the many that Genevieve had procured from the bank to hold their burgeoning files.

As Vivi bent over the envelope, a strand of hair fell from her ponytail into her face. Just as she was about to push it back, Buggy reached up and did it for her. For just the blink of an eye, Buggy let her hand linger gently against her daughter's cheek. But it was long enough for Vivi to sense the clumsy tenderness. Looking up, Vivi asked, "What's the candle for, Mother?"

"I was wondering," Buggy said, "if yall might want to pray with me tonight—for just a moment." Her voice sounded unsure, almost shy.

Vivi looked at Teensy, who shrugged her shoulders.

"Okay," Vivi said. "We'll pray with you."

Reaching into the pocket of her robe, Buggy pulled out matches. She lit the candle, then set it on the bedside table. Kneeling at the side of her daughter's bed, Buggy began to pray.

"Blessed Lady," she said softly, praying in the language of the ancient Mary masses. "Virgin greeted by Gabriel, Light for the Weak, Star in the Darkness, shining with brilliant light, Comforter of the Afflicted, you know the sorrows of all your children. Take our pain into your heart and bless it. Gracious Lady, gentle and sweet, we cry to you for solace. Be with us in our time of sadness. Holy Mother, shining with brilliant ray, remember the soul of Jack Whitman, who has been called to your loving bosom. Remember Newton Jacques Whitman, whom we have loved."

With those words, Buggy Abbott pierced Genevieve Whitman's delusion, which had held her daughter in its grip. The candle flickered beside her daughter's bed, and its tiny flame released Vivi.

That night Vivi, who had up to that point thought she knew what suffering was, suffered even more. In her sleep, she let go of Genevieve's fantasy, and when she woke the next day, it was to a new world in which her loss was real.

When Vivi and Teensy attempted to confront Genevieve about the implausibility of Jack's having survived the crash, she would not listen. "*Sans aucun doute,* without a doubt," Genevieve muttered, over and over, as if the words were an incantation, a mantra that could make her fantasy come true.

Vivi remembered all this as she pulled into Teensy's drive. How could five decades have passed so quickly? How many years went by unnoticed, unembraced?

French mulberry bushes grew near the brick wall that ringed Teensy and Chick's huge yard, and rows of thick mondo grass and large camellia bushes edged the circular drive—all plantings put in by Genevieve many years ago.

Remember the soul of Jack Whitman, Vivi prayed as she reached to open the door of her Miata. Remember Newton Jacques Whitman, whom we have loved.

❧

Ten minutes later, as Vivi sat on the pool patio with Teensy, she fell into the shorthand of their long friendship. A luxuriant honeysuckle supported by a trellis hung lazily over their heads, while caladiums, impatiens, and elephant ears grew in wild profusion around a fountain from which sprang a stone mermaid. It was an old patio, an old tile pool, and the feeling was one of a meticulous balance of cultivation and wildness.

"The Sidda thing with the scrapbook has me thinking about Genevieve," Vivi said.

Teensy said nothing for a moment, then asked, "'Without a doubt'?"

"Exactly," Vivi nodded, comforted by the fact that she was not alone with this memory.

Arriving with a tray with drinks for the two women, Chick looked at Vivi and Teensy and tried to gauge their mood. "Yall want me to put on a couple of filet mignons?"

"Give us an hour or so, please, *Bébé*," Teensy responded, blowing him a kiss through the air.

"*Sans moi?*" he asked, looking at the two old friends.

"Yep," Vivi said, giving him a smile. "*Sans toi.*"

"Holler if yall need anything, *mesdames*," he said, giving a stagy little bow. "I'll be inside marinating—vegetables, that is."

Vivi and Teensy reached for their drinks, then sat in silence. The hissing of lawn sprinklers and the soft slap-slap sound of water as it circulated out of the swimming pool mixed with the growing songs of crickets and the trickling sound from the fountain. Early-evening sunlight hit the pool water as Vivi sipped her bourbon, and Teensy, her gin.

Amazing how that one phrase "without a doubt" held such meaning. How it recalled Genevieve's long decline: her inability to accept Jack's death; the short-wave radio in her bedroom; the middle-of-the-night calls to the White House; the all-night "strategy sessions" to stage Jack's return. Then finally after the war, the disastrous trip to France, where there was, of course, no trace of her son. Only devastation, disorientation, displacement. And the years that followed, years when Genevieve did not leave her bedroom, which had become a pharmacopoeia.

"It's the things that aren't in that scrapbook," Vivi said elliptically. "The little big things. Dog tags."

She heard a sharp intake of breath from Teensy.

"Oh, if there had been *anything*, Teens," Vivi continued. "*Anything*. His dog tags, his boots, the Saint Jude scapular. *Anything*. Genevieve could have accepted it if there'd only been something for her to touch, some little piece, some stupid tiny object. I have sent my oldest daughter—The Grand Inquisitor—our 'Divine Secrets of the Ya-Ya Sisterhood.' But there is so much I didn't give her, cannot give her. Cannot give myself."

Vivi took a deep breath.

"I don't suppose yall have any Goddamn cigarettes around here, do you?" Vivi asked. "I know none of us smoke anymore, but I could use something to gesture with."

Teensy walked over to a hutch at the outdoor kitchen end of the patio. She returned with a silver cigarette case, which she opened and offered to Vivi. Vivi took two cigarettes and handed one to Teensy.

"Shall we light?" Teensy asked.

"Will Chick find out?" Vivi asked, sounding like a girl.

"He knows," Teensy said.

"Let's light, then," Vivi said, and allowed Teensy to light their cigarettes with a box of matches that sat on the glass patio table beside them.

"Every time I light a cig these days, I say a 'Hail Mary' for Caro," Teensy said.

Vivi turned to look at her old friend. Teensy was still tiny, with stylishly cut, subtly colored dark hair, with just the right amount of silver peeking through. She wore a pair of red silk pencil-legged pants with a black shell. On her size-five feet were a pair of little black-and-white-striped espadrilles. As she smoked, Vivi could see the sun spots on her friend's small hands.

"*Maman,*" Teensy said, as though the word itself were an incantation. "There is no escape from our mothers. I don't even want to escape anymore."

Gazing out at the pool, then over at the fountain, Vivi thought: Maybe we aren't *meant* to escape our mothers. What a Goddamn scary thought.

She pictured Genevieve wearing a turban, dancing and singing while she cooked crayfish *étouffée*. Genevieve with that Cajun patois, that laugh of hers, those misbehaving eyes. Genevieve hauling the four Ya-Yas to Marksville for the pirogue races, the hot *boudin*, the *cochons de lait*, the thick black café at four-thirty in the morning on the way to the Fisherman's Mass. Genevieve hauling her out of that hellhole of a boarding school. Vivi Walker's life would not have been the same without Genevieve Whitman.

"Sidda wouldn't be such a worry wart if she'd known Genevieve," Vivi said.

"Don't kid yourself," Teensy said, "*Maman* retreated to some bayou in her head long before Sidda saw the light of day."

Vivi knew that was true, but still could not help wishing her daughter had known the woman who had been such a beacon. Why were memories flooding in like some internal levee had burst? Was it age? Was it the fight with Sidda?

As Vivi smoked, she remembered how she'd visit with Genevieve when she was pregnant with Sidda and the twin. Sometimes, on good days, the Ya-Yas would spend whole afternoons with Genevieve in her bedroom. Vivi six months and huge; Teensy, four months, but barely showing; Necie pregnant for the second time, and beginning to put on weight all over; Caro, the biggest of them, fit and strong and big as a horse. The four of them, beached whales, surrounding Genevieve, snacking on sandwiches and Bloody Marys that Shirley brought up on a tray. Genevieve's boudoir on a good day had the feeling of an intimate if slightly bizarre bistro.

Genevieve would be propped up, dressed in one of her gorgeous bed jackets, ten thousand pill bottles on her bed table, her thick black hair piled up on her head, her nails perfectly done, surrounded by freesias, her favorite flower. She'd listen to every single detail of the Ya-Yas' pregnancies, no detail bored her. Then, lapsing into her patois, Genevieve would give them remedies she'd learned growing up on the bayou.

"To keep the devil away, let the *bébé* teethe on a necklace of alligator teeth. Show dem spooks who is boss! For teething, take crawfish, rub de chillun's teeth, will make them cut easy."

"Always remember," Genevieve would say to the expectant Ya-Yas: "Sometime the *bébé* she has to get sick to get well."

On bad days, the boudoir lamps weren't even turned on. Genevieve's room was kept dark. She wanted no light. The bad days finally stretched to weeks, then to months. Finally, only Teensy was welcomed into her mother's bedroom.

One afternoon when Sidda was a little over a month old, Vivi stopped in to show Sidda to Genevieve. It was Vivi's first trip out after losing the twin, and she was trying to pull herself out of depression. She intended to ask Genevieve to be Sidda's godmother.

Caro had driven Vivi and the baby to the Whitman home. When they arrived, Shirley met them at the front door.

"Miz Vivi, Miz Caro, yall kindly wait in the living room?"

When Teensy came down the stairs, she looked exhausted. Her swollen body looked like a volleyball had been placed in the waistband of an adolescent girl's skirt.

"*Maman*'s sleeping today," she said. "I'm sorry. She's not doing so good."

"Is she sleeping," Caro asked, "or did they give her another shot?"

"Another shot," Teensy whispered. She lifted the baby blanket to peek at Sidda sleeping in Vivi's arms.

"Lashes to die for."

"Like Shep's," Vivi said.

"Little one," Teensy whispered to the baby. "I don't think my *maman* can be your *marraine*." Then she folded the blanket back over Sidda's tiny head. She did it quickly, as if she couldn't bear to see the baby's face for another instant.

"Vivi," she said, "ask Caro to be the godmother."

"Why?" Vivi asked. "It doesn't matter if Genevieve can't be at the baptism. I want Genevieve to be—"

"Don't argue with me, Vivi," Teensy said. "Please."

"Couldn't I just show Sidda to Genevieve?" Vivi asked.

Teensy looked as though she were barely holding on. "I'm sorry, Vivi," she said.

Sidda never got to meet Genevieve St. Clair Whitman.

A month after Sidda's baptism, Vivi was lying on a green-and-blue-plaid spread on top of the daybed. Sidda lay next to her, sucking on her bottle. It was a moment when she had managed to put the lost twin in God's hands for a few hours, and cuddle up inside her life, and she was thankful. Shep was in the kitchen, mixing a drink and slicing some cheese to go with crackers. He was the one who took the phone call from Chick.

Vivi could hear the sound of him talking, but couldn't make out what he was saying. She was in a sweet, dreamy time with her new baby. My husband is going to bring me appetizers, then broil me a steak, she thought. I look pretty damn good for a woman who has just had a baby.

"Baby," Shep said, walking back into the room with her bourbon.

"'Baby' yourself," she said, patting the bed. "Come sit."

Vivi wanted her little family curled around her. She was a new mother with a handsome husband and a beautiful and healthy red-headed daughter. She might have lost a child, she might have been doing battles with the demons, but that evening she was in a glow and she knew it. Vivi could feel the bright center spotlight shining on her.

"Look at this darling girl," she whispered to Shep. "Just look at her."

Vivi took a sip of her drink, then set it on the table next to the day bed. She began to whisper to Sidda. "You have pretty eyes big as plates and a perfect nose and sweet little lips. You have ten yummy toes and ten yummy fingers and pretty little legs. I just want to eat you up."

Shep looked at his infant daughter for a moment, then at his wife. He hated to ruin the sweetest moment they'd had since the twin died.

"The good French lady has left us, Vivi," he said, softly.

Vivi wasn't paying attention to him. She was in Sidda's sweet, powdery little world. She was holding the bottle to Sidda's lovely lips. She watched her daughter's eyes starting to get heavy as she finished the bottle.

Bending down, Shep started to pick up Sidda. He had slipped one of his hands under her tiny back.

"Don't pick her up, yet, Baby Doll," Vivi said. "Let her drift all the way off, then I'll burp her and put her to bed."

Usually Shep let Vivi tell him what to do with his daughter. He didn't touch Sidda without Vivi's instruction or permission. This time, however, he left his hand under Sidda's back for a moment, hesitating. Then he scooped her up, taking the bottle out of Vivi's hands.

"What are you doing, Shep? You want to finish feeding her?"

Shep stood holding Sidda in one hand at his hip.

Vivi sat up, still in a good mood, ready to indulge her husband.

"Vivi, Genevieve has passed over," he said, watching his wife closely.

The taste of iron seeped into Vivi's mouth. She stood up. Strange, she thought. I did not taste iron when the twin died. I have not tasted it since Jack died.

"What happened?" she asked, not wanting to know.

Shep looked down at the baby girl in his arms. He did not want to tell his wife what he had to say. "Babe, I'm awful sorry. But I think the alligators got her."

Vivi looked down into her daughter's sleepy eyes. For a moment,

Vivi could not see her daughter. She could only see her own shocked expression reflected back to her from the baby's large hazel eyes.

"Can I do something, Vivi?" Shep asked. "Is there something I can do for you, Babe?"

Vivi shook her head. "There's nothing you can do for me. Finish feeding your daughter. Then burp her and check her diaper. I'll be in the bedroom on the phone. Please don't disturb me."

Then Vivi turned and walked out of the room, and Sidda began to cry. Shep Walker lifted the infant up in the air so that Sidda's baby body was slightly above his face. He did not know why she was crying. He did not know how to make her stop.

"Hey, Little Butterbean," he said. "Everything's okay. You got your papa's eyes, you know it? You got your mama's set of lungs and your papa's eyes."

"Can I talk?" Vivi asked Teensy, who was now stretched out on a lounge chair, her shoes kicked off.

"What do you mean *can you talk*?!" Teensy said. "The only way any of us are going to stay out of The Betty is to talk."

"I have realized that I do not forgive Holy Mother Church," Vivi said. "I thought I had, but I haven't. They should have let us bury Genevieve in the Divine Compassion graveyard."

"HMC still doesn't like final exits via barbiturate-vodka cocktails," Teensy said, sounding vulnerable in spite of her tough words.

"I kept going to Mass," Vivi said, "even though you quit. Even though Caro gave up on Confession. I kept up everything, just like Necie. Even after I had to switch confessors after Sidda told the world I was the Hitler of motherhood. All my life I've been a sucker for that pure, light feeling you get for two and half minutes after you've come clean in Confession. The feeling that if you got run over by a truck you'd be just fine."

"I gave up on that when they told me my striptease was a mortal sin," Teensy said.

"You're smarter than me, Teensy-boo."

Teensy laughed. "In the land of the blind, the nearsighted man is king."

After taking a sip of her drink, Teensy continued. "I am not smarter, Vivi. But I know *Maman* loved me. She did not kill herself because she did not love me. She killed herself because she believed she had let my father kill my brother. She left that in her note. My father is the one she punished the most."

Teensy sighed, then took a sip out of her drink.

"Do you miss him?" Vivi asked.

"I miss Jack every day of the world," Teensy said softly. "But not in the way you do. He was my brother. I have spent my life with the man I love."

"I can still close my eyes and see Jack," Vivi said. "See him running down the court with the basketball, jumping off that rope swing at Spring Creek. Teensy, I can still see him—I don't know if you even remember the time at the Gulf when—"

Vivi paused to look away. "God, am I crazy, still carrying on like this? Am I one of those nuts who never get over high school, for Christ's sake?"

"My brother was your true love, *Bébé*," Teensy said.

"Yes," Vivi said, and took a sip of her bourbon. "And I would still give everything I have to smell his scent one more time before I die.

"That's something I don't forgive," Teensy said.

"What?" Vivi asked.

"God taking Jack. I'm glad we beat the Japs and I'm proud we stopped Hitler, but I still don't think my brother should have died in that war. It's how come you and I understood the kids when they were against Vietnam. Patriotism is a crock. True love is not a crock, but patriotism is, *cher*."

"The Catholic Church and the United States military really ought not to mess with the Ya-Yas," Vivi said.

Opening the set of French doors that led from the living room to the patio, Chick said, "Do I hear yall plotting against Church and State? Please, Teensy, I don't want the FBI bothering us again."

Teensy and Vivi laughed.

"You crazy fool," Vivi said. "How's your marinade?"

"Just call me Julia Child," Chick replied, affecting the famous chef's voice. "Yall need refreshing?"

"*Oui, oui, s'il vous plaît*," Teensy said. "And, *Bébé*, we're almost ready to eat. What can we do to help?"

"I've got it," Chick said. "Yall stay put. I'm enjoying myself."

"Love you," Teensy said, standing up and kissing him lightly before she sat back down.

When Chick turned to go back inside, Vivi caught Teensy's eye. "How many years?" she asked.

"Almost golden," Teensy replied.

"Golden from the beginning," Vivi said.

"He's been there through it all, I don't have to tell you about that," Teensy said. "I could not have lived my life after Jack and *Maman* if Chick hadn't been by my side. Chick and the three of yall."

Vivi looked at her friend. "You are both blessed."

"Blessed and lucky, and neither of us sweat the *petit caca*," Teensy said. "It also hasn't hurt that we haven't had to worry about money a single day in our lives. *Mais oui*, my marriage has survived even when it looked like my children wouldn't."

"That's part of what worries me about Sidda—what she witnessed in my marriage."

"Come on, Vivi," Teensy said. "You and Shep have stuck it out."

"We were never like you and Chick," Vivi said. "But that's no revelation."

They were interrupted by Chick, who stepped back out on the patio with fresh drinks.

"You know," Vivi said, "you are an adorable waiter. How much do they pay you in this joint?"

He winked at her before stepping back inside.

Vivi took a sip of her drink, letting the warmth of the bourbon settle into her body. "God, is it a full moon or something?"

"Who knows?" Teensy asked, lighting them each another cigarette. "There are some months when I could swear it's a full moon for thirty Goddamn days. And we're supposed to be postmenopausal and serene. That's a joke."

She handed Vivi a cigarette. In unison, they said, "Filthy habit."

Then they each took a puff.

"I had the dream once when I was still sleeping in the same bedroom with Shep," Vivi said.

She paused for a moment to see if it was all right with Teensy to continue. When Teensy nodded, Vivi proceeded.

"The one where Jack is smiling that long, slow grin of his. You know the one I mean. He's giving me that smile from the basketball court. He's turning and giving me that grin. I see his strong jawline and that hank of thick, black hair. And I feel exactly the same way I did back then, the same warmth in my groin, the same heart pounding.

"I lower my head to toss my hair out of my eyes the way I used to do back when I still parted it on the side. And when I raise it again, Jack's jaw has been blown off. Same thing every time."

Vivi took a sip of her drink and stared out at the pool. She took a deep breath before continuing. "Shep put his arms around me one night when I had the dream. He got up and mixed me a drink, brought it to me in bed. I was touched by Shep's concern, but I never told him why I was crying."

Vivi frowned, then inhaled deeply from her cigarette, letting the smoke out slowly. "Kids know everything. My daughter knows that I held back the core of myself from her father, from my husband of forty-some-odd years. She knows that my marriage wilted on the vine and just hung there. She witnessed me hold back the precious part of me that I buried when I was a teenager. Even when Sidda was not in the room, she saw."

"Vivi, you're being too hard on yourself," Teensy said.

"No, I'm not," Vivi said, firm. "I have held on to your brother. That dream has torn me up hundreds of times in the past five decades. The only time it left me was when my babies were little. *And I missed that dream, Teensy. I wanted it back. I begged that dream to return.* And it did. With a roaring vengeance in 1963, when I dropped my basket. And part of me was *thankful*. Because as much as that dream destroys me, it gives me *back* that part of my life."

Teensy did not speak. She put down her drink and just listened.

Vivi stubbed out her cigarette. "What my thoroughly analyzed daughter doesn't understand is that you don't have to spend thousands of dollars in therapy to consider things like this. I think. I try to work it out. You don't have to pay someone a hundred bucks an hour."

"I like to think my rates are quite reasonable," Teensy said.

Laughing, Vivi stood up and kissed her friend. "I love you so much, Teens."

"Talk to Sidda," Teensy said.

"Oh, no," Vivi said. "No, no, no. Not my style. This is *my* luggage. These are *my* trunks."

She walked to the French doors, as if looking for Chick. "I carry these stories. They have my name tags on them."

Shaking the ice in her glass, she said, "Now where *is* that darling little waiter? We could use some service in this establishment."

Looking up at her, Teensy said, "Any baggage you have, *Bébé*, ceased to be only yours the minute that sperm hit that egg."

Vivi turned away from Teensy so that she could see the water as it spurted out, in a small arc, from the breast of the mermaid statue.

"Don't you miss her?" Teensy asked.

"I miss Sidda horribly. I think about her all the time."

"Then why in the world don't you call her, talk to her, listen to her? Try to answer her questions."

"I don't have any Goddamn answers," Vivi said.

"Forget answers, then. Just tell her what happened. Try to mend this thing."

Teensy stared into her glass, took out a piece of ice, and plopped it in her mouth.

"Don't chew on that, Teensy, you'll ruin your teeth," Vivi said.

"I have been chewing on ice for sixty-six years, and I still have every single one of my own teeth," Teensy said, "which is more than I can say for some people."

With that, Teensy bit down on the ice and glared at Vivi.

"What?" Vivi said. "Why are you looking at me like that?"

"If you don't tell Sidda about the hospital that nobody called a hospital, then I will," Teensy said. "It's not pretty to lose your mother, at any age."

Vivi studied Teensy to see if she was serious. "That was not the only time I left my children."

"I know," Teensy said gently.

Vivi closed her eyes for a moment, then looked at Teensy. "Okay, it's in your hands. Do whatever you think is right."

"I have no idea what I think is right, *Ma Petite Chou*," Teensy said. "I simply know that for me to do nothing would be a sin."

"Let's not get too Sarah Bernhardt about it," Vivi said, and reached out her hand to Teensy.

"No," Teensy agreed, "let's not."

Affecting a mongrel European accent, Vivi swung back around to Teensy and asked, "How much do I owe you for today's session, Dr. Freud?"

"The name is Pootwell," Teensy replied, "Dr. Pooty Pootwell."

When Chick stepped onto the patio with a platter of filet mignons, and wearing an apron emblazoned with a crayfish that read, "Suck de heads!" he found the two women in each other's arms, laughing and crying at the same time. He was unfazed. He had found them this way eighty-four thousand times before.

24

The address on the envelope was barely legible, but Sidda recognized the hand immediately. It was the almost-hieroglyphic handwriting of Willetta Lloyd, the black woman who had worked for Sidda's family for as long as she could remember. The envelope was so thin that the handwriting within was visible.

The letter read:

December 1, 1957

Dear Miss Vivi Walker,

Why sittin down I think of you and decide to write and thank you for the cashmere coat you done give me. It pretty and warm. I done let it out in the sleeve and hem and now it fit me fine. Chaney and me is fine and send you our good wish and prayers and hope all is fine with you and your family.

Love,
Mrs. Willetta T. Lloyd

How different this letter was from the others Sidda had found tucked in the scrapbook. Written on cheap, lined paper, the page was ragged at the top, where it had been torn from a tablet.

God knows Willetta deserved whatever nice things my mother gave her, Sidda thought. My mother's life, my own life, would not have been possible without Willetta. What we owe her is so complex I'll never figure it out.

Sidda contemplated the date the letter was written. What had prompted her mother to give Willetta a cashmere coat? She wondered if the long, soft, cream-colored coat she remembered Willetta wearing for years was indeed the one referred to in the thank-you note. Letter in hand, Sidda walked into the kitchen. Leaning against the counter, wondering if she should make a bite to eat, she half expected to smell that peculiarly Willetta scent: part Ajax, part Lipton tea. She thought of the tall, stately black woman who had fed her, dressed her, hand-washed her "delicates," played with her, sung to her, and listened to her with tenderness. She thought of the letters that still arrived from Willetta in that scrawling hand. She thought of how, each time they spoke on the phone, Willetta would say, "Oh, we misses you ever day here at Pecan Grove." She remembered Willetta's six-foot frame, her slightly Indian face, and she ached for this woman who had been a mother to her.

Willetta had begun baby-sitting for the Walker children when Sidda was three years old, then became their full-time maid a few years after that. "Maid," however, does not describe what Willetta was to Sidda. Forced by circumstance to spend more time caring for the Walker children than her own, Willetta loved Sidda in spite of the slave wages she was paid for her days, and often her nights. Living just down the lane from the Walker home, in a shotgun house with her husband, Chaney, and her own two daughters, Willetta had given Sidda an acceptance and affection that were miraculous, given the relationship she had to Sidda's parents.

Of the countless cruelties of racism, Sidda thought, one is the unspoken rule that white children, once we reach a certain age, are supposed to renounce the passionate love we feel for the black women who raised us. We're supposed to replace it with a sentimental, patronizing affection. We're supposed to let the thinly veiled jealousy of our own mothers obscure what we feel for the women they hired as maids.

❦

Something about the cashmere coat disturbed Sidda. Once, years ago, Sidda had dreamed of seeing her mother standing in a doorway. In the dream, when Vivi unbuttoned the coat, she had been naked underneath, with gashes all over her body, as though she had fallen on a bed of knives.

Sidda stood in the kitchen of the cabin and recalled the kinds of meals Willetta used to cook for them: stewed okra and tomatoes over rice, pork chops smothered in onions, hot biscuits dripping with butter and honey. She was suddenly seized with longing for a Willetta meal. Something with tons of fat and cholesterol, something to see her through.

Instead, Sidda grabbed an apple out of the wooden bowl on the counter. Then she stepped out on the deck into the warmth of a Pacific Northwest summer morning. She looked out at the tall fir trees that surrounded the cabin. She bit down into the apple. I know nothing, she thought. She looked around at the tall fir trees that surrounded the cabin. I know nothing but the smell of the sun hitting those countless needles from these old evergreens.

25

*T*he next day Vivi went wild cleaning out her closets. She made a thermos of coffee, went back in her dressing room, and started pulling clothes off their hangers. She set out a box for Willetta, a box for the Garnet Parish women's shelter, and a box for a sassy twenty-something girl who lifted weights at the club with Vivi. That little girl would adore the outrageous things that wouldn't fit Willetta and would seem too frivolous for the women's shelter.

Once she finished with her closets, Vivi climbed to the attic and started going through boxes and boxes of clothes that went as far back as the fifties. When she got to a box marked CHARTREUSE MOIRÉ MATERNITY JACKET, she had to stop and mix a drink.

Carrying the box to the kitchen with her, Vivi put "Judy Garland Live at the Palladium" on the CD player. She mixed a drink, lit a cigarette, and opened the box to examine the jacket.

It was one of the numbers she'd designed for herself when she was pregnant with Baylor, her last child. Cut like a painter's smock from a gorgeous piece of fabric, with oversized rhinestone buttons. She'd worn it with matching earrings, black cigarette pants, and a kicky little gold velvet beret.

She could only stand to look at the jacket for so long.

Walking into the den with her drink, Vivi lay down on the window seat and stared out at the bayou.

It isn't easy to lose a mother.

She propped a pillow under her knees and closed her eyes. That maternity jacket brought it all back.

Vivi, 1957

I could not take it any longer.

Seventeen straight days of rain in Central Louisiana. November. Damp to the bone cold. A week before Thanksgiving, when the in-laws would come and scrape me to the bone. Four babies who hardly stopped crying long enough to eat and shit. Four of them. It would have been five if my twin baby boy had not died. I adored them, but I was sick to death of them. Beautiful children can also be cannibals. I longed for someone to swoop down and take them off my hands long enough for me to think one single thought without an interruption.

Sidda, four years old, was still coughing from bronchitis, and asking so many questions I wanted to slap her because I did not have the time to talk, because there was Baylor three months old, who still was not sleeping through the night. And Little Shep, three, who scooted around so fast I couldn't keep track of him. He toddled faster than grown-ups walk, could make it out the front door and out onto the driveway before I could wipe myself. Lulu Walker, two, who ate *constantly*. Always starving. If I heard her say, "Mama, I hungry," one more time, I would kill her.

Shep was out at the duck camp all the time, with no Goddamn telephone.

If I asked the father of my children when he'd be back, all he said was, "I'll *be* back when I *get* back."

I couldn't even make myself talk to the Ya-Yas about how sick I was of my four little monsters. I did not want even my best friends to know how fed up I was. I tried once to explain to Caro.

"Tell Shep you want more time away," she said.

That wasn't it. I could have a baby-sitter any time I wanted out. But it wasn't enough. It still left me the responsible one.

For a while, I had Melinda, this big black baby nurse that the kids called Lindo. She came home from the hospital with me for every one of my babies. My children had gotten used to her.

So had I.

Melinda stayed for three months to nurse Baylor and then she left me. She had to. She had another baby to take care of.

I begged her to stay. I stood in the kitchen and said, "I need you, Melinda. Can't you just tell Mrs. Quinn to find another nurse? She can get somebody else."

"I can't be doing that," she said. "I done nurse two Miz Quinn's babies and she be countin on me. Already got my room fixed up. Miz Quinn fix me up a nice room."

"You mean I don't?" I said. "I know it's tiny—I'm sorry—I know it's not a real bedroom. But it's all we have in this place. I'll order a new bed if you want, get new curtains, you just tell me what you want. I had no idea you didn't like your room here. Is it the bed? I mean, I know it's not a great bed."

She just stood there in her big brown body, with that starched white uniform so clean and white you could smell the Clorox rising up off it.

"It ain't that, Miz Vivi," she said. "I got me another baby coming I got to look after. I can't be staying here. Done been here three months with this new baby, Baylor, just like I done with all your other babies."

The monsters were all asleep for once. It was quiet. I could hear that low hum of the refrigerator. I did not want to beg a colored person to help me, but I couldn't stop myself.

"Melinda," I said. "I am begging you. Please don't leave me. I cannot take care of these four babies by myself. Please, please do not leave me. I will pay you anything you want. I will make Mr. Shep get you your own car. How about that?"

I thought for a minute I had convinced her, thought for a minute she would stay. After all I had done for her and her family, I thought she might at least stay and help me.

"Miz Vivi," she said, "they you chilren and you gonna have to tend them one of these days."

I put my head in my hands and leaned down on the kitchen counter. That entire house smelled like baby formula. Baby formula was all I had smelled for the past four years. Baby formula, baby poo-poo, and baby throw-up.

Melinda took out three bottles from the icebox.

"Use the little saucepan to heat them," I said, "and go ahead and give Sidda a bottle. I know she's not supposed to have one, but she's quieter if she gets one with the others when they wake from their naps.

"Yes, ma'am," Melinda said.

My heart started skipping and I could feel the fist in my stomach. My skin itched all over. It was red from scratching. I had told myself that I would be ready for it. Ready for Melinda to leave me with all four monsters. I handled two kids, didn't I? I handled three, didn't I, with another on the way? I handled it, didn't I?

"Miz Vivi, you be wanting me to warm you something up? You need to have you a bite."

"No, thank you, Melinda," I said. "Maybe I'll have something later. I'll just have a Coke now."

"You done had you enough Coca-Colas," she said. "You need you some food."

I pulled the aluminum icetray out of the freezer and ran water over it. Took out one of my squatty crystal glasses and filled it with Coke. Coke was my friend. It settled my stomach; it was the one thing that always stayed down no matter how upset my stomach was. I drank so many Cokes I had to hide the bottles from Shep and Mother. I didn't want to hear their comments.

It was almost twilight and still raining hard when I put the kids in the car and drove Melinda home. I pulled up in front of her house, and left the car running. Two long-legged boys ran out to greet Melinda. They must've been eight or nine years old. I had no idea she had children that young. They could have been grand-children, for all I knew. You could never tell with colored people.

"Melinda," I said, "won't you please change your mind? You could visit with your family and I could come back and get you later on tonight."

"No, Miz Vivi," she said. "I can't go be letting people down. I got my *work* to be thinking of. What if I let *you* down when you be bout to birth a new baby?"

I could not believe what I was hearing. I looked at that colored woman and I wanted to slap her. "All right, Melinda," I said. "I understand. God forbid I should interfere with your *career*."

I handed Melinda my last ten for a tip, and she climbed out, holding a folded newspaper over her head so she wouldn't get soaked.

"M'dea! Oh, M'dea!" the little colored boys called out, hugging her, reaching to help her with her suitcase.

That's when Sidda realized Melinda was leaving, and started to bawl. "Don't go, Lindo!" she whined, and tried to climb out of the car. You would have thought someone was torturing the child. You would have thought *I* was leaving, not some colored nurse.

"Shhh, Dahlin," I told Sidda, "stay in the car. It's raining. Mama's going to buy you some new cutout dolls."

But Sidda scrambled out of the backseat, and the next thing I knew she and Little Shep were both following Melinda out into the pouring rain.

Oh, my God, there was not one, but two filthy yard dogs standing on the edge of Melinda's porch. All I needed was for one of my babies to get bit by some rabies-infected colored dog. All I needed was for them to get even sicker with that damn bronchitis.

"Get back in this car!" I hollered. "Yall get back here this instant!"

When Baylor, the baby, who was lying on the front seat next to me, heard me holler, he started howling. Just after Melinda had finally gotten him quiet on the way out here. Only Lulu was behaving, sitting in the back sucking down her third bottle since she'd woken up.

"Stay right where you are, Tallulah," I told her. "Don't you move a muscle."

Then I climbed out of the car, and stepped down right into a puddle. There was not one Goddamn sidewalk out here in Samtown, and there I was wearing my good brown suede flats.

A bunch of coloreds were up on Melinda's porch all dressed up like for a party. "Whoa, Melinda!" they called out, hooting and whistling. "Get yourself in here, girl! We been waitin on you, Honey! We got fried chicken just jumping off the plate waiting for yo mouth!"

"Oooh, chile," Melinda said, and headed toward the porch, my two oldest children tagging right along behind her. "I done got me a welcome-home party!"

You could tell from the tone of her voice that she had forgotten all about me and my children. Like we did not exist.

"Melinda," I said, my hair dripping wet, "would you be so kind as to help me get my little children back into the car and out of this pouring rain?"

"Oh, yas'm," she said, and handed one of the colored boys her purse. "Yall go on up and wait on the porch," she told them. "M'dea be right behind you."

It has always amazed me the way colored people call their mothers "M'dea." Short for "Mother Dear." I don't know where they get it.

Melinda scooped both Sidda and Little Shep into her arms, and brought them back to my car. Those two kids would not stop screaming. God, I was sick of their screaming.

"Yall be good chilren for you Mama, now," Melinda told them. Then she wiped the mud off her dress, where their feet touched her outfit.

"Thank you, Miz Vivi," she said, and slammed my car door.

Just slammed the door to my car and walked up to her house where all the lights were blazing and her family and friends were waiting to throw her a party.

I got back in my car with my screaming children and my ruined shoes. I knew it didn't make a grain of sense, but my feelings were hurt. If Melinda was going to walk off and abandon me like that, then the least she could have done was to invite us in for a minute.

"Mama, where we going?" Sidda asked from the backseat.

"Mama, we get hamboigas!" Little Shep said. I do not know where he got it, but the child said "hamboigas" like he grew up in Brooklyn or something.

I lit a cigarette. "I don't know where we're going yet. Just sit there and be still."

Both Sidda and Little Shep still had bronchitis. They coughed so hard their whole bodies shook, coughs so deep I couldn't bear the sound. I couldn't bear the look in their eyes when they coughed up mucus and almost choked on it.

"Spit it out!" I had to tell them. "Don't swallow it, Baby Dahlins, it'll make you sicker."

But they didn't understand. They got that bronchial thing from Shep. I had never seen anyone cough that hard. Nobody ever did that kind of thing on my side of the family. I had listened to their coughs for weeks on end. Thank God for the cough syrup Dr. Poché had prescribed. It stopped the coughing and made them sleepy.

The thing about Melinda was she knew just when to take

Baylor. She knew just when he was about to drive me right over the edge. She would step into my bedroom, where he was crying, just when I was about to slap him. She would reach down and take him out of my arms, like she was a fat black angel sent to me to stop me from harming my baby. She did that with all my babies. Sometimes I wondered how she knew. Wondered if something in her huge body vibrated so she picked it up like a radio station when I was *this* close to slapping my babies just to get them to shut up.

I did not like to spank. It was not something I wanted to do. It just happened, before I knew it. I couldn't talk about it. Oh, Caro would joke in those days about driving off and forgetting one of her boys at a gas station and not remembering him until the next day, but she was kidding. I could not tell my friends about the things I did to my children when they pushed me too far.

If things got too bad, Mother would send Ginger over, and sometimes Ginger's granddaughter, Mary Lee, but she was just a girl herself. It wasn't enough. Nothing was enough. If Delia were still alive, she would see to it that I never had to call for help.

When I finally got the kids home and in bed that night, I was so exhausted I was shaking. The son of a bitch, Shep. How could he have left me when he *knew* it was Melinda's last day?

I could not sleep. I was too keyed up. I could feel the inside of my body vibrating. I could feel twelve million nerve endings. Necie's kids had the measles, Caro was on a new kick of going to bed early. So I called Teensy, but she and Chick had already gone out.

"Where did they go?" I asked Shirley, who was baby-sitting.

"To Mr. Chastain's dining room," she said.

I rang the restaurant and had them page Teensy.

"I need adults," I told her.

"I'm flattered you think we qualify, *cher*. We haven't ordered yet. Shall I get you some gumbo to start with?"

"Whatever," I said. "I'm not very hungry."

I hadn't had an appetite since Baylor was born. My stomach wouldn't settle down enough; eating was a chore.

I could have called Mother to baby-sit, but I didn't want to see that constipated look of blame on her face when she asked me why I couldn't just cook supper at home. So I called Willetta

Lloyd, whose husband, Chaney, worked for Shep and his father on Pecan Grove, where we'd be moving when our new house was built and we got out of that rat-trap rental house we were in back then. Willetta cleaned at Dr. Daigre's house at the time, but she baby-sat for me, what with the Daigre kids being almost grown.

"Don't tell me no, Willetta," I said. "Please don't tell me no."

I threw on a pair of camel wool slacks and a black sweater, and reapplied my lipstick. I looked tubercular. My hair was getting thinner every day. I found hairs on my pillow when I woke up in the morning.

After I drank my dinner at Chastain's, I could not bear to say goodnight. "Oh, don't be party poopers," I told Teensy and Chick. "Please don't call it a night yet. Let's drive over to the Theodore for an after-dinner drink."

"Love to, Vivi Dahlin," Chick said, "but we've got to get home and see if our *petits monstres* have destroyed the house yet."

"Teensy, can't *you* stay? I don't want to go home yet. Come play with me."

"Vivi *Bébé*," she said. "I am exhausted. My babies woke me up early this morning, and I didn't get my nap today. Rain check?"

"Absolument," I said, then I kissed them both goodnight.

"Vivi," Chick said, "why aren't *you* tired? We've only got two kids, you've got four, for God's sake."

"Not to mention the fact that Shep seems to think that *he* has none," Teensy said. The Ya-Yas didn't like the way Shep left me for the duck camp. Necie called me the Duck Widow.

"I'm not in the least bit tired, really!" I told them. "I could go all night."

"Gimme whatever you got, then," Chick said. "We could make a million if we bottle it!"

The truth was I was tired way underneath my skin. I was tired where even I couldn't see. I do not know how that happened. How I ended up like that. It all happened so fast.

I loved the sound of Shep's voice. I loved the way the sun shone on the blond hairs on his forearms. I thought: we will have beautiful children, he has good bones, good eyes, he's from an old family. I thought: he is not Jack, but I cannot have Jack.

Shep brought me to see Pecan Grove. He drove me across the

eight hundred acres in his convertible, showed me the spot where he wanted to build a house. I felt sexy with him. I felt something like love.

I did not know what it would take to wake up every day and see Shep. He was not the man I wanted, he was not the man I truly loved.

I adored actually being pregnant. I adored walking into a room with my latest p.g. outfits that I designed myself and had Mrs. Boyette tailor.

But then there were these four creatures who depended on me. They wouldn't go away. You couldn't take them back because they kept getting bronchitis. I didn't mean for it all to happen. I didn't mean for it not to happen. I just drifted into the mother club like a boat without a rudder. I did not know what mother-hood would smell like.

I did not know that being a mother meant I would lie awake in torture, the weight of responsibility biting into my skin. Was I doing it right? Was I giving my babies what they needed? Was I doing enough? Was I doing too much? *Would I burn in hell if I did not put them before me in every Goddamn thing I said and did?* Did I have to be the Blessed Virgin Mary, the Holy Mother herself, rather than Vivi Abbott Walker?

If I had known what I was getting into, I would have said no to all of it. Would have taken off running at the mere mention of babies.

Willetta left when I got back from Chastain's. I gave her a tip for coming over at the last minute. She would not spend the night like I asked. These colored women were suddenly all saying no to me. Chaney came and got her. He came up to the door and brought her an extra sweater, and they turned around and walked down the side-walk to the pickup truck with PECAN GROVE written on the side.

I had not slept more than five hours a night in over four years. I was a woman who used to sleep ten, eleven hours a night. Sleep was so sweet to me I could taste it. I could taste a good nap like a bacon, lettuce, tomato sandwich on fresh French bread.

It was not only the rest I missed. I missed my dreams, God, I missed my dreams. Even the dark ones. Even the Jack dream. It had been so many years since I'd dreamed. Always being uprooted to warm a bottle, lead a sleepy-eyed kid to the bathroom, and return to bed angry as hell, knowing I'd be exhausted the next day.

On good nights, I used to dream of lying in a pool under a waterfall and how my body could dip under the water and live without air, then pop up and begin to fly. I used to fly all over the place during those good deep sleeps, and when I awoke I would be smiling.

With my kids and Shep, I couldn't do what I wanted. I wanted to run away with a stranger and be rich rich, filthy rich. I wanted no responsibility. It's not that Shep was a bad man. He wasn't. We were building a big new house on a Goddamn plantation. In the meantime, though, we lived in that ratty little rental of his father's. Six of us living in two bedrooms where I could not breathe.

How was it that I came to hate Shirley Fry for winning the U.S. Women's Singles? I used to love winners. I used to *be* a winner. I used to play tennis, I mean really *play*. I was so strong. My stomach so flat, my legs so tan, my hair so blonde.

I mixed another drink, a stiff one. I watched the television sign-off, cried at the "The Star-Spangled Banner." Lit a ciggie in bed. I tried to read, but that last bourbon must have been stronger than I realized. Hard to focus on the words.

So I peeked in on the four of them again. God, they were beautiful. My children were perfect, each one of them more gorgeous than I could have ever imagined. I thank God for not giving me an ugly child. It's so much easier to love them when they're beautiful. I made good babies.

Lulu snored like her father, but her eyes were bigger. Sidda with those cherry-stained lips, perfect little lips, and red hair any one of the Ya-Yas would've died for, not to mention those lashes. Little Shep with his toy tractor that he *insisted* on taking to bed with him every night. Such a muscular little boy terror.

Baylor in his crib. I stared down at him, tufts of cotton-top hair sprouting, little pea thumb in his mouth, puffy little breaths like he was blowing feathers.

The night light was on, but I tiptoed over and turned on the closet light as well. If they woke up, I didn't want them to be afraid. I didn't ever want my children to be afraid.

Back in my room I closed my eyes and thought about Jack. Pictured his neck. Pictured him lifting me high into the air the way he used to do, out of nowhere, just out of sheer joy. Pictured what our babies would have looked like.

I must have drifted off. I was pulled back by somebody coughing. I waited for it to stop. Where was Melinda? Why wasn't she taking care of this?

My body was heavy. I tried to lift my arm, but it would not move. I thought I'd gotten out of bed and slipped into my robe.

More horrible coughing. Sidda, unable to clear the phlegm from her chest. I had to get up. I had to go to her.

I thought I was on my feet. Thought it was Father coughing. I brought him hot lemon juice in his chair by the fire in the house on Compton Street. He did not see me. "Father," I said, "here, drink this."

And then I woke with a start. My father was dead. He rounded the curve going too fast when Sidda was an infant, soon after I lost her twin, not long after we lost Genevieve.

Sidda was standing next to my bed. Her hair was tangled. It was not hair like mine. She was not a true blond. She could not stop coughing. I imagined I could see the inside of her body, could see her small ribs about to crack. I sat up in bed, pulled her to me, and circled my arms around her rib cage.

"Baby," I whispered, "try to hold on to just one long breath."

It only made her cough harder.

"It hurts, Mama," she said.

I reached for the glass on the night stand. "Darling, here, can you swallow just a little sip of water?"

I held the cup to her mouth and she swallowed.

"Yes, sweet baby, good, that's good. Swallow slowly, darling. That's it."

She gagged and spit the liquid out of her mouth and started coughing worse. I took the glass from her hand and smelled it. It was not water. It was bourbon. If I had had a knife I would've used it to cut my heart out.

"I'm sorry, Buddy. I'm sorry all this is happening to you."

"It's okay, Mama," she said. "I came to tell you that Lulu and Baylor are sick."

"What do you mean, they're sick, Dahlin?" I asked her.

"They made a lot of poo-poo."

When I stepped back into the children's room, I was slapped in the face by the smell of shit. It was pouring rain outside, all the windows were shut tight, heat was blasting up through the floor furnace, and the whole room smelled like crap.

Lulu was sitting up in her bed sobbing. When I went to her, I could see she had diarrhea. It was dripping out of her diaper, all over her legs and onto the covers. Somehow it had even managed to get in her hair.

I picked her up. "Oh, Baby. Shh-shh, Lulu-Cakes, it's okay."

Her baby poo-poo rubbed onto my gown, against my arms. Baylor started crying when he heard the sound of my voice. I walked over to his crib carrying Lulu, reached down to feel his diaper. It was full. The world was filled with baby crap. I thought it was all I would ever smell.

"Baylor," I said to my youngest baby, as if he could understand, "I beg you, please do not start up."

He cranked it up, though, wailing at the top of his range.

Then Sidda started that deep coughing again. I turned to look at her, and that is when Lulu threw up on me. Her baby puke soaked my gown. I could feel the wetness against my breasts. I could feel my whole body start to itch.

I ran to the bathroom with Lulu, the overhead light so cruel and bright. As I bent down to position her over the toilet, I caught a glimpse of myself in the mirror and I did not know who it was.

The wet washcloth was in my hand. What to wipe first: Lulu's face or bottom. When would I get to wipe my own soiled body?

Then Sidda was in the doorway, her long red hair falling down over the shoulders of her nightgown. Her coughing racked her body, shook her shoulders.

"Is that all you can do is cough?!" I said. "Stop that coughing this instant! Can't you see I've got my hands full? Go back into the bedroom and pick up your baby brother. I need some help around this house!"

My four-year-old daughter looked at me, covered her mouth with her hand, and then obeyed. When she returned, she had Baylor in her arms and Little Shep by the hand. I wanted to kill them for putting me through this.

Where was my husband? Where was the father of those four children? You show me where it is written that only mothers are supposed to smell crap. I could've shot him for leaving me alone like that.

"Sidda, wipe off the baby. Just take that washcloth and wet it and clean Baylor up."

Holy Mary Mother of God, where are your *soiled gowns? Didn't the Son of God crap all over the place, the odor mingling with the animal smells in that manger? Why do you always look so Goddamn sweet and serene?*

Sidda had Baylor in the bassinet, changing his diaper as best she could. When she started coughing again, Little Shep said, "Bad Siddy. Mama say no cough!"

Lulu finally stopped throwing up, and I cracked open the bathroom window. Still pouring rain and freezing outside, but I could not take the stench any longer. The wind blew in on the five of us, on the little Holy Family as we puked and shat and cried and coughed and slowly lost our minds.

Finally they were all clean. I had changed the shit- and puke- and snot-filled sheets and diapers and underwear and pajamas. I had flung the bedroom windows open and cranked the heat up to ninety.

Outside it was still raining.

Lulu, exhausted, had nodded off, her pudgy leg sticking out of the covers like it always did when she slept. I'd given Little Shep, who was now wide awake, a box of animal crackers, and he sat in his bed playing with his tractor and biting the heads off giraffes.

The baby was on his stomach, making little fretting noises. I rubbed his back in little circles. "There, Bay-Bay, be quiet. Please be quiet for Mama."

Sidda's next coughing jag went on forever, making me close the windows, although I hated to.

I crossed to her in her bed and looked at her. Why was her face pinched? She was only a child. "Siddalee Dahlin, when did we last give you cough syrup?"

"I don't know, Mama," she said, and started to cough again.

I got the cough syrup out of the medicine cabinet in the bathroom and returned to her side. "Sit up, Dahlin," I told her. "Here, let me prop up your pillow."

I poured the amber liquid into a spoon. "Here, Sidda, swallow slowly, okay?"

Her coughing momentarily stopped. I looked at the cough syrup and decided to pour myself a spoonful. It couldn't hurt.

My hands were shaking. I pushed Sidda's hair out of her face. I placed my hands on her cheeks.

"Feels good, Mama."

"You're my big girl, Sidda," I whispered. "You're my oldest. You have to help me take care of the little ones, you promise?"

"Yes, Mama," she whispered, her eyes starting to close.

Back in my bedroom, I lay down, my eyes wide open. It took me a while to realize that the stench now came from my own nightgown, which I hadn't yet changed. Without getting up, I slipped the gown off me and lay on the bed naked. I looked down at my body and tried to pray.

But the smell was too strong. I rose, walked to the closet. I took out my ankle-length off-white cashmere coat, a Givenchy that I bought for myself with part of my inheritance after Father died. The single most expensive, extravagant item I had ever bought for myself. I pulled on socks and boots and stepped out onto the small side porch.

The rain was still falling, and an oyster-colored light was starting in the east. It was cold and damp, but at least it didn't stink.

Holy Mother of the Redeemer, if only once I could see baby throw-up stains on your lovely blue garments, if only once I could see your own palms itching to slap the Savior in his bawling face, then maybe I would not now feel like such a piece of human crap. You Goddamn Eternal Virgin, if you would wipe that insipid pastel smile off your face for one moment and look at me like we were in the same shoes, then I might not despair.

I was no virgin. I stank. My hands smelled like baby poop and puke and tobacco. Even the Hovet I sprinkled on them could not erase the stink. There was nothing to erase the stink of being alive. I was afraid my children would die. I was afraid we were all dying.

In the dawn air the cold turned my breath into fog. Fog was all around me. Soon I could not see my own hands.

I made myself wait until six-thirty to call Willetta. I told her it was an emergency, and she came. While she made the kids breakfast, I put on lipstick and combed my hair. I was still trying not to cry. I went to the drawer in the bureau where Shep kept his cash, but there were only two fives. I needed more than that.

"Willetta, do you have any money?" I asked.

I was asking my colored baby-sitter for money.

"No, ma'am, just my bus money. What you need?"

"What I need is a lot of money," I told her.

"You need you Mr. Robert B. Anthony off the TV to give you a check for a million dollars is what you need," she told me while she gave Lulu a bottle with 7-UP in it for her upset stomach.

"Make sure Little Shep eats his oatmeal," I said. "Otherwise he'll be into the cookies before you can turn around."

"Yas'm," she said, buttering Sidda a piece of toast. "Where you going in all this rain?"

"I'm going to Confession," I said. "I'm going to get absolution."

"Them old cat-eyed priests mean," Willetta muttered. "You got to look out for them old cat-eyed priests."

"I'll be back in an hour or so," I said.

"Good, Miz Vivi," she said, "because I got to get over to Mrs. Daigre's soon as you get back. She having her a bridge party this evenin."

They did not know me over at Saint Anthony's. It was all Italian there. The church was darker and older than Divine Compassion, and they loved their artificial flowers, those Italians did. I had not been in that church since my childhood, when Mother took us there for the funeral of one of her friends.

Underneath my Givenchy, I was wearing only my bra and panties. Who would've known the difference? It was not a sin. I had my chapel veil on.

"Bless me, Father, for I have sinned. My last confession was two weeks ago."

I tried to take a deep breath but it got stuck in my chest. My heart slammed and I could not breathe.

I didn't know this priest. I couldn't confess at Our Lady of Divine Compassion. What I had to say was too Goddamn much for my own parish.

I could smell him sitting there on the other sign of the screen. I leaned my nose in and smelled the screen. Scents of incense and leather-bound hymnals. The worn velvet of the kneeler scratched against my knees. I had no comfort. My whole body itched. Had been itching for four and a half days. I itched all over. It would drive me crazy if it didn't stop. I had already gone through two bottles of calamine lotion, which had stained half my outfits, and it did no good. I called Dr. Beau Poché for something stronger, and he was supposed to have it waiting for me at Bordelon's. Thank God for Beau. He was a baby doctor, but he took care of me too.

I was twenty-nine years old, almost thirty. I could not breathe. My sins left me breathless. "Bless me, Father, for I have sinned. It has been two weeks since my last good confession."

I pulled my Givenchy coat tight around me. "Father, I accuse myself of bad thoughts toward my family."

"Were these thoughts impure?"

"No, Father."

"Have you borne hatred toward your husband?"

"Yes, Father. And toward my children."

"How many times have you borne these thoughts of hatred toward loved ones?"

"I don't know, Father. Too many times to count."

"What are these bad thoughts?"

I knew I had to tell him. He was a priest, the representative of God on earth. I had to tell my sins. Then maybe I could eat, then maybe I could sleep.

The palms of my hands itched. They itched right into the center of my skin. I pushed my thumbnail as hard as I could into my palm. I did not want to tell my innermost thoughts to this priest. I did not trust his cooked-cabbage smell.

But I needed absolution. I needed a prayer that would carry me back into that tiny house without murdering those four dear little children.

"In my thoughts," I whispered, "I want to abandon my children, I want to injure my husband. I want to run away. I want to be unattached. I want to be famous."

"Do you have the courage to make sacrifices?"

"Yes, Father."

"Have you the necessary health and abilities to fulfill your duties as a wife and mother?"

"Yes, Father."

"Well, then," he said, and shifted his weight in the chair. "The married state is a road which passes over hilly regions. You accepted a life of duty and responsibilities when you received the sacrament of matrimony. Precious lessons of patience and resignation may be learned from the lifelong sorrow of the Blessed Virgin Mary, Mother of Our Blessed Lord. Ask her to teach you how to bear your cross silently, patiently, and in perfect submission to the will of God. We are put on this earth to suffer. It is through suffering that you reach happiness, through humiliation that you attain glory. Your chief duty is to live together in love, concord, and fidelity with your husband, and to raise your children in the Catholic faith. You must banish these bad thoughts."

"But, Father," I asked, "what if I cannot make the thoughts stop?"

"Then you commit a sin of faithlessness in the Passion of Your Redeemer. For your penance, make a good Act of Contrition, say three Our Fathers and seven Hail Marys while slowly meditating each of the Seven Sorrows of Mary. Now, by the power of God invested in me I grant you absolution for your sins in the Name of the Father and the Son and the Holy Ghost. Go in peace and sin no more."

I walked out of the church and got in my car. It smelled like my babies. I lit a cigarette. You must do penance in order to be forgiven. The car was cold. I pulled the Givenchy cashmere around me. I lit another cigarette.

I stared at the velvet box that held the ring from my sixteenth birthday. Shep did not own that ring. I did. My father gave it to me. I could not get money unless Shep gave it to me. I could charge wherever I wanted, but Shep had to hand me money. I did not have a checking account. I had nothing of my own except that ring.

Five hundred dollars. The man at The Lucky Pawn just handed over the money. Did not want to hear where the ring came from.

"I don't want your story, lady," he said. "I just want your pawn item."

On the map, the Gulf of Mexico didn't look far. Still, it was farther than I had driven by myself in years. I drove fast. Faster than that Ford had ever been driven.

That old-lady sedan came with my second baby. I had nothing to do with picking it out. It appeared in the driveway with a note from Shep, and I was supposed to say thank you. Didn't my husband remember my Jeep? Didn't he remember I was the queen of the road, roaring through the night with the Ya-Yas, my bare foot heavy on the pedal, my painted red toenails bright as the dials on the dash?

Nobody knew where I was. *Not even the Ya-Yas.* I would go somewhere and start a new life where no one knew me. I would have no roots. I would leave my husband, my children, my mother, that piss-ant priest, even my best friends behind. I would wipe the slate clean and stand naked and try to find out who was there. I would look for Vivi Abbott, a missing person.

I didn't stop until I got to the Gulf of Mexico. I stood at the edge. All I could see was water, stretching clear down to Mexico. The air was clear. I had left poo-poo diapers behind in Louisiana. Nothing in front of me but water. It was blowing and lightly raining, but I craved a hurricane. I am a woman who loves hurricanes. They put me in a party mood. Make me want to eat oysters on the half shell and act slutty.

I leaned my body against the wind and walked. I was not the kind of woman to take off her coat and walk into that ocean, giving up. But the thought crossed my mind.

I thought of that lovely, exquisite trip the Ya-Yas and I took to this same Gulf. Was it '42? '43? Drove all the way here by ourselves, no chaperone, no nothing. Jack and the gang drove down later. Stayed at Caro's family's beach house, woke up in the mornings, threw on our swimsuits, and headed straight for the beach.

I thanked God that that beach was still there. That the water was still raging. That nothing was crying but seagulls. No baby puke, no mouths to feed.

I walked for hours, and did not miss my children for a moment.

"Give me the best room you have," I told the desk clerk at the Hotel of the Gulf Coast. "Water view."

Postcards in a little holder on the desk read, "An Institution in Keeping with the Grandeur and Beauty of the Mississippi Gulf Coast. In a Tropical Garden on the Beach."

I signed the register as Babe Didrikson. The clerk only nodded. Fool, I should have signed Grace Kelly.

"Have room service send up a bourbon and branch water, please. A double. Your best name brand."

The first thing I did was draw a hot bath and climb into the tub with my drink. When I could no longer smell baby crap on my fingers, I got out. I dried my body with the plush white towel, and applied the lotion. I pulled my Givenchy around me, put on fresh lipstick, headed downstairs, and tried not to scratch in public.

The dining room looked out on the Gulf. I sat down and unfolded the linen napkin in my lap.

I ordered another bourbon and branch water and drank it quickly. I felt my shoulders relax.

I ordered a third drink. When I finished it, I felt my stomach relax. But I still itched.

I ordered a dozen oysters, and ate them with cocktail sauce hot as hell, with extra Tabasco sauce. I was nobody's mother. I was the queen of my own sovereign nation.

A gentleman approached my table. He was graying at the temples, not hard to look at, but I didn't like his shoes. Cheap and lacking originality.

"Excuse me," he said. "I can't help but notice you are alone this evening."

I looked at him square in the eyes, and spoke with a British accent. "I am working on a story for *The London Times*."

"*The London Times* is writing a story about Gulf Shores?" he asked, impressed.

"Very confidential," I said. "Sorry."

"What a shame," the man said. "A pretty thing like you."

"Pretty is as pretty does," I said.

The man went away.

I polished off the oysters, then ate a salad, and ordered bread pudding for dessert.

"We are known for it," the waiter said.

"Lovely," I said. "And a snifter of brandy, for a nightcap, if you'd be so kind."

I sat at the table with plenty of room to breathe. Nothing tight on my waist. I should've dressed like that all the time. I should've shredded my girdles with a potato peeler. My belly was full and rounded, and I was very sleepy.

My sobbing woke me.

The smell and taste of bananas and peanut butter was in my mouth. Our favorite snack on that summer trip to the coast. Necie and Caro and Teensy and I sitting on the beach eating bananas smeared with peanut butter. The softness of the fruit, its sweetness, the nutty flavor of the peanut butter, the caramel color against the pale flesh of the bananas. The sun on my skin, my toes dug into the sand, the sound of our laughter. Jack's arrival. Turning cartwheels, climbing up onto his shoulders, wading into the Gulf. My body, agile, in constant motion. Eating when I was hungry, sleeping when I was tired. Being kissed when I wanted. Never having to beg for anything.

I flicked on the light in the room and lit a cigarette. When I opened the window, I could hear the Gulf. Cold air hit my face.

I put out my cigarette and walked into the bathroom. I turned on the heater full blast, stood in front of the mirror, and looked at my body. There was my body. *Do not cry. Nobody likes a woman with saddle bags under her eyes.* But I could not stop sobbing. My breasts would never be firm again.

I did not feed my babies from my breasts. Nobody but coloreds did. It was the 1950s. I had thought I might breast-feed the twins. I had wanted to breast-feed the twins. But after my baby died, my milk dried up.

I was dried up. I could not go back to that house full of hungry mouths. I would start over in a new town, get myself a newspaper job. People did these things. People started over.

I hugged myself around my waist. I had to hold on to myself. I had to hold my own body so I would not dry up and blow away.

In the bed I kept holding myself. I tried to concentrate on the smell of the salt air coming in through the open window. Empress of the Heavens, I prayed, Gracious Mistress of the Singing People, send me a sign. Otherwise, I will drive my car as far as my money will take me, then I will stop and report the news in an unknown town. Sweet Lady, who carried the Divine, give me a signal.

In my sleep, my twin boy came to me, my precious one, the one I lost, the one whose body was not sturdy enough to stay. Melinda held him in her arms. She wore blue robes and a crown. When she saw me, she smiled, and gently set my baby down. He was only an infant, but he stood by himself.

He took a breath, locked me with his eyes, and began to sing. No accompaniment, just one perfectly pitched, bell-like voice singing a lullaby and love song rolled into one.

When the Deep Purple falls
Over sleepy garden walls,

And the stars begin to flicker in the sky,
Thru the mist of a memory
You wander back to me,
Breathing my name with a sigh.

In the still of the night,
Once again I hold you tight,
Tho' you're gone, your love lives on
When moonlight beams.

And as long as my heart will beat
Lover, we'll always meet
Here in my Deep Purple dreams.

When my boy twin finished his dream song, he stepped forward and raised his arms to me. I bent down and took him in my arms. His gaze was steady and so was mine. I held him to my breast for a moment. I did not need anything else. After a while, he climbed down from my arms and started to walk away. Just before he disappeared, he turned and said, loud and firm, "Wake up!"

I obeyed.

I woke and walked to the window. It was light outside, and my body felt rested and hungry. My itching had stopped. My nipples were party-girl pink.

Picking up the phone, I said, "Good morning, Room Service, how are you? Could you be so kind as to bring me up two poached eggs, biscuits, and a side of bacon? With a tall orange juice and some coffee? Oh—and what day is it?"

"Friday, ma'am." I had slept for days.

"Wake up," the baby said.

I picked up my coat off the floor and reached into the pocket. The card read "The Lucky Pawn Shop, Fultonville, Louisiana, Telephone 32427."

I picked up the phone. "Front desk? Will you get me the long-distance operator? Thank you, Dahlin."

"This is Vivi Abbott Walker," I told the pawn man. "Do you still have my diamond ring? I sold it to you for five hundred dollars."

"Yes, lady, we still got the thing."

"It's not a *thing*. It's a twenty-four-carat diamond ring that was a gift from my father, the lawyer Taylor Abbott."

"Look, lady, I don't wanna know where my merchandise comes from—"

"Oh, shut up, and listen to me. Don't you part with that ring. I'm coming back to get it."

"The piece is my property now," the jerk said. "Someone walks in ready to fork over the right amount, it's gone."

"Listen to me. You sell that ring and I'll swear you stole it from me. I'll drag your butt into court so fast your head will spin. I know the city judge. I know all the judges. Do you hear me?"

Finally, the jerk said, "I don't want any trouble. I run a clean operation. When you gonna come get this item?"

"Tomorrow," I said. "Maybe the next day. You hold on to it until I get there."

"I'll hold it till the end of the day today. That's it, lady. Don't waste my time. I got a business to run." Then he hung up.

I was thirty-one years old. I was still alive. I would take chunks of myself and store them in a root cellar. I would take them out when my children were grown. My twin boy gave me a sign.

Life is short, but wide. Genevieve told me that.

When I get home, I thought, I will give my Givenchy coat to Willetta. It has served its purpose. Willetta *deserves* a luscious cream cashmere. She deserves a Goddamn mink. When I get home, I'll tap dance for Sidda and Little Shep and Lulu and Baylor and feed them peanut butter and bananas and we will talk about summer. We will talk about Spring Creek, where the sun beats down so hot on the pine needles that when you step on them they release a fragrance so pungent that you want to pick them up off the earth and tuck them inside your clothes, just to bring that piney smell in closer to yourself. I will roll on the clean rug with my babies and tickle their backs, and I will tell them stories about sailing through raging storms in a boat I built myself. We will play Columbus and journey together to worlds unknown. When I get home, I will dump that Goddamn Ford sedan. By hook or crook, I'll have a new Thunderbird. When I get home, I will hug my four babies. I will hug the man I have married. I will do my best to give thanks for gifts, strangely, beautifully, painfully wrapped.

26

To say that Sidda was startled by the sight of the three Ya-Yas
pulling into the drive of the Quinault Lodge in a teal-colored
Chrysler LeBaron convertible would be an understatement. She had
just stepped out of the front door of the lodge, where she'd been on
the phone with her Jungian analyst in New York. Having recounted
several mysterious dreams, having analyzed her latest feelings about
marriage, her mother, and the frustration of finding no answers, she
was hardly prepared to be hit head on with the sights, sounds, and
scents of Caro, Teensy, and Necie.

All three women wore sunglasses. Necie and Teensy wore hats; a
New Orleans Saints baseball cap sat on top of Caro's short silver hair.
Teensy wore a pair of black linen slacks with a crisp white linen
blouse. On her feet she wore a pair of little Robert Clergerie sandals,
which probably cost more than her airfare from Louisiana. Necie was
clad in a light-blue-and-white-striped skirt and blouse, looking very
Talbot's. Caro wore khakis and a white shirt—she could have been in
a Gap ad.

The backseat of the convertible was loaded with the kind of luggage that one does not normally see at park lodges in the Western
United States. It was the kind of luggage one associates with

Southern women of a certain era who believe that it is their duty to make sure that doormen and porters make a good living, and that it is impossible to arrive in a new place without a pair of shoes to match every possible change of clothes.

For a moment all Sidda could do was stand and stare. Two young male cyclists had already stopped to ask Teensy if she needed any help with the luggage. Necie was already chatting with a young mother carrying an infant in a pack. Caro was examining a rain gauge that was built into a totem pole. Sidda shook her head in amazement as she witnessed the unself-conscious way these women interacted with strangers. She knew that later, when they saw these same people in the lodge, the Ya-Yas would greet them like the oldest of friends.

Stepping toward the car, Sidda lowered her sunglasses.

"Excuse me," she said, "don't I know yall from somewhere?"

"*Mon Dieu!*" Teensy exclaimed. Then, quickly dismissing the two young cyclists, she said, "Pardon me, boys, the reason I'm here is here."

Then she embraced Sidda with a quick, intense clutch, before releasing her to Necie's more gentle, lingering embrace. Caro put her hands on Sidda's shoulders and studied her closely before she gave her a warm hug.

"You're as beautiful as ever," Teensy said.

"You're so thin," Necie said.

"You look pretty good for someone in the middle of a midlife crisis," Caro said.

After catching her breath, Sidda said, "I suppose yall were just in the neighborhood?"

"*Exactement!*" Teensy laughed. "We figured as long as we were out of the house . . . "

"I don't want to sound rude," Sidda said, "but what in the *world* are yall doing here?"

"We are," Necie explained, reaching into the backseat for a red-and-white ice chest, "here on a matter of Ya-Ya diplomacy."

"It's four P.M. Pacific time. Does my mother know where yall are?" Sidda asked.

"More or less," Teensy said.

"In her heart your mother knows everything," Caro said.

After checking in, the Ya-Yas walked down the hall of the comfortable, 1920s-era lodge to their room. A baffled-looking teenage boy following behind with their mountains of luggage. Caro had also brought an oxygen tank—in case she needed it. Leaving them to unpack and freshen up, Sidda went downstairs to the bar to get the drinks they had requested.

Patiently, she explained to the woman behind the bar exactly how to make Teensy's Gin Risqué and Necie's Betty Moore's Whiskey Cocktail. Caro's Glenlivet with a splash was easier.

"I don't get a lot of requests around here for drinks with preserved kumquats in them," the bartender said wryly. "These cocktails wouldn't by any chance be for the three old hot tamales who pulled up in the convertible, would they?"

"How did you ever guess?" Sidda said.

"Are they old movie stars or something?"

"No," Sidda replied, "they're Ya-Yas."

"Excuse me?"

"Fairy godmothers," Sidda said.

"Oh," the bartender said, "I always wanted one of those."

When Sidda delivered their signature drinks, she found Necie and Teensy lying on the bed, their feet propped up on pillows. Caro was standing at the window, looking down on the lawn that sloped to the lake.

"Dinner at your place in an hour and a half?" Teensy asked.

"We provide the entrée, of course," Necie said.

"Of course," Sidda said. "But aren't yall a little tired?"

"A petite nap is all I require," Teensy said.

Sidda smiled. "I can't believe yall aren't more wiped out. I'm always exhausted when I fly across the country."

"Oh, good heavens," Necie said. "We didn't fly in today! We got to Seattle yesterday. Caro got us a suite at the Inn at the Market, and we had the loveliest meal at Campagne."

"Outside in the courtyard," Teensy added. "Delicious *foie gras*."

"We slept late," Caro said. "Stopped twice on the way to the Peninsula. Would have stopped four times if I allowed Necie to have her way. Comfortable car."

"Not exactly the type of car any of us would drive at home," Teensy said, taking a quick sip of her drink. "But it'll do for a rental."

"How are the cocktails?" Sidda asked.

"My Gin Risqué is very *rain forest*," Teensy said, gesturing toward the window dramatically, as though to invoke the trees.

"My Scotch is positively part of the ecological web," Caro added.

Sidda burst out laughing. She had forgotten that of all the secrets of the Ya-Ya Sisterhood the most divine was humor.

Later, after Sidda had returned to the cabin and the Ya-Yas had rested, the ladies bombed up to the cabin in the convertible. Sidda knew they had arrived because no one else in the world would blow the horn quite that madly. The three women climbed out of the car, bearing two bottles of wine they'd bought at the lodge, and the ice chest Sidda had noticed earlier.

"All you need to do is pop this in the oven on 350," Necie said, lifting a casserole dish from the ice chest.

"What's in here?" Sidda asked.

"Your mama's crayfish *étouffée*, made from crayfish your daddy raised at Pecan Grove, and succotash made from his corn," Necie explained.

"Mama sent this to *me*?" Sidda asked.

"Well," Teensy hedged, "she didn't exactly *say* it was for you, but she dropped it off at my house the morning we flew out. There was a note on it that said 'Seattle.'"

With her first bite of crayfish *étouffée*, Sidda could see her mother in the kitchen at Pecan Grove. She saw Vivi first melting butter in a large cast-iron skillet, then slowly stirring flour into the butter, and cooking the roux until it became a chestnut brown. She smelled the onions, celery, and green peppers as Vivi added them to the roux. She saw the dish change color as Vivi added the crayfish tails, along with fresh parsley, cayenne pepper, and generous shakes of the ever-present Tabasco bottle. With each bite, Sidda tasted her homeland and her mother's love.

After she paused to brush the tears from her eyes, Sidda said, "So much good seasoning. It makes my eyes water."

"Right," Teensy said.

"Tabasco and cayenne can do that," Necie added.

After dinner, the four of them took a stroll along the lake, heading south along a trail cut out of the rock. Translucent red huckleberries hung like tiny Christmas balls on the nearby bushes, and on the rock face, vine maple leaves were already turning orange. The last rays of the sunset were bouncing off the lake water at the same time a summer moon was rising, cream-colored against a Wedgwood-blue sky. The four women stopped to take it all in.

"Never seen that happen before," Caro said. "Sunset and moonrise all at once. Must mean something."

Back at the cabin, as the long northwest twilight stretched in front of them, Necie pulled a pound of Community French roast coffee out of her bag.

"Anyone for a demitasse?" she asked, before heading to the kitchen to put on a kettle.

As though the Louisiana coffee weren't enough, when Necie reappeared she bore a plate of tarts. "Petite pecan tart, sweetheart?" she asked as she offered the plate to Sidda.

"My God, Necie," Sidda said, "where did these come from?"

"I brought them in my carry-on."

"Mama did not make these too, did she?"

"Oh, no," Necie said. "*I* made these. Your mama won't fool with sweets. That's why she still wears an eight and I have to pray my way into a twelve."

Caro, having examined the collection of CDs, put on Itzhak Perlman playing old standards with Oscar Peterson.

Teensy and Necie sat comfortably on the sofa, Caro took the easy chair. Hueylene had crawled up into Teensy's lap, where the cocker was content to stare out at Sidda as if to say: See, we should have company more often. Sidda pulled up yet another chair and sat so that she could see all three women.

The strong coffee and the sinful tarts with their heady combination of dark corn syrup, nuts, and powdered sugar produced a happy buzz in Sidda's body. "These are delicious, but I better only have a tiny bite and a sip. Otherwise, I'll be up all night."

"So," Teensy asked, casual. "Where are you keeping the 'Secrets'?"

"Beg your pardon?" Sidda asked.

"The 'Book of Divine Secrets,' *chère*. Let's have a look."

When Sidda returned from the bedroom with her mother's scrapbook, the three Ya-Yas stopped their conversation abruptly. Handing over the scrapbook, Sidda watched the women's reactions closely.

Briefly, the women opened the album and gave it a cursory scan. After a few moments, Teensy spoke. "There's a lot in this book."

"There's a lot that isn't in that book," Caro said.

Sidda closed the scrapbook and set it on the coffee table between them.

"Sidda," Necie said, "Caro told us you had some questions."

"Yes, ma'am," she said, automatically falling back into the manners of her childhood.

"Sidda, please," Caro said, "let's eighty-six the 'yes ma'ams,' okay, Pal? It's from another regime."

"I have no idea where that came from," Sidda said, laughing nervously.

Teensy looked at Caro, then at Necie, before she picked up her yellow straw bag.

"My God, Teensy," Sidda said. "Not more Louisiana goodies!"

"Well," Teensy said, removing a large manila envelope from her bag, "goodies of a sort."

"Caro said you were asking about the time your mama got sick and went away," Teensy said.

Sidda's breath caught in her throat.

"I have some letters you gave me a long time ago," Teensy said, "when you were a girl. You asked me to give them to your *maman.*" She paused and took a deep breath. "But I never did."

Teensy handed Sidda the manila envelope. "There are also some letters of your mama's that I—that we've saved over the years."

"We thought about mailing them to you," Necie said. "But it didn't feel right. I don't know if you still pray to the saints, but I prayed to Saint Francis of Patrizi—"

"Saint Frank Patrizi," Caro interrupted. "Not Frankie of Assisi."

"—He's the Patron Saint of Reconciliation," Necie continued. "Anyway, it seemed better if we were with you when you read the letters."

Sidda looked at the envelope, then at the three women. "Thank you. I'll look forward to reading them."

"Why don't you go ahead and read them now, Pal?" Caro said, standing. "Stretch out and read while we do the dishes."

"Oh, no—" Sidda said—"I can't let yall do that. I'll clean up after yall leave. After all, yall provided the meal."

"We insist," Necie said. "A good guest always helps clear."

"But aren't yall tired?" Sidda asked.

"Not a bit," Teensy said. "Matter of fact, I'm wide awake."

"Me too," Teensy said. "You know it's two hours earlier here than at home."

"I just get started at this time of day," Caro said. "Take as long as you want. We aren't going anywhere."

❧

While the Ya-Yas cleaned up, Sidda lay down on the sofa, the old feather pillow propped under her head. The letters were divided into two different stacks. The first was a series of unposted envelopes in a child's hand. It took her a moment to realize it was her own penmanship. She stared at the loopy letters on the first envelope. It was addressed to "Mrs. Shep Walker," but there was no address. The name seemed to hang misplaced, off-center, floating in space with no coordinates to anchor it. As she stared at the blank white space where the address should have been, Sidda's stomach tightened. Without being aware of it, she drew her knees close in to her body, so that she became smaller.

The first letter read:

April 2, 1963

Dear Mama,

Nobody will give me your address. Teensy said I can give my letters to her and she will get them to you so I hope she does. Mama, I am so sorry we were bad and got you upset. Buggy said we are too much for you. She said we can only write you cheery letters. Please get well soon.

I am sorry we were bad and got you upset.

I am taking good care of the others.

Sunday night we stayed at Buggy's. Then Necie came and got me and Lulu. Little Shep and Baylor went to Caro's. Daddy is gone. I don't know where he went. I wish I could stay at Teensy and Chick's so I could swim in their pool.

When I asked Necie where you are she said you are out of town getting well. Are you in the hospital, Mama? Are you visiting friends? I watched *The Little Rascals* and *Superman* on TV, and me and Lulu played Barbies with Malissa and Annie. We slept in Necie's attic guest room. I am sorry. I will write you again soon. Please write me and come home soon.

Love,
Sidda

Sidda closed her eyes. Sunday evening, winter. Third or fourth grade. Her father's cowboy belt in her mother's hand. The landing of the silver belt tip against her skin. Her wild attempts to protect the other children. The leather against her thighs, across her back. The hot craziness; Vivi's talk of hell, of burning; Sidda's shame at urinating on herself; her voice hoarse from crying out. Above it all, the belief that she could have stopped it all from happening.

These images were not new to Sidda. Her body knew them well. Nothing—not distance, not career, not Connor, not her therapist's suggestion that Vivi had suffered a breakdown—nothing had ever fully relieved her of the belief that she had been the cause of that Sunday's punishment.

Lost in the images, Sidda flinched as Necie leaned down and gently draped a light cotton blanket over her. She opened her eyes to see the look of concern in Necie's eyes. Without speaking, she went back to reading.

April 12, 1963
Good Friday

Dear Mama,

Willetta came to see me today and guess what. She brought us Lucky the hamster who was at home all alone without us. He was lonely she said. Willetta was feeding him every day but he wanted us!!! So now we have him here at Teensy's where we all are now!! He is on his wheel going crazy. You should see him. He misses you.

I am waiting for a letter from you. Teensy said she thought I might get one soon. Teensy took me to see Hayley Mills at the Paramount. The others didn't get to go, just me and Teensy.

I prayed for you at the Stations of the Cross. This Lent is too long. I don't believe it's only forty days. Only one more day till Easter and I can eat candy again. I kept my Lent sacrifice to give up M&Ms. Please be home by Sunday. OK?

Teensy bought me and Lulu Easter dresses. Uncle Chick is real funny. We are having an Easter-egg hunt

and you are invited. Shirley their maid and us are dye-
ing eighty-four thousand eggs. I called Willetta on the
phone yesterday and she says everything is fine at
Pecan Grove. I don't see why we can't stay at home
with Daddy. Everything is not fine because you aren't
here.

We will see you on Sunday. OK?

Love,
Sidda

❧

> Easter Sunday
> April 14, 1963

Dear Mama,

We got dressed up and went to 10:30 Mass and then
came back to Teensy's. Necie and Caro and everybody
came over and we had a brunch. Willetta and Chaney
and Ruby and Pearl drove all the way over here to
bring us a Easter cake. Willetta had on a big yellow
hat with flowers on it. Daddy came too and picked me
up in the air.

When I kept asking about you, he made me be
quiet and play with the other kids. Uncle Chick
dressed up like the Easter Bunny. We looked for eggs
in the tall grass and on the lawn and by the sides of
the flower gardens and in the pots around the swimming pool. Baylor found the golden egg and he got a
big stuffed bunny and we all got prizes too.

The grown-ups had drinks by the pool, and when
Daddy got ready to leave, Lulu bit him on the leg.
Then it got all crazy. Daddy said, "Goddamn it to
hell." And Daddy started crying, Mama.

Then Daddy stayed and we had pork sandwiches
with Teensy and Chick and watched Ed Sullivan.
Then Daddy left. I don't know where he went.

THEY WON'T TELL ME WHEN YOU ARE COMING
HOME. I got mad. I sat in Caro's lap and told her
made-up stories about the people on Ed Sullivan. I
don't want to talk about the people on Ed Sullivan. I
hate Ed Sullivan. I hate everybody.

Siddalee Walker

❧

May 23, 1963

Dear Mama,

We are all staying with Necie now. Please come and
get us. Necie's house is too loud. There are eleven kids
here now, and I don't have any room to myself. I can't
do my homework.

You need to come home now, OK? Lulu is chewing on her hair again and I can't make her stop. The
other children miss you too bad. Little Shep got in a
fistfight. He gave Jeff LeMoyne a bloody nose and the
nuns punished him and made Caro come pick him up
from school. Lulu won't wear her uniform to school
anymore, even Necie can't make her. Baylor is acting
like a baby again, Mama. He is talking baby talk and
spitting and everything. So you see you have to come
on back now, OK? We miss you. I am being so good
you wouldn't recognize me, Mama! Come on back, you
won't believe how sweet we are. I am sorry we made
you mad and made you get sick. Are you having fun
without us, because we aren't having fun without you.
You will see when you return how we have changed.
NO kidding! Ask Daddy or the Ya-Yas. Please, Mama.

Love from your oldest daughter, Siddalee Walker

P.S. We got our report cards before Easter vacation. I
made straight As! (Except in conduct.) I did better
than anybody!

June 6, 1963

Dear Mama,

You didn't write me. I thought you were going to. I
don't think it's very nice to leave and not write me. I
am not writing you one more letter. School is out and
you aren't home. I hate you.

Sidda

⚘

June 7, 1963

Dear Mama,

I'm sorry for my last letter. I'm sorry for everything.
Everybody here misses you and wants you home. You
would not recognize me, Mama. I am so good. Please
come home. OK? Necie is going to take us to Spring
Creek but I don't want to go without you. Pretend like
I never wrote that other letter, OK?
    I love you.

Your loving daughter,
Siddalee

Sidda folded the last letter back into its envelope. She felt hot and
dizzy, flooded with anger toward the Ya-Yas for exposing her to such
graphic reminders of the past.
    But I asked for it.
    She sat up and peeked her head over the top of the sofa. She
could see the three Ya-Yas seated at the table, perhaps the first time
she'd ever seen them together without nonstop conversation. Necie
was working on a needlepoint, and Teensy was playing solitaire. Caro
had found a jigsaw puzzle, which she was avidly working on.
    They are sitting sentry, Sidda thought.
    Teensy looked up. "How you doing, *chère?*"

Sidda nodded.

"Holler if you need anything," Teensy said.

"Want another pecan tart?" Necie asked.

"No, thank you," Sidda said. "I don't dare."

Looking up from her jigsaw puzzle, Caro said, "I find if I take my glasses off and kind of blur my focus these puzzle pieces come together more easily."

Sidda felt comforted by their presence. She hadn't realized until now just how alone she had felt. She reached for the second batch of letters.

There were three envelopes, one to each Ya-Ya, addressed in Vivi's hand. The envelopes were Vivi's personalized Crane stationery, and still had a soft plush feel after thirty years. But, as Sidda opened the first envelope, she saw that the letter itself was not written on her mother's stationery, but rather typed out on a piece of typing paper. Although the typing paper was yellowed slightly at the edges and the folds, the typing still looked strong, black, and immediate against the paper. The palms of Sidda's hands itched as she began to read.

> July 11, 1963
> 2:30 A.M., my 9th day home

Teensy Baby—

The only soul I could stomach at the Hospital That Nobody Calls a Hospital said it would be good for me to write about my feelings—since I seem to have trouble talking for the first time in my life. Thus my old Olivetti, which Shep went and got for me from Mother's attic. At least you'll be spared my hand, which isn't too steady.

Teensy, I cannot bear to tuck my children in these days. I cannot bear to hold them or hug them or watch them brush their teeth. I do not dare let myself get too close to them. Except when they are sleeping.

I wait until everything is quiet and then I tiptoe into their rooms. First into the boys' room with its little-man smell of spiciness and their leather baseball mitts hanging on the bedposts. I lean over Little Shep's bed. My fierce little trooper. He sleeps hard, that kid does.

Plays hard, sleeps hard, does everything full-tilt. And then I watch my baby, Baylor. Oh, Teensy, he still sleeps curled into a little ball.

And then I go in my girls' room. The minute you step in there, you know it is a little girl's room with their smell of powder and Crayolas and some scent like vanilla. There is Lulu, who kicks all the covers off her bed every night of her life. She lies there, her little darling chubby body, asleep on her stomach, wearing that lovely nightgown you bought her with the yellow roses. She loves that gown. Willetta can hardly get her out of it long enough to wash it.

And then there is my oldest. On the nights she doesn't wake gasping from her nightmares, Sidda sleeps with all the covers pulled tight under her chin, a second pillow clenched in her arms, her right arm flung over her head. That beautiful white gown you gave her. How did you find something so perfect? It makes her look like a little girl-poet. Underneath that gown is a scar on her shoulder blade that I put there. Oh, God, she took it the worst. She is still taking care of the others, a little bitty mama. The nurse at the hospital told me to write even if I am crying; she said to keep on writing. Necie told me how you picked Sidda up and took her to the movies with you once a week, just the two of you. And how you had to convince her that it was okay for her to just sit there in the dark and watch Hayley Mills and sip her Coke and run to the lobby to use the phone to check on the other kids. Oh, I want to thank you the most for Sidda's nightgown because it reminds me that she is a little girl.

I have to be so careful, Teensy.

Merci bien, merci beaucoup, mille mercis, tata.
Vivi

Sidda put down the letter and pressed her palm against her chest to calm her breathing.

I want to thank you the most for Sidda's nightgown because it reminds me that she is a little girl.

Sidda wanted to hide. She stood up and feigned a stretch. "I'm getting a little uncomfortable on the sofa. I think I'll go in the bedroom."

"You vant to be alone?" Teensy asked, in a Garbo voice.

"Yes," Sidda said, "I do."

"Well, then, we'll just follow you into the bedroom," Caro said.

"That's right," Necie said. "We'll just bring ourselves right in there with you."

Hueylene looked up from where she lay, and gave her tail a loud thump on the floor. Sidda felt surrounded; her usual retreat into isolation when faced with pain was being thwarted.

"You've been out here long enough on the edge of nowhere," Teensy said. "We just arrived. Do you want word to get back home that you were a poor hostess?"

Try good manners.

"Absolutely not," Sidda said. "May I go to the bathroom unaccompanied?"

"No, you may not," Teensy said, grinning. Dropping her cards on the table, she went to Sidda's side, and stuck there like glue as Sidda tried to walk in the direction of the bathroom. When Sidda stopped to stare at her, Teensy pulled Sidda to her in a tight embrace.

"There is nowhere you can hide from the Ya-Ya Sisterhood," Caro called out.

Laughing in spite of herself, Sidda kissed Teensy on the cheek.

When she came back from the bathroom, the ladies did not look up. Sidda tucked herself under the cotton throw, and picked up the letters. Before she began to read, she took a moment to absorb the room she was in, the sights and sounds around her. The playing cards lightly slapping the wooden table, the breathing of the women, the sound of Hueylene's gentle snoring, a loon crying somewhere along the lake path. Sidda let these sounds enter her before she returned to that dark Lent season that extended long past Easter.

The next letter read:

July 14, 1963

Caro Dahlin—

My dearest friend—I am—maybe for the first time in
our lives together—at a loss for words to thank you
for all you have done for me and my gang. Taking

care of my boys for almost three solid months.
(Months that for me were not so solid.) Having Shep
over for dinner, when he could be found. You are one
of the few people he feels comfortable enough to talk
to. When I got home, he said, "That Caro is no bull-
shit." That is praise of the highest order from a man
who used up his stock of compliments sometime
around 1947.

Buddy, it is all such a cloud. I remember you
standing next to me somewhere in a hallway in the
hospital that nobody calls a hospital. I remember you
holding my hand. Shep told me you were the one who
came first, after I did what I did, after I did what I will
never forgive myself for. After I dropped my basket
and could not pick it up.

Willetta brought my girls in yesterday evening to
kiss me goodnight, and after they left, I said a prayer
that they would be lucky enough to have a friend like
you. Some women pray for their girls to marry good
husbands. I pray that Siddalee and Lulu will find girlfriends half as loyal and true as the Ya-Yas.

I think of you, Caro, when I climb in my bed.
When I wrap my arms around my shoulders and rock
myself to sleep like you did that first night I was
home. Shep might seem gruff sometimes, but since I
have been back, he has surprised me. The way he
asked you to spend that first night with me. I think he
suspects that he will never be as essential to me as you
and the Ya-Yas. We have to keep these men in the
dark, you know, or the whole world would fall to
pieces. Just ask me, I am an expert on falling to pieces.
And you are an expert in helping put the pieces back
together.

I love you, Caro. I love you, my Duchess Soaring
Hawk.

Your Vivi

The final letter, as Sidda suspected, was written to Necie.
It read:

July 23, 1963

Dear Dear Necie,

I do not know how you do it, Countess Singing
Cloud. We kid you about your pink and blue
thoughts, we laugh about your ditziness, and yet you
are the one of all of us who manages to stay organized
and do it with style.

I cannot talk about what happened. My life was a
basket and I dropped it.

You were the one who kept my world running
while I was gone. How did you do it? The ten thousand basketball games and altar-boy practices and Girl
Scout and Brownie meetings and dentist appointments and God knows what else. Baby doll, you must
have *lived* in your station wagon between taxiing your
kids *and* mine.

Welcoming my girls into your already huge
household. Tucking them into that darling attic
room with the big windows and the canopied beds.
Feeding them, keeping Lulu's hands away from her
hair munching, listening to Sidda practice her endless piano. Handling my mother in her attempts to
"calm" my kids. Your novenas, your countless
rosaries.

And Shep. He cooked me a steak the other night
after the kids were asleep. Poured me a drink—a short
one—and told me what all you did for him. He is
ashamed of how he acted after taking me to the hospital nobody will call a hospital. For the drinking. He
told me how you drove out to the duck camp when
nobody could find him. How you sobered him up and
got him back to town. Kept him sober for the Easter-
egg hunt.

Darling Girl, you have an admirer for life in my
husband. Please be patient with him because I'm sure
he will only show his thanks in the most bumbling
ways. But maybe that's all any of us have, bumbling
ways of giving thanks.

Thank you from my clumsy heart. You are most
dear to me and I am your

Grateful Vivi

Sidda lay very still for a moment. Then she carefully tucked all the
letters back in the manila envelope, and placed it on the coffee table.
Turned over on her stomach, leaned her head over the edge of the sofa
so she could see the Ya-Yas.

"Hey, yall," she said softly.

All three women looked up.

Only then did Sidda start to cry.

Sobbing, she stood up, with her pillow in her hand, and crossed to
the table. Her hair was smashed against her head where she had been
lying down. She looked sleepy and sad and lost.

"I changed my mind," she said, in between sobs. "Can I please
have some more coffee and pecan tarts?"

"Of course," Necie said, heading to the kitchen. "I brought eighty-
four thousand."

Clearing away her game of solitaire, Teensy looked up at Sidda.
"*Ma Petite Chou*," she said, "come sit. Bring your pillow and come sit
by me."

"So, Pal," Caro said, "how're you doing? Sure you feel like staying
up late with the alleged grown-ups?"

"I want to know the truth," Sidda said.

"We don't deal in truth," Caro said. "But I've got some stories.
Will that do?"

"That'll do," said Sidda, as she bit into one of the tarts Necie
handed her. "That'll have to do."

27

*C*aro closed her eyes for a moment, gathering strength. Then she opened them and began to speak.

IT STARTED JUST before Mardi Gras. The four of us had all decided to give up drinking for Lent. Necie took it seriously—she was the only one who stayed on the wagon the whole time. I saw the whole thing as a test of will. Teensy amended abstinence to mean every day *except* Sunday. Then your mother modified it to mean every day except Sunday—or any time at all if we happened to be outside of Garnet Parish.

Well, Pal, we put a lot of miles on Teensy's Bentley—driving to Lafayette, Baton Rouge, or even Tioga, just to have a drink. *Anything* to cross the parish line. Then one weekend your mama and Teensy lit out for Marksville. I would have gone too, but one of the boys had strep throat. They left early that Saturday. Hit a few of the Cajun dance halls, where dancing and drinking beer start at nine o'clock in the morning. They went all day and into the evening. On the way back they put the Bentley in a ditch. Nobody hurt, just the car in a ditch and the two of them too smashed to deal with it. They called Necie to come get them because they were too scared to call Chick or Shep, and they knew I had a sick kid.

When Necie found them, Vivi and Teensy were at Dupuy's Lounge eating *boudin* balls, sipping gin-and-tonics and acting up. This was the second week of Lent. Maybe the third, I don't know. Lent is a long stretch, Pal, a long desert of a stretch.

Necie called a tow truck for the Bentley, then drove them back to Thornton.

The next thing I knew, your mama had gone to some new priest—I've blanked out his name. He sent her to Dr. Lowell. A big Knights of Columbus man, had priests referring patients to him right and left. I'd never heard of the man till Vivi got the prescription. Dexamyl. I'll remember that name until the day I die, half Dexedrine, half Miltown. Shot you up and threw you down. It was supposed to get your mama off alcohol and make her a better Catholic all at the same time.

Vivi adored those pills, couldn't stop raving about them. Gave her energy, she said, kept her mind off drinking, no appetite at all, and she could get by on four hours' sleep. Flying high. Too high.

Two weeks before Easter she took off on some four-day retreat with that same priest, somewhere in Godforsaken Arkansas. She went cold turkey off bourbon, straight onto pills and penance. It kills me to think I didn't spot her headed for the rocks. Friends are supposed to act like harbor boats—let you know if you're off course. But it ain't always possible, Pal.

I don't know what happened at that retreat. Over the years, Vivi's told me a little. She didn't know a damn soul there. All Catholic lay women, no nuns, just that Goddamn priest. The place where it was held evidently used to be a small sanitarium for TB patients, can you imagine? She had packed her stash of Dexamyl, her missal, her rosary, one change of clothes, and a lipstick. All-day lectures, prayer, fasting, Communion, plenty of Confession, I'm sure. Stick-your-fingers-in-the-wounds-of-Christ shit. She was going to get pure.

I am not a psychologist, Pal. I don't know what fine filament got stretched too tight. I think a lot of it was the Dexamyl. People did not know how bad that drug was back then. Ten times worse than booze.

Caro stood up from the table and walked to the sliding glass door to look out at the lake. She ran her hands through her short hair and began to cough.

Sidda was worried. The cough sounded so ragged. "Are you okay, Caro? Can I get you anything?"

"I don't suppose we could skip the rest of this tale," Caro said, "and I could divulge to you my world-famous Ramos Gin Fizz recipe instead?"

Sidda went to Caro, and put her arms around the older woman's waist. "This isn't easy for you, is it?"

"Nope," Caro whispered.

Sidda looked at Teensy and Necie. "Why did yall come?" she asked. "I mean, this is no picnic, is it?"

"Your *maman* misses you," Teensy said, standing and walking over to the sofa, where she kicked off her shoes.

"We're like her ambassadors, you know what I'm trying to say?" Necie said, unsure.

"Did she *send* you?" Sidda asked.

"Not in so many words, no," Teensy said.

"Then why did you come?" Sidda asked. "Why didn't she come herself? Why doesn't she—why *hasn't* she told me this story herself?"

"*Because,*" Caro said. "That's all: *because.*"

Sidda waited as the older woman walked into the kitchen and returned with a glass of water. Crossing to the easy chair, Caro sat down. The light was minimal, and she took out a pack of matches. In horror, Sidda thought she was about to light a cigarette. Instead, Caro reached for the candle that sat on the table next to the chair. She lit it, then reached into her pocket, pulled out a cigarette, and placed it, unlit, between her lips. From that point forward, she used the cigarette to gesture as she told the story.

BY THE TIME Vivi got back to Pecan Grove, Caro continued, she was convinced—at least this is what she'd pieced together—that the four of you kids had been entered by the devil.

Caro stopped to look at Sidda, who was still standing near the glass door. "Pal," she said, "why don't you come get comfortable? I'm kind of lonely over here."

Crossing toward the easy chair, Sidda pulled over several large lounging pillows, and plopped down on the floor beside Caro. Necie went to lie on the sofa with Teensy, their heads at opposite ends. Caro got up and, without speaking, crossed to the table where Sidda had left her feather pillow.

Handing it to Sidda, Caro smiled. "Here ya go, trooper."

"I imagine you remember the next part, Sidda," Caro said, sitting back in the easy chair. "Vivi beat the four of you violently. She struck you repeatedly with a belt while you were naked. By the time I got there, after Willetta had cleaned yall up, the welts were horrible and the four of you were almost hysterical. Willetta and her husband had seen the beating out in the yard and gone over to your house, where they stopped Vivi, and took yall back to their house. Willetta called your grandmother, and your grandmother called me. At your grandmother's instruction, I went to Willetta's house first."

At that point, Caro paused.

"Caro?" Teensy said, getting up. "You okay? I worry about you talking this much."

Caro put down her unlit cigarette, and pulled her oxygen tank closer to her. Swiftly, without drama, she began to attach the tube that ran from the tank to her nose.

"Can I do anything, Caro?" Sidda asked. "Can I get you another glass of water?"

Struggling to keep breathing herself, Sidda went into the kitchen, where she poured Caro a glass of water. The kitchen was dark, and Sidda could smell the strong coffee on the stove. She laid her cheek down against the cool countertop for a moment and took a deep breath.

Steady. You have already lived through this.

Caro took a sip of the water Sidda handed to her, then a swallow of black coffee, and continued her story.

"Buggy took yall home with her, and I went up to your house. I found Vivi lying on the kitchen floor alone, naked. I thought at first I could reason with her. I thought I could *will* Vivi to snap out of it. My mistake.

"I have loved your mother like a sister, loved her like family, loved her as much as I love my children, probably more than I loved my husband. Ever since the day I met her at the concession counter of my father's movie theater in 1933, wearing a little yellow dress with red tulips on the pockets, buying an Orange Crush. Seeing her on the floor like that wasn't easy."

Caro paused for a moment and rubbed her eyes. Then she continued:

I TOOK HER to the bathroom, put her on the toilet. *And she could not remember what to do.*

Pal, I said. Just try to relax and let the water come out.

Vivi's body was so tense you could see the veins in her face. That's when I decided to call Beau Poché, yall's baby doctor—you probably remember him. I had no idea where your father was. Shep was never home. So I called Beau Poché myself, knowing damn well he was only a pediatrician. He'd known us all for years, though, played trumpet in the band when we were in high school, made countless house calls on every one of our kids. I was not about to call the sons of bitches who called themselves psychiatrists in this town who let us lose Genevieve.

Beau was at the house within thirty minutes. Vivi was on the hall floor, naked underneath the robe I threw on top of her. She could not tell Beau what year it was. She could not tell him her name. He gave her a shot—some kind of tranquilizer, and she didn't fight it. A truck pulled into the driveway. I signaled to Beau that I'd go see who it was.

It was dark by then. I met your father just as he was climbing out of his truck. "Shep," I said, "Vivi's sick. She's cracked up. We've got to get her some help."

"Where are my children?" he said, angry. "Are they okay?"

"With Buggy," I said.

He turned his back, took a step toward his truck.

"Don't you even think about getting back in that truck," I told him.

Your father covered his eyes with his hands.

"Where is Vivi?" he said.

"Inside with Beau Poché."

"You called that man out to my house?"

"Yes, I did, Shep, and I don't want to hear one word about it."

"She could just be behaving actressy, Caro," he said. "You know how Vivi can be."

When your father walked into the house, he ignored Beau Poché. He spoke to Vivi.

"Vivi, Babe," he said, "you look like you could use a good meal. How bout I fix you a little something to eat?"

Then your father went into the kitchen and fried a pound of bacon. Your mother followed him in there. She sat on the floor by the stove and stared at his feet. I stood there and watched your father fry bacon, slice tomatoes, tear lettuce, and toast bread. I sat at the kitchen counter and watched him get down on the floor next to your mother and try to make her take a bite of the sandwich he'd just made. She could not remember how to chew. The food fell out of her mouth.

Shep looked up at us sitting there at the counter on those rattan stools. "Can't either of yall get my wife to take a bite of this bacon, lettuce, and tomato sandwich?" he asked, tears streaming down his face.

"No, Shep," Beau Poché said. "I'm afraid we can't."

Then your daddy picked the bacon off Vivi's lap and wiped the mayonnaise off her face.

This must have been what—the fourth Sunday in Lent.

The next day Chick drove Teensy, Shep, your mama, and me to a private clinic outside New Orleans. Necie took care of yall. It was a long day. At the hospital, we wanted Vivi to sign herself in. Shep did not want her to feel like she was being put away.

But when the administrator asked Vivi what her name was, she said, "Queen Dancing Creek."

The man looked at your father.

"Ask her one more time," Shep said.

The man asked again.

"Rita Abbott Hayworth," Vivi said, "love child of H. G. Wells and Sarah Bernhardt."

I would have laughed if your mama hadn't accompanied that comment by picking up a paperweight from the administrator's desk, and throwing it so it barely missed his head. Right away, Chick put his arms around Vivi like he was hugging her. Really, he was trying to constrain her because we had no idea what she would do next.

"I'm afraid if your wife cannot give me her legal name," the man said, "this will have to be an involuntary commitment."

Your father stepped up to the man. "Listen to me, Nimrod," he said. "I'm paying the bill in this sonavabitch joint, and if my wife wants to sign herself in as the President of the Goddamn United States, that's how you'll do it, you hear me? *Her name is Rita Abbott Hayworth.* My wife signs in however she wants, and then you take Goddamn good care of her. She is a precious woman. Am I clear?"

Man, was he clear.

Your father kissed Vivi on the forehead before we left her. Then he cried all the way to the Monteleone Hotel, got smashed in silence, and passed out before we even ordered dinner.

There are no records of Vivi Walker's ever having checked into a psychiatric clinic for three months. No one ever knew, except us. When Vivi got home three months later, she made it clear that she did not want anyone to know.

When your mama got home she'd stopped hallucinating. She could speak coherently again. She'd lost tons of weight. The only thing she would eat at first was peaches.

We tried to get her to talk about her breakdown, but she would not allow it. The most she would say is "I dropped my basket." That is the phrase she made up to refer to the whole episode.

Only once, when Vivi and I were alone one night, years later, at Spring Creek, did she talk about it. It was late and we'd been drinking gin. She made me describe to her exactly how I found the four of you kids that Sunday afternoon. She made me tell her everything—every single mark on each one of your bodies. She watched my every expression, my every eye movement, waiting for me to judge her. But I didn't. And I won't.

What I regret the most is that none of us ever talked with you, Sidda—or Little Shep, Lulu, or Baylor. We hid behind some archaic belief that you do not interfere with another person's children.

Caro looked at Sidda in silence for a moment. "Here's what I want you to know: *not one bit of this is your fault.* Something just cracked in Vivi. Maybe people are more like the earth than we know. Maybe they have fault lines that sooner or later are going to split open under pressure.

"And, yes, your mother was an alcoholic. *Is* an alcoholic. I admit it. I know that has been hard for you, Sidda. I am not denying one bit of it.

"But of all the loony, imperfect souls you'll ever meet, my friend, Vivi Abbott Walker is one of the most luminous. When she dies, the remaining three of us will ache like part of our body has been cut off."

Caro looked at Teensy and Necie, and gave a little laugh. "We're surviving members of a secret tribe, Pal."

Then, focusing her gaze on Sidda, Caro said, "You've got Ya-Ya blood, Siddalee. Whether you like it or not. And sure, it's tainted. But what the hell in life isn't?"

Caro leaned back in the easy chair and let out a sigh. No one spoke for a while. Then Sidda unfolded from her position on the floor and walked to the glass door. She slid it open and stepped out onto the deck. The heat of the summer day had been replaced by a cool Northwest night. She looked out across the lake, and it occurred to her that she could walk down the steps of the deck and onto the lake path, walk straight out into the night and never return.

She looked back into the cabin, where the three women remained in their same positions. Inside, the candle still burned. Hueylene waited at the door with her head cocked to one side, trying to keep an eye on all of them.

Sidda felt very young and very old at once as she watched Caro, then Teensy, then Necie slowly rise from their spots and walk toward her out on the deck, Caro leaning on Necie's arm. She stood quietly as the three women put their arms around her. She breathed in their scents, the lake air, the scent of the towering old trees. She breathed in the vast world of suffering and pure, dark love, and as she did, a well of compassion began to flow in her. The moon was dropping behind the ridge of trees on the opposite side of the lake; something caught Sidda's attention. It was the tiny key she'd hung in the window, glowing in the fading moonlight.

28

*I*t was early afternoon when Sidda began to stir from her sleep on the sofa. She had collapsed there the night before, after giving the Ya-Yas her bedroom. Someone was whistling "When You Wish Upon a Star," and at first she thought she was dreaming. She let her body sink down a little deeper into the covers. The air was warm and the scent of cedar and lilies drifted in through the open deck door. The whistling floated in and out of Sidda's dreams before she realized that there was only one person in the world who could whistle "When You Wish Upon a Star" with all its wonderful Walt Disney intricacies.

Hueylene smelled Connor before Sidda saw him. The cocker ran to the deck door, her barks quickly turning to happy whines of adoring welcome. Sidda flung the covers back and stood up.

When she saw Connor standing on the deck rubbing Hueylene on the belly, her heart gave a sudden lurch. She paused for a moment and pressed her hand over her heart to quiet it. It was kicking so hard she thought for a moment she might be having a heart attack. Then she remembered that very thing used to happen all the time when she was a lovesick teenager. But now that she was forty, the power of the response made it hard for her to stay standing. She took a deep breath. Then, clad only in a baggy T-shirt, she ran across the room, through the open door, and out onto the deck, where she jumped up onto Connor, her bare legs wrapping around his waist, her hands at his neck. Connor cupped her naked butt, spun her around in the air, and they began to kiss.

He had been thinking about her for almost two weeks, but he'd forgotten the swiftness of her small body, her wild spontaneity, the softness of her smell when she'd just awakened.

Hopping and jumping around them in a clumsy, happy dance, Hueylene barked excitedly, angling for attention.

"Hueylene, Hueylene, you old blonde bombshell of a governor, you," Connor said in between kissing Sidda's lips, neck, eyes, ears.

"Happy happy happy!" Sidda said.

Gently, Connor set Sidda down on the deck railing. "Pretty good shape for forty, Hot Little Chili Pepper."

"Old cheerleaders don't die," Sidda said, "we just dye our hair."

The two of them stood looking at each other, unable to stop smiling.

"Hey, Sidd-o."

"Hey, Conn-o."

"Hey, both of you," Caro said at the edge of the deck door. "Give an old lady a thrill, why don't you?"

"Caro!" Sidda said. "Good morning."

"Afternoon is more like it," Caro said, stepping out onto the deck.

"Grocery delivery?" she asked, glancing down at two large bags from Pike Place Market, which sat on the edge of the deck.

Tugging slightly at the bottom of her T-shirt, Sidda smiled at Connor. "Yes, actually. My deliveryman drove all the way out from Seattle just to bring me some sugar."

"And they claim chivalry is dead," Caro said.

"Caro Bennett Brewer," Sidda said, "meet Connor McGill."

Extending her hand, Caro said, "Who taught you to whistle, Pal? You're not half bad."

Connor shook her hand and smiled. "My mother taught me to whistle. I accept your compliment on her behalf. A pleasure to meet you."

"Oh, my God!" Necie said. She had just appeared at the door, along with Teensy. "Nobody told me there was a *man* here. I haven't even brushed my teeth!" With that, she vanished back into the cabin, leaving Teensy standing at the edge of the deck looking out at the others.

Stepping forward, Connor said, "I bet anything you're Teensy. I would've recognized you anywhere after Sidda's description."

Teensy stared at Connor for a moment, frozen. Sidda thought for a moment that she might not have heard him.

"Teensy," Caro said, punching Teensy on the shoulder, "where are your manners?"

"*Excusez-moi,*" Teensy said. "I—uh—you look like someone I used to know. Are you Connor McGill, the *fiancé*?"

Connor laughed and looked at Sidda. "Yes, at least I think I am."

"You better be, *cher,*" Teensy said, reaching out to give Connor a kiss on the cheek, "because you are some kind of gorgeous."

"I simply cannot get over it," Necie said. "These croissants are perfect. They get crumbs *all* over you, just like they should. Where did you say you bought them, Connor?"

Sidda, Connor, and the three traveling Ya-Yas were enjoying *un petit déjeuner* out on the deck, compliments of Connor's grocery delivery.

Before Connor could answer, Necie said, "Connor, you *must* come visit us in Louisiana. I would love to prepare some of our local delicacies for you."

Connor put down his coffee cup and smiled. "With an offer like that, I don't know how I could stay away."

"*Promise* me," Necie said.

I'm in trouble *now,* Sidda thought.

After breakfast, the Ya-Yas swung by their room at the lodge to get fresh clothes and change into their swimsuits. Then the five of them spent the afternoon on the lake. They swam and lay on the dock in the sun, the ladies announcing that while Lake Quinault was not as warm as a good swimming hole ought to be, it did have its quaint qualities. Later that afternoon, Connor barbecued some halibut steaks he'd brought from town. Caro helped with the fire, and Necie did kitchen prep, watching Connor closely to see what kind of cook he was. Teensy kept their glasses of Merlot filled, and Sidda was in charge of dessert— fresh blueberries with a hint of Necie's Courvoisier on top.

It was not yet eight o'clock when the Ya-Yas said goodnight. One by one, they hugged Sidda goodbye. One by one, they whispered into her ear.

"He is *au coeur tendre*," Teensy whispered.

"Marry a man who cooks!" Necie whispered.

"Don't worry about your mama," Caro whispered. "One breath at a time, Pal, it's the only way."

Once alone, Sidda and Connor did what they'd been longing to do for weeks. As each undressed, their eyes never left the other's body. Lying on the bed, Connor gently pressed down Sidda's lower lip and held it there for a moment before he kissed her. The gesture made her shiver, and soon their bodies went where their imaginations had been traveling.

As they caressed, stroked, and entered each other, Sidda felt as though she were being reintroduced to her own body. Each stage of their lovemaking seemed to open her not only to sensual pleasure but to a grief that lay in her bones and muscles. Her rapture, which was almost simultaneous with Connor's, was accompanied by a shout. As she shuddered with release, she began to weep. She felt untied, unfolded, unsecured. As if her borders had dissolved, leaving her open, penetrable on every level. Along with love and longing, she felt a mixture of abandonment and grief surge through her, and it left her raw and wide open.

"I'm sorry," she whispered to Connor. "I'm sorry, all I do is cry."

"Sweet Pea," he said softly, "whatever it is, it's okay."

Sidda tried to make herself laugh, but she could not.

"Baby-cakes," Connor asked, "what's wrong?"

Pulling away from him, Sidda sat up in bed. Briefly, she recounted the Lenten story she had learned the night before. He watched her closely as she spoke, and when she finished, he tried to pull her toward him. But she pulled away. She felt she had somehow handed him a piece of kryptonite.

"She should have told me herself," Sidda said.

Connor touched her hair softly with his hand. "She dispatched her emissaries, didn't she?"

"It's not enough," Sidda said softly, her words catching in her throat.

She got out of the bed. "You don't deserve this, Connor. I'm a wreck."

Connor watched her naked body, still flushed, as she walked out of the room, closing the door behind her. He lay in the bed, studying the room he was in. The sight of Sidda's books, her robe hanging on a hook on the back of the door, a vase of lavender and blue hydrangeas on the bedside table, a marked-up version of May's latest draft of *The Women: A Musical*. He loved these everyday signs of Sidda, he loved her forty-year-old body, her mercurial mind. He told himself he would not go to Sidda until the Swainson's thrush he could hear outside the cabin had stopped its singing. In the meantime, he lay in the bed and tried to name the other birds he could hear singing in the distance.

In the big room, Sidda stood at the round oak table and opened the scrapbook. The night was still quite warm, and she could hear the sound of moths hitting the door to the deck.

She turned to a photo of a twenty-something Vivi lying on a picnic blanket outdoors. Her mother's face was propped in her hands, and she was gazing at a baby girl whose little sunbonnet revealed wisps of strawberry-blonde hair. The baby returned Vivi's gaze, and the two of them appeared oblivious of anything but each other. The world they shared in that moment seemed utterly private, utterly complete.

Sidda turned the snapshot over. On the back it read, "Queen Dancing Creek with Royal First Daughter." She turned the photo back over again, and her eyes filled with tears. Why have I left the warm bed of my lover to return, yet again, to these artifacts?

She set the photo aside and reached for the packet of her mother's thank-you letters to the Ya-Yas. Gently lifting each letter and examining it, Sidda began to perceive the love inherent in her mother's words. She remembered a phrase she had read somewhere. "Words lead to deeds. They prepare the soul, make it ready, and move it to tenderness." Wasn't it Saint Teresa who'd said that?

Sidda remembered her inexpressible joy at seeing her mother's face when Vivi had finally returned. The joy of smelling Vivi again, after the seemingly endless, unexplained separation. Vivi's cotton nightgowns. The outline of her thin frame when she stood in the doorway to tell Sidda goodnight. Sidda's longing for her mother to step closer, to crawl into the bed and hold her, to promise she would never go away again. The sound of Vivi's feet in the hallway. The yearning, the aching for her mother taking precedence over the hideous anger Sidda felt at her leaving.

She did not hear Connor walk into the room. When he reached out to touch her on the shoulder, she jumped. Slipping away from him, she grabbed the cotton throw off the sofa.

The lamp in the corner glowed softly. Sidda pulled the throw tightly around her naked body as she stepped back to the table. Connor stood, his arms hanging beside his naked body.

"I was just looking at this book of supposed divine secrets," Sidda said.

Reaching out, Connor turned a few pages of the scrapbook. "Ya-Ya maidens with child," he said, stopping at a photograph.

Sidda glanced at the image. She'd come across the snapshot earlier, but never really studied it. Captioned "Beauties of 1952," it showed the four Ya-Yas, in their early twenties, all eight or nine months pregnant, sitting around a kitchen table. Caro's feet were propped on the table, and one of her arms was around the back of Vivi's chair. Necie's head was slightly lowered, her eyes almost closed in a smile. Teensy's hands waved in the air as though she were telling some outrageous joke. Her feet were propped on the table next to Caro's. Vivi's head was thrown back in a big laugh, her mouth wide open so you could see her teeth. Each one of the women was dressed in a maternity smock of some kind. Each held a drink in one hand and a cigarette in the other—with the exception of Necie, the only one who had never smoked.

"Fetal abuse captured in a Kodak moment," Sidda said.

Connor leaned his hands on the table and dropped his head down closer to the image. "1952," he said. "She was carrying you, Sidda."

He pointed with his finger to Vivi's huge belly. "Looks like the tribe is having fun," Connor said. "You were nestled in that big double-basketball belly with your twin, huh?"

"I'm sure my twin thrived on all the alcohol and tobacco smoke," Sidda said.

"Look at these women, Sidda," Connor said. "They're drinking and smoking, but doesn't the other stuff count too? Look at it. Look at that image."

He held the book up closer to Sidda's face. "Look at them. Look at them like you look at actors, without yourself in the way."

"Stop it, Connor."

"No, Sidda, I won't stop it."

Sidda forced herself to study the snapshot. To look at the glimmer in their eyes, the tilt of their heads, their facial expressions, the lack of tension in their bodies, their relaxed gestures. She let herself receive the photo until she felt, as she did with actors, the very energy that radiated from their bodies.

"What do you see?" Connor asked.

Sidda held on to the edge of the table. "Ease," she said, barely audible. "I see lightness and ease. I see suffering somewhere in my mother's eyes, but I also feel the camaraderie. Laughter. Friendship."

Connor watched her, listening.

"But—" Sidda said, and stopped.

"But what, Sidda?" Connor asked.

Straightening up, Sidda turned away from the table and started toward the kitchen. Catching her arm, Connor repeated the question.

"But what?"

"But," Sidda said, "she did not know how to love me and I don't know how to love you."

"No," Connor said, and pulled her back to the scrapbook. "That is not the way it works."

He pointed again to the photograph. "*Look* at them. I met these women, Sidda. They're still full of the same lightness and ease at seventy. *And they love you. They want you to be happy.* I realize I haven't met the divine Vivi yet, but I promise you she feels the same way. Doesn't their laughter count for something? Doesn't that sisterhood and the laughter and the not being so damn alone in the world count for something? Didn't you absorb some of that spirit along with whatever else passed through the placenta?"

Sidda turned away from the scrapbook, but Connor took her face in his hands and forced her to look at him. "Sid, I'm not your mother. And I'm not your father. And I want to take you for better or worse."

Sidda was silent for a moment. "There's such a thing as alligators that get in the way for some people," Sidda said.

Connor's eyes were wet and his breathing was a little ragged. "I'm stronger than alligators. Smarter too."

A sob shook Sidda's body. "You can't do this for me, Connor," she said. "I have—"

"I don't want to *do* anything for you, Goddamn it!" He broke away, so that he stood naked, in front of the door to the deck. He was shifting his weight from one foot to the other, almost like a boxer. Sidda could hear his bare feet as they slapped the floor. She could see his lean, muscular forty-five-year-old body, utterly unself-conscious in its focus and intensity.

He locked her with his gaze. "I don't want to *do* anything. I just want to love you."

She could not respond.

"Look, I'm five years older than you are, and I've never even *wanted* to get married before. I'm making this up as I go along. You think I've felt *tranquil* since you postponed the wedding? I've been dangling by a thread over the canyon of fucking doom. I'm not cut out for limbo, Sidda."

Connor opened the door and stepped out onto the deck.

A horrible little line from her Catholic catechism surfaced for Sidda: "Limbo is not hell. But the baby souls suffer there, nonetheless, because they cannot see the face of God."

As Sidda stepped out onto the deck, fat cumulus clouds passed by the moon, now a little less than full. She walked to where Connor was standing, his hands on the railing, facing out at the lake. Letting the cotton throw fall from her body, she leaned her body against his back.

"I don't have too many boogeymen for you?" she whispered.

Connor McGill stood perfectly still as he stared out at the lake. He watched the clouds cross the moon, obscuring it briefly before they moved on, revealing once again the lunar snowiness. He chose his words with care. "No, you do not have too many boogeymen for me. You have just the right number."

Sidda embraced him then. She held him tightly, breathing in the meaning of his words. They stood that way in the moonlight for a long time, Hueylene sitting patiently at their feet.

Finally Sidda asked, "Maybe a little midnight swim?"

They walked down the steep stairs to the dock, where, naked, they slipped into the freezing Northwest water. On their way back, they swam on their backs so they could look up at the moon, their strong flutter kicks sending plumes of water into the air.

When they returned to the cabin, they were both wide awake. As they dried each other off on the deck, Connor spotted the small key Sidda had hung in the window.

"What's the wee little key belong to?" he asked.

Giving her hair a swipe with the towel, Sidda looked up. The moment she spotted the key, she froze. Her body leaned slightly forward, and her head tilted to one side. She looked as though she were listening to a faint call that was trying to reach her from a long distance away.

Then, breaking her almost trancelike stillness, Sidda stepped into the cabin, stood on tiptoe, clasped her hand around the key, and pulled it down from where it hung. A smile spread across her face.

Reflexively, she covered her mouth. She looked like a child who had just discovered hidden treasure.

Finally, Sidda emitted a delighted laugh. "Connor, would you be interested in sharing a bottle of Moët that mysteriously appeared in my refrigerator within the past twelve hours?"

"You could twist my arm to 'sip some stars,'" he said.

When Connor returned with the Moët, he found Sidda sitting in the moonlight, stroking Hueylene with one hand and fingering the key with the other. Brandishing two jelly glasses, he popped the cork, poured the champagne, and set the bottle in an empty tin olive oil container that he'd filled with ice.

"What shall we toast to?" he asked.

"Lawanda the Magnificent," Sidda said, giving the tiny key a kiss, then holding it up for Connor to see. "That's what this key unlocks."

"Lawanda?" Connor asked. "Is there a story behind that name?"

"Funny you should ask."

"I've got all night," he said. "And then some."

"Good," she said. "I'm in an Isak Dinesen mood."

"Well, then, Ms. Walker," Connor said as he pulled her feet into his lap and began to rub her toes, "fly me to the moon."

Sidda closed her eyes for a moment, as though she were calling the story to her. Slowly, she brought the glass of champagne to her lips and took a sip. Opening her eyes, she glanced for a moment at the little key she held in her hand. Then she began to speak.

29

*L*AWANDA, THE MAGNIFICENT, a huge female elephant, came to Thornton in 1961, the summer after I finished second grade.

Local developers had just paved over acres of farmland to build the Southgate Shopping Center, the very first of its kind in Central Louisiana. Thornton was a town of about ten thousand. When someone opened a new business, let alone a whole shopping center, it was big news.

In those days everybody still shopped downtown, along the river. Still stepped gratefully into the few stores with the Kool penguin sign that read "Come on in. It's Kool inside." Old codgers still sat on chairs in front of River Street Café and chewed the fat about Earl Long's latest antics. The Colored water fountain was still around the back by the storeroom, although a few bold souls were already refusing to use it. Only the lucky or the rich had air conditioning at home, and while my family was both, we were still used to sweating the semitropical Louisiana heat, where a comfortable summer day meant anything below 98 degrees and 98 percent humidity.

There had been all kinds of publicity about the shopping center's grand opening. Billboards, radio ads, and a television ad that ran for weeks advertised it as "Cenla's Entry into the Twentieth Century!" Of course, the unspoken subtext was integration: the coloreds were trying to sit at what was supposed to be *our* counter at the downtown Walgreen's, they were trying to ruin *our* downtown. Come on out to the shopping center, where things are still white!

For the grand opening ceremonies they were offering free elephant rides to every white kid in Garnet Parish. Promoted as "Lawanda the Magnificent, Straight from the Wilds of Darkest Africa," the elephant's picture had been plastered all over Thornton. I had been thinking, dreaming, reading, and talking about elephants for weeks, and when the day finally came for the grand opening, I was beside myself.

The Ya-Yas, with all sixteen of us kids in tow, arrived early at the new shopping center and set up a little tailgate party in the parking lot—Cokes, cocktails, snacks. It was the biggest parking lot I'd ever seen. I had to blink and rub my eyes; I was disoriented to see stores and pavement where all my life there had been nothing but cotton. I'd never seen a field disappear before. I didn't know such a thing could happen. I thought a field was forever. At that age I thought that everything was forever.

When we arrived, the Thornton High School band was playing and there were teenage girls tap dancing on a stage in front of the brand-new Walgreen's. At a table, a lady straight off *The Price Is Right* gave each one of us a little key just like the one I have in my hand.

Sidda held up the key so Connor could see it.

"It used to hang from a key chain that had a blue plastic elephant attached. The elephant had a number stamped on it that indicated your place in line for a ride."

"Vivi Dahlin send that?" Connor asked.

"Vivi Dahlin sent this key," Sidda said.

She took another sip of champagne and leaned back in her chair. She could feel the generosity of Connor's listening.

I WILL NEVER forget my first glimpse of Lawanda. She was an enormous, magnificent beast, her height and her bulk in perfect proportion. There was a surprising grace to every element of the animal. Feet big as basketballs. Majestic jutting brow, eyes big as platters with foot-long lashes. Ears big as card tables, and feet so big her toenails looked like dinner plates. When her ears fluttered, I could feel the air move. Of course, I've no idea of her actual size—I was seeing all this from a seven-year-old's perspective.

In typical fashion, Mama and the Ya-Yas were the only mothers who *insisted* they be allowed to ride on Lawanda, along with their children. They weren't worried about our safety. They just didn't want to miss an opportunity to ride an elephant.

When it was our turn, we climbed a few steps up onto a wooden platform that had been set up so that kids could be helped up onto Lawanda's back. Mama stood at my side, holding my little brother Baylor's hand. He must have been around four. I remember Mama had him dressed in a little red-and-white-striped shirt, with a small straw hat. Of course, she'd dressed all four of us in her idea of elephant-riding outfits.

"Siddo Kiddo!" Mama said. "It's your turn now. Climb on."

I stared at Lawanda, whose huge back held Lulu, Little Shep, and Baylor. I don't know what happened, but I just froze.

"Let's go, Buddy," Mama repeated.

The elephant handler's assistant reached out to help me onto Lawanda. But I was paralyzed.

"Sidda Dahlin," Mama said, "don't be a party pooper. Climb on Lawanda with the rest of us."

Sidda took another sip of champagne. "Need I tell you that being a party pooper is a cardinal sin in the Church of Vivi? It's the eleventh commandment, which Moses forgot to bring down the mountain: Thou Shalt Not Be a Party Pooper."

Giving Hueylene a pat on the forehead, Sidda continued.

"I CAN'T, MAMA," I whispered. "I'm too scared."

"Will you be all right?" Mama asked.

"Yes, ma'am," I whispered, my head hanging in humiliation.

"All right then," she said, and she climbed onto Lawanda's back along with my three siblings.

With each step of Lawanda's enormous feet, my terror grew. *They will all be killed*, I thought. *Lawanda will throw them off her back, and stomp them to death. She will kill them like ants, then smear their bodies like ketchup on the fresh blacktop.*

I climbed down from the platform, but once back in the crowd, I couldn't find the Ya-Yas anywhere. It was too crowded. Everywhere I turned, there were strangers, and they were all taller than I was. It was the first time in my small-town life that I'd been in a crowd and not been able to find a single face I knew.

I worked my way to the edge of the crowd, and stood there. I could not spot Lawanda and my family, no matter how high I stood on tiptoe. I was hotter than I'd ever been in my life. The blacktop parking lot was bubbling, it was such a scorcher.

I pressed my elephant key chain into my palm and went looking for Mama's T-Bird. I should have ridden that elephant, I told myself. I would rather die with Mama than be safe on the ground without her. If I lose Baylor and Little Shep, and Lulu, I'll be sad. If I lose Mama, I will die.

I walked through rows and rows of cars looking for the red bandanna on Mama's antenna. "Saint Anthony, Saint Anthony, won't you please look around? Something has been lost and must be found." I said the prayer over and over till I found the T-Bird.

The metal door handle was so hot it hurt to open it. Inside, even though the windows had been rolled down, it was so hot I almost swooned. I grabbed the beach towel Mama kept in the car and spread it across the front seat so I could sit down in the driver's seat. I turned the wheel back and forth and pretended to be my mother. I blew the horn; turned on the radio. I pretended to light a cigarette. Then I slammed on the brakes and yelled, "Goddamn it to hell! Get out of my way!"

I could not stop my morbid thoughts. What will I do when they tell me Mama is dead? How will I find Daddy? Will the Ya-Yas adopt me?

Closing my eyes, I sent messages to Lawanda. *Don't do it, Lawanda. Please. Don't kill my mother.*

I smelled Mama before I saw her. I had been dozing in the driver's seat, and what woke me was her scent. I recognized it right away. Her personality smell, Coppertone, and the sun on her skin, and somewhere underneath, her Jergen's lotion and her Hovet perfume. I opened my eyes, and her hand was on my shoulder. She was standing just outside the car.

I jumped out of the car and buried my head against her thigh.

"You're not dead, Mama! You're not dead!"

She lifted my hair up and blew on the back of my neck.

"Have they been spreading rumors again of my untimely passing?" she asked, laughing. Then she reached into the ice chest to pull out a beer and a cold Coke.

"Dahlin," she said, gently pressing the cold Coke bottle against the back of my neck, "you missed the ride of a lifetime!"

On the way home, with the Ya-Yas following behind us, caravan-style, Mama declared, "I don't care if they build a Saks Fifth Avenue there, *Lawanda* is the most fun I will ever have at that shopping center! They should have Lawanda every day— instead of that ridiculous Singer Sewing Center for the 4-H crowd."

"Lawanda is leaving," Little Shep said. "Lawanda only came here for one day."

"Lawanda the Magnificent is a busy elephant," Mama said.

"Will Lawanda know me if I ever see her again?" Lulu asked.

Mama thought for a minute, then said, "The question is: Will *you* know *Lawanda*?!"

I was sitting in the front passenger seat holding Baylor in my lap. Suddenly I became overwrought at what I had missed. I had looked into Lawanda's huge eyes and she had looked back. I had sent her messages not to kill Mama and she had heard me. Lawanda had offered me the chance to climb onto her broad back, *and I turned it down.*

I burst into tears.

"Sidda," Mama asked, "what on earth is wrong with you?"

"I don't feel good," I mumbled. I didn't want to tell her why I was crying. Not in front of the others, who might make fun of me for chickening out.

Mama handed me a Kleenex from her purse, then reached over and felt my forehead: "I don't feel any fever."

I continued to cry uncontrollably. I pushed Baylor out of my lap and made him crawl into the crowded backseat of the T-Bird with the others.

When we got to Pecan Grove, the other kids scrambled out into the yard, pretending to be elephants. Mama got out of the car, but I stayed in my seat. I stretched the top of my sunsuit out and covered my face with it. I could feel the tears dropping down on my hot belly.

"Do not try my patience, Buddy," Mama said. "Either tell me what is wrong or forget it."

"I want to ride Lawanda," I mumbled into my sunsuit.

Mama leaned closer to me. "Get your head out of your sunsuit and speak up. You'll never get anything in life if you mumble like that."

I lifted my head and looked up at Mama. I could see my face reflected in her sunglasses.

"I will die if I don't get to ride Lawanda," I said.

"Why didn't you ride when it was your turn?" Mama asked.

"I don't know. I got scared."

"What spooked you, Dahlin?" she asked, sitting down on the grass beside the driveway.

"I looked at Lawanda and I got scared and then yall left and I thought you were going to be trampled to death."

"Ah," Mama said, "the alligators can get you at any age, Buddy. But the worst thing you can do is freeze. You understand what I'm saying?"

"Yes, ma'am," I said.

"So," she said, "you *absolutely* must ride Lawanda. Is that it?"

I nodded.

"You'll never be able to live with yourself if you don't. Is that it?"

"Yes, ma'am," I said, "that is exactly it." I felt an enormous relief that she could read my mind. I stopped crying.

"Okay," Mama said, reaching into the car to blow the horn. "Time to implement Plan 27-B."

Caro, who'd gone into the house with the other Ya-Yas, stuck her head out the door. "What's up, Pal?"

"Sidda and I have to see a man about an e-l-e-p-h-a-n-t," Mama called back. "We'll be back later. There's shrimp in the fridge, vodka in the freezer, and Oreos in the cookie jar. My house is your house."

I climbed into the car next to my mother and we roared off, in the direction of Lawanda.

The parking lot was almost empty. The elephant keeper was hosing down Lawanda's legs, and the lady assistant was pitching hay to a pile in front of the elephant. I stood transfixed as I watched Lawanda lower her trunk, curl it around some hay and plop it in her mouth.

"Hello, sir!" Mama said. "I know you've had a long day and

must be utterly exhausted. But could you *possibly* consider being so kind as to give my little girl a ride?"

He checked something on Lawanda's huge foot. "Nope," he said.

Mama stepped in a little closer. "Please, you must. She panicked when it was her turn and now she's just dying to ride."

"Too bad," he said.

I looked at Lawanda's feet. She had pieces of blacktop stuck between her toes.

"Just one short ride?" Mama said. "Of course, I'd be happy to pay you. Hold on just a second, and I'll be right back."

Mama ran back to the car and returned with her purse. She rummaged through it until she found her wallet.

"Here you go," she said. "I can pay you two dollars and seventy-two cents."

"No way," the man said. "Cost you more than that. The girl is tired. We have to drive all the way to Hot Springs, Arkansas, tonight."

He called Lawanda a girl.

Mama tore through her wallet, looking for more cash, but all she had were Daddy's charge cards. The entire time I was growing up, my mother never had a checking account of her own. She was completely dependent on my father's numerous charge accounts and whatever money he felt like giving her.

"I don't suppose you'd consider charging it to my husband, would you?" Mama said, joking. "How about Green Stamps?"

"I got work to do," the man said.

I was devastated.

"Will you wait long enough for me to come back with some more money?" Mama asked.

"Depends on how long that is," he said.

"Give us five minutes," Mama said.

We jumped back in the T-Bird and sped over to Johnson's Esso, at the edge of the shopping center. It was where we always got gas, one of the many places where Mama simply said, "Charge it to Shep, Dahlin."

Mama pulled right up next to the station office, where Mr. Lyle Johnson sat at his desk, a girlie calendar hanging on the wall above him.

"I need some quick cash, Lyle," Mama said. "Would you just

charge five dollars to Shep's account and give it to me?"

Mr. Lyle picked up a windshield wiper off his desk and started fooling with it. He wouldn't look at Mama.

"I'm sorry, Miz Vivi," he said, "I can't do that."

"And why in the world not?" Mama said. "You've done it countless times before."

"Shep done come in here two days ago," he said, "and told me I can give you all the gas and service you want, but I can't give you no more cash."

For a minute I thought Mama was going to hit the man. She bit on her bottom lip and looked out the window for a second.

Then she turned back to Lyle Johnson and acted like she had just discovered he was actually Paul Newman.

"Oh, Lyle," she said, "be a big sweetheart and just do it for me. I'd be ever so grateful."

"Sorry," he said. "Shep said just gas, no cash."

Mama started to leave. Her face was red and I thought she might start crying. She didn't though. She turned back around, and in one of the deepest voices I'd ever heard her use, she said: "Listen to me, Lyle: I need five Goddamn dollars right this instant. I need it for my daughter."

"I'm sorry," he said. "I take my orders from Shep. He's the one that pays the bills."

I could see my mother's humiliation. It mixed with my own embarrassment and disappointment. I wanted to kick Lyle Johnson for the way he treated her. And I wanted to yell at my mother because she didn't have cash in her pocket like my Daddy.

We stepped out of Lyle's office and went and stood by the T-Bird.

"I guess we have to give up," I said.

Mama looked at me and squinted her eyes as she watched a white Galaxy sedan pull up to a gas pump. "Don't let me ever hear you utter those words again," she said.

She took my hand and walked me over to the Galaxy.

"Good evening," Mama said to the lady.

"Evening," the lady said.

The woman was rather large, and she was wearing a man's workshirt that was raveled where the sleeves had been cut off. Her dashboard was crammed with matchbooks, a fly swatter, and a bunch of candy wrappers.

"I've got a proposition for you, Dahlin," Mama said.

The lady gave Mama a look. "Look, hon," she said, "you're not a kook, are you?"

"Absolutely not!" Mama said, laughing. "Listen, you're paying with cash, right?"

"That's right."

"How much gas are you planning to buy?"

"Four dollars' worth," the woman said, and reached into her shirt pocket.

"Tell you what," Mama said. "Let me put five dollars' worth on my husband's charge account and you pay me the cash. What do you say?"

The woman looked at us for a moment, then said, "Well, I don't see what harm that can do."

"You are an angel from God," Mama said.

"I don't know about that," the woman said.

Mama made Lyle Johnson himself pump the gas. When she signed for the woman's gasoline, she said, "Lyle, I'm looking forward to the day when you have to ask *me* for a favor."

Mama winked at me, and I winked back. Then we climbed back into the T-Bird with our cash money and sped back to Lawanda.

"Monsieur Elephant Keeper!" Mama said. "We have returned! With cash on the barrel head!"

The man laughed. "How much you got?"

"Four big ones," Mama said, squeezing my hand to let me know she was bargaining.

"Forget it," the man said.

"Make it four-and-a-half," she said.

"Four-and-a-half," I repeated.

The man smiled at her. My mother smiled back.

"Six," the man said.

"Highway robbery!" Mama said and started to walk away.

"Oh, all right," the man said. "Five-and-a-half."

"You got yourself a deal, Mister!" Mama said.

Mama and I climbed onto Lawanda's magnificent back and greeted the animal. "Good evening, Lovely Lawanda," Mama said. "You're more splendid than ever."

"Good evening, Magnificent One, oh Lovely Lawanda," I said. "Thank you for waiting for us."

My arms circled around my mother's waist, and in the pink-orange light of a summer twilight we set out across the parking lot. The elephant keeper walked beside us, a pole in his hand. Soft evening light shone on my mother's freckled skin, and on Lawanda's flat gray hide, with its thousand wrinkles. As Lawanda lumbered in her slow, undulating walk, it felt like soft cushions were tied to her basketball feet, so quiet and soft was each step. For an animal that massive to move so gracefully seemed miraculous. She had the power to destroy us with a flick of her trunk. Instead, she let us climb on her beautiful, tired back and ride.

"Siddalee," Mama said, "close your eyes, just for a minute." Then, in her most magical high-priestess-European-queen-gypsy-fortune-teller voice, Mama began to speak.

"Lawanda, oh Magnificent One, spirit Siddalee and Vivi Walker away from this hot blacktop parking lot! Return us to the untamed green jungle from whence we came!"

"Are you ready?" Mama asked. "Are you willing?"

"Yes, Mama! I'm ready. I'm willing!"

"Then open your eyes! Open your eyes and witness Vivi and Sidda of the High and Mighty Tribe of Ya-Yas as they commence their great escape on the back of Royal Lawanda!

"Great Scott! Look at this! Lawanda is jumping the ditch! She's out of the parking lot! Oh, my God! I don't believe it! We're crossing the highway. Sidda, look at them, will you?! Just look at those people jumping out of their cars to watch! Oh, they've never seen the likes of an elephant breaking free with Ya-Ya royalty on her back!

"We're too much for them! Wave to the people, Dahlin, wave like the Queen and Princess we are.

"Oh yes! We're on the Lawandamobile! Listen to her roar and trumpet! Hold on now! Look at her! We're charging across the highway, faster than a plane! Past the beauty shop, past Hampton's Funeral Home, where the sight of us stops all the mourning! Past *The Thornton Daily Monitor*, which has never touched news this big! Past Father's old law offices, past Whalen's Department Store, where there's nothing we want to buy anymore! Past the River Street Café, and—

"Oh! Oh, Buddy! Hold on to your hat! We're climbing up the side of the levee now! Look! The sky is fading to blue-purple and filling with stars. There's the Big Dipper and the Little Dipper.

There's Pegasus! Reach up, Buddy, scoop down some stars with your hand! Up here on Lawanda's back, we can touch the heavens!

"Into the Garnet River, now, the red flowing river. What a mighty swimmer! Feel how Lawanda submerges, breathing through her snorkel trunk! Even alligators know better than to mess with Lawanda! She could stay down longer, but she surfaces so we can breathe.

"Oh, no! Look up on the levee! It's the jealous pissants, gunning for us. They've got their spears, they've got their guns! Well, they will not take our ivory trunks, they will not take our broken hearts! We are not trinkets to put in a jewelry box! Oh, no, they'll tell their children's children about us, Buddy! The mother and daughter team that got away!

"Come on, sweet, strong Lawanda, you can do it! Just a few more feet to the other side of the river where safety awaits. Ah, yes, yes. We made it. Now we can rest. Now rest, Sweet Big One, that's it, rest, eat all you want.

"My darling daughter, we're finally here! Home in the wild, green verdant jungle. Do you *feel* the velvet air?! Do you *feel* it on our skin? Do you smell the bananas and ancient trees? Do you hear the rare birds and millions of monkeys? Do you see them swinging from tree to tree? This is our true home, no need for air conditioning, no call for cash, just walking barefoot all year long. Where the trees and animals know our names and we know theirs. Yesssss! Say it, Sidda! Say it with me: 'Yesssss!' There is nothing, anywhere, to be afraid of! Lawanda loves us and *we are not afraid!*"

Sidda paused for a moment. She looked down at the key, which still lay in her hand.

"All we had done was circle that puny shopping-center parking lot, but when that ride was over, I was a different little girl.

"We climbed back into the T-bird and drove down Jefferson Street in the early darkness. I looked at my mother behind the wheel, barefoot and humming. Without taking her eyes off the road, she reached out her hand and placed it on top of mine. Her skin was cool and soft. We drove past the familiar landmarks we saw every day. But the world outside our car seemed charged with mystery, all new and unknown."

Sidda glanced at the key one last time. *It's life, Sidda. You just climb on the beast and ride.*

Then she crossed to Connor, took his champagne jelly glass out of his hand and sat down in his lap, facing him. She began to kiss him all over, while at the same time unfastening the jumper she'd put on after their swim.

They began their lovemaking on the deck, with Sidda still straddling Connor. Then they moved to the bedroom. When she closed her eyes, Sidda felt like they were a satellite tumbling in wide-open space, and this did not scare her. For once it did not scare her to open to this man, to herself, to the endless wide universe she had no control over. This time, when their pleasure joined, Sidda did not weep. She laughed out loud, the way a child does when she is deeply and completely delighted.

After Connor fell asleep, Sidda got out of bed. She walked into the big room and chose a cassette tape from her collection of music. Bringing a small boombox out onto the deck, she poured herself the last of the champagne. She slipped in the home-edited tape she'd made of Aaron Neville singing "Ave Maria" over and over. She stood naked in the moonlight.

My mother and I are like elephants, she thought. In the stillness of night, out of sight, out of acoustic range, separated by barren, dry savannas, my mother has been sending me messages. In my dry season, when I froze in the face of love, my mother did not abandon me. My mother is not a stage character to be fathomed from fragments, and I am not a scrawny, anxious child waiting for her perfect love. We are each flawed, and in search of solace. Mama longed—still longs— to bust free of the hot, dry place where fear keeps her frantic and bourbon keeps her hazy. She still longs to return with me on the back of a graceful beast to the fertile jungle where wild things flourish.

Sidda held the glass of champagne up so she could see the bubbles in the moonlight. My mother is not the Holy Lady, she thought. My mother's love is not perfect. My mother's love is good enough. My lover's love is good enough. Maybe I am good enough.

Twenty minutes or so passed before she spotted a shooting star. Then a meteor shower filled the sky. Sidda stood perfectly still, watching and listening. Hueylene came out to sit at her feet. The sky was so clear, the setting moon so kind. There were no city lights to interfere. The meteor light from so very far away was older than she could even imagine. There was nothing to figure out. There was Sidda's heart beating. There was the heart of the planet beating. There was enough time. She was not afraid.

30

*C*onnor and Sidda sat out on the deck in their shorts and T-shirts after having slept till noon. Van Morrison played on the CD and Hueylene was almost sobbing she was so happy to be eating bits of bacon that Connor snuck her from his plate. He had cooked Sidda's favorite breakfast: fresh sour-dough French toast with maple syrup.

Pausing for a minute to look at her lover and her dog against the backdrop of the lake and the mountains and the trees, Sidda felt a shiver of happiness. "Thank you, Connor," she said. "For listening. For loving me."

He gave her a slow smile, then put a piece of cantaloupe in his mouth. "What's this Vivi birthday shindig the Sisterhood was talking about?"

"The Sisterhood?" Sidda asked, smiling.

"The Ya-Yas," Connor said. "If you and your mother are like elephants, then the other three of them are the sister elephants. You know, the ones that tag along and help mothers with the calves."

"You amaze me."

"Hey, I watch Public Television. When is Vivi's birthday?"

"It's actually in December. But this year they're celebrating at the end of October because Mama wants an outdoor party when the weather's still good."

"Why don't you return her scrapbook to her in person?"

Sidda put down her fork and stared at Connor.

"Are you nuts? She's still enraged about *The New York Times*. She'll kill me on sight."

"You know," Connor said, "no one would ever suspect you worked in the theater, Sidda."

"Am I being melodramatic?" she asked, laughing. "*Moi?* Never."

"Of course not," Connor said.

"Of course not," she said.

"I don't hear much about your dad," Connor said, reaching for his cup of latte. "He must be a brave man."

"What do you mean?"

"Come on," he said, "marrying a woman as strong as your mother. Finessing his own way through that band of women. What's the French word for *sisterhood*? *Communauté de soeurs*."

Sidda helped herself to a slice of cantaloupe. She thought of how much she'd missed her father. "He was never around much. I've been so obsessed with my mother I guess I haven't paid much attention to Daddy."

"You might want to," Connor said. "Teensy told me you've got his eyelashes."

"Teensy said that?"

"Yep. Said your mother's lashes 'disappeared when she swam.' She told me that while we were in the lake."

Sidda shook her head. "God only knows what else they told you when I wasn't listening."

"You have no idea," Connor said.

Unable to resist, Sidda dipped her finger into the remaining maple syrup. Then she put her finger in Connor's mouth for him to lick it off.

"You know," she said, "October is my favorite time in the South. There's nothing like Halloween in the Gret Stet of Loosiana."

"Necie said she'd cook for me," Connor said. "Teensy wants to introduce me to Cajun music, and Caro has already challenged me to a whistling contest. I hear Louisiana calling."

"October," Sidda said, thinking out loud. "Harvest time. Not too hot, perfect weather. We'll be done at the Rep. The American Playhouse project will be under control."

Connor McGill winked at Sidda. She winked back. She fed Hueylene the last scrap of bacon. Then she stood up, walked to the railing overlooking Lake Quinault, and flung her arms wide into the air.

"Are you listening, Holy Lady?" she called out. "Gods and Goddettes? Angel-gals? Thank you for making Connor McGill and me the same species. Thank you for his kisses sweet as Aaron Neville's falsetto! Thank you for not knowing, for guessing, for leaping into the dark!"

"I take it that means we're going to Louisiana together," Connor said.

"Uh-huh," Sidda said. "Shots and passport up to date?"

"I like to live dangerously," he said.

September 8, 1993

Dear Mama,

I have never properly thanked you for lifting me up
onto Lawanda's back. For our trip to the wild jungle,
for your bravery, for the way you were true to me on
that hot blacktop of the Southgate Shopping Center.
There is a lot I haven't thanked you for.

The Ya-Yas told me about your early birthday
party in October. Would an out-of-town daughter and
her sweetheart be welcome?

Thank you also for the crayfish meal you sent. It
was your kitchen, it was the best of Louisiana distilled
into one dish. It moved me to tears.

I love you,

Sidda

September 16, 1993

Sidda Dahlin—

I do deserve to be thanked. But so does Lawanda,
Mother of Us All. Glad you remembered something
good for a change.

As for my birthday, you'll have to take your
chances. I have no idea of whether I'll be in a welcoming mood or not. It's my birthday, and I'm not in the
least bit interested in having the party scrutinized in
the national media.

You *must* let me know about your wedding—is it
on or what?

Love,
Mama

⌘

September 20, 1993

Dear Mama,

Wedding plans are still on hold. We'll just play the
party by ear, what do you say?

I love you,
Sidda

⌘

September 26, 1993

Sidda Dahlin—

Life is short, Buddy. Don't keep your wedding on hold
too long or you won't have anything to *hold on to*.

As for my early birthday party at Pecan Grove on
October 18, which starts around seven in the evening:
I play *everything* by ear.

Love,
Mama

On the night of October 17, the day before she and Connor were
scheduled to fly from Seattle to Louisiana, Sidda very carefully photographed the old snapshots and memorabilia contained in the scrapbook of "Divine Secrets." The photo she took the most care with was
a picture she hadn't discovered until she'd returned to Seattle. Tucked
into the folds of one of the back pages was the image of a woman,
blonde with dark eyes, holding an auburn-haired baby girl in her lap
as she sat on a porch swing. Each of them was dressed in a fetching
summer dress, and back-lit by the sun. Sidda photographed the image
several times. With each advancement of the film, she dropped deeper
into an appreciation of the moment recorded on that Southern swing.
When she finished photographing the image, she turned the snapshot
over and photographed the inscription on the back. In Vivi's hand
were written the following words: "Vivi and Sidda, 1953. A beautiful
day, a pink dress. Photo by Buggy."
After finishing eight rolls of film, Sidda closed the scrapbook and
set it on the dining-room table. On either side of the album, she set
sanctuary candles, one with an image of Our Lady of Guadalupe and
one with a depiction of Saint Jude. She lit both candles, turned out all
the lights, and said a little prayer of thanks to the Holy Lady and her
angels. Tenderly, she took the "Divine Secrets of the Ya-Ya Sisterhood"
album, and wrapped it in a silk pillow case, and placed it in a gallon-
size Ziploc bag. Then she tucked it into her carry-on bag, along with a
tiny, gift-wrapped package.

For the fourth time since she'd boarded the plane, Sidda checked
her carry-on to make sure the scrapbook was still safe. Then she took
a sip of her Diet Coke and settled back for the flight.
"Have I lost my mind?" she asked Connor. "I mean, Vivi Dahlin
still sounds angry. There's no telling what will happen."
"Your mother doesn't own Louisiana," Connor said.
"Yes, she does," Sidda said. "She is the Queen of Central Louisiana.

But she's getting old. She won't live forever. I want to see her."

"What do you want from this visit?" Connor asked.

"Oh, just the perfect healing of all wounds, transcending of all pain. That sort of thing. What do you want?"

"To marry you in your hometown."

Sidda choked on a peanut and quickly reached for a quick sip of her Diet Coke. When she recovered, she said, "I'm not going to touch that right now. Okay?"

"Definitely do not touch it right now," he said. "Not in public."

As they flew over the heart of the country, the earth tinged by the reds and golds of October, Sidda and Connor played game after game of gin rummy, betting everything from trips to Tuscany to back rubs to little private pleasures only the two of them knew how to broker. They didn't stop playing until the Boeing 707 landed—just barely—in Houston, where the weather had grown melodramatic. A mean, exciting storm born somewhere off the coast of Africa had Houston in its grip.

Sidda's perfectly calculated plans—to arrive in Thornton in plenty of time to check into their lodging, shower, change, and make a shining entrance just as Vivi's party kicked off—were blown off course. During a three-hour wait in an airport café, Sidda had plenty of time to wonder if her reentry into the land of tropical depressions and storms was a crazy mistake.

"It is hurricane season, after all," she told Connor. "We should have never attempted to make this trip. Jesus."

"The last time you were home—when was that—couple of years ago? That was October too, wasn't it?"

"Right," Sidda said. "My goddaughter Lee's baptism."

"No hurricane then, right?" he asked.

"No," she replied, "just your run-of-the-mill psychic squalls and mental typhoons."

"Well," Connor said, testing her, "maybe we won't make it after all. Maybe we should just check into a hotel here in Houston."

"Are you kidding? And miss the birthday party?! No, no, no, if that plane doesn't take off soon, we're renting a car and driving."

"That's what I thought," he said.

"Smarty pants."

When the small puddle-jumper plane from Houston to Thornton was cleared for take-off, Sidda took it as a sign. Visibility has increased: this means my mother will not kill me.

By the time the plane landed at Thornton's tiny airport, it was almost ten o'clock at night. They rented a car, cracking up when the only one available was a big silver deluxe Chrysler New Yorker Fifth Avenue with burgundy leather interior.

When they turned off Highway 1 onto Jefferson Street, Sidda wished she smoked. "Cocktail hour has come and gone," she told Connor. "No telling what shape Vivi Dahlin will be in. Daddy either."

"You know how to wing it."

"Yep," Sidda said, trying to control the nausea, "I know how to wing it, but I'd sure as hell rather have a finished script in my hands."

At the sight of her parents' home, Sidda slowed the car to a crawl. The long brick house on the rise above the bayou looked different than it did in her memories. The pine trees seemed taller. The pecan trees and azaleas were older, and ivy now covered almost the whole back side of the six-bedroom brick house. Everything felt more settled and peaceful-looking than she remembered.

She could see the small wood frame house at the edge of the field, where Willetta and Chaney lived. Something about that little house helped her keep driving toward the much larger house in which she'd grown up.

"We've made it this far," Sidda said, creeping the car up the long drive, "I guess we might as well at least *drop in*."

She slowly drove past the bayou to the front of the house. The first thing she saw as she turned off the motor was her parents. They were sitting on a wooden swing under two old pecan trees in the front yard. White Christmas lights were strung around the swing set, and Vivi and Shep sat inside their glow. Vivi was wearing a rust-and-gold-colored silk pants suit, her ash-blonde hair cut in a smart page boy, which swung from side to side as she moved her head. Shep wore a pair of light gray Dockers and a blue-and-gray-plaid shirt. They both had aged in the past two years.

Sidda watched for a moment as her mother gestured animatedly with her hands. She did not recognize the person sitting in an Adirondack chair opposite the swing, which surprised her. Sidda believed she should be able to recognize every person in her hometown, in spite of the fact that she hadn't actually lived there in over twenty-five years. There were very few other cars. Most of the guests had already left.

Clearly, her parents did not recognize their unfamiliar rental car. Taking a deep breath, she said a prayer to the Holy Lady and her band of Louisiana angels, then Sidda started blowing the horn.

"Hold my hand and tell me I'm not insane," Sidda whispered to Connor.

"You're not insane," he said, "and I love you."

As Sidda watched her mother rise from the swing and walk toward the car, she noticed how Vivi moved more slowly than she remembered. Her mother seemed to have shrunk a little in height, but other than that, she looked positively robust. With each step Vivi took, Sidda's heart beat faster.

When Vivi reached the car, Sidda rolled down the window. "It's me, Mama." Her voice sounded foreign. She tried not to feel five years old. She tried to feel at least eleven.

As Vivi leaned her head into the car, Sidda could smell bourbon on her breath, mixed with the painfully familiar Vivi scent.

"Sidda?" Vivi asked, unbelieving. "Is that really you?"

Sidda was relieved to hear that her mother was not drunk, only lightly tipsy.

"Yes, ma'am," Sidda said, "it's me."

Vivi didn't respond for a moment. Sidda wondered if she would turn and walk away.

After a beat or two, Vivi put her fingers in her mouth, and let rip one of her famous Ya-Ya whistles. "You crazy fool! What in the world are you *doing* all the way down here?"

"I came for your birthday," Sidda said. "I decided to take my chances."

"Holy Mother of Pearl!" Vivi said, then turned to Shep and the other guest, "Would yall believe it?! It's Siddalee! *It's my oldest child!*"

Sidda stepped out of the car and into her mother's arms. "Happy Birthday, Mama," she whispered. They embraced for an instant before Vivi's body stiffened and pulled away.

"I can't believe it!" Vivi said, nervous. "You *nut*! I didn't think you'd really come!" Leaving Sidda, she crossed to the car's passenger side, and peeked in.

"Who are *you*?"

"I'm Connor McGill, Mrs. Walker," he said and gave her a slow grin.

The minute Connor smiled, Vivi gasped, and stepped back from the car, momentarily shaken.

Sidda held her breath.

Stepping back to the car window, Vivi said, "Gloriosko-Zero! I do not believe it! What are you doing just sitting there, Dahlin? Get out of this car and let me *see* you!"

Folding his long legs out of the car, Connor stood next to Vivi, who appeared absolutely tiny next to him. As he stood there, relaxed, open, Vivi surveyed him from head to toe. The whole time she studied him, she kept one hand clasped to her chest, like she was trying to keep her heart in place. Sidda had absolutely no idea what her mother might say or do next.

"Oh," is all Vivi said at first. "Oh," she said a second time, in a small, young voice.

Then she wrapped her arms around her waist, which was not a gesture Sidda could recall ever seeing her mother make. Vivi was silent for so long that Sidda wondered if she were experiencing pain.

Finally, almost abruptly, Vivi shifted her hands to her hips. "Sidda," she said, "for God's sake, why didn't you *tell* me Connor looked exactly like Jimmy Stewart in *Mr. Smith Goes to Washington?*"

Connor laughed.

"My, my," Vivi said, as she extended her hand to her daughter's lover. "I have always *adored* tall men."

Connor then completely shocked Sidda by refusing to shake her mother's hand. Instead he kissed it. He lowered his lips to Vivi's hand and kissed it. Sidda almost fell on the ground.

"It's a pleasure to finally meet you, Mrs. Walker," he said.

"Oh," Vivi said, "*please* call me Vivi, or you'll make me feel terribly old."

"You *are* old, Babe," Shep Walker said, stepping over to the car.

"Oh, shut up," Vivi said, laughing. "Don't give away my secrets. Shep, this is Connor McGill. Connor, meet my first husband," she said, playfully, making it sound like she'd had several.

"Shep Walker," Sidda's father said, extending his hand to Connor.

"Connor McGill, sir," Connor said. "A pleasure to meet you."

For a moment, Sidda was left out of the triangle as her mother wrapped up the introductions between the two men. She stood to the side as she witnessed her mother in her favorite two-men-to-one-Vivi ratio in the old time-honored sport of competitive flirting. Sidda watched her father as he waited for a sign from Vivi that it was all right to welcome his daughter.

"Lucky yall made it down here with that old storm that was messing around," Shep said.

"The wind and rain in Houston were pretty bad," Connor said.

"That's why we're late," Sidda said.

"Storm was heading our way," Shep said. "Sure glad it changed its mind and headed out into the Gulf."

"The grand old Gulf of Mexico," Vivi said, linking her arm in Connor's. "It's absorbed many storms. Do you know the Gulf, Connor?"

"No," Connor said, "I don't. But Sidda has sure talked about it."

After Connor's subtle refusal to continue excluding Sidda, Vivi turned to her husband and said, "Shep, you remember Sidda, don't you? Our child with the national-media connections."

Sidda and her father stepped toward each other at the same moment. Hugging his daughter tightly and quickly, Shep whispered in her ear, "Missed you, Babe, missed you."

Sidda was aware of how her mother policed their hug. I've got to stay alert, Sidda thought. Mama is like a hurricane. Same ferocity, same beauty. And you never know where she'll strike down.

"Beautiful place you have here, Mr. Walker," Connor said.

"You'll have to come back in the daylight," Shep said, relieved. "I got me some surprises out in that field. Along with my rice and crayfish, of course."

"Gadzooks!" Vivi said, "I've utterly forgotten my guests! My manners are going to hell in my dotage!"

"Dahlin, come over here right this minute!" she called out to the person they'd been chatting with when Connor and Sidda arrived.

A small wiry man of around seventy stepped toward the car. He was wearing a plaid bow tie and a finely tailored shirt, looking a little like a cross between an aging horse jockey and Mr. Peepers. "Sidda *Bébé*," he said, and without hesitation gave her a long, warm hug. "Teensy was right. You look ravishing."

"Chick," Sidda said, "it's wonderful to see you."

"You must be Connor," Chick said, giving him a kiss on the cheek in the European fashion. "I'm La Teensy's lesser half. She raved about you. Welcome to Thornton, where the sin-loving Southern half of the state meets the atonement-hungry North."

Putting his arms around Sidda again, Chick looked at her face. "And the nose looks terrific."

"The nose?" Connor said.

"She took half of that little upturned beauty off on our diving board doing her first cut-away," Chick explained. "Thrilled to see it grew back."

It felt luxurious to have Chick's arms around her. *The smoking bunny,* she thought, as she remembered the Easter he and Teensy helped keep her family pasted together.

"You darling man," she said to him, smiling. "Where is Teensy? Where are all the Ya-Yas?"

"La Teens needed her beauty rest," Chick said. "Necie and Caro followed suit. I'm the last of the red hots, *chère,* and I'm not red hot for long. About time for me to *vamoose.* I've probably worn out my welcome as it is."

"*Nevah,*" Vivi said, "you know that."

"Terrific party," Chick said, stepping away from Sidda to give Vivi a kiss. "Happy Birthday again, Viv-o. Impossible to believe you're thirty-nine. Gives new definition to the word 'timeless.'"

Vivi laughed and kissed him again.

"Night, Chick," Shep said, putting his arm around the smaller man's shoulders. "Thanks for all your help."

"*Bon soir,* Sidda, Connor," Chick said, heading toward an immaculately restored Bentley. "Sidda, please don't snitch and tell your *amoureux* that I'm a *faux* Cajun. I can't help if I only married into majesty."

As Chick was driving off, Shep said, "I believe I'll turn in. I'm not good for much after ten P.M. these days."

"I'm shocked you lasted this long," Vivi said.

"Little bird told me we might have a surprise tonight," he said, giving Sidda an almost indiscernible wink. "You know how Ya-Yas can talk."

Sidda gave her father a quick peck on the cheek. "Goodnight, Daddy," she said. "Love you."

"Love you, Butter Bean," he said. "Love you bunches."

As Shep walked back to the house, Sidda became aware of raucous laughter coming from somewhere behind the house. "Who's that? Are there still guests out back?"

"Our Lady of Pearl," Vivi said, "I almost forgot about them. That's your Uncle Pete and the boys out on the dock. They have been back there playing *bourrée* for God knows how long."

"*Bourrée?*" Connor asked, his eyes opening wide.

"But, of course," Vivi Walker said, raising her eyebrows.

She led them in the direction of the bayou. "Do *you* play, Connor?"

"Oh, no, ma'am," Connor said.

It floored Sidda to hear Connor say, "No, ma'am." She knew those words had never crossed his Yankee lips before.

"Sidda's only told me about *bourrée*," he said. "I've always wanted to sit in on a game."

"Connor's an ace poker player, Mama," Sidda said. "He has regular poker nights in New York, Maine, and Seattle—every theater he designs for, he's got a group of poker buddies."

Sidda knew that Vivi Walker automatically liked anybody who played cards. It didn't matter if they were liars or embezzlers or Republicans. If they played a decent hand, they were okay by Vivi.

"What in the world could *Sidda* tell you about *bourrée*?" Vivi asked. "She's never played in her life."

"You're right, Mama," Sidda said. "I told Connor what a cracker-jack *bourrée* player *you* are."

"Said you were one of the best in the state," Connor said.

Vivi stopped for a moment and looked first at Connor and then at Sidda. "Yall are trying to *please* me," she said, giving them a wide, grateful grin. "Okay, I'm easy."

It made Sidda want to cry when she saw how much this small effort delighted her mother.

"I am thoroughly impressed that you have taken up with a card-playing man, Siddalee," Vivi said as she continued walking. "I shall look forward to taking his hard-earned money away from him some-time in the near future."

Vivi led Connor and Sidda back to a little dock that extended out over the bayou behind the Walker home. On the dock sat a card table and two old floor lamps, from which ran a long orange extension cord that disappeared in the direction of a small playhouse, where Sidda used to stage her tea parties. A small camp stool that held a platter of food was positioned between the lamps. On folding chairs around the table sat Sidda's brothers, Baylor and Little Shep, her mother's brother, Pete, and her cousin, John Henry Abbott. Irma Thomas was singing the blues from a portable CD player positioned next to a cooler. Spanish moss hung like wild witch hair from the trees that leaned out over the bayou.

Ain't no doubt, Sidda thought: I'm right smack in the heart of Louisiana. She wanted to lift the tableau up, set it down on a stage, and say: *This is where I come from.* But this wasn't a scene she could direct. She was in the middle of one sweet, messy, unpredictable improvisation.

When the four card players spotted Sidda, each man's jaw dropped. Sidda knew exactly what they were thinking: hold on to your seat—Vivi and Sidda in the same state. If they'd been wearing holsters, their hands would have been on their pistols.

Sidda knew the scenes they'd had to witness down there in the thick of things: Baylor refusing to represent Vivi in a lawsuit against Sidda. Vivi's letters, sent certified mail to everyone in the extended family, announcing that she had disowned her oldest daughter. Vivi's highly publicized (in Thornton) firing of the lawyer who'd represented the Walkers for decades because he dared advise her to think it over before she cut Sidda out of her will. Vivi's monthlong attempt to reach Arthur Ochs Sulzberger Jr., publisher of *The New York Times*, to give him a piece of her mind. Vivi's wild attempt to force the Garnet Parish Library to burn their issue—and the microfiche—of *The New York Times* that carried the offending article. Then Vivi's desperate cancellation of her library card when they refused. And of course her delight in the subterfuge when she later reapplied for a card under an assumed name. Baylor had kept Sidda informed of all this, hoping to make her laugh at the small-town drama, but it had only broken her orphaned heart.

Now, as she looked at her four male relatives, she did not blame them for hesitating before they spoke.

Baylor was the first to break their standstill. He made the Sign of the Cross, then slapped his hand of cards down on the table and sauntered over to Sidda. Once he reached her, he picked her up in the air, swung her around, and pretended he was about to throw her into the bayou.

"Go ahead!" the other *bourrée* players yelled. "Do it! She's been dry too long! She needs a bayou baptism!"

"Don't you dare!" Sidda hollered, delighted.

At the last minute, Baylor stopped short. Instead, he set her feet back on the ground and gave her a bear hug. "What is this, you little sneak! How'd you ever get into Hooterville without me, the grand gatekeeper, knowing? I thought they confiscated your passport."

"She's a sly one," Vivi said.

Turning to Little Shep, who had not yet risen from the card table, Sidda said in Pig Latin, "Eyhay, Epshay!"

"Come over here, big sister," he said, "and gimme a hug."

"Thought we'd never see *you* again," Little Shep said as he stood and hugged Sidda with all his nearly two hundred pounds.

"God, you're beautiful!" he said, looking at her. He stroked her hair. "Your hair, your skin. How come you look so good?"

"Luck? Love?" Sidda said. "A nearsighted little brother?"

Little Shep laughed. "No, I mean it. Women down here don't stay looking as good as you, Sidda."

"I beg your big fat pardon," Vivi said.

"No, Mama," Little Shep said, "I mean the ones in my age group."

"Better stop while you're ahead, son," Uncle Pete said.

"How you been, Shep?" Sidda asked.

"Can't complain, Sis," he said. "Playing the hand I been dealt. Sorry I never wrote you back. You know how life is, huh?"

"Sidda," Uncle Pete said, stepping over to give her a hug. "Glad to see you home. It's been too long."

Immediately after hugging Sidda, Pete protectively put his arms around Vivi's shoulders.

"Birthday Girl," he said with fondness. "How's my little Stinky doing?"

Laughing, Vivi held her brother's hand to her heart. "This just might turn out to be one of my favorite birthday *fêtes* so far," she said. "Everybody's here except Lulu."

"Where *is* Lulu?" Sidda asked. Sidda's younger sister didn't stay in touch, and since *The New York Times* upset, Sidda had lost all track of her.

"Tallulah is in Paris," Vivi said. "Left her interior-design business with her partner and took off for France."

"Took off with a Frenchman is more like it," Baylor said.

"His family owns a winery somewhere, and his divorce should be final any day," Vivi said.

Turning to Connor, who'd been quietly watching the reunion, Sidda said, "I want yall to meet Connor McGill, my Yankee sweetheart. He is, by the way, a hell of a card player."

Connor groaned loudly. "No, no," he said, "she's got it all wrong. She has me confused with some other Yankee—we all look alike. I don't know a queen from a deuce—I mean a 'two.'"

"Yeah, *right*," Baylor said, reaching out and shaking Connor's hand. "I've heard about you Maine boys. Killers. All those long winters. Pull up a chair, pal, have a brewsky. We'll be happy to take you to the cleaners—I mean, introduce you to the cutthroat world of Louisiana *bourrée*. My big brother and I here learned the game at our mother's feet while she was weaning us on bourbon-spiked baby bottles."

"You crazy fool," Vivi said, loving every minute. "It was *Tabasco,* not bourbon!"

Laughing, Connor asked, "What's a foreigner got to do to get a beer on this dock?"

"Help yourself, Connor," Uncle Pete said. "Some cold shrimp and fried frog legs still left."

"Guess I better if I'm going to swim with the bayou sharks," Connor said, opening a bottle of beer and pulling up a chair.

Everybody laughed. They liked Connor. Sidda liked Connor. She could not stop smiling as she watched her Yale-educated scenic designer release the Good Ole Boy within.

Connor took a long swig of his beer, then stood up. He put his beer on the table, walked over to Sidda, and leaned her back in his arms. Then, for no good reason other than bayou voodoo, he planted a huge wet kiss right on her lips.

The whole *bourrée* gang let out a holler as Vivi watched, eagle-eyed. Sidda loved it.

As Vivi led Sidda back in the direction of the house, she said, "Most of the food has been put away already, but come on, let me fix you a plate."

While Vivi went inside the kitchen, Sidda walked out to the front yard and sat down in the swing. A Cajun cooker was set up nearby, along with several tables. *Laissez les bons temps rouler,* Sidda thought. A birthday crayfish boil.

Sidda watched as her mother walked back out toward the swing. She's not as *feverish,* Sidda thought.

Vivi paused for an instant, a momentary hesitation that seemed to border on shyness. It was only for a beat, then she continued on to where Sidda sat on the swing.

She handed Sidda a glass of champagne and a plate piled high with boiled crayfish, new potatoes, corn on the cob, and hunks of buttered French bread.

"Thank you, Mama," Sidda said, realizing just how hungry she was.

"Your daddy prepared the whole meal," Vivi said. "I didn't have to do a thing. I'm sorry there's so little left. My guests just gobbled everything up."

"This is plenty," Sidda said.

"Can you handle eating that crayfish here on the swing, or should we move to the table?"

"Mama, I have not forgotten how to suck the heads of a Louisiana crayfish *wherever* I'm sitting."

"Here's a couple of napkins," Vivi said, pulling two large squares of pink linen out of her waistband.

After tucking one of the napkins into the collar of her blouse as a bib, and the other under her plate, Sidda began to shell the crayfish. "Will you join me?" Sidda said, gesturing to a spot beside her on the swing.

"Thank you for offering me a seat on my own swing," Vivi said in a tone that Sidda couldn't quite read.

Vivi sat down, although not so close that their bodies touched. She stared straight out, keeping one hand behind her back. Sidda could hear her mother breathing. For the first time Sidda realized she hadn't seen her mother light one cigarette since she'd arrived.

Afraid to say the wrong thing, Sidda said nothing. She shelled the crayfish and ate. "This is delicious."

"Thank God Louisiana men know how to cook," Vivi said.

"Not as sophisticated in its flavoring as your *étouffée*, of course."

"Necie made sure you had some?" Vivi asked.

"I had forgotten food could taste like that," Sidda said.

"You really thought it was good?"

"Good?! Mama, the *étouffée* you sent up with the Ya-Yas would have made Paul Prudhomme weep over his cast-iron skillet. That man is a short-order cook compared to you."

"Well, thank you. I am *known* for that dish, if you recall. I learned how to cook it from Genevieve Whitman."

"Thank you for sending it to Quinault, Mama."

"The one thing I did right was feed yall well," Vivi said.

Something in Vivi's tone struck Sidda. Mama is as nervous as I am, she thought. She turned to Vivi and said, "You did more right than wrong."

Vivi did not respond. Neither mother nor daughter knew what to say next.

"You look good, Mother. Really good."

"*You* look terrific," Vivi said. "I think you've lost weight."

Sidda smiled. Her mother's highest compliment.

"*I've* filled out," Vivi said. "It's the weight lifting: adds bulk. And the not smoking: adds Snickers bars."

Sidda laughed. "You are amazing with your weight lifting. I keep telling myself I should, but I never do."

"Do I look too fat?" Vivi asked.

Sidda could not count the number of times her mother had asked her that question. Now, for the first time, she thought she heard what her mother was really asking: Is there too much of me? Do I need to trim myself back for you?

"No, Mama," Sidda said, "you don't look fat. There is just enough of you. Not too little. Not too much. In fact, you look exactly right."

Vivi kept staring straight ahead, out at the fields, only barely lit by moonlight.

"Your father," she said, holding back tears, "has put in over three hundred acres of sunflowers out there. It's his second crop this season. Not cotton, not soybeans. *Sunflowers.* Wait until you see them in the daylight. He claims it's to attract birds for hunting, but he's not fooling anybody. You don't need *three hundred acres* of sunflowers to attract a few little doves. I mean, all he does at the Labor Day Dove Hunt anymore is take photographs."

Vivi took a deep breath before she continued. "*It's a Van Gogh out here, Sidda.* You think you know a man that you've put up with for nearly fifty years and then he does something like that. All for beauty."

Vivi began to cry a little, but gave a deep sniffle, and stopped. She patted lightly around her eyes with the tips of her fingers. "Splotchy-splotchy saddle bags."

Vivi turned so that Sidda could clearly see her dark brown eyes, her faintly freckled milky skin, her aging chin. Then, in an exaggerated, petulant little-girl voice, she said: "It's my party and I'll cry if I want to."

Then Vivi burst out laughing.

Sidda joined her in laughter. God, it felt good to laugh with her mother again!

"What made you do it?" Vivi asked, looking at Sidda. "What made you get on a plane and fly all the way down here?"

"Lawanda," Sidda said. "Lawanda made me do it."

Vivi turned away. She was silent for a moment. "You didn't remove anything from my scrapbook, did you? You didn't lose anything, did you? Because that stuff is priceless. You can't put a price on any of those treasures."

"I brought 'The Divine Secrets of the Ya-Ya Sisterhood' with me, Mama. It's in the car. Let me get it right now."

"No, don't get up—that's all right."

But Sidda was already walking toward the car.

When she opened the car door, Vivi could see her daughter's wrinkled forehead in the illumination from the car light. So beautiful and *intent*, Vivi thought, just like when she was little.

Sidda walked back to the swing, carrying the scrapbook and a small gift-wrapped box, which she concealed in the pocket of her linen jacket.

Sidda handed the scrapbook to her mother. "I hand-carried it onto the plane with me. I didn't want anything to happen to it. 'I want this safely returned to me,' your note said."

Vivi stared at the album in her lap. She ran her hands over the package, then brought her hands up to her mouth. "It's not the scrapbook I wanted safely returned," she whispered.

"Mother," Sidda said, smiling, "your note expressly said you'd take out a contract on me if—"

"It was *you* I wanted to return safely to me," Vivi whispered.

"Oh, Mama," Sidda said, hardly able to speak.

She laid her hand on her mother's shoulder. She could smell her mother's Hovet perfume, with its pears and violets and orris and vetiver chords so miraculously mixed. Underneath that scent, Sidda smelled Vivi's natural scent, the one that came from her skin, from the very molecules that made up her body. In the Louisiana night air, Sidda could smell again the first scent she ever breathed in.

A light attached to a telephone pole at the edge of the driveway gave off an old-fashioned country light. It combined with the white Christmas lights strung around the swing to illuminate Vivi's face. Sidda could see the lines on her aging, almost translucent skin, lines formed from years of charm hiding fear. She could see her mother's courage, and she could see her pain.

As Sidda joined Vivi in staring out into the darkness of the fields, where hundreds of sunflowers grew, she thought: I will never fully know my mother, any more than I will ever know my father or Connor, or myself. *I have been missing the point. The point is not knowing another person, or learning to love another person. The point is simply this: how tender can we bear to be? What good manners can we show as we welcome ourselves and others into our hearts?*

There, in the front yard of Pecan Grove Plantation, in the heart of Louisiana, which had not yet had its first freeze of the year, Siddalee Walker gave up. She gave up the need to know, and she gave up the need to understand. She sat next to her mother, and felt the power of their combined fragility. She returned home without blame.

When Vivi reached out her hand to Sidda, she took it. Their hands rested on the swing between them. At the same moment, each of them looked down and noticed the similarity of their hands' coloring, the shape of their fingers, the veins that carried their Ya-Ya blood through their female bodies.

"Oh, my," Vivi sighed.

"Oh, my," Sidda echoed.

With those few sounds, it was as though mother and daughter exchanged the same breath. Then, without a word, they began to push against the ground with their feet, so that the swing began to rock ever so gently. Nothing rambunctious, just a smooth swaying, as if the swing were a cradle holding both mother and daughter, two separate and equal planets tumbling through space on a night in late autumn.

"I want to give you something," Vivi whispered. She reached into the pocket of her silk pants. Then, taking Sidda's hand in hers, she slipped something into her daughter's palm.

When Sidda unfolded her fingers, she beheld a small velvet jeweler's box. She opened the lid, which snapped back on a tight little hinge. Inside sat the diamond ring Vivi's father had given her over fifty years before.

"My father gave me this on the night of my sixteenth birthday," Vivi said, simply. "I almost lost it once, but I got it back."

Then, like a priestess, Vivi took the ring from its box and slipped it onto her daughter's finger, her own hands shaking and soft and spotted with age. Once the ring was on, she raised Sidda's hand and kissed it. Not like you kiss a lover's hand, but like you kiss a baby's fingers because they are so pink and pudgy and because you love them so.

Feeling her mother's tears against her palm, Sidda lifted Vivi's hand to her lips and kissed it before pressing it against her cheek. Then each of them began to cry. No shoulders shaking, no big gasps, just tears rolling down on their cheeks in silence.

"Thank you, Mama," Sidda whispered, "for all the divine secrets you've shared."

"*Secrets?*" Vivi said, between sobs. "Oh, Dahlin! If you're talking about my scrapbook, that was nothing! I don't even *remember* half the junk that was in there. You should see the stuff I *didn't* send you. Now that's where the *real* secrets are!"

This is my mother, all right, Sidda thought.

"I tell you," Vivi said, tears still falling, "it is a sin and a shame they don't make Wanda Beauty anymore."

"Would sure come in handy for sinners like us," Sidda said, "breaking the 'Fifth Rule of Beauty and Allure.'"

"My love lights are going to be dingy and lusterless as hell."

"Sparkleless in a setting of bags and puffs,'" Sidda said. "A girl has enough handicaps in the campaign for love.'"

"Goddamn right," Vivi said.

"Okay," Sidda whispered, "it's my turn." Reaching into her jacket pocket, she pulled out the tiny gift-wrapped box she had carried on the plane. Before she handed it to her mother, she gave the small gift a kiss, then slipped it into her mother's hand.

Vivi tore the rose-colored handmade paper off the box. She reached in and very gently lifted out a tiny glass vessel about the size of a fox-glove blossom. The vial was very old, made of sterling silver over glass, with one jade stone in the center of its little screw-on lid. Gingerly, Vivi unscrewed the top and held the vial to her nose to sniff it.

"It's not for perfume. It's for something else, isn't it?"

"Yes, it's for something else, Mama."

Vivi tilted her head slightly to the side, thinking. "Tell me."

"It's called a lachrymatory. A tiny jar of tear drops. In olden days it was one of the greatest gifts you could give someone. It meant you loved them, that you shared a grief that brought you together."

"Oh, Sidda," Vivi said. "Oh, Buddy."

"This one dates back to Victorian times, I think. I found it in London a few years ago while scouring antique shops for props."

"Are your tears in here?" Vivi asked, holding up the vial.

"Yes, but there's room for more."

Vivi looked at Sidda and winked. At least it looked like she was winking. She may have been trying to blink a tear. Because in the next moment she was holding the tiny jar under her right eye, bobbing her head up and down, trying to shake her tears down into the container.

Sidda looked at her mother and started laughing.

Vivi looked at her and smiled. "What are you laughing about, you crazy fool? I have been waiting for this gift my whole life."

"I know," Sidda said, now laughing and crying simultaneously. "I know."

Then Vivi stood up from the swing, still holding the jar under her eyes, and began to hop. First on one foot, and then on the other.

Once she realized what her mother was doing, Sidda got up from the swing and began hopping too. She hopped first on her right leg and then on her left, leaning her eyes down in the direction of the lachrymatory so that her tears might fall in. Vivi, holding a jar of tears in her hand, and Sidda wearing a once-pawned, now-redeemed ring on her finger, hopped and cried. Hopped and cried and laughed, and made wild impromptu whooping sounds. If someone had happened upon them, they might have thought the two women were performing a strange ritual tribal dance. The Ritual Mother-Daughter Dance of the Almost-Lost-But-Still-Mighty Tribe of Divine Ya-Yas. An ancient passage of tears and diamonds. Diamonds and tears.

32

*I*t was after one in the morning when Sidda and Connor checked into the Tante Marie House on Cane River.

"It's straight out of a movie," Connor whispered as they walked up to the front door of an early Creole Greek revival home. Columns lined the deep porch, and the air was fragrant with thick, sweet smells. The flickering of gas lamps created shadows that danced along the shutters and brick walls, making Sidda and Connor feel they had stepped back into another century.

The owner introduced himself as Thomas LeCompte. By the time he had led Connor and Sidda through a courtyard garden and up a flight of stairs into a gallery apartment in the old slave quarters beyond his house, he'd decided that not only did he know Sidda's family, but there was probably a good chance that the two of them were *related*.

"As a matter of fact," Thomas said, stepping through the French doors out onto a gallery that looked down upon the garden, "that camellia bush over there, a Lady Hume's Blush, came from plantings your maternal grandmother gave my father. I think her name was Mary Katherine Bowman Abbott, wasn't it? A tremendous gardener, your grandmother. My father was, too. A camellia *nut*. When a camellia blossom fell, he spoke of it as a *beheading*. Daddy would kill me if he saw the way my gardener has pruned your grandmother's jewel."

Beside him on the gallery, Sidda and Connor looked down on the garden, a wild profusion of blooming begonias, impatiens, and the remnants of big, showy caladium leaves. The sweet scent of butterfly ginger, its white flowers glowing in the darkness, reached up to greet them. Surrounded by the tangled masses of Spanish moss hanging from giant live oaks, the garden was enclosed by old brick walls, which were covered by a few remaining Rose of Montana blossoms. A fountain with a small pool sat in the far corner of the garden, buttressed on one side by a chinaberry tree and on the other by a crepe myrtle, its leaves gold and red with autumn. Lush plantings of a variety of camellias, azaleas, roses of all kinds, salvias, and jasmine filled the space so completely that the red brick floor of the courtyard was barely visible.

Sidda looked at the huge camellia bush, its buds full and swollen. "I never knew Buggy—that's what we called my grandmother—was such a great gardener," Sidda said.

"Oh, well," Thomas said, "that sort of thing is only known among the true gardeners, you know." Then, making the Sign of the Cross, he muttered, "Daddy, forgive me."

Connor, a true gardener, said, "That variety of camellia is legendary, Sidda. A Lady Hume's Blush that size is comparable to a black pearl. I didn't think they really existed."

"I must let you get to bed," Thomas said.

Connor and Sidda watched as he descended the stairs.

"I can't believe I'm in America," Connor said.

"You aren't," Sidda said. "You're in Louisiana. And we're about to spend the night in converted slave quarters that look like they're straight out of *Southern Living*. It makes me feel a little guilty. All the misery these four walls have held."

Connor looked around the living room, filled with antiques, plush carpets, and Audubon prints. "A lot of misery, yes. But life happened here, too. Couples made love, babies were born, people sang as well as wept. These walls have probably witnessed joy along with the suffering."

After they'd fallen back into the huge four-poster bed, Sidda told Connor the bare bones of her reunion with her mother. She did not feel much like talking, though. They made love briefly, intensely, sleepily, sweetly. They were both exhausted. After their lovemaking, Sidda did not fall asleep. Connor stroked her back and made up little bits of a song for her. Something about a little bulb growing underground in winter. He sang softly until finally his voice drifted off and he fell asleep.

If God is good to me, Sidda thought, I will be sharing a bed with this man when I am eighty.

After a few moments, Sidda climbed out of the bed, careful not to wake Connor. Naked, she walked barefoot across the wide cypress-plank floors and down into the garden, into the warm, humid Louisiana night. She stood in front of the camellia that was her grandmother's black pearl. Then she crossed to the fountain and dipped her hands into the small pool. Her fingers wet, she touched her eyes, then her lips, then her breasts. She breathed in and out, she offered herself mercy, she gave herself forgiveness. *Sometimes lost treasures can be reclaimed.*

The next morning Sidda spooned up against Connor and suggested they do things together she had never done before within a hundred-mile radius of her hometown. After that, she whispered a few decisive words to him. When he heard what she had to say, he pulled her to him without speaking, and held her. He kissed her forehead, her eyes, then her nose, her lips, then the tips of her fingers.

"I'm sorry for all my crazy indecision," she said, "for making you hang on a thread over the canyon of doom."

"Ah, Sweet Pea," Connor said, rolling back onto his side so that he looked into her eyes. "We're all hanging by a thread in the canyon of doom. We're all each other's keepers."

The deep kindness in his eyes, the tenderness in his voice erased any smidgen of doubt that she had made the right decision.

By noon, they were at Pecan Grove, drinking ice tea with Vivi and Shep on the back patio. Willetta was also in attendance, to witness Siddalee Walker's announcement that she would marry Connor McGill in exactly seven days in the sunflower field in front of her parents' home. Within approximately thirty minutes, three cars appeared in the drive. The Ya-Yas had arrived.

Now the show could get on the road.

33

*I*n her father's field of sunflowers, early on the evening of October 25, wearing her mother's wedding dress, Siddalee Walker said yes to Connor McGill.

Surrounded by her parents; her brothers and their families; her sister, Lulu (who'd flown home from Paris); the Ya-Yas; the Petites Ya-Yas and their families; Willetta and her family; her friend May Sorenson (who'd arrived at the last moment from Turkey); Connor's parents, one grandparent, and two sisters; Wade Coenen (who'd escorted Hueylene, and who had recut Vivi's wedding dress so that it plunged and dipped and showed Sidda's shoulders); and a host of other friends who'd rearranged their lives to fly to Thornton on a week's notice, Siddalee Walker said to Connor McGill: "I will love you with tenderness in the best way I know how."

Sidda's seven-year-old niece Caitlin Walker, one of Baylor's twins, was responsible for the fact that all the children (and also several of the adults) were wearing Halloween costumes. A stranger happening on the ceremony might have mistaken the gathering for a well-heeled group of pagan worshippers, if it hadn't been for the fact that Teensy's cousin was playing "Amazing Grace" on a Cajun fiddle.

At the party afterward, that same fiddler and the rest of his band—Alligator Gris-Gris—played a combination of Cajun and Zydeco, mixed in with old standards from the forties they'd been forced to learn in order to make a living on the South Louisiana country-club circuit. Under the huge, old live oak, which Baylor had strung with a million tiny Christmas lights, Shep Walker supervised a *cochon de lait*, delighting the New Yorkers with heaping plates of roast pig and dirty rice. Willetta's husband, Chaney, stood over a huge black kettle filled with fresh shrimp, and long tables stacked with fresh French bread, salad, and a thousand Louisiana specialties lined the dance area.

Sunflowers and zinnias, which Necie had arranged, were everywhere, and bales of hay circled a bonfire tended by Little Shep. The weather was perfect, with just a little nip in the air, so everybody could dance without getting too sweaty. It was about as loose and happy a wedding party as folks had ever witnessed.

Midway through the party, once everyone had eaten, the band stopped playing, and the squeeze-box accordion player announced that a special treat was in store. With that, he stepped aside and introduced the four Ya-Yas.

Stepping up to the microphone, Vivi Abbott Walker lifted her glass of champagne to the heavens, winked, and said: "Siddalee Dahlin, this song is for you."

After taking a healthy sip of the champagne, Vivi signaled to the others. Then, in four-part Ya-Ya harmony, accompanied by a fiddle, accordion, and bass, the four old friends began to sing. Their voices were not particularly fine, their harmony was a little slippery. But when they opened their mouths, what came out was part lullaby, part love song, part benediction. They sang:

Nights are long since you went away,
I think about you all through the day,
My buddy, my buddy,
No buddy quite so true.

Miss your voice, the touch of your hand,
Just long to know that you understand,
My buddy, my buddy,
Your buddy misses you.

By the time the song was over, Sidda had reconciled herself to the fact that in every single one of her wedding pictures her face would be streaked by long black threads of mascara from crying so much. When her father came up from behind and handed her his handkerchief, she was grateful.

"Your mama and them were still rehearsing when I went to bed last night," Shep said.

Sidda looked at her father and smiled. "Thank you for growing those sunflowers, Daddy," she said.

"You know that's my second crop this year. Don't know what possessed me to grow sunflowers this late in the season. I caught a lot of ribbing about growing flowers after spending my whole life growing money crops clear up to the front door. That was a different time in my life, though. I had four of yall to feed, buy cars for, send through college. Now I grow things for different reasons. Still, I'm glad you and Con came along and made it look like those sunflowers have some reason for being there. Keeps me from looking like I've gone all soft. Got to keep up my image, you know."

Sidda reached up and gently wiped the tears away from her father's cheeks. "I love you, Daddy."

"I hope your marriage is a good one, Baby doll," he said. "Maybe we can all be more like a family now, if you know what I mean."

"Yes, Daddy," Sidda said, linking her arm with her father's, "I know what you mean."

"Don't you think it's time for a father-daughter dance?" Vivi said as she stepped up. She gave Sidda a kiss on the cheek, then kissed her husband. "I think what the American family needs is more *dancing*, don't yall?"

Sidda looked first at her mother, then at her father. "I think you're right, Mama. In fact, I think somebody should include that in a presidential platform."

As the band kicked back in, Vivi took Sidda's face in hers and kissed her once more. Then, taking Sidda's hand and placing it in Shep's, she gave them a little push toward the dance floor.

"Shake a tail feather, Dahlins!" she said. "Cut a rug!"

With that, Vivi went off in search of the Ya-Yas, and soon the four of them were dancing together, their dresses swirling, their eyes shining.

After the wedding cake (baked by Willetta and decorated by her daughter Pearl with Halloween colors) was cut, everybody hit the dance floor again. Even though it was getting late, and the toddlers were sleepy-eyed, nobody wanted to leave Pecan Grove Plantation. Nobody wanted to stop celebrating. Instead they stayed and danced. They waltzed, they jerked, they Cajun two-stepped, they mash-potatoed, they jitterbugged, they fox-trotted, they boogied their little hearts out.

From her perch on the crescent of the harvest moon, the Holy Lady looked down and smiled at her imperfect children. The angels attending her that night felt little twinges of longing to be in human form, if for only a few minutes. They wanted to rock, they wanted to roll, they wanted to feel the peculiarly human feeling of having a perfect night in an imperfect world. They wanted to taste the saltiness of tears the way Sidda did, the way Vivi did, the way—if truth be told—almost everyone did on the night Sidda Walker wed Connor McGill.

So it is when an umbilical cord of love flows up from the earth and down from the sky. So it is sometimes near Halloween in the State of Louisiana when the divisions between heaven and earth crack open a little and spirits gather from all over. Perhaps the souls of Sidda's twin and Jack and Genevieve Whitman joined in the festivities that night. Perhaps little unborn spirits in the cracked hearts of each of the guests were called forth. When the dancers spoke, breathless, happy, in between songs, they told each other the night was charmed. They told each other it felt like some kind of spell had been put on them.

To this the Blessed Mother only winked. To this she would only say, "Them that know don't tell; and them that tell don't know."

For Siddalee Walker, the need to understand had passed, at least for the moment. All that was left was love and wonder.

Acknowledgments

With special thanks to the following:

MAURINE HOLBERT-HOGABOOM, my mentor, whose love, acceptance and inspiration has taught me how wide and sweet and wild motherhood—and sisterhood—can be.

TERRY GIBSON, a lighthouse with a steady beam.

DIANE REVERAND, my editor, who intuitively and enthusiastically embraced the Ya-Yas when this book was a *bébé*.

JANE ISAY, unbidden angel, who appeared, and, with great kindness, helped me refine and structure my thoughts.

DONNA LAMBDIN, Louisiana Sister, and BOB CORBETT, who introduced me to Lake Quinault.

JAN CONSTANTINE, for her generous advice and friendship.

TOM WELLS, my brother, whom I love.

And to these essential ones:

Randy Harelson, Nancy Chambers Richards, Willie Mae Lowe, Bobby and Althea DeBlieux, Darrell Jamieson, Jennifer Miller, Lori Mitchell, Brenda Peterson, Torie Scott, Barbara Bailey, Brenda Bell and Stanley Farrar, Honi Werner, Steve Coenen, Lynne and Bob Dowdy, Linda Buck, Jane and Gene Crews, Janice Shaw, Libby Anderson, Uli Schoettle, Julia Smith, Barbara Fischer, Sherry Prowda, Colleen Byrum, Jan Short, Karen Haig, Mary Colegrove, Myra Goldberg, Bard Richmond, Jay Morris, Jerry Fulks, Lou Maxon, Meaghan Dowling, David Flora, Marshal Trow, Bainbridge Island Public Library, Bainbridge Island Arts and Humanities Council; The Seaside Institute and community, especially Nancy Holmes, and Robert and Daryl Davis; Sally and John Renn, Tom and Barbara Schworer, and Lulu, (the Judy Holiday of the cocker spaniel world, whose cheerful companionship exemplifies why "dog" is "God" spelled backwards). And my extended family whose love and outrageous sense of humor set the stage for who I am. Especially my mother, who taught me how to swim.

Note to the Reader

I am grateful to Liz Huddle and Burke Walker, who shared their experiences of being stage directors with me and thus helped shape the character of Sidda Walker.

I will always be thankful to Adrienne Rich for her seminal book, *Of Woman Born*, which inspired and coached me as I wrote this novel. Thanks also to Diane Ackerman, whose ability to express the beauty of the physical world woke me up. I thank Denise Levertov for her poem, "The Annunciation," which sparks the Holy Lady to show up sometimes when the moon is right.

I'm grateful to *Weavings* for publishing "Forgiveness: The Name of Love in a Wounded World," an essay by Henri Nouwen. I'm grateful to *The Sun* for its wonderful "Sunbeams," which published both the Mary Antin and H. L. Mencken quotes that are used as epigraphs.